A World Away

Pam Rock

LOVE SPELL  NEW YORK CITY

LOVE SPELL®

August 1995

Published by

Dorchester Publishing Co., Inc.
276 Fifth Avenue
New York, NY 10001

Printed in the United States of America.

Love in another time, another place.

SWEET LOVE

"Garner, look what I've found!" Alena held out a bundle wrapped in a single huge leaf and uncovered a waxy yellow chunk riddled with comblike holes.

"What is it?"

"Taste it!" She dipped her finger into the mass and licked away the stickiness. "It's wonderfully sweet."

She dipped her finger and brought it to his lips covered with a thick golden syrup. At first he resisted, but she softly teased his lower lip until he took her sticky fingertip between his teeth and gently sucked it.

"Would you like more?"

"Yes," he said, speaking with his heart, not his head.

She dipped her finger again and brought it to him, losing a tiny drop on his chin, then parting his lips.

"I'll share with everyone when we get back to camp," she assured him, again offering him a dab on her finger. "Am I wicked to eat my fill first?"

"Not as wicked as I am for accepting a share from you," he said, taking her hand in his and guiding it to his mouth.

Other *Love Spell* Books by Pam Rock:
LOVE'S CHANGING MOON
MOON OF DESIRE

To Haley

A World Away

Chapter One

Garner Rie inhaled deeply, puzzled by his inability to find the source of the strange odor circulating through the spaceship's air ducts. He'd walked the length of the skyliner on both the upper and lower levels without finding anything to explain the faint but disturbing smell.

"You've run a complete check of the electrical system?" he asked the stocky, silver-haired chief engineer, Hail Benay.

"Yea, sir, and I've had the greasers doing a manual inspection bow to stern. They've used the heat and radiation sensors to check everywhere except in the captain's quarters and Highness Yor's stateroom. Captain Blaz said any man who mucks with the First Minister's daughter will be blown out with the waste."

Garner's frown deepened, but he clenched his jaw, holding back his angry reaction to the captain's threat. As executive officer and second in command, he was obligated by the Code of Service Rules to uphold the commanding officer's decisions. The captain of the vessel had life-and-death power over his crew in space, but Garner's last superior officer had had congenial relations with both officers and greasers. Things were different under the command of Captain Hurex Blaz, and Garner was liking the maiden voyage of the *Moon Courier* less with each passing hour.

"That ain't the whole of it, sir," Hail went on. "One of the passengers complained because the light in his stateroom was flashing on and off. We all but tore the system apart and couldn't find a bad connection."

"Nothing showed on the control board?"

"No, sir. I ran the check myself. According to the computer, everything's as smooth as a joy-girl's thighs—no offense, sir." The older man flushed and wiped his palms on the sides of his regulation green coverall.

"None taken. Any report of meteor hits?"

"Seven—too many for this sector. No damage yet, but I'd give half my pay to change course. Perdition! I don't know why it's so blame important to break the fifty-five-hour record on this run. I like to break in a new vessel easy-like, not push to the max on the first voyage. You won't be telling the captain I said that, sir?"

"No, but keep checking. Also, keep a close eye on the gravity generators. I'll get back to you as soon as I can."

Garner glanced around the engine control room, crowded with the latest instruments of space technology, and wished he knew more about the crew of greasers. The chief engineer had a good reputation, but he couldn't do every man's job. If one greaser was slacking off, taking shortcuts, something could be overlooked. Garner didn't share the blind faith some space officers had in machines. He'd seen man's ingenuity make the difference between life and death too many times.

He used the crew's walkway past the galley to reach the lower-deck corridor, then hurried forward to the command bridge. There the second officer, Lon Weal, had the duty, and the helmsman was monitoring the command computer that piloted the ship.

"Where's the captain?" Garner asked.

"In his quarters, sir," Weal said, standing at attention to answer.

Garner shook his head, wondering if he'd ever get used to the exaggerated formality on the *Moon Courier*. In his seven years of space service, he'd never been on a vessel where the staff officers didn't address each other by their given names.

The captain's office and living space occupied a double stateroom next to the command bridge, across the corridor from Garner's small cubicle. He pressed his palm on the sensitized identity panel and waited for the captain to respond to the low hum that announced him.

"Rie, I'd expected you to be dressed for meal-call by now."

"Something's come up, sir," Garner said, belatedly remembering to throw back his shoulders and tighten his buttocks in the exaggerated stance of attention this captain demanded of every crew member who addressed him. Garner hadn't had to assume this ridiculous posture since his cadet days, and he had to bite back his resentment to make his report.

"I don't think you realize how important it is to demonstrate what the ship can do on the maiden voyage," Captain Hurex Blaz said, stretching his thin lips into a scowl, when Garner had finished.

Garner stared at the fair-skinned, long-faced space captain and steeled himself to conceal his disapproval of the commander's handling of the ship. He'd disliked his new superior officer since their first meeting, and had made up his mind to put in for a transfer as soon as the vessel returned to Prima—even if it meant a severe setback to his career.

"I want that stubble off your face, and your best dress blues had better be presentable when you report to the dining room. I want this midpoint banquet to be an example of Space Service hospitality and efficiency," the captain said.

Blaz stood ramrod straight, his pale, almost colorless hair cropped so short it gave the illusion of a bald skull. He was exercising his commander's privilege by wearing a white dress tunic over sharply creased white trousers, a ceremonial uniform Garner had never seen worn in space.

"Yes, sir, but I'm concerned about the odor coming through the air ducts. It smells like burning wire. The chief engineer checked out the electrical system, and the computer isn't showing any malfunction, but . . ."

"Rie, do you own a surface vehicle?"

"No, sir." Garner felt his cheeks burn with humiliation. Unlike most space officers, he had to live on his pay, and only the rich could afford a private surface vehicle. Blaz never passed up an opportunity to remind him that he'd risen above his rightful place by becoming a space officer.

"If you'd ever driven a new vehicle away from the mart, you'd recognize the scent of newness.

Everything on board this vessel is fresh from the assembly site. The equipment, the metallic skin, even the fabrics and the glue have a distinctive odor that doesn't fade until the vessel's made a few runs."

"Sir, that isn't what I smell. As second officer, I insist on filing a report of a possible malfunction. We've already taken seven meteor hits. I recommend a slowdown and a change of course until we've done a thorough breakdown on all systems."

"Mister Rie, I'll make that decision when and if I deem it necessary. I was commanding space vessels while you were still sweating out your time at the training academy—at government expense."

"Are you declining to file my report, sir?" Garner felt suffocated by anger, but he'd learned all too painfully how to deal with that as a charity appointment at the Academy. Defying authority was a no-win proposition.

"That's correct, Rie."

Chafing at the captain's lack of respect for his opinion, Garner could only do what any Prola would so in his situation: try to avoid his upper-caste superior as much as possible.

"Request permission to be absent from the midpoint banquet, sir. It's my watch on the command bridge."

"Weal has been assigned to your watch. I want you at the meal, Rie. Our distinguished passenger has expressed an interest in seeing the Space Service's token low-caste officer, and naturally we'll accommodate her. This is Highness Yor's first trip to the moon base. I want her to speak highly of the *Moon Courier* and tell her father she was accorded every consideration. Do you have any idea what First Minister Yor can do for a man's career?"

"No, sir, I don't," he said, trying to swallow his resentment at being treated as a low-caste exhibition. "But Weal has already served a double watch." Even as he spoke, Garner detected the metallic odor again. "The scent is stronger now. It seems to come through the air ducts. Request permission to take the bridge and supervise an investigation." He added "sir" after a pause that made it sound grudging.

"You'll follow my orders as they stand, Rie, or confine yourself to quarters to await an insubordination hearing on Prima. Is that clear?"

"Yes, sir."

Garner backed out to the corridor and leaned against the metallic-gray wall to suppress the tremors in his arms and shoulders. He wanted to strangle Hurex Blaz! The space liner was hurtling through a meteor field with a possible malfunction the computers didn't detect, and all that jackass cared about was impressing some high-caste woman!

He thought of talking over the danger to the ship with the second officer, but Lon Weal's only qualification for his position was the knack of looking neat after a long watch. The rumor among the greasers was that his politician father had bought his appointment to the *Moon Courier,* but Blaz was entrusting the inexperienced officer to do extended duty with no sleep break. Standing three consecutive watches on the command bridge was almost unprecedented, but Garner knew the Code of Service Rules by heart. No cadet left the academy without having it drummed into him. The captain had the authority to order a triple watch.

In the washroom Garner scraped his bristles so furiously that he broke the skin, leaving a deep nick on his strong jawline. He hardly recognized the angry face reflected in the highly polished steel mirror. His deep-set blue eyes were narrowed in rage and shadowed by fatigue. His high cheekbones and straight nose had the chiseled look of stone, and the tight set of his mouth made indentations at the corners.

The band of brass encircling his wrist, designating his Prola caste, chafed his skin and his soul. How different his life might be if wearing a band of platinum was his birthright.

By the time he stanched the flow of blood from the razor cut and slicked down his unruly black hair with water, he had only minutes to change into his dress tunic and report to the dining room. He could only hope the chief engineer and his greasers would get lucky and discover the source of the biting, metallic smell.

In her stateroom Alena Yor stared at the luminous numerals on her timekeeper and twisted her platinum bracelet, trying to will time to pass more quickly. She couldn't concentrate on anything but the hours of flight that loomed ahead like endless torture. She didn't know how she could endure the rest of the trip.

She pulled out her cosmetics case and swabbed her face with astringent cleansing fluid, holding the saturated bit of cloth over her closed eyes while she tried to pretend her stateroom was as large as a meeting hall on Prima. Unless she got a grip on herself, she'd be a babbling lunatic before she met her father at the domed research facility on the moon Bedir.

He was so proud of her! For his sake, she had to overcome her claustrophobia. She lay back on the narrow bunk that folded into the wall when it wasn't in use. Maybe if she didn't look at the silvery walls of the coffin-like cabin, she could get over the sensation that the walls were closing in on her, squeezing the breath from her body.

"Think about pleasant things," she said aloud. "Think how fortunate you are to have Stanko Yor as your father."

Her father was her whole world. Her mother had died before Alena was old enough to remember her, but Stanko Yor had spared no effort or expense to raise his only child as befitted a woman of the elite Scientifica caste. When he'd discovered that as a child she'd had an uncanny sense of direction, he'd gathered together the best tutors to prepare her for a career as a cartographer. He'd been waiting for years for an opportunity that would allow her to use her exceptional skills. Now she was on her way to prove herself to him and to the scientific community. She was going to assemble data to make the first complete three-dimensional map of the only fully explored moon in the Zorya solar system. When it was finished, she would merit the title of Highness for her own accomplishments, not just because of her father's high caste.

She moaned aloud. Not even thoughts of a glorious career could distract her from the misery of close confinement. In fact, it was partly because of her elite standing that she was suffering so much. Mingling with lower-caste passengers was beneath her. There was no one with social status as illustrious as hers on the vessel, with the possible exception of the captain, and he was vague about his genealogy. This meant she had to take all her meals alone in her stateroom—although she had so little appetite she didn't touch most of the food brought to her, putting it into the waste-disposal unit to save the chef from disgrace.

Another of her caste privileges had worked against her. Her father's high position in the government had prompted the authorities to waive all the fitness tests required of space travelers. Now she fervently wished she'd taken them, even if her claustrophobia had disqualified her from the flight.

In a perpetual state of terror, she'd done a rash thing: asked to dine with others on board. Now she had to worry about what her father would say when he learned she'd encouraged the captain's attempts at familiarity by allowing him to include her in a meal with the crew's officers and higher-caste passengers.

She sat up, still clenching her eyes shut, and ran her fingers through long red-gold hair that fell to her waist. She wanted to coil the thick strands into an elaborate coiffure around her head, but her hands were trembling. The captain didn't know it, but he might be saving her sanity by giving her a reason to spend time in a roomier chamber. She also planned to lead him into offering to escort her to the observation lounge. If she could think of some excuse to linger there for a while, she might summon enough courage to get through the rest of the trip. Unfortunately, when she used the observation lounge, other passengers couldn't enter it until she left. She hated being selfish, but she had to see the heavens, had to know that a universe of space still existed outside the suffocating confines of the cubicle someone had ironically named a stateroom.

She was a little embarrassed by the reason she'd given Captain Blaz for wanting to dine with others. She'd claimed it was to see firsthand if a low-caste cadet made a satisfactory officer. Her father had been instrumental in initiating a program that allowed one candidate per year from the lowest caste to gain admittance to the Space Academy. It was a revolutionary concept, training a Prola at government expense, but her father saw the need for a greater pool of candidates for the arduous Space Service.

Usually Alena gave little thought to the world of politics and the rigid caste system that had existed on her home world of Prima for more than 3,000 years. Although it was much different now in the technological age, her planet still clung to the societal structure that had served it well in a primarily agrarian era.

Science was the primary concern of the highest caste, the Scientifica, whose rulers governed the planet. Her father was on Bedir observing an important series of experiments. As the First Minister of Science, he was the overseer of all government-funded research projects and one of the most powerful men on Prima.

Reluctantly opening her eyes, Alena looked at her timekeeper and saw it was finally time to get ready for her unprecedented appearance at a meal and she was thankful. She dressed quickly, slipping into a high-collared gown that fell to her ankles in a swirl of midnight-blue sheena, the cloth woven especially for her from almost invisible strands of fiber produced by tiny tree-worms. Although the garment left her arms bare, it was the most modest of the seven gowns she was taking to Bedir. Her father would expect her to dress elegantly for their shared meals, even if she spent the rest of her time in more practical work tunics.

She pushed her slender feet into silver thongs and swept back her hair on the sides with ornately carved combs. She was still too unsteady to attempt an elaborate hairstyle, much as her father would disapprove of letting her tresses hang free.

When she stood, the sensation of being compressed by the walls of the cubicle was even worse. Her head was only inches from the metal above her. She was tall for a female, but her father towered over her. How did he endure a space voyage in a compartment where his head brushed the ceiling?

She had to get out! Even if she disgraced herself, she couldn't stand the confinement another moment.

Pressing the door release, she cautiously slipped out, but the corridor was too low and narrow to be much of an improvement. The stateroom doors on either side were closed, and at the far end, the stern of the vessel, there was nothing but the entrance to the section housing the escape pods. To get a grip on herself before entering the elevator to the lower level and the dining room, she looked into the observation lounge that occupied the nose of the upper deck.

The marvelous lounge was blessedly empty of other passengers. Above and in front of her, costly transparent sheets of plasticon served as windows on space. She entered the lounge and pressed her forehead against the front of the ship, looking out on the dark, star-studded universe. If only she could think of a way to spend the rest of the voyage in this spacious room!

Breathing deeply again and again, she felt some of her gnawing anxiety ebb away. She was less nauseous, and her legs were no longer in danger of collapsing.

Stateroom doors slid open silently, so she didn't realize someone was coming until she heard a man's deep voice calling out to someone else in the corridor.

"I say, Font Lea, care to join me in the observation lounge?" a man's voice said. "I think we can get a glimpse of Brona before we hie down to the meal."

Alena didn't have time to dwell on her exasperation. It would be terribly embarrassing to ignore the pair of space travelers, but speaking to them was unthinkable. Their approach blocked the corridor, and there was only one way to escape: the spiral staircase that led from the observation lounge to the lower level. A sign warned that it was for emergency use only, but it was the only way she could avoid contact with men of lower caste or less status within her own caste.

Eager to avoid a confrontation, she picked up her skirt and rushed down the steps that circled around until she reached the lower level, a section of the vessel she hadn't seen.

In his quarters, Garner finished changing, pinning his insignia of office on the stiff collar of his tunic. He hated dress blues. They reminded him of Academy days when corporal punishment was mandatory for any cadet with a tarnished button or a soiled cuff. He'd suffered for dress infractions too many times to have any appreciation for the showy side of the Service. In fact, the scratchy tu nic and tight-fitting trousers represented everything he didn't like about the Space Service.

He tried to focus on what he did like about it: the prestige it brought his caste; the pride his family had in him; decent wages and the right to better housing. Even these advantages paled compared to the elation he felt when he took the command bridge and knew he was challenging the enormity of the universe by piloting a thin-skinned, man-made vessel through the depths of the solar system. He didn't think he'd ever be able to love a woman the way he loved space flight.

His timekeeper warned him against delays, but he couldn't force himself to sit through the captain's blasted banquet without checking on the second officer. He had little confidence in Lon Weal's ability to get through even one uneventful watch. His stomach knotted at the thought of an emergency challenging the inexperienced officer when he was bleary-eyed from a triple shift.

Hurrying to the command bridge at the bow of the vessel on the lower deck, Garner felt grateful that his duties kept him in the bowels of the ship most of the time. He lacked the temperament—the patience—needed to deal with high-caste passengers.

Weal was sitting in the command chair, his head slumped forward suspiciously. Garner would be justified in relieving him of the watch if he were sleeping, but the second officer didn't give him that opportunity. He bounded up, pink-cheeked but alert.

"Sir."

"I'm not the captain," Garner said caustically, comparing Weal unfavorably with the scrappy young second officer who'd shared his last freighter run. Space officers often forged friendships that lasted a lifetime, but Garner didn't think he and Weal would ever grow close. This second officer worked hard to ingratiate himself with the captain, but did nothing to earn the respect of the crew.

"Second Officer Weal," Garner said, addressing him formally to give the impression he was speaking for the captain, however untrue this was. "Are you confident you're alert enough for an additional watch?"

"Yea, sir."

"Be especially watchful for malfunctions. Report anything the least bit unusual to the captain at once—even if you have to interrupt his meal." He spoke loudly to be sure the first helmsman could hear. The man who entered commands into the computer control console could take action without orders from the watch officer if an emergency demanded an instantaneous reaction. Garner hadn't worked with this helmsman long enough to know whether he had enough confidence to act independently in a crisis.

But Garner realized he'd done all he could. Turning to hurry toward the meal room, he collided with an intruder. He reached out to avoid toppling the trespasser, and found the most beautiful creature he'd ever seen trapped between his arms.

"The stairs are for emergency use only," he said, sounding gruff because she'd taken his breath away. "There's a sign in the observation lounge."

"I'm sorry. . . . "

He looked down into warm brown eyes fringed by the thickest lashes he'd ever seen. He nearly whistled through his teeth, so stunned by her beauty that he forgot to release his accidental prisoner.

"I didn't know where the steps led," she said, averting her eyes and gently laying her hands on his chest, as though she'd intended to push him away but had lost her nerve.

"This is the command bridge. No passengers are allowed without the captain's permission."

"Perhaps you can direct me to the meal room?"

"I'll be glad to," he said, disarmed by her shy, almost frightened look.

He'd seen faces like hers, but only in periodicals that chronicled the lives of the elite caste's most prominent members. His sisters saved their coins to buy the brightly colored publications, aping the classic hairstyles of what they called their "betters."

"Where is it?"

Her melodic voice reminded him that she was waiting for directions from him, but his own voice seemed to be lost somewhere in his midsection. He'd never seen red-gold hair like hers; never dreamed that a woman's face could be so perfect and so patrician without losing the warmth of living flesh. Her eyes were slightly slanted, her nose delicate and straight, and her cheekbones elegantly high, but it was her mouth that mesmerized him: lips so pink and full and sensual that he nearly forgot himself and ran his fingers over their shapely fullness.

"Perhaps you could escort me there?" she asked, her voice husky and low.

"It would be my privilege," he said, remembering that any tardiness on his part would be sure to bring the captain's wrath down on his head.

She stepped backward and placed her slender hand on his arm, then quickly pulled it away as though she'd surprised herself with the gesture.

"Down this way," he said, gesturing for her to precede him, regretting that the corridor was too narrow for him to offer her his arm again. He fervently wished he could capture her delicate hand and cover it with his, a thought that made his palms feel damp.

He didn't regret the opportunity to watch her glide down the narrow walkway ahead of him.

Her bare arms excited him; they had the peachy glow of pampered skin with the firmness of sleek muscles under the skin. She held her shoulders back and moved with only a slight, provocative sway of her hips.

For the first time since coming on board, he thought dealing with passengers might not be all bad.

When the corridor divided, he lightly touched her wrist to guide her toward the right. The vessel's designer had installed two separate curved walkways, one leading to the meal room and the other to the galley. Until now Garner had thought it was silly to spare passengers the sight and sound of food being prepared, especially since it meant quite a few extra steps for the overworked servers. Now he was glad this elegant woman wouldn't have to pass any sweaty greasers on her way to dine.

"Thank you," she said softly, her voice as melodious as musical chimes.

"My pleasure." He followed her through the entrance, surprised again when she placed her hand on the crook of his elbow and seemed to expect him to act as her escort.

The individual tables had been moved into two long rows joined by a head table, not an easy task for those who had to loosen the bolts holding them in place and tighten them again in alternate screwholes. Garner felt a resurgence of his resentment when he thought of the wasted man hours that could have been used trying to detect the source of the burning odor.

A conversational din filled the room, allowing them to get close to the tables before anyone noticed them. All the passengers seemed to be present, as well as the off-duty officers. The ship was filled to capacity: 52 passengers and 18 crew members. Only the nine greasers—three of them doubling as servers, the chef, and the on-duty officers were absent.

"Highness Yor, my deepest apologies!" Captain Blaz rushed forward, and all conversation stopped at once. "I went to your stateroom. I never intended to have you find your way here unescorted. Please forgive me."

"There's nothing to forgive. This gentleman very kindly brought me here."

Blood thundered in Garner's ears as he met Blaz's stare, but he didn't need a rebuke from the captain to know he'd trespassed against an inflexible caste tradition. He should have averted his eyes in her presence and refrained from touching her in any way. His thoughts had been even more damning. Her comely face and voluptuous body had played havoc with his senses. He was angry at himself for being attracted to a female who was as unobtainable as the most distant star.

"Executive Officer Rie has overstepped his authority," the captain said in a stern voice.

"Oh, don't think that, please. I humiliated myself by wandering onto the command bridge. High Rie did me a great favor," she said.

"And you do him a great honor by addressing him with a title of honor, Highness Yor. Garner Rie is the Prola you wanted to see—the first low-caste officer to serve under my command."

If she was shocked, she immediately concealed it with a sweet, almost sad, smile directed at Garner. "His caste doesn't detract from the service he did in escorting me here."

Somehow Garner managed to move stiffly toward the table, urged on by the communications officer, Vane Col, one of the few staff members who didn't seem to resent a low-caste executive officer. Garner felt stripped of his dignity and exposed as worthless trash in spite of the courteous words of the Minister of Science's daughter.

"Honor me by sitting on my right," the captain was saying, seating his guest of honor beside him at the head table.

Garner heard only fragments of the captain's welcoming speech. He could still feel the touch of her fingers through his sleeve, and he would never forget the way her lustrous hair trailed down her back, stopping just above her slender waist. She walked like a goddess, the sway of her hips more seductive than the naked gyrations of an exotic dancer he'd once seen in Danica, the crowded capital city on Prima where he'd grown up in the poorest of slums.

He was a seasoned spaceman; he took care of his carnal needs during furloughs, but in flight, the ship was his mistress. He'd never expected—or wanted—to meet a female who could arouse him in space. He hated the way he felt: his groin ached, his palms were damp, and his collar was choking him. In self-defense, he carefully kept his eyes averted, afraid of his reaction if he met the gaze of her warm, honey-brown eyes.

He would never forgive Hurex Blaz for demeaning him in the eyes of the high-caste woman!

The meal was extravagant, but Garner ate sparingly, scarcely tasting the succulent meat pudding, spicy preserves, or the pre-baked breadrolls heated in the galley's oven. The passenger across from him, a heavy-jowled man with iron-gray hair cropped almost as short as the captain's, tried to sound him out on flight safety standards, but his questions seemed designed to make Garner expose Blaz's lax attitude toward navigational concerns. Garner responded in monosyllables, knowing the captain was covertly watching him. Even if Blaz didn't issue an official reprimand—and Garner didn't think he would go that far—the captain was in a position to make his life miserable and sully his reputation.

"Officer Rie is a conscientious officer," the captain said, seemingly agreeing with a comment someone else had made. "In fact, he's expended a great deal of energy trying to figure out why our shiny new ship smells so . . . new."

Garner wanted to throttle him for ridiculing his safety concerns, but he'd worked too hard and put up with too much to give Blaz the opportunity to demote him. Nothing the captain did, nothing he said, was going to make Garner give him a reason to relieve him of his duties, not after the humiliation he'd suffered as an outcast at the Academy and the grueling struggle he'd had to prove himself worthy of being a space officer.

"I've noticed an odd smell," Highness Yor said. "It seems to come and go, as though the ventilating system is blowing it in and out."

Oddly, her support made Garner even angrier. He wasn't a charity case anymore. He didn't need or want her pity. Let Blaz ridicule his caution. Garner had a bad feeling about this maiden voyage; a less skeptical man might call it a premonition. Things weren't going well on the *Moon Courier.* The ship wasn't as space-worthy as it should be, but the captain was only concerned with enhancing his own reputation by flattering the passengers and breaking the speed record. Garner hoped he was wrong about both the ship and its commander; he was more interested in surviving the flight than in being right.

Chapter Two

Her claustrophobia was like a bad dream that kept creeping into her consciousness, even though the utilitarian dining room was spacious compared to her stateroom. She couldn't put her fear out of her mind even though she was enjoying the novel experience of sharing a meal with a group of strangers.

"Will you be making your return trip on the *Moon Courier,* Highness Yor?"

The captain's question wasn't welcome; Alena didn't want to think about another agonizing flight.

"I understand this is the most spacious liner in the fleet," she said, unwilling to commit herself to anything.

"It certainly is." Captain Blaz's smile was ingratiating. "And history will record that Highness Yor honored us with her presence on the maiden voyage."

"I'm honored to make the trip," she said, making a conventional response and forcing herself to smile.

She glanced up from the creamy confection she was eating with more appetite than she'd felt since boarding the vessel, then quickly returned her attention to the sweet pink dab on her eating utensil. Her eyes had strayed to the low-caste officer too many times during the meal. The captain was watching her, his gaze so avid he seemed to be storing her image in his brain. She wanted to squirm, but her status made it mandatory that she conceal her discomfort.

Resolved not to look in Officer Rie's direction again, she tried to enter into the conversation flowing around her. Captain Blaz made it difficult. He seemed determined to monopolize her attention, perhaps thinking his caste status made him the only one worthy of conversing with her.

She didn't need to look at the executive officer to remember his rugged, almost overpowering attractiveness. His eyes were vivid blue, in startling contrast to his dark brows and thick black hair. Spacemen were known for their pallid complexions; certainly the captain's was as pale as a land slug's underbelly. Officer Rie's skin either had a natural tan shading, or he spent his furloughs basking in solar rays. She wondered if his whole body had this pleasing coloration, but the thought of seeing his naked torso brought heat to her cheeks. She'd felt oddly light-headed when she realized how powerful his arm was, and she still couldn't believe how boldly she'd overstepped the bounds of propriety by touching him. What had prompted her to behave so outrageously? If he were a Bellicosa, a man of the military caste, or even a Guilder of the merchant class, he might have been worthy of a covert glance from her. A Prola was different. On Prima she would have been censured by others of her caste for even looking at him. Even her curiosity embarrassed her, but she still wondered how he felt, elevated so high above others of his caste.

The captain was asking something about her map project, but she had to ask him to repeat his question.

"I don't want to be presumptuous. I'll understand if the details are still classified as secrets," he said.

"Oh, no. My father hopes the map will generate much publicity when it goes on display in the capitol building. He wants to stimulate moon investments."

"A worthy goal, I'm sure," Blaz said. "I hope the *Moon Courier* can do its small part in helping Bedir to prosper."

"No doubt it will under your command," Alena said, flattering the captain to atone for her inattentiveness.

A slender young man in a server's apron approached the captain, his face betraying reluctance to interrupt his superior.

"Sir, I have a message for you."

"This is neither the time nor the place."

"Sir, the chief engineer needs to speak to you. He said I'd be on report unless I tell you it's urgent."

"Tell him to wait for me in the engine control room." Blaz smiled at Alena. "Before I take care of mundane navigational problems, I would be honored to escort you to the observation lounge. We should have an especially good view of the planet Brona by now. As you know, probes landing there have shown all the necessary elements to sustain life. There are no signs of intelligent life inhabiting it, but it's almost certain Primans can survive on the surface. The Space Service is planning a manned expedition in the near future. No doubt there are abundant resources to be harvested on that warm neighbor of ours once regular flights are a reality. So far, no one has attempted to land there, but we're very close to the time when a trip to Brona will be as commonplace as a moon run."

"Captain, I could never forgive myself if my presence interfered with your pressing responsibilities," Alena said, eager to separate herself from the captain and his pedantic lectures, even though she still feared returning to her tiny cubicle. "Perhaps you could appoint someone of lesser importance to escort me to the lounge."

"Highness Yor, you are my most important concern."

"Please, don't burden my conscience by letting me keep you from your duties. Perhaps Officer Rie could escort me. I have several questions I'd like to ask him on my father's behalf." She was telling a blatant falsehood, and she didn't dare examine her motive for doing so.

"Of course, that can be arranged."

Blaz's words were cordial, but the blood rushing to his face betrayed his disapproval. His pale skin was mottled by angry red splotches, and she hoped her rash request wouldn't cause trouble for the Prola officer.

"Rie, put yourself at Highness Yor's disposal," he ordered before bowing deeply to his passengers and leaving the room.

"May I escort you now?" the low-caste officer asked, standing at attention beside her chair.

His voice was flat, devoid of emotion, but she

was unnerved by the anger she saw in his eyes. His expression was disciplined, but his rigid stance betrayed his discomfort.

"Please do," she said, rising from the bolted-down chair and nodding at the other passengers, taking silent leave of them as befitted her position.

He led the way to the small lift that carried passengers between levels, letting her enter first. Although the enclosed cage was designed to carry up to six passengers, it was much too small for her comfort. She shut her eyes and steeled herself for the moment of horror when the door slid shut.

Mercifully, the upward ride was quickly over. In a few moments the door was sliding open again, but her forehead was damp and her dress was clinging to the skin between her shoulder blades.

"Is there anything I can tell you about the ship, Highness Yor?"

Alena couldn't fault him for a lack of courtesy, but his stiff formality was oddly hurtful. She suddenly wanted very much to see him smile.

"I'm embarrassed to admit how eager I am to stand on firm ground again," she said impulsively.

"I'm sorry you find the flight unpleasant." His words were correct but his voice was cold.

"Not through any fault of the crew!" she hastened to assure him. "It's a weakness of mine that has worsened on the ship—the staterooms are so small!"

"I understand. Claustrophobia disqualifies more people from space travel than any other consideration."

He smiled sympathetically, and the narrow corridor seemed less ominous.

The observation lounge was unoccupied; all the other passengers had heard her request and, of course, they wouldn't intrude while an elite-caste female was present.

"It's beautiful," she said quietly.

The transparent panels in the bow were windows on space, and she admired the view.

"A sight like this is worth the trip," she admitted, reaching out with both hands as though she could catch a glittering star.

She turned to the young officer and smiled broadly without analyzing the reason for her sudden sense of well-being. He was so close she could detect his pleasing masculine fragrance. On his skin the strong disinfectant soap used on board the vessel was enticing to her nostrils. He was almost as tall as her father, and she liked the sensation of looking up to speak to him.

"Do you ever grow accustomed to such a glorious sight?" she asked.

"Never."

She knew he was looking at her, not the heavens, and a shiver of excitement ran down her spine. She was used to respect and deference from men of all castes; she had yet to be courted by a male suitable for mating. For an instant she wished Garner Rie had been born into the Scientifica caste—although he could raise his professional status by serving as an officer in the Space Service, he could never change his caste. She had never met such a handsome man or one so likely to breed sturdy offspring. Unfortunately, she knew because he was born a Prola, he would die a Prola.

Her cheeks burned at the intimacy of her observations, and she turned her face away, hoping he didn't suspect what she was thinking.

Garner shifted his weight from one foot to the other, anxiety gnawing at him as he tried to imagine what emergency had prompted the chief engineer to summon the captain away from his banquet. As executive officer, his place was on the command bridge, but he had another reason for wanting to be free of the responsibility for Highness Alena Yor. It took all the self-discipline he possessed to keep from touching her.

"Look over there," he said, his voice strained for reasons he could never admit to her. "That bluish light. It's the planet Brona."

"How exciting! My father says someday we'll colonize there."

"It's possible, but I wouldn't want to be among the settlers. Early probes have shown that it's hotter and wetter than any region on Prima. The vegetation has a stranglehold on the surface."

"I don't think I'll ever go there either. I can't imagine being confined in a space vessel long enough to reach it."

"It's not as distant as you think. Probes from Prima have reached it in about three weeks. The problem is landing and taking off again."

He hadn't intended to stand so close. It was a torment not to run his fingers through the red-gold hair that cascaded down her back. Usually he disliked the spicy oils women used to scent their bodies, but her skin was subtly enticing, like the first blooms of the moura plants his mother cultivated on the tiny plot of land behind his family's hovel.

Shifting his stance to put more distance between them, he wondered how he could ever again be satisfied with one of the joy-girls employed by the Space Service to satisfy the needs of crew members on furlough. Until this moment he'd thought the system was commendable; he liked the ready availability of female flesh with no commitment. Few spacemen mated for life; those who did were usually ambitious and wanted a powerful family connection on Prima.

"I smell that odor the captain mentioned," she suddenly said, detecting it at the same instant he did.

"Yes."

"It smells like electrical wires melting."

"I tried to tell the captain that," he said without considering the consequences of contradicting Blaz.

"It's horrible—but now it's fading."

"That's why it's so puzzling. Nothing shows on the computer; the warning system is ignoring it."

"Surely the crew is investigating?"

"As many as the captain will allow," he said, knowing he should be with them instead of tormenting himself by wanting to stroke the arms of an untouchable female.

"Would you like to help them?" she asked.

He was more troubled by her understanding attitude than by her striking appearance. In the few high-caste women he'd seen, beauty seemed to conceal icy hearts. He'd been warned since childhood never to trust a member of the elite; he was genuinely sorry that he couldn't confide in her. He just couldn't depend on her not to repeat anything he said.

"I'm honored to be your escort, Highness Yor."

She smiled up at him, revealing small, perfect teeth, and he imagined how her love bite would feel on his overheated flesh.

"Your words are gallant, Officer Rie, but your eyes betray you. You're anxious about the safety of the ship."

"You're very perceptive, Highness."

Instinct told him he could safely share his concerns with her, but he was oddly reluctant to alarm her. Nor was this the time or the place to change his long habit of reticence with strangers—with anyone who wasn't wedded to space flight as he was.

"Please leave me now. I have no further need of your presence."

Her words sounded arrogant, but he couldn't take offense. Her eyes were sympathetic, and she smiled broadly to seal their conspiracy. She was helping him circumvent the captain's order that kept him away from more urgent duties.

"I thought you wanted to question a low-caste specimen," he said without a trace of bitterness, surprised at how easy it was to talk with her.

"You've caught me out! It was only a ruse to free Captain Blaz for more pressing duties."

"I thank you for doing the same for me. Please let me escort you to your stateroom."

"No! I mean, it's only a few steps to my door. Don't let me detain you."

Garner hesitated, knowing there was no real reason to remain by her side. Usually he was the first to welcome any release from protocol, but she made him feel oddly protective.

"Stay in the lounge," he urged, smiling at her as he would a friend. "The other passengers won't intrude, and I doubt very much if any will resent your privilege."

"Will you tell me what the problem is when you discover its source?"

"Gladly."

He hadn't meant to respond so fervently; he compensated by bowing stiffly and backing away.

A shuddering impact suddenly caught him off balance, throwing him forward against Highness Yor. They both fell to the floor, momentarily blinded as the lights went out.

Incredibly, his first fear was that he'd injured her. Her legs were pinned under his torso, and he rolled aside, kneeling beside her with his heart pounding in his chest.

"Are you all right?"

"I think so." She sat up, her face a blur illuminated only by starlight, and reached out for his hand as though it were a lifeline. "What made the lights go out?"

"I'll have to find out," he said, not wanting to frighten her with any of the alarming possibilities. "Can you stand up?"

"Yes, I think so."

He stood and helped her, reaching under her arms and lifting her.

He'd never experienced such a severe impact on a space vessel. The ship was in serious—maybe disastrous—trouble, but he still felt a shiver of arousal when he touched the sensuously soft cloth of her gown. His hands slid to her waist as she steadied herself against him.

"Don't leave me alone," she said in a soft, breathless voice.

"I won't," he answered, bending his head close to hers, her lips only inches from his own. How easy it would be to release all his fear and frustration by claiming her mouth in a long, deep kiss. He knew the Code of Emergency Procedures as well as he knew his own name—he wasn't responsible for any passenger's peace of mind, and another moment with her would unsettle his own mental state even more!

"I have to report to the command bridge." He only now remembered that Weal still had the watch, and cold dread cooled his ardor.

"I'll go with you!"

It was an outrageous suggestion. He should use his emergency powers to confine her to her stateroom, but it would be inexcusably cruel to leave her alone in a pitch-dark cubicle.

"All right, but only until the backup generator gives us some light," he agreed. "Take my hand and be careful on the steps."

They cautiously descended the spiral steps, aided by a muted glow at the bottom. The backup power for the command bridge was separate from the rest of the vessel's. It ensured that both computers would stay on-line regardless of any other malfunctions. Garner felt a flicker of relief that at least one system was functioning as it should.

Lon was seated, crouched over the watch officer's desk, while the helmsman manned his station at the computer.

"Weal, what's the status?" he demanded, horrified when he realized the second officer was weeping, blubbering like an unweaned whelp.

"By all that's holy, Rie! We're doomed!"

"Pull yourself together!" he ordered harshly, appalled by the incompetent officer's emotional reaction to a crisis.

Weal's assignment on the *Moon Courier* was another example of a man's caste counting for more than his abilities. Garner clenched his fists, wanting to pummel the coward, but the situation was too urgent to vent his anger in that way.

The second officer made a sloppy attempt to stand at attention, apparently executing the only maneuver he hadn't forgotten under duress.

"Highness Yor!" Lon's voice was squeaky with surprise when he saw her, but her presence seemed to impart a measure of composure to the devastated watch officer.

Garner considered whether to relieve him of the

bridge command, a drastic step that would certainly end Weal's career—or his own if he couldn't justify the action to the satisfaction of a review board.

Where was the captain? He hadn't made his way to the bridge, so it could mean he was caught in an emergency situation in the engine control room.

Garner made his decision. Weal was useless on the bridge, but he probably couldn't do any harm at this point. The low-caste officer walked over to the helmsman and they conferred in urgent whispers, the helmsman confirming that all communication was cut off. He couldn't speak to the captain on the intercom system, and so far all attempts to reach the Prima base had failed.

"Carry on. You're doing fine," Garner said to encourage the helmsman.

"If you're leaving, I'm going with you!" There was determination but no fear in Highness Yor's voice.

"The crew . . ." He couldn't imagine the high-caste female coming into contact with greasers.

"It doesn't matter," Alena said, surprised by her audacity. She didn't know why it seemed so urgent to stay with Officer Rie.

The dark, narrow corridor intimidated her, but she didn't hesitate to follow him into the gloom.

"Stay close," he warned, reaching back and catching her hand with his hard fingers.

She closed her eyes, trusting him to guide her, until the ship shuddered again, nearly causing her to lose footing.

"Another hit," he said grimly. "The *Moon Courier* isn't going to set a speed record on this trip. It may go down in history for sustaining the most meteor hits in a single voyage."

"We'll be—" She bit off her words, realizing it was unfair to ask him for reassurance before he knew their situation.

Ahead she heard furious pounding. Rie stopped beside what had to be one of the second-class staterooms and called out loudly.

"Don't panic, sir. You'll be able to open the door as soon as the auxiliary power unit is activated."

He pulled her away from an outburst of profanity too loud to be muffled by the corridor wall.

"If it weren't for you, I might be trapped in a dark stateroom too," she said. "Those poor people who are, they must be terrified!"

She thought of her father for the first time since the meteor hit. If he knew what was happening to her, would he be more disturbed by the damage to the vessel or the way Garner Rie's fingers circled her wrist? She was sure Garner had looked at her in the lounge with the gaze of a man who desired a woman, and it had excited her beyond reason. All her life she'd been warned against contamination by low castes, yet this officer's courage was the only thing holding her fear at bay.

"The engine control room," he said, pulling her into a surreal scene illuminated by the ghastly green glow of a lantern sitting on the deck.

"The chief started tearing down the engine monitor," a young greaser with a stricken face said. "When we got the big hit, it shorted and fried him!"

Alena clung to the rim of the entrance as she realized what was causing the hideous smell permeating the area: burning flesh. Her stomach churned, and she clamped a hand over her nose and mouth, determined not to succumb to weakness.

"Does the captain know?"

"Yea, sir. He said to take the remains to the waste chute . . . the waste chute . . ." The young man's voice broke.

"He was a good man," Rie said, "and we'll have a proper eulogy later. Do as the captain said. Where is he now?"

"Went to find the high-caste bitch, sir," a voice said from the shadows.

Alena was appalled that the commander of the vessel had put her welfare above that of the ship and all aboard it. She'd never heard the word "bitch" spoken aloud, but she didn't blame the speaker for resenting a passenger who took precedence over everything else in a dire emergency.

"Watch your words, greaser!" Rie snapped, standing aside so two men could carry away the remains. "Does anyone know what prompted the chief to disassemble the monitor? It's never done in-flight."

"We all know, sir," the young greaser said. "The chief told us it was risky, but he was at his wit's end to know what that stink was. Getting worse, it was. . . ." His voice had a catch in it, but he didn't break down as the second officer had.

"Did he say anything—anything at all about what was wrong?"

"He said plenty," another crew member said. "Most of it not fit for the ears of a female."

Alena had stepped aside to let the men carry out their chief's body, then entered the engine room, acutely conscious of the stir her presence caused.

"Pretend I don't exist," she said to encourage the speaker. "I'll be grateful beyond measure if you forget you've ever seen me in this place."

"What did he say?" Garner demanded impatiently.

A swarthy young man with a grimy face and

massive shoulders stepped out of the shadows. "The first meteor shower caused electrical disturbances and shorted out the damage-control subsystem in the computer. That's why the sensors didn't pick up on the smell of burning wire. The module that should have detected the problem was damaged."

"Eli Moke, from now on you're chief engineer. Can you activate the backup generator? I've got passengers trapped in their staterooms."

"I'm working on it, sir. The chief said whoever rushed this vessel into service should be set adrift in space."

"If you can't get it working soon, send two men to force the doors with prybars. We've got enough trouble without passengers going crazy in the close quarters. Where's Officer Col?"

"Here, sir," the communications officer said, moving into the green glare. "I think the intercom will work when the generator starts up."

He broke off, thrown against a greaser when another impact made the deck tilt sharply.

"Rie, if we don't get out of this meteor storm . . ." Col said, forgetting formality and calling his friend by name.

"Priority number one is the generator. Then all hands stand ready to activate the engines."

Garner glanced at Highness Yor, wondering how much she knew about space flight. He feared the worst: the ship drifting into uncharted parts of the solar system until the oxygen supply gave out. The escape pods, highly publicized to encourage travelers, were useless unless there was a habitable environment within their limited range. In the vast reaches of the solar system, there were only two safe harbors: Prima and the moon base on Bedir. Theoretically Brona could sustain human life, but it was unexplored except by remote mechanical probes that had showed it was dangerous beyond imagination.

Small meteor hits couldn't be felt inside the heavily insulated ship. In order to shake the vessel, a meteor had to be large enough to be potentially lethal. They couldn't risk more battering from the storm around them but, unless the captain was dead or totally incapacitated, only he could order a course change.

"I have to find Captain Blaz," Garner said grimly. "If the generator isn't working in ten minutes, start freeing the passengers manually."

Alena watched the bizarre scene in the engine room, almost able to convince herself she was caught up in a nightmare. Maybe she had space fever, a mental state caused by the anxieties of space travel. She'd read lurid reports of the symptoms: delusions, hallucinations, incessant screaming, and, in extreme cases, self-mutilation or homicidal rage.

Officer Rie started to leave, then looked at her as if belatedly remembering she was there. He nodded his head, and she took it as a signal to follow him. She did so thankfully. The engine control room occupied a good portion of the lower-deck stern, but it was so crowded with men and equipment that it was little better than her stateroom. She followed, clutching the back of his coarse-fibered tunic when he didn't offer his hand.

Corridor lights flickered briefly, then came on before they reached the command bridge at the opposite end of the lower level. The concealed tubes provided just enough illumination to make the corridor seem like deepest dusk in the moments before the solar light on Prima gave way to the dark of night. She didn't need to be told energy had to be conserved in every possible way until the emergency situation was resolved—if it ever was!

Garner could hear the captain raging at Lon Weal before he could see either of them.

"Imbecile! You should have placed Highness Yor under bridge protection while she was here. How could you let her wander in the dark with that slum-bred interloper? You're a disgrace to your birthright! You have no more caste consciousness than a braying, long-eared beast!"

His heart pounding with anger, Garner froze in the corridor outside the command bridge, temporarily unseen by the other two officers. He heard Alena gasp, and for a moment he feared she might try to defend him. Nothing could be worse than to have her champion his cause. He knew the scorn some officers had for the low-caste graduates of the Academy. Enduring it was the price he paid to travel in space. No matter how harsh and unfair it was, the attitude of men like Blaz wouldn't drive him out of the Service. But if Blaz even imagined that a female like Alena Yor looked on him with favor, he would draw up bogus charges to force him out of the Space Service.

The oldest and most strictly enforced laws on Prima forbade the mingling of castes. Men and women who crossed caste lines in the name of love became the Uncasted, banished from their families and sent to live in the wild, harsh Outlands of Prima—a bleak region far from civilization where people reverted to savages. Besides a bestial struggle for survival, those condemned to the Outlands had to live with the knowledge that their whole family would be made to suffer economic and social hardships as a consequence.

A simple thing like kissing Alena in the observation lounge could have cost him his career, even though he suspected she would have betrayed her caste but not her femininity by parting her lips and responding to him.

He stood in the corridor for a few more moments, allowing Blaz to change the subject. It was wiser not to bring the captain's enmity out into the open. He couldn't challenge a superior officer without risking his own career, and he didn't think Blaz would publicly slander him, not as long as some high-placed officials, including High Yor himself, wanted a few token low-castes in the service.

"Say nothing," Garner urged Highness Yor, holding her back a while longer so Blaz wouldn't suspect they both had overheard.

For the first time in his 31 years, Garner wondered how it would feel to be an elite female. Did they experience anything like the urges that tormented men? Did high-caste women bestow their favors only to breed more of their own kind, or did they sometimes lose themselves in passion like the joy-girls they scorned and denounced? If it weren't for the danger to his career, he would gladly learn more about this elegant, detached creature who held herself so far above him.

He partly turned and found Highness Yor's hand, unable to resist touching it one more time before the captain placed her beyond his reach for all time. Her skin was wonderfully soft, but there was strength in her slender fingers and uncalloused palms. He maneuvered his fingers between hers, surprised that such a simple gesture seemed so intimate. With guilty haste, he explored it from her smooth, hard nails to the delicately veined wrist, gratified but also alarmed when she squeezed his fingers and brought his hand to her cheek.

He was ready for the act of mating, yet he'd neither seen nor touched any secret part of her body. He felt like some demented stranger stroking Alena's satiny cheek and pressing his knee against her slender limbs, parting her thighs as easily as a knife went into solidified oil.

"This can't be," he murmured for her ears only.

"No, it shouldn't be happening."

"The Service is my wife and my mistress." He was reminding himself of what he had to lose, not explaining his situation to her.

"As it is with all who challenge space, my father says."

This was insanity, to fondle the daughter of the Minister of Science in the corridor of the ship. He was risking more than his career!

"I have my duties." He brought her hand to his mouth in one more rash, impulsive act, and pressed it so hard with his lips that he feared she'd carry a mark there for many days.

"It's my fault you neglect them," she said. She pressed her hand against her mouth, as though she were tasting the imprint of his lips on her skin. "I'll go."

He watched until she disappeared inside the elevator, and only then did he remember her dread of enclosed spaces.

At least he knew the elevator was functioning; the door closed with its usual silent efficiency, and she was whisked away from him.

He slowly counted to 100, grateful for the first time in his career for the tight trousers that effectively girdled his loin.

"Rie reporting for orders, sir," he said, stepping onto the command bridge and forcing his attention back to the disastrous situation that could make all other considerations meaningless.

Chapter Three

Alena saw several people in the dim upper corridor, but no one saluted or yielded the right of way to her. Deference was forgotten as people sought companionship in the crisis.

Because her stateroom was in a privileged position near the observation lounge, she couldn't help hearing the agitated din of many voices coming from there as she entered her quarters. Her cubicle seemed lonely beyond endurance after she closed the door, and she fervently wished her father were traveling with her. How ironic that he'd urged her to wait for the *Moon Courier* rather than go earlier with him on a more cramped, uncomfortable freighter!

Her heart was thudding, but she fought against panic, knowing part of her agitation came from being touched by Garner and wanting more of his forbidden caresses. The walls seemed to close in on her, and she took deep breaths to steady herself.

What would her father do in this situation?

When she forced herself to think calmly and rationally, she knew exactly how he would react: by gathering as much information as possible, then deciding what he could do to improve the situation. He wouldn't cower in his stateroom waiting for other people to take action.

The interior of the stateroom was as murky as the corridor, but she could see well enough to open the wall compartment where her traveling cases were stored. She was dressed for a formal meal, not a crisis. Working more by touch than sight, she found a pale blue, hooded tunic and a pair of dark insulated trousers. The room was cool, and it would get colder if the vessel was dependent on the backup generator for very long.

Working by feel, she gathered her long tresses into a bun at the back of her neck and pulled the hood up to cover as much of her head as possible. With her feet encased in thick stockings and heavy shoes intended for working at the moon base, she felt as ready as she would ever be to mingle with the other passengers.

The observation lounge was packed; most of the 51 other passengers had crowded into this upper-level lookout post where they could see the stars. There was much conversation, but most people were either intensely curious about what was happening or upset because they might face delays in getting to Bedir. No one sounded as frightened as the person trapped in the stateroom two doors down from her had.

Standing near the entrance, Alena was able to brace herself when the next large meteor battered the ship, but not everyone was so fortunate. Several people cried out as they were knocked to the deck, and someone moaned in pain.

"My ankle—I can't get up," a woman called out from the center of the lounge.

Alena had been well tutored in the healing arts as part of her career preparation. A cartographer had to be able to survive on rugged terrain, although so far she had only worked briefly in the field as a student apprentice.

"Let me see," she said, surprising herself by boldly speaking out.

She knelt beside the female and carefully examined the ankle as best she could in the dim light. "It's swelling already. It needs to be elevated with a cold pack."

"Get the medical officer," the woman's mate said, too agitated to realize the hooded figure was the high-caste female.

"I think it's just a sprain," Alena said.

"You don't know that. I want a qualified person to look at it," the man insisted, lifting his spouse and carrying her to one of the launch seats bolted to the back wall of the lounge.

Alena tried to lose herself in the crowd. She'd never been contradicted by a lower-caste male, and humiliation was a new and unpleasant experience.

She watched from the dark shadows until the medical officer, Velma Pitt, was found and brought to the lounge. Alena had noticed her, the only female crew member, in the dining room and wished the medic belonged to the highest caste instead of the middle caste. Pitt was a sturdily built woman with heavy legs and arms and thick black hair coiled around her head in braids. Her friendly, open face and warm hazel eyes made Alena feel they could become friends if it weren't for the difference in status.

"It appears to be a sprain," the medic confirmed when she had made a cursory examination. "Go down to the galley and ask the chef for a cold pack," she told the husband. "Tell him I authorized it."

Alena watched the medic until she disappeared from sight at the end of the dim corridor. What she was feeling wasn't all admiration; she actually felt a tinge of envy. Velma Pitt led a purposeful life; she had a role to play in this crisis, unlike Alena, who chafed at the restrictions that kept her from helping. She had healing skills, but physical contact with the lower castes was totally unacceptable.

Alena wondered if she would ever reach the moon base and fulfill her father's hopes for her. The map project could confirm her tutors' expectations, but when it was completed, how long would it be before she had useful work to do again? It was unthinkable for a high-caste female to work as a commercial mapmaker or an instructor of cartography. She would be idle until her father found another suitable project.

On the lower level Garner left the command bridge with his stomach knotted in anger and frustration. Blaz had convened an Officers' Council, an emergency measure that gave every crew member with officer's ranking a vote in the decision that should have been made by the commander alone. But while the captain had waited for that obscure provision in the code book to be carried out, the ship had floundered in a meteor storm, sustaining two more hits. With the computer malfunctioning, there was no sure way to confirm how much damage had been done, but

Garner had seethed with impatience. He had seen no way of saving the vessel unless a course change was ordered immediately.

At last, after maddening debate and possibly fatal delay, Blaz had called for a vote of the Officers' Council. They had unanimously supported a course change, but even then Blaz had procrastinated, insisting that every officer sign the log to verify the vote. Garner had had to sign, as had the second officer, the new chief engineer, both helmsmen, the communications officer, and the medic.

Garner swore under his breath as he entered the engine control room. He'd never served under a captain who'd exercised his code-book right to convene an Officers' Council instead of making a crucial decision himself. Blaz had put the ship and the people aboard it in even greater danger by delaying the course change. He was only thinking of his own career; he didn't want a blot on his record if the *Moon Courier* had to go far off course.

Eli Moke immediately began instructing his crew of greasers when he and Garner reached the engine room. The new chief's face had a sheen of perspiration even though the temperature had dropped drastically. He knew how desperate the situation was, and it was his responsibility to start the engines that would alter the ship's course.

"The starboard fuel tank took a hit," he said quietly. "It's dry."

"You're sure?" Garner whispered, containing his own dread so the crew wouldn't be more alarmed than they were.

"Worse, we've been knocked off the moon course by meteor hits. By all that's sacred, why did he put us through the farce of an Officers'

Council? There was only one possible decision! To get out of this hell-storm!"

"All he cares about is covering his ass—that's why we had to put our signatures in the log. Once a captain convenes an Officers' Council, the decision is binding on him. By ducking the responsibility, he makes it nearly impossible for a review board to hand down a faulty-judgment charge against him."

Garner knew that speaking against the captain could get him thrown out of the Service, but he was sure none of the crew members anxiously waiting for the firing of the engines would denounce him, not after Blaz had put their lives in greater jeopardy by shirking his responsibility.

"I'm ready but . . ." Moke said.

"Fire the engines then, man!"

"The captain said he'd see me floating out in space if I did it before he gave the word," the chief said miserably. "I think he meant it."

"I'll take responsibility—"

His words were cut off by an outburst of static coming from the ship's intercom.

"Col got it working!" Garner said with relief. "That should be Blaz with his order."

His moment of relief turned to dismay when the captain started speaking.

"My honorable passengers, regretfully my duties won't allow me to speak to each of you personally. . . ."

Garner snorted in disgust, unable to imagine Hurex Blaz even acknowledging the existence of the less-prestigious travelers quartered in lower-level staterooms.

"The ship has sustained some damage—hopefully very minor. Let me assure you that the hull of the *Moon Courier* is impenetrable. This is the finest liner ever built. If it were a water vessel, it would be unsinkable."

Garner had to hold up his hand for silence; even the greasers were mumbling against the captain now.

A burst of static muffled the man's next words. Then he continued with what sounded like a prepared speech.

For the first time in his life, Garner seriously worried about the competence of a commander. Was Blaz one of those captains who appeared efficient for years, only to snap in his first real crisis? If he did, what could Garner do? The greasers were muttering against Blaz now, but their discontent wasn't deep enough to endure for long. He knew they wouldn't risk their careers and lives by going against a high-caste officer. Even if the captain was dead wrong in his actions, there was no way Garner could assume command of the ship himself. Except for the greasers, there were no other Prolas on the vessel, and higher-caste passengers and crew members would never tolerate mutiny by a low-caste executive officer.

"Men," Garner said, "if he doesn't give the command to fire the engines in the next two minutes . . ." He paused to listen to the speaker for another instant, then thanked the fates that he hadn't said more.

"If you haven't already done so, go immediately to a launch seat and secure the harness," Blaz said. "In exactly seventy-five seconds the engine crew will fire the engines to alter course. Don't be alarmed if you feel an abrupt thrust, but it should be much milder than our launch from Prima. We don't have to contend with gravity in space. This is your captain. I repeat, secure all launch harnesses immediately. Thank you, ladies and gentlemen."

A clicking noise indicated that the public address system was off. The captain came on again, this time speaking only to the crew in the engine room, alerting them for his order. Garner automatically backed against one of the launch stations built into the hull at intervals between pieces of equipment and storage lockers. Throughout the room, others were doing the same. Unlike the passengers' harnesses, the crews' were flexible, allowing them to move a few feet from the hollowed-out depressions that served as seats so they could perform their duties. A hard thrust would automatically cause these lifebelts to tighten, pulling the wearers into their seats and locking them there. Garner had been caught out of position once on a launch. The result had been unpleasant but not life-threatening. His buttocks had been black and blue and his back had ached for the rest of the flight, but the alternative, being unsecured, could have been fatal. Course changes weren't as dangerous as launches, but the captain had rightly ordered everyone to find a station. Unfortunately his wordiness had been one more unnecessary delay.

In spite of the tension in the engine room, Garner thought of Highness Yor. Was she safely secured? Passengers had to practice emergency procedures that included finding a launch seat wherever they were on the vessel in 30 seconds or less. Ordinary passengers practiced; had her privileged status excused her from the drills? Would she panic and be unable to lock the ends of the harness together?

He forced his attention back to the situation in the engine room. Although the crew was spared from hearing it, a warning gong was sounding throughout the ship. There were plenty of seats available, and the high-caste beauty wasn't his worry!

"Forty-two seconds," Blaz shouted over the intercom. "The helmsman has completed entering the course adjustments in the computer."

Chief Moke was already standing by the switches, wiping his palms on the sides of his coverall. At the crucial moment, it was his responsibility to trigger the automatic system. If for any reason the engines didn't fire within the ten-second grace period, he had to throw on the manual override.

Garner saw beads of sweat on the young officer's forehead. For ten seconds, the fate of the vessel was on Moke's shoulders. If he froze and didn't activate the manual override when it was needed, the computer would go into a lockdown. It would take a series of complicated commands to ready the engine for a second try. They didn't have time for this kind of delay. The sensor screens showed no letup in the meteor storm, and Garner didn't share Blaz's faith in the invincibility of the *Moon Courier.* It was true that the hull could resist the impact of a meteor half the weight of the ship, but the fuel tanks and even the engines were still vulnerable, positioned as they were outside the main body of the vessel.

It was extremely unlikely that the *Moon Courier* would be destroyed by a fiery explosion, but it could float into deep space with no means of returning. Garner feared an instantaneous death far less than a slow, agonizing end in the forbidding vastness of the solar system.

"Fire engines," the captain bellowed into the stillness of the engine room.

Garner's instincts told him it was too much responsibility for a man who'd only been the chief engineer for hours. He wanted to rush to the switches himself and intervene, but it was unthinkable for an executive officer to interfere. The chief had supreme control of the engines; not even the captain was authorized to touch those switches.

Moke activated the automatic control, and the engine room was totally silent, not a man among them even daring to breathe.

The engines didn't fire; even the least-experienced greaser knew that the untried vessel had failed them again.

Garner's heart stopped, but he didn't dare make a move that would disturb the chief engineer's concentration. He counted to himself and tried not to see the terror etched on every face around him. They were running out of time.

Then the incredibly costly, highly touted new engines made a small noise not unlike the whistling of wind through a canyon, and every man present relaxed with an audible sigh.

"Engines activated, sir," Moke said, grinning with relief one instant and screaming in terror the next as he was thrown face-first into the unyielding surface of a storage locker. The unfastened ends of his launch harness whipped around like demented serpents as the ship spun like a child's toy caught in a whirlpool.

Garner fought for consciousness, but felt himself slipping back into bottomless darkness. Pinpricks of light exploded inside his lids, giving him an immeasurably small instant of grace to accept the finality of death.

* * *

His hearing returned first, with a steady hammering noise, a rhythmic pounding both familiar and frightening. He was cold, icy cold, and he was curiously reluctant to open his eyes. Slowly he realized what he was hearing: the pumping of his own heart.

He was alive; he'd survived, but the realization didn't bring him relief or joy. He was too weary to be responsible for his own fate or anyone else's. All he wanted to do was sink back into unconsciousness.

A flaming image teased his mind, and he tried to focus, dimly aware that the red-gold tongues of fire existed only in his mind. Then a female rose out of the inferno, and the flames became luminous locks of hair that swirled around a naked torso like none he'd ever seen. She raised her arms to beckon him, and her pink-tipped nipples made him harden with desire.

His erotic hallucination burst like a bubble, and icy rivulets of perspiration ran down his forehead. Called back to reality by the vision of Highness Yor, he reluctantly opened his eyes. A short distance from him one of the greasers was stirring in his launch seat, beginning to fumble with the catch on his safety harness.

Garner was revived by this sign of life. Calling on deep reserves of stamina, he looked around the engine control room, steeling himself for the worst. The dim auxiliary lights showed other crew members still secured in their harnesses, some showing signs of recovery.

With arms and legs trembling, Garner fumbled with the buckle on his harness and managed to release it, slowly piecing together what had happened. They'd collided with another meteor only moments after the engines fired. The force of that hit had made all the earlier ones seem trivial. There was no way of knowing how long the ship had spun out of control, but the force of the impact had, mercifully, made the humans aboard black out.

He stretched his arms and legs, a groan escaping his lips as he heaved his aching body into a standing position. The deck was steady under his feet; the vessel hadn't exploded, and the fact that he could breathe reassured him that the thick hull hadn't been breached. He took a small tentative step, and his foot hit against an obstacle.

Garner had seen men die, but never in space and never so violently as the young chief engineer. He was lying on his back, his features little more than bloody pulp. His head and legs lay at improbable angles, and the stink of death assaulted Garner's nostrils. He didn't need to check Eli Moke's pulse to know he was gone.

"What a terrible waste." Garner spoke aloud without realizing it.

"Sir, why did his harness come apart?" the young greaser asked, attempting to rise from his seat.

"I don't think we'll ever know that." As executive officer, he felt an obligation to say something reassuring, but he was appalled by the senseless accident. Had Moke been so anxious about starting the engines that he hadn't properly locked his harness? Or was this one more equipment failure to blame on the builders of this damned vessel?

He was momentarily paralyzed by even blacker thoughts. Blaz should have changed course at the beginning of the meteor storm. He'd been so obsessed with setting a speed record, he'd allowed the ship to sustain hit after hit before finally convening an Officers' Council to further shirk his responsibility. Two good men were dead, and there was only one person to blame: the captain of the *Moon Courier*.

Garner tormented himself, wondering if he could have done anything to head off the disaster. Blaz was in command, and caste as much as rank made him a total autocrat. Armed resistance was impossible. The few weapons on board were securely locked away in the captain's quarters. Even before Chief Engineer Hail Benay's death, Garner could only have called upon a few Prola crew members to oppose the captain, and a lifetime of conditioning made it unthinkable to most of them to disobey their superior. Weal would undoubtedly have stood with Blaz in any situation, and it was unlikely any of the others would have supported a low-caste officer if he'd tried to circumvent the captain's orders.

Had he hesitated because his own career would have been destroyed? Garner thought of the 52 passengers, most of them men in fit condition who were reporting to assignments at the moon base. Would any of them have supported his disobedience if he'd altered the course without Blaz's permission?

Garner knew the answer; any attempt at mutiny had been doomed to fail. Even the passengers quartered on the lower level with the crew came from higher castes. Mechanics and sanitary technicians traveling to Bedir had more status then Garner did. Going to the Space Academy hadn't changed that. The passengers would mindlessly follow the lead of a high-caste captain, even if it led to their deaths.

"Is he dead, sir?"

The greaser was standing, still bracing himself,

and staring in horror at the bloody remains of Eli Moke.

"Yes, I'm afraid so."

"A ship has to have an engineer!" the greaser cried out, rousing muffled sounds of alarm from others who were slowly reviving.

Garner didn't want to tell him the awful truth: that the ship's destiny was out of the hands of men. They had neither the power nor the fuel to put the ship back on course. The *Moon Courier* was adrift in space; the computer might clarify their situation, but instinct told him there was no way to remedy it without help from Prima. And that might not be a possibility.

"One of the helmsmen will be appointed as chief," he said, hoping none of the crew members knew how poorly prepared the computer men were for engine-room duty. His own choice would be to appoint the best-qualified greaser, but none of them had enough caste status to be considered by Blaz.

"I'm going forward to assess our situation," Garner said in a crisp, authoritarian tone, deciding brusque orders would help the men more than pointless sympathy. "As soon as two men are steady on their feet, I want the chief's remains carried to the disposal."

"Sir, his eulogy . . ."

"There's no time. Prepare a thorough damage report and get this place cleaned up," he ordered, almost envying the men who were groggily trying to put their world back into perspective. They were accustomed to obeying their superiors; they weren't burdened with the necessity of making decisions.

With heavyhearted dread, he started down the corridor to the command bridge, torn between fear of what he'd find and a murderous urge to strangle Captain Hurex Blaz.

In her stateroom Alena bent forward, her head between her knees, trying to keep from blacking out again. There was a maddening buzz in her ears, and she'd lost all sense of up and down.

Slowly she remembered the awful sequence of events before she'd lost consciousness. The captain had sought her out, urging her to assume launch position in her stateroom. He hadn't tried to conceal his shock at finding her in the observation lounge with a mix of castes. His pale eyes had been icy with disapproval, which made his flowery words all the more unwelcome. She'd complied, however, reopening her door as soon as he'd had time to leave the area.

His speech on the intercom had been more alarming than reassuring, and when people started tramping down the corridor, silently intent on reaching safety seats before time ran out, Alena had had the terrible feeling that the *Moon Courier* would be her coffin.

Now she was conscious, alive and uninjured except for nagging aches from the back of her neck to the bones in her ankles. Yet she was more frightened than she had been during the crisis. With nothing to do but wait for news, she felt more claustrophobic than she had at any time since meeting Officer Rie.

She thought of him now—in fact, she'd thought of little else since he'd taken her to the bridge and engine room. Was he all right? Had the crew fared worse than the passengers during that horrible collision, if that was what it had been? She remembered little, only that the vessel seemed to spin out of control, making her unbearably nauseous before she blacked out.

In fact, she didn't know if any passengers or crew members had survived. No one passed her open door; no sound broke the eerie silence. She might be the only living person on the ship.

So frightened she nearly fainted again, she tried not to imagine floating alone in space with no hope of rescue. A scream was building in her throat, but she clutched her face and clamped her lips together, determined to fight her rising panic.

Was she imagining things? The truth couldn't be much worse than her frenzied speculations, so she released her harness buckle and tried to stand upright. Twice her legs failed her, and she plopped down again, bending to dangle her head between her knees before trying again. On the third attempt, she managed to take the few short steps to the door, hanging on until she felt strong enough to go on.

To her immense relief, a man was staggering out of a stateroom near the murky centerpoint of the corridor, and ahead in the lounge she could hear muffled words from those who'd used the launch stations there. She wasn't the only one alive!

Her relief was tempered by anxiety. She desperately wanted Garner to be alive. She tried to tell herself it was only because he seemed like such a competent officer—someone who was dependable in a crisis—but embarrassing images kept passing through her mind: a shock of midnight-black hair falling over his forehead; the way he'd parted his lips and touched them with the tip of his tongue; the tight fit of his trousers on powerful thighs.

"This must be space fever," she said aloud, wondering how long it would be before she started raving and screaming.

No, she was calm and rational. Leaning her backside against one wall of the corridor and her hands on the other, she braced herself, waiting until the tremors in her thighs stopped.

Garner found her leaning against a wall in the walkway, her face deathly pale and her hair spilling down her back in complete disarray. He was carrying the passenger list, dispatched by the surly, almost-silent captain to account for every soul on board. Blaz had found the first casualty among the travelers: a lanky agri-specialist who'd come to the command bridge to demand an explanation after the captain's warning. He'd managed to harness himself in a spare seat there, but his heart had given out during the crisis.

They'd left Prima with 70 people; now there were 67, and Garner had only begun to check. It was his first experience with death in space, and he dreaded finding more corpses.

"Highness Yor, let me help you back to your stateroom." For a moment he forgot everything but his image of a flame-haired female, the curls on her groin as fiery as the wondrous locks streaming over her shoulders.

"Oh, no! I can't go back there. Tell me what's happened. Is the ship all right?"

"The hull is still sound. One fuel tank was ripped off, according to the computer monitor." He didn't tell her the monitor was as unreliable as the man who commanded the vessel, nor did she need to know the remaining tank was empty.

"But we'll still reach Bedir, won't we? Can't we get to the surface with escape pods?" She reached out and steadied herself by grasping his arm.

"Highness . . ." He was at a loss for words.

"You can't be secretive now, not after everything that's happened," she begged. "Please—Garner—tell me the truth."

Hearing her speak his name nearly broke his composure. He wanted to cradle her in his arms and assure her that everything would be fine, but he respected her too much to lie.

"Come sit in your stateroom, and I'll tell you everything I know."

He was disobeying Blaz's order by not concealing the truth from a passenger, but the captain's wrath meant little now.

He knelt beside her when she was seated, not sure why he thought it would help to take her hands in his.

"It's very bad, isn't it?" she whispered.

"It could be worse," he said, although he could scarcely imagine a more desperate situation. "When we manage to contact Prima, they'll be able to send a relief vessel to retrieve us."

"You make it sound like we've broken down on a thoroughfare." Her laugh was forced. "Are we very far off the course to the moon?"

He sighed and squeezed her fingers, not realizing how tight his grasp was until she leaned forward and pressed her knee against his arm.

"We're leaving Bedir behind us. The only thing between the *Moon Courier* and the sun is Brona."

"Surely the captain will change course soon!"

"It's out of his hands, Highness. The meteor destroyed the last of our fuel."

"Then we'll just drift—forever?"

"Not forever." He knew that sometime in the future the *Moon Courier* would be incinerated by solar heat, but by then the vessel would be a ghost ship, fragile human life snuffed out when water, food, and oxygen gave out.

Impulsively he stood and pressed the door control, shutting the two of them in the silver-walled cubicle.

"You don't expect rescue, do you?" she asked solemnly.

"Don't give up hope, Highness."

He could hear the soft rhythm of her breathing, and he wanted this wondrous woman to continue living more than he'd ever wanted anything. He'd sworn an Oath of Duty to give his own life if need be to save the lives of passengers entrusted to the care of the Space Service, but for the first time this responsibility seemed like a sacred trust. He desperately wanted to tell her everything would be all right, but he couldn't find words for a glib lie. He was torn between comforting her and honoring her intelligence and worth with the truth. Everything he thought of saying seemed hopelessly inadequate.

"I feel so unready for this," she said, "as though I'm disappointing my father after all his years of raising and educating me. He desperately wants a male heir, but he hasn't even found a suitable mate for me. He thought there was plenty of time. . . . " Her voice trailed off.

He knew she was thinking of a future that might never come. He lowered his head and groped for words, knowing he had many other passengers to console but unable to tear himself away without giving her some encouragement.

"I'm so frightened I'll never have a chance to really live," she murmured, so close her hand brushed against his.

"Don't give up." He'd never felt so inadequate, sure as he was that they would all die a slow, agonizing death.

"Garner." She took his hand and squeezed with a strength born of panic. "I don't want to die without knowing how it feels to be a whole person, not just my father's dutiful daughter."

His heart constricted, and he couldn't bear the thought of her death.

"Highness, I'm not going to let you die."

She was silent, but her grip on his hand loosened, making him hope his words had given her a glimmer of hope. He didn't want her to suffer the agony of fearing death through the many long days before it became a certainty.

"I don't believe you, but I thank you for wanting me to be comforted."

"Believe me, Alena. I swear I'll find a way to preserve your life."

He rose and opened the door, knowing he had to leave her before his voice broke and unmanned him. He retreated from the stateroom, stricken by the enormity of what he'd done: He'd promised Alena, Highness Yor, that he wouldn't let her die.

He meant to keep that promise.

Chapter Four

Garner finished checking on the upper-deck passengers, relieved to find only minor injuries among them. A few had harness burns, painful but not serious, and one passenger was suffering from a probable wrist fracture. Under the circumstances, the calm attitude of the scientists and technicians bound for Bedir was much more important than their physical condition. Instead of panicking, they'd bombarded him with complaints about the flight, and had tried to impress him with the urgency of reaching the moon base on schedule. No one seemed to suspect the vessel was doomed.

No one but Highness Yor.

For the first time since childhood, he felt like screaming in frustration. If—when—her life was snuffed out, it would be like the death of brilliant star, a loss of radiance that would dim the universe.

He felt cold sweat trickle down the small of his back, and his knees were still trembling from the devastating impact of the last meteor. What had possessed him to promise Alena he wouldn't let her die?

Forcing himself to think of his duties instead of his rash words, he staggered down to the lower deck, guided by the dim emergency lights that made safe movement through the passageways possible.

He'd soothed the passengers with platitudes and half-truths. He wouldn't try to deceive the crew members who avidly gathered around him when he stepped into the engine room.

"The first thing to do is appoint a man who understands the engines to serve as acting chief," he said.

"What use? We're adrift on this death trap—"

"We're all going to die!"

"Enough of that talk!" Garner shouted over the agitated muttering of the greasers. "I'll personally eject any coward who spreads panic or shirks his duties!"

"I know engines better than any greaser in the Service," a surly crewman named Tacka said. "It's only the book learning I lack, or I'd be a chief by now."

"No doubt you're qualified, Tacka, but there's more to being chief than being a mechanic."

Garner fervently wished he'd had time to learn the greasers' strengths and weaknesses before this crisis. Tacka was gifted with mechanical ability, but he was a loner, quarrelsome and mean-spirited. He was older than the others, and had been reprimanded by Hail Benay for hazing the only crewman new to Space Service, a stocky youth named Gullaner.

"Tacka, your assignment is to begin a complete engine appraisal immediately. I can't spare you from that to do the chief's other duties. Roar, you'll serve as acting chief engineer."

The old greaser's face was sickly green in the ghostly emergency light, and Garner knew he'd made an enemy by not giving Tacka the rank of chief, however briefly he might live to enjoy it. But he couldn't give authority to a man who was addicted to cruelty.

"Yea, sir," Tacka said, making no attempt to hide the hatred on his face, "but I reserve the right to appeal to the captain."

"Noted," Garner said, knowing Blaz was likely to overrule him just to keep a Prola officer in his place. But the captain hadn't taken any responsibility in the engine room since liftoff from Prima, and they could all be dead before he paid attention to Tacka's complaint.

"Clean this place up!" Garner ordered. "Roar, see that Tacka gets all the help he needs. Gullaner, find some rations for the crew. No man goes off duty until every wire and bolt on this vessel has been inspected and evaluated."

Playing the part of a brisk, efficient executive officer made Garner feel more like one. He hoped hard labor would have the same effect on the greasers. As long as they were busy, they wouldn't have time for despair.

He made his way down the dim corridor to a much more serious problem: the captain and his reaction to the crisis.

Privacy was a luxury no crew members enjoyed on the *Moon Courier.* Garner heard sounds of violent retching as he passed the entrance to the officers' sanitary facility. He went into the cramped cubicle and found what he'd expected:

Lon Weal puking like an overfed babe.

"As second officer, your place is on the bridge, Weal. You have three minutes to put yourself in order and report for duty unless you want to be assigned to an outside engine check."

"You can't. . . . " His voice quaked with terror.

"Read your Code of Service Rules. When there's an emergency shutdown of the vessel's engines, it's the sole responsibility of the executive officer to select personnel to inspect the exterior mountings. The captain can't save you from a space walk in this situation."

"By all that's holy, Rie . . ."

"You now have two minutes. And change that filthy tunic."

Garner didn't feel any satisfaction when Weal streaked past him down the dim corridor to his quarters. He didn't enjoy being a bully, but the harsher he was with the men, the more he felt there might be hope. Maybe he could do something to save the ship—and the life of Alena Yor.

On the command bridge, the captain was watching the helmsman at work on the computer. Vane Col was lying on the floor, his face contorted by agony, russet hair plastered damply to his forehead. Velma Pitt had slit his trouser and was easing an emergency leg splint under the exposed limb, crooning softly with a tenderness that surprised Garner. He didn't need to ask the medic to know Vane's leg was broken, but he did wonder about the affectionate murmurs that passed between them.

"I gave him an injection that should start working soon," she said to Garner. "I'm not going to try to move him until it kicks in."

She sounded grim, and Garner knew there was

another temporary opening on the command staff: communications officer.

"There's a possible wrist fracture and some harness burns topside," she added. "Nothing urgent."

"Get upstairs and see to them, Pitt," the captain called over to her. "I won't have passengers whining to Space Service headquarters that their injuries were ignored." He didn't look away from the control computer where Baren, the senior helmsman, was frantically tapping out emergency signals. The captain was still wearing his white dress uniform, but the ill-fated banquet seemed like a distant, hazy memory to Garner.

"Sir, I appointed Greaser Roar as acting chief engineer." Garner stood at attention, shoulders back and buttocks tight, ridiculous as the pose seemed in the circumstances.

"Don't bother me with that now, Rie. We have to reach the Space Control Center on Prima. The passengers won't tolerate a long delay in being rescued."

"Sir, we're adrift!" Garner couldn't have been more stunned if Blaz had suggested they put on space suits and try to fly back to Prima without a ship.

"Are you questioning my priorities, Rie?"

"No, sir." Garner ached from the effort of maintaining his rigid stance in the face of lunacy. "But no ship in operation today is capable of carrying enough fuel to intercept and retrieve our vessel. Space Service won't risk losing a second ship when the odds against a successful rescue are a million to one."

He braced himself, sure the captain would lash out at him. A verbal attack would have been less shocking than the captain's response.

Blaz smiled, a smug leer that sent chills down Garner's spine.

"You may be an officer, Rie, but as a Prola, you're not privy to the grand scope of the space program. Even as you challenge my judgment, a ship is being made ready for the first manned flight to Brona. We're drifting toward that planet. What could be more logical than to use the prototype for the Brona project to rescue the *Moon Courier*?"

Garner's fists were balled so tightly, his nails bit into his palms. He knew the captain scorned his low caste, but this was the first time Blaz had humiliated him in front of other crew members. He'd endured abuse before, and he could stomach it now, but he was shocked by the ranking officer's belief in rescue. Blaz might as well rely on heavenly spirits carrying the ship back to Prima in their arms! The first manned flight to Brona was in development, but when it was ready, the Scientifica who controlled the government and the Bellicosa who staffed the military would never risk losing a second vessel on a fool's mission.

Rescue in space was a child's dream, costly beyond calculation even if it were possible. Garner knew it wasn't, not with the technology available.

"Pitt, get up to the passengers!" the captain bawled out. "I intend to note your lax response to a direct order in your Service file."

"Sir, I need to prepare Vane Col for immediate surgery," she said anxiously.

"Unless you plan to spend the rest of this voyage confined to your quarters . . ."

"Yes, sir. I'll go under protest."

"We need a communications officer, sir," Garner said, controlling his anger with superhuman effort.

"Baren will serve as acting communications officer," the captain curtly assured him. "Now don't trouble me with non-essential details. Just keep those greasers on the lower deck where they belong, and see that the passengers get the best possible meals under the circumstances."

"Yes, sir. I'll institute rationing procedures immediately."

"Did I mention rationing?" The captain turned on him again, giving him a tongue-lashing that vilified generations of his ancestors.

Garner heard Blaz's tirade as meaningless babble. To control his fury, he let his mind focus on the most compelling image he could summon: his dream of a woman with hair like golden flames. She was reaching out to him, naked as she'd come into the world, her breasts full and her rosy-brown nipples erect, her secret place as brilliantly colored as the locks that swirled around her head.

". . . let bastard Prolas like you in space," the captain was shouting. "Now see to your duties, mister, and don't bother me with petty concerns, or you'll rue the day you weaseled your way into the Space Service."

Garner stepped over Col's drugged form, outraged at being made to leave him there to suffer from the captain's indifference.

Without knowing it, Highness Yor had just saved his life. If her image hadn't blocked out the captain's vile braying, Garner might have strangled the space ship commander with his bare hands. The penalty for mutiny in space was harsh and swift: ejection into space, a sure and terrible death.

Gratitude was one more reason to save Alena's life, but he still didn't see how it could be done. The planet Brona was all that stood between them and sure death as the ship drifted closer to the sun. In a few weeks the *Moon Courier*—moving in excess of 30,000 kilometers an hour—would skim the fringe of Brona's atmosphere. Their vessel would heat up and begin to disintegrate unless the engines could put out enough thrust to put them into orbit around the planet. If this happened, and he had no faith in such a miracle, they could use the escape pods to reach the planet's surface. If the pods functioned properly . . . if a safe landing site could be found without survey maps or contact with the Prima control center . . . if they could survive on the unexplored planet . . .

For the first time Garner was thankful for the exacting, often harsh training at the Academy. He remembered every emergency procedure drilled into him as a cadet, and he drove himself even harder than he drove the crew of greasers, trying not to overlook the smallest detail, the tiniest repair that might mean the difference between survival and death.

Conditions aboard the vessel seemed to worsen by the hour. By the second day after the collision, passengers were wearing multiple layers of clothing, attempting to stay warm.

"We're freezing in here," an irate passenger told Garner when he went to the upper deck on yet another fool's errand for the captain. "I thought the *Moon Courier* had plenty of fuel cells."

"For a normal run, yes, sir," Garner said, chafing under the dictates of courtesy. "But we're on backup generators, and it's imperative that we conserve power."

He couldn't believe a scientist qualified for a moon-base assignment would question the need to use a minimum of their available oxygen for the mixture of hydrogen and oxygen that produced electricity in space. This time the passenger grumbled assent. But Garner wondered how hostile the high-caste scientist would become when his belly was empty and his bones ached in subzero agony. At the captain's insistence, there was no rationing, only a gradual decrease in the portions allotted to both crew and passengers. But without adequate electricity, there was no way to thaw or heat the frozen provisions. The *Moon Courier* was a luxury vessel, and most of the stores required some preparation, unlike the rations on a freighter, most of which were dried or preserved in thin-skinned aluminum storage units.

Night and day lost all meaning, but Garner rarely slept more than a few hours each cycle. On the eighth day, he prowled the upper deck while the passengers were still in their cubicles. His stomach was a hollow ache, but he wouldn't allow himself a morsel more than the lowliest greaser received. Gullaner was already up, trying to thaw enough food packets with the galley's small ration of electricity to make a stew that would sustain 67 people for another day.

Garner suffered more from the chill dampness than from hunger, which had been part of his youthful experience growing up in a large family on the meager pay his father earned as a laborer for the transport authority. The colder it got on the ship, the damper the air became. The high humidity made the cold more penetrating, and runny noses were as common as goose bumps.

No one was allowed to bathe; water was too precious. The passengers were dangerously idle, unable to pursue any interests in the dark staterooms or public rooms. Complaining became their only release from the monotony of their days.

Garner went into the upper-deck lounge, the one place where life still seemed tolerable. It was always crowded, except during the mandatory sleep hours, essential to further preserve energy by extinguishing most corridor lights and cutting back on the already minimal heat. At this hour the lounge was deserted and he could be alone, gazing out at the universe and remembering the thrill he'd once felt traveling through space. If he was going to die soon—and he fully expected to—he could still be grateful that he'd seen the heavens as few living beings ever had.

"Garner Rie."

Her husky whisper sent shivers down his back. He'd imagined that resonant voice so often he was afraid to turn around, afraid he was hearing things.

"I've wondered. . . . " She came up beside him where he stood facing an observation panel. "I've wondered if you were well," she said softly, every word caressing his mind like the feathers joy-girls used for erotic torture.

He knew how inappropriate it was to think of this high-caste female in the same way a man thought of a professional pleasure-giver. He bowed his head, ashamed but excited by her presence.

"I can't thank you enough for what you did for me," she whispered.

"I did nothing."

"You gave me hope. I believed you when you said I wouldn't die. I still believe what you told me, High Rie."

"I only did my duty, Highness, and it's not proper for you to give me a title denied to my caste." He kept his eyes riveted on the distant stars.

"I don't understand why people need castes!" she cried out unexpectedly.

He turned to look into her face, surprised that this regal beauty could speak like a child denied a sweet treat, astonished that a member of the Scientifica would question the caste system. He didn't have an answer for her.

"Think of it, Garner. Tradition says castes have existed for three thousand years, but in that distant age, people lived on the soil, tended beasts, and harvested grain. What use did they have for Guilders before they learned to coin money? What use were the Scientifica when there was no science, only the art of using herbs for healing?"

"No doubt the Guilders were the first merchants, just as the Bellicosa were the warriors and the Scientifica the rulers," he said. He couldn't bear to mention his own caste; the Prola had been little better than beasts of burden, working fields and caring for animals they were never allowed to own. As for the Uncasted, they must have been beggars, slaves, and outcasts, perhaps no worse off than the banished people of the current era.

"We're all prisoners now," she said with a weary wisdom that made him forget her childlike outburst. "Look at this."

By the light of the stars, he saw her hold up her arm, pushing up the heavy garment that concealed her wrist.

"I've seen enough platinum bracelets. I've no wish to examine yours," he said dryly, clenching his hands together to keep from taking her delicate hand into his.

"Without this cursed band, I'm naked in my father's eyes. Tell me how it differs from a slave bracelet, when it keeps me from doing so many things I long to try?"

"You shouldn't speak to me this way, Highness."

"No, I should stay in that horrible dark hole, alone because no one is fit company for the daughter of Minister Yor."

"I'm sorry." He regretted her suffering, knowing as he did how much worse conditions would become.

"Don't be sorry for me! I'm ranting like a spoiled child! I have no right to burden you with my petty concerns."

"Nothing you could ever say would be a burden to me, Highness." He'd shocked himself by speaking the truth, but no power in the universe could make him retract those words.

"Will you do me one great favor, Garner?"

Her voice enchanted him; her words beguiled him. He would gladly do anything if it would bring her solace before the fate that awaited them.

"Gladly," he said, wishing there was a word adequate to express what he felt at this moment.

"Let me hear my given name on your lips: Alena. Call me Alena."

"Alena." He said it slowly, the way a priest intones the sacred words. "Alena, Alena, comely Alena, sweet Alena." Once he'd started this magical litany, he couldn't seem to stop repeating her name.

She touched his arm and smiled up into his face.

"You've given me courage to return to my dark prison before the others leave their beds."

"A moment . . ." He lifted her hand from his arm so she wouldn't feel it tremble.

"I wish we had a million moments together," she said, turning and running from him.

* * *

Alena closed the door of her stateroom, not wanting any eyes but Garner's to see the rapture she felt. She lost her fear of death when he was near; her claustrophobic terrors receded like the nightmares of childhood. He made her feel fully alive.

She lay back on her narrow bed, wishing she had light to see her own reflection. She felt transformed, like a creature of light and air who could change her image at will. Touching her eyelids with her fingertips, she played with her spiky lashes, imagining how Garner's thick lashes might feel against her cheek.

"Am I beautiful?" she asked aloud, too insecure at this moment to trust the opinions of people who had confirmed that she was. She meant: "Does Garner think I'm beautiful?"

She traced the outline of her lips, wondering if he found them alluring.

Alluring! It was a word she'd only read, and not often at that. Her father had chosen all her reading matter until she was old enough to devour the romantic tales she'd bribed their female servants to smuggle into her quarters. In those half-forgotten stories, the heroine was always alluring. She whispered the word again: "Alluring."

A sober realization overcame her: She was infatuated with Garner.

She knew some of the symptoms because she'd once been giddy over her music instructor: obsessively dwelling on every aspect of his appearance; constantly analyzing his character; feverishly daydreaming even though her fantasies left her limp and unsatisfied.

"It's just the same with Garner," she said, trying to convince herself this attraction would quickly fade.

She rolled on her stomach and propped her chin in her hand, wishing for some diversion, anything to tear her thoughts away from the handsome space officer. If she could read or write or send a message to a friend . . .

She sat up, disturbed but no longer able to deny the truth to herself: What she felt for Garner was nothing like her crush on the music teacher. It was much deeper—and more dangerous—than girlish infatuation. She knew what her father was capable of doing to any unsuitable man who caught her attention, although she'd never given him reason to take action.

Not only could she bring about the ruination of a good man by showing him favor, but her own life might take an unwelcome turn. Her father loved her more than his own life, or so he told her, but he would be the first to banish her if she disgraced herself and him by having congress with a Prola.

She desperately needed bright lights, firm ground, and people of her own caste to talk, work, and laugh with her. This harrowing, solitary flight was making her crazy! She could more easily reach up into the heavens and pluck a star to wear in her hair than she could fulfill her wild fantasies with a man of the lowest caste, however handsome and appealing he was. They stood on opposite sides of a great chasm, and any attempt to be together would send them both crashing into a bottomless inferno.

Garner resolved never to return to the lounge during the quiet hours of slumber. He couldn't risk meeting Alena again, couldn't trust himself to be alone with her. Nevertheless, she was with him constantly in spirit, pushing him to make the ship as sound as possible.

He studied their situation with all the intensity of a driven man. They had one, and only one, chance to survive. The *Moon Courier* was streaking toward Brona, where it would burn up in the atmosphere unless one of the ship's battered engines could deliver a final thrust to put them in orbit. They could start an engine once using the residual fuel in the undamaged tank, but if the initial attempt to achieve orbit was unsuccessful, they were doomed.

Life aboard the frigid ship became insufferable, with minor illnesses plaguing crew and passengers, making their lives even more miserable. The captain fretted to excess over each small ailment reported by the travelers, and nothing Garner said dissuaded him from squandering precious power to address the passengers on the speaker system every day.

"My esteemed guests," he said at the beginning of the 22nd day of drifting, "I humbly regret the outbreak of respiratory infections, and I apologize again for the poor quality of your meals and accommodations. I want to reassure you that everything possible is being done to ensure your safety and well-being. We're continually dispatching emergency signals to the Space Control Center on Prima. We aren't able to receive their responses, but we're completely confident that a rescue mission has been launched. Please bear with us on the inconveniences."

Garner listened to Blaz with disgust; the man should have been an innkeeper, not a space commander. At least the captain was too preoccupied with passenger welfare and futile messages to

Prima to interfere with the crew or their work in the engine room.

The *Moon Courier* had been designed as a fully automated vessel, requiring only a minimal crew for routine operations. But the computer had failed them. The meteor-damaged system had already caused the internal meltdown that had first alerted Garner and the engine crew. Garner no longer trusted automation for any but the most mundane tasks, like ejecting the daily waste. The nine remaining greasers had had to assume chores far beyond the dictates of their job contracts, and it was the executive officer's responsibility to see that they did all that was asked of them. Although they were trained space technicians, the captain had no scruples about asking them to see to the needs of the passengers, no matter how trivial their requests. Garner managed to keep Tacka and Roar in the engine room by assigning double and even triple shifts to all the men. Everything that could be checked was given the most thorough examination possible in space.

If the men grumbled, they did it out of his hearing, but even surly Tacka seemed to recognize that their survival was in the executive officer's hands.

After the captain's daily speech to the passengers, Garner gathered the greasers in the engine room.

"After we achieve orbit—a little over seven hours from now—the sirens will sound for a pod drill. The passengers will be calmer and more efficient if they don't know it's the real thing. The best we can hope for is an unstable orbit; we don't have the power to ensure that the *Moon Courier* will completely circle Brona even once. A minute's delay in leaving the ship might mean the difference between survival and death. There won't be time to deal with passenger panic or pathetic attempts to take forbidden hand luggage into the pods. The success of the operation—and our survival—depends on you."

Their hushed assent told him they recognized and feared the gravity of the situation.

"You should know the pod arrangements so well you can execute the drill in pitch darkness if necessary. As dictated in the Code, the first helmsman will eject Pod Number One. Ferrick, I've given you command of Pod Number Two because you're the only crew member on board who's ejected from a pod in space."

"Yea, but we came down on Prima, not a nasty hellhole like Brona."

"Look at the bright side, Ferrick. You'll go down in history as one of the first of our species to set foot on a new planet."

"And who knows what beastly thing might be waiting to bite it off!"

The men's laughter was forced.

"The second helmsman will eject Pod Number Three," Garner continued, "followed by Roar, Tacka, and Vane Col. Officer Col is still immobile after surgery, so there will be no passengers in his pod. I expect the crew assigned to him will show every courtesy due a disabled officer.

"The captain, medic, and second officer will eject with their passengers in that sequence." He didn't need to tell them the executive officer would be the last to leave. It was the oldest tradition in the Space Service: The captain had to be spared to command on landing; Garner had to make a final check of the whole ship for stragglers before leaving with the last pod.

"Are there any questions?" he asked.

"Only one, sir." The acting chief engineer shuffled uneasily. "If the computer doesn't activate the engine . . ."

"We aren't going to rely on the computer, Roar. We'll use manual start."

"Sir, I've never done it before."

"You won't be doing it this time. I'll take the responsibility and do it myself."

The greasers, bedraggled in work-stained blue tunics and dark gray insulated leggings, were silent, but several heads nodded approval.

"Okay by me," Tacka mumbled.

Even Garner's worst foe in the engine control room preferred to trust his life to the executive officer.

Seven hours and counting: Garner knew he had to make the captain listen to reason. They weren't going to be rescued. The vessel was doomed, but the people aboard had one chance to survive. He reported to the bridge, ready to use any means, even mutiny, to evacuate the passengers and crew before the inevitable incineration.

"Sir, we're ready to put the ship in orbit in exactly six hours and forty-two minutes." He stiffened into an attention stance to convey the urgency of his purpose and mollify the captain. "If we succeed, we'll immediately sound the sirens for a pod drill. I strongly urge not telling the passengers it's the real thing. We can avoid panic and—"

"There's still time to think about it," the captain said. "I anticipate a lockup with a rescue ship within the next few hours. Prima has been fully informed of our predicament."

"I hope you're right, sir, but if we do achieve orbit . . ."

"Once we're in orbit, we can consider our options."

"There are none, sir! We're out of control. We have enough fuel for one thrust. No more. There's no chance of maintaining a stable orbit."

"Rie, I've had enough of your arrogance."

"Sir, I respectively request that you convene an Officers' Council."

"I intend to, excluding, of course, that Prola you appointed acting chief. I've never commanded a ship where all the officers weren't Bellicosa. Hail Benay had his faults, but he proved his caste lineage to my satisfaction before I requested him for this mission."

"The chief engineer is always included in an Officers' Council, sir."

"Mister Rie, your attitude will be duly noted in your Service file, and you may expect a fitness review before you're assigned to another flight."

"We may be dead in a few hours, sir."

"I hereby convene an Officers' Council," Blaz said, his usually pallid face mottled by angry red blotches of rage. "Helmsman, note that the following are in attendance: yourself, the second helmsman, the second officer, the executive officer, and Captain Hurex Blaz."

"Vane Col and Velma Pitt should be here," Garner insisted.

"Col is medically unfit for duty; Pitt has urgent medical duties among the passengers. Now state your proposal for the record, Rie."

He did so, stressing the urgency of immediate action if they achieved orbit.

"Noted. We'll take the vote," Blaz said.

Garner had to intervene. "Weal, this is the only chance any of us have to survive!" he said appealing to the weakest officer, hoping he was more afraid of a fiery death than the captain's censure.

"I vote for Mister Rie's proposal," Weal said, his face sickly white with fear.

The vote was four to one in favor of immediate evacuation. Garner knew the captain would make him pay if they both lived, but at least he'd have a chance at keeping his word to Alena.

Shortly before the crucial moment, he had Vane carried to a seat near the escape pods, with two greasers nearby to evacuate him when the drill sirens went off.

When all preparations were completed, Garner sounded the alarm for launch positions. He didn't make Eli Moke's mistake. His own harness was securely in place as he stood before the control board, ready to execute a manual engine start.

He tried not to see the terror etched on the weary faces surrounding him. Every greaser was locked in a launch seat; the navigational data was flickering on a screen monitored by the second helmsman.

He could only imagine the scene on the command bridge: Blaz urging the first helmsman to send more frantic signals to Prima; Weal cowering in his seat, unmanned by his bodily functions, a coward facing death because his family's privileged position had robbed a more worthy man of the appointment.

Garner's hands were stiff with cold, and he tried to warm them in his armpits, bringing back enough flexibility to manipulate the levers. He didn't allow himself the luxury of preparing for death. He didn't beg forgiveness from a deity he only half believed existed; he didn't review his transgressions or catalog his regrets. If he tried to bolster himself with metaphysical hopes, he would have to accept that Alena and all the others might soon die a grisly, fiery death.

He did allow himself a fleeting fantasy, wondering how it would feel if he could go to her now and press his mouth against her full, pink lips. Then he called on all the self-control he possessed to concentrate on starting the one functioning engine.

"Countdown, sir." The helmsman's voice was husky with fear, but it didn't waver. "Ten . . . nine . . . eight . . ."

Garner discarded his gloves and frantically rubbed his hands together for maximum warmth and dexterity.

"Seven . . . six . . . five . . . four . . ."

His fingers were in place. All he could see was the red knob that would determine their fate.

"Three . . . two . . . one . . . engage!"

His hands acted without conscious direction from his brain. He strained to hear the swoosh of an engine coming alive. An instant of silence seemed like an eternity.

"Your seat, sir!"

The greaser's scream sent him hurling backward, the harness tightening as his backside made contact with the hard launch seat built into the shell of the engine room.

Things happened too fast for his mind to absorb them: a great rumble, a shrill whining, involuntary human screams, and a violent lurch that brought the vessel out of its fatal plunge toward Brona's atmosphere.

Garner lapsed into another state of consciousness, but he was still aware of the great ship shuddering like a sleeping beast aroused to do battle. He felt lurching and twisting, the impact of immense pressure on the shell of the *Moon Courier*, and frantically prayed the vessel would hold together. Time stood still; he screamed as a million needles of pain stabbed his joints. Yellow dots bombarded him from the dark underside of his lids, and blessed darkness wrapped him in a cocoon of oblivion.

He opened his eyes, stunned and then jubilant because the vessel had survived. He wanted to rush to an observation panel and see the dark, mysterious planet below them, but he'd practiced the evacuation procedures so many times he acted automatically. He shouted to alert Roar, and in seconds the pod-drill signal was bombarding them with shrill, unmerciful blasts of sound.

To his surprise and horror, the captain overrode the siren and started talking on the speaker system.

"This is not a drill. The *Moon Courier* must be evacuated. I repeat, this is not a drill. Proceed to your assigned pod immediately. This is Captain Blaz. This is not a drill."

The captain's voice was like the drone of a doomsayer, one of Prima's morbid psychics who claimed they could predict natural disasters by going into trances and speaking gibberish. Garner felt a surge of panic, even though he'd lived for this moment, practiced for it, steeled himself for the worst possible consequences.

The captain was literally driving the occupants of the ship into a frenzy. The orderly drill became a stampede as the greasers reacted to the hysterical voice booming out at them.

Garner stopped and took a deep breath, then blocked the way of a screaming runner: Weal.

"You fool! You're an officer! Act like one!" He cracked his open palm against the man's tear-streaked cheek and shook him by the front of his tunic. The second officer whimpered and disappeared into the lift, forgetting the cardinal rule of pod drills: always use the stairs. Garner wasted precious moments pulling him from the conveyance, disconnected to conserve power, and shoved him toward the spiral stairs, already deserted by swift-moving greasers better prepared for survival.

He vowed never to question the mercy of his deity if Alena was spared the consequences of the captain's folly.

Chapter Five

Garner heard the shrill whine as Pod Number One ejected from the upper-level stern. Every survival instinct he had urged him to follow Weal to the pod chamber directly above where he stood. The *Moon Courier* could tear away from its unstable orbit at any moment and soar toward the raging inferno of the sun.

He didn't know if the vessel was trembling or his legs were. His teeth chattered, either from cold or fear, and icy perspiration ran down his forehead into his eyes, momentarily blinding him. If he followed Weal up the spiral stairs, he could enter his pod and be poised for escape in less than a minute.

His conscience prevailed, and he regretted wasting precious seconds deciding whether to carry out his final duty on board the great doomed space vessel. Breaking into a run, he negotiated the long corridor to the command bridge, calling out and checking the staterooms as he moved past doors that had opened automatically when the pod-drill siren sounded. The lower deck was deserted.

He scrambled up the stairs from the bridge to the passengers' lounge, forgetting to count the shrill sounds that numbered the departing pods. He didn't expect to find stragglers, but a panicky passenger might have been immobilized by fear or injured in the mad scramble provoked by the captain. He started down the dim corridor, hoping to see nothing but deserted staterooms.

In his rush to complete the final check of the vessel, he nearly missed seeing her. Alena was bent over a storage compartment in the dark recess of her cubicle, tugging on a jammed door.

"You should have left!" he said frantically. "What's your pod number?"

"I must get my equipment!" she cried out in desperation when he came into her stateroom.

"You can't! The storage compartments lock automatically when the pod drill begins."

"But I need—"

"Highness," he said, unceremoniously grabbing her arm, "even if I could force the automatic lock, you can't take personal luggage in a pod. There's no safe place to put it."

"I'll hold the case!"

"Impossible. Most likely it would brain someone on descent." He pulled roughly, yanking her into the corridor and propelling her in front of him along the narrow width.

By the time they reached the pods, seven of the ten silvery-gray escape vehicles had left the ship. Number Eight, Velma Pitt's, was moving into position in front of the long ejection tube, the high whine deafening to unprotected ears, and Number Nine had a closed hatch, sealed for the descent to Brona.

He half-pushed, half-carried Alena to Number Ten and lifted her up to the open hatch. His pod had no assigned passengers, only a heavy load of supplies and space for stragglers he might find. By Space Service law, he was expected to be the last to leave. No others were expected to share his late departure—especially not the high-caste Alena. He heard her gasp as she dropped down into the small interior; then, after a final check for stragglers in the corridor, he followed her, locking the hatch cover behind him and scrambling for one of the seats built into the pod.

"Fasten your harness," he ordered, hurriedly punching in the code to activate the pod before securing his own.

Pitt's pod disappeared, and Number Nine with Weal in command was close behind it, already in position in front of the tube.

Garner glanced at Alena and was horrified: She was frozen on the edge of her seat, the harness still recessed in its holder.

"Put on your belt!" he shouted, trying to startle her into acting.

He could have been giving the order in an alien tongue. Her only response was to wrap her arms around herself and press her body back against the seat.

Their pod was automatically moving into position, and he didn't dare stop it. If he switched on manual override, he would have to go through a complicated, time-consuming series of steps to reactivate it. The *Moon Courier* was shuddering, its metal shell threatening to crack, weakened as it was from the great strain endured during the orbital thrust.

He released his own harness and rushed to her, knocking her backward and yanking the harness over her head and shoulders. She resisted, too caught up in her claustrophobia to realize what she was doing, but he forced the clasp between her legs and engaged it in the lock built into the front of the seat. The pod was poised at the entrance to the tube when he scrambled back to his own seat; they were entering the air lock as he blindly fumbled with his clasp and locked it in place between his legs.

He was awestruck when the little pod emerged from the mother ship and started its downward descent toward the night-shrouded planet below them. The people of Prima had dreamed and planned for generations, hoping someday to send manned expeditions to Brona. He felt reverence for being allowed to have this unique experience, no matter what the consequences. Adrift in space with only the flimsy pod sheltering him from the overwhelming forces of the universe, he felt tiny and insignificant, but at the same time tremendously blessed to be seeing what lay below them: another world.

When he recovered the use of his voice, he was still angry at Alena for failing to go to her pod when the siren sounded. He'd been deathly afraid during her dangerous, unresponsive lapse when she'd failed to engage her harness, but now that they were safely away from the mother ship, he was furious at her again. Against his better judgment, he began berating her as he would a disobedient greaser, fearful for her safety on the new world if she couldn't execute a simple survival measure in strange and new circumstances.

"Have you no sense at all? How could you flaunt the rules and neglect the most elementary procedures? Do you think the laws of physics will be suspended so High Yor's daughter can bring her pretty things along on a pod ejection?"

"No! It wasn't like that!" Her soft voice did nothing to divert his anger. "I'm a cartographer. I only wanted to be useful. . . ."

"You could've begun by fastening your own harness." He was more agitated than angry when he remembered the way he'd forced her thighs apart to secure the catch.

"I . . . I couldn't remember how . . . I read the manual, but . . ." She looked stricken, but he wouldn't allow himself to be swayed by her distress.

"The manual! Didn't you learn to fasten a harness during the pod drills?"

"I was excused from them," she said, looking up with just a trace of haughty defiance. "The captain didn't think it was fitting for me to mix with other castes in the confusion of getting to the pods."

"Is it more fitting to be tossed around inside a pod, injuring others as well as yourself, possibly being battered to death?"

"You can't talk to me that way!" She sounded stunned.

"Someone should! Did you skip all the training sessions required for travel in space? If you were a woman of my caste, I would castigate your backside with my own hand to punish your foolishness."

She gasped, making him feel guilty for speaking so harshly, even though he knew she deserved severe punishment for putting both their lives in jeopardy.

"Look through the video screen," he said, unnerved by her unspoken remorse. "You can get a glimpse of two—no, three open parachutes."

"Brace yourself," he added more kindly, remembering her terror of enclosed places. "You'll feel a lurch when our chute opens. Then we'll float down as though we had giant wings."

He hoped for her sake this was true. He didn't know how much turbulence there would be during their descent. Once the pods were ejected, there was no way to control them, and the wind currents might be tempestuous. If the main chute worked as it should, and they didn't have to contend with strong winds, they might be fortunate enough to have a smooth descent. The second chute would ensure an easy touchdown on water or land—if everything went as it should.

A sudden lurch released a billowing, fluorescent-yellow chute in their wake, but the impact was enough to make Garner's stomach turn over. He fought a twinge of nausea, and noted that Alena didn't seem affected by it. Apparently she didn't suffer from motion sickness. He sagged with relief as he tried to restore his equilibrium by swallowing hard.

She gingerly peeked through the tiny screen in their pod, the only way to view the outside.

"What is that orange flare down there?" she asked.

He quickly switched his focus from her to the dark surface below them. A pinpoint of orange blazed up, and his minor discomfort was forgotten in the horror of recognizing what he saw: The first pod had crashed and exploded. Staring intently, he made out the fluorescent dot of another chute not far from the site of the accident. As he watched, a second fiery pinpoint flared up near the first, and he could only draw one conclusion. Two pods had landed with tragic results.

The gray haze of early dawn was creeping over

the horizon of Brona, and he strained to make out some details of the planet below them. What he saw explained the fiery flare-ups, but it also made his blood run cold. The first two pods had touched down in a range of rugged mountains with jagged peaks reaching skyward.

"The fires are pods, aren't they?" she asked, her voice husky with fear. "What happened? Why are they burning?"

"They crashed in a mountainous area. Something set off the oxygen—electrical sparks, friction from the impact—we may never know."

"We're all going to die."

Her voice was so matter-of-fact, he was afraid she'd gone into shock.

"Not necessarily. We're riding a strong current of air, and we still have time to pass beyond the mountains before we get near the surface. We may come down to the east of those peaks."

Before he could say more, a third ship flared up with fleeting brilliance that allowed no hope of survivors.

"We're going to die," she repeated.

"No!"

He inched forward as far as he could without releasing his harness and grasped the tips of her fingers, trying to concentrate on the woman across from him, not those who had perished in the first three pods: both helmsmen and the greaser Ferrick, along with the passengers assigned to those pods.

"I've been so frightened since we left Prima," she said softly, straining forward to lock fingers with him. "But there's an odd peace in knowing your fate, isn't there? We're certainly going to die when our pod touches down. It's a relief of sorts to know it's out of my hands. Nothing I can do will change it. And I won't disgrace my father by turning into a raving lunatic. I would've lost my mind if the voyage had lasted much longer. You gave me temporary courage, but if I'd been trapped much longer in one of those awful staterooms on the *Moon Courier* . . ." She shook her head, looking so sad his heart ached for her.

"Don't give up yet!" He squeezed hard, trying to hurt her fingers just enough to distract her from morbid thoughts. "Look below. I can make out three—no, four other chutes. The wide is strong. There's a chance. . . ."

They both stared, straining to see more. He realized that her grip was almost as punishing as his. Her long, sharp-tipped nails bit into his fingers like the talons of a predatory winglet, the fiercest airborne creature on Prima.

"I think I see . . ." She didn't finish her thought.

"It's a river. Broader by far than any on Prima. The pods are designed for water landings. In fact, it's equally safe to touch down on flat land or water."

"But if they hit the mountains . . ."

"Look directly below. Aren't most of the pods, including ours, beyond the range of mountains?" He held his breath, not releasing her hands as the fourth pod floated down to the surface.

Moments later it was bobbing on the surface of the river.

"No explosion!" She pulled away, pressing her knuckles against her lips, as though savoring the taste his touch had left on her skin.

He felt abandoned without her fingers locked with his.

"Will they drown?" she asked after what seemed like a long interval of silence.

"Unlikely. Flotation devices come out on impact. The pods automatically release an anchoring weight to stop the craft from drifting while the passengers board an inflatable raft. Every pod carries one."

Another pod went down on the water as they watched. Garner tried to determine who had survived so far. Roar and his passengers must be among those who'd landed safely. Even though he'd only been acting chief for a short while, he was one of the men Garner trusted most. He felt immensely relieved this man had survived. There were too few reliable crew members among those still descending in the pods.

He and Alena had drifted downward enough to see a great splash when Tacka's pod came down in shallow water closer to land. Garner held his breath as Number Six, Vane Col's pod, missed the river and landed on the shore, no doubt a rough touchdown for a man with a broken leg held together by a metal pin. At least the communications officer had survived. Of the original officers, he was the most congenial. If they were permanently stranded on Brona, men of good heart would be urgently needed.

The next pod—Number Seven with the captain in command, if Garner's observations were correct—came down smoothly on land, the fluorescent chute billowing down with it.

"Velma Pitt is next," he said aloud, hoping this valuable officer wouldn't meet with disaster.

"I wish . . . no, never mind," Alena said.

"I think we've gone beyond the need to conceal our thoughts," he said, letting a faint smile soften his stern expression.

"Look, another safe touchdown. Who's next?" she asked evasively.

"Number Nine, Second Officer Weal." He had a

hard time saying his name without showing distaste for the man. "Then it's our turn. Sit back with soles of both feet flat on the floor," he said, explaining the safest way to get through the landing, trying to relax himself to lessen the chance of injuries.

"Officer Rie—Garner—will you make a pact with me?"

"A pact? You sound like a conspirator."

"Only for our mutual benefit. If you'll promise not to speak of my foolishness to anyone, I swear I'll never tell that you threatened me with physical punishment."

"Highness Yor, I only commented on your lack of preparations for the flight. Emergency procedures never seem important until they're desperately needed, and then it's too late to learn them. It was never my intention to administer—to inflict . . ."

"Do you agree to a bond of silence?" she asked, squirming in her seat, her face revealing the humiliation she felt at the mention of it.

Even in the dim light he could see the high color in her cheeks. Was it possible a woman of high caste could blush like a bashful Prola maiden?

"You want me to promise never to mention your reason for lingering, for failing to get to your assigned pod before it left without you?"

"I was supposed to leave in Number One," she said, a tremor in her voice.

"Sometimes fate takes strange turns that work to the good. I was tempted to leave without checking all the staterooms," he confessed, hating the thought that she could have been extinguished in the first fiery pod crash or left behind to perish alone in the *Moon Courier*.

"Why didn't you leave when the siren first sounded?"

"The executive officer is responsible for the final inspection of a doomed vessel."

"To see that no one is left behind?"

"Yes. Brace yourself, Highness!" The ground was rushing up to meet them.

"Our pact!" she screamed over the rush of air as the second, smaller chute slowed the pod.

"I swear to keep it."

"As do I!" She shrieked on impact as the pod dug into soft ground on the alien planet.

Before they recovered enough to unfasten their harnesses, the hatch was thrown open and the captain's pale face confronted them through the opening.

"Highness Yor, I was terrified! I thought you perished in Pod Number One. Your safety means more to me than my own life!"

"Please, forgive me for worrying you, Captain Blaz. I turned my ankle in the rush to the pods and couldn't get to my assigned place. Officer Rie saved my life by remaining behind when all others had left."

The captain glared at his second in command, obviously not pleased Garner was the recipient of her gratitude.

"It's not fitting you were alone with a Prola," he said, "but I'm relieved our emergency procedures insured your safety, Highness. Now that you've landed, be assured I'll be personally responsible for your well-being. If any low-caste crew member inflicts his presence on you, he will be severely punished."

Alena pulled herself through the open hatch, pretending she hadn't seen the captain's hand extended to assist her.

Nothing seemed real; this couldn't be happening to her! She'd behaved badly: flaunting rules and risking her own life and Garner's. Panic was no excuse. She hadn't prepared properly for the evacuation; she'd been arrogant in avoiding the pod drills, as though reading a manual was a substitute for learning proper procedures. She was embarrassed, ashamed of her cowardly behavior when the pod ejected, and agitated by the stern way Garner had treated her. No man had ever pushed her as he had, forcefully maneuvering her down the corridor to the pod. Worse, she could still feel his rough hands parting her thighs to engage the seat harness. He'd saved her life, but the price was high: her peace of mind.

There was no graceful way to exit from a pod. She pushed off from the edge of the hatch and hoped for the best, relieved when she landed on her feet instead of plopping down on her backside as she'd feared.

Garner had said she deserved to be punished, as a Prola female would be for such unacceptable behavior. She walked a few paces away from the pod, trying to erase an image of lying prone across the executive officer's knees while he pummeled her posterior, an indignity not even children of her caste had to endure.

Slowly she became aware of her surroundings, distracted from her unsettling thoughts by the stifling atmosphere outside the pod. She'd never felt heat like this. The mist that crept off the river was more like steam from a boiling pot than the fog on Prima. She gasped for breath, wanting to be free of her insulated clothing: the many-layered black tunic and silver trousers that had made life tolerable on board the frigid vessel. Here on the surface of Brona, even her feet felt overheated in the thick-soled ankle-high boots she'd brought for field work on that distant moon where her father was waiting for her.

"Keep together," the captain ordered. "Our first priority is to designate operators to send emergency signals to Prima."

"Sir, request permission to assess our situation and set up a temporary camp," Officer Rie said.

"First we need to see how many survivors are qualified radio operators," the captain said.

Alena watched the two men, as did all the survivors huddled around them. Rie was standing ramrod straight, correctly addressing his commanding officer even though he must have been as hot as she was. His calf-high military boots had insulated silver trousers stuffed into the tops, the same as all the officers she could see. There were five in all: Garner; the captain; the pale-faced communications officer, leaning on a stocky greaser; the second officer, a pinched-face younger man named Weal; and the female medical officer, Velma Pitt. They all wore padded dark gray jackets, unbuttoned now to reveal skin-hugging black bodysuits.

As she became more aware of her surroundings, she felt an overwhelming surge of excitement. They were the first of their species to set foot on Brona, the mysterious inner planet. She looked around and saw a mixture of awe and fear on the faces avidly watching the exchange between the *Moon Courier*'s captain and executive officer. For better or worse, these people, herself included, were the first Primans to explore this alien world.

The sun was rising, a great orange orb clearing away the steamy mist, allowing the first clear view of the terrain. If she hadn't seen it from the pod, she wouldn't have recognized the vast expanse in front of her as a river. It was too wide to see across to the opposite shore, and the sluggish, mud-brown water reminded her of a swamp. Wherever people stepped on the soft, boggy shore, their feet left water-filled impressions. Some distance away, the vegetation grew thick and high, a near-solid wall of glistening green leaves dotted with brilliant splashes of color, perhaps the blooms of exotic plants. She was too far away to be sure they really were flowers.

The surviving passengers and crew members were abnormally quiet, no doubt subdued by the strangeness of their surroundings. Only the captain and Garner were speaking, and she realized their exchange was curt and hostile.

"Sir, without knowing the swiftness of the current or the buoyancy of the pods, we should make every effort to tow them to shore immediately. We desperately need all the supplies we can salvage."

"Mister Rie, are you telling me you refuse to dismantle the communications equipment before towing the pods?"

"No, sir. I'm only suggesting the job will go much faster if a flotilla of rafts can tow them to shore first."

"Get the greasers on it immediately then. I hold you personally responsible for seeing there are no delays."

"Yes, sir, but the greasers alone won't be able to salvage the pods as quickly as you'd like, and we need to set up a secure camp before dark. I suggest we invoke Code 726 giving Space Service status to all passengers, so every able-bodied person can be assigned to tasks as needed."

"That's outrageous!" one of the passengers said, finding his voice.

Alena recognized the protester as Catton Sur, a

Scientifica, but not as aristocratic as those of Yor lineage. She'd exchanged a few words with him at the captain's dinner, as was permissible between males and females of her caste, but she'd found his speech too boastful and his manners atrocious.

"Captain, I believe my father would support an extreme measure like invoking Code 726 in this situation," Alena said, impulsively lending her father's prestige to Garner's proposal.

"I beg your pardon for disagreeing, Highness Yor, but there are fifteen surviving crew members, more than enough to do the mundane tasks necessary for our survival," Catton said. "I appeal to you, Captain Blaz, to do the right thing. I counted thirty-one passengers: eleven Scientifica including Highness Yor, twelve members of your own Bellicosa, and the rest Guilders. Certainly you intend to uphold the laws and traditions of Prima's caste system even in this remote place. It's unthinkable that any of us labor beside Prolas, much less take orders from one, no matter how well intentioned his political appointment was." Catton's bland, unlined face was pink with indignation, and his wispy gray hair was too thin to cover the round skull that glistened wetly under the hot rays of the sun.

"The Space Service Code is very clear, sir," Garner said, speaking to the captain, not the irate passenger. "Until the members of this party set foot on Prima again, all authority is vested in the ranking officer. If we're going to survive at all, every living soul will have to participate in the labor under one command."

"I don't have time for politics, Rie. We have one priority: contact Prima so they know where to look for us. High Sur, honored passengers, I beg your cooperation. Naturally caste laws and traditions will be honored here, but we will need your skills and expertise to make contact with the homeworld and man the receivers around the clock."

Alena looked at the faces of the survivors, and saw fear. Catton Sur tried to disguise his with bluster; Captain Blaz practiced denial by putting blind faith in communicating with Prima: but like all the others, these two men were also afraid. She looked at Garner, perhaps the one person present who wasn't motivated solely by fear. His sure voice and concrete proposals were keeping her own panic at bay.

"Sir, I would like to take the Space Service oath of obedience, and I urge my fellow passengers to do so," she said loudly so all could hear. Her voice sounded hollow and unfamiliar in the strange atmosphere.

Alena risked meeting the executive officer's eyes. What she saw in them wasn't fear, only puzzlement and something else—an intensity that made her knees feel weak.

"It's only a formality," Blaz said apologetically to Catton Sur and a small band of passengers standing near him. "Our primary task is to communicate with the Space Control Center. I beg your indulgence until then. Naturally, if any of you want to be released from the oath after we've established contact with Prima, I'm authorized to allow that."

Catton Sur looked at his follow passengers and perhaps saw what Alena had seen: shock and apprehension. Failing to find visible signs of support, he reluctantly raised his hand with the others and began repeating the words of allegiance every officer was compelled to memorize at the Academy: "I hereby attest and swear. . . . "

Alena repeated the words without thinking about what she was saying. Garner went back into their pod and emerged again before the long oath was finished. He'd stripped down to his black bodysuit, a smooth-fitting garment that made her avert her eyes, then glance back, forgetting to mumble the words after the captain said them. She'd always thought of Prola men—when she thought of them at all—as poor physical specimens: too thin or too chunky, with harsh, lumpish faces. How crass of her to stereotype all Prolas as the same kind of males who tended her father's vast gardens. Officer Rie had a magnificent body, muscular without being heavy. His broad chest, lean waist, and flat belly must make lesser men envious, no matter what their caste.

He carried a coil of rope over his shoulder, tugging on a loose end to test its strength. She was mesmerized by the bulge of muscle on his flexed arm, but she didn't dare let her eyes wander to areas more mysterious to those of her gender.

He tossed the rope to a stocky crew member standing nearby and climbed back into the pod, as agile as a performer of acrobatics, emerging in moments with the collapsed raft they hadn't needed. This too he tossed to the waiting greaser, whispering quick instructions that sent the youth racing toward the mud-colored river.

She was unbearably warm, yet she dreaded exhibiting her body clad only in her own pale blue undersuit. As though reading her mind, Garner looked in her direction and smiled, a fleeting upward curve of the lips that made her tingle.

Father, why aren't you with me? she asked miserably, feeling out of her depth with the Prola officer and more than a little frightened by the power he exerted on her will. He'd made the idea of emergency enrollment of the passengers into the Service seem so logical and pressing, she'd stood up to Catton Sur, a male of her own caste, and prodded the captain into taking action. She was confused by her rash support of the first officer, but also exhilarated. Yet when Garner led a party of men, all the greasers and a few passengers, toward the water, she felt more alone than she ever had in her life.

"In the circumstances," the captain was saying to those left on shore, "I'm declaring bodysuits to be the uniform of the day. No one can function on this vile planet dressed in survival garments intended for a frigid space ship." He looked upward, perhaps mourning the *Moon Courier*'s demise, then started removing his own heavy clothing.

Alena looked around, wanting to talk to someone, needing to share her feelings and find release by discovering another person as frightened as she was. There was no one. Of the four other women, one was Mavro Tut, a Scientifica famous in research circles but a shy, diffident female who, like many lower-status members of the upper caste, spoke only to her husband and, in public, only when he first addressed her. Velma Pitt, whom Alena admired for her usefulness, was a Bellicosa, as were the other two female passengers.

How strange, Alena thought, to be in this desperate situation and still be unable to reach out in friendship to those few people who shared her plight. She needed them, and she had skills and comfort to offer in return, but the gulf between the castes was so great, she was virtually alone. Even if she had enough spirit left to defy caste tradition and seek out Pitt as a companion, the medical officer was totally occupied trying to ease Vane Col's sufferings and checking on less serious complaints of others.

Suddenly Alena felt dizzy, whether from heat, thirst, or anxiety she didn't know. Instead of calling out for help and taking someone away from more urgent work, she went back to the pod. Steeling herself, she managed to crawl into it. Sitting in the seat Garner had occupied, she put her head between her legs until the danger of fainting passed, then drank sparingly from a container of water she located among the supplies in the floor storage area Garner had left unlocked.

Officially she was a member of a military community under the command of Captain Hurex Blaz, but she knew her status hadn't changed in any meaningful way. No one was going to assign a task to her; she would be as useless on Brona as she had been on the *Moon Courier*.

Slowly she peeled off her oppressively warm outer garments, feeling self-conscious even in the cramped seclusion of the pod. The soft knit undersuit clung like a second skin, outlining every feature of her body. Yet no matter how exposed and immodest she felt, she would have to join the other stranded passengers to learn what plans were being formulated for their survival.

The child in her wanted to scream, weep, and shout curses at the unseen force that had brought her to this pass, but this time she wasn't going to fail herself or others. She vowed to contribute to the group's survival, no matter what she had to do. She never again wanted Garner to look at her with scorn because she'd been too arrogant or too ignorant to do what was prudent and right.

"Help me!" she pleaded to the distant deity who sometimes seemed so remote from the traditional worship in the Scientifica temple she attended with her father. She didn't have exotic oils or ritual lights to appease this sacred unseen force, but she prayed to the Universal Power for help. She didn't want to disgrace herself or her father's name again. She didn't want to be a burden to anyone, least of all the Prola officer who seemed to be a better man than many who held themselves above him.

Chapter Six

"What are the odds a solar system will have more than one habitable planet?" asked Erasma Dee, one of more sociable of the Scientifica.

"Slight, I imagine," Garner said, trying to conceal his impatience with idle conversation from the wiry little man who had proven to be the most eager, if not the most efficient, worker among the passengers.

"Astronomical—one in a million! I still can't believe I'm here." Dee wiped muddy hands on the front of his white undersuit, already filthy from hours of laboring on the muddy shore of the river. "Can you believe—"

He was cut off by a shrill, inhuman shriek, distant but still threatening enough to make the men working on the shore freeze and listen.

"Sir, do you think . . ."

Garner raised his hand to cut off Gullaner's question.

A second cry followed, then a third.

"There's a sound that gives me cold chills," Erasma whispered.

"Something big made that noise," Tacka said, glumly staring at the distant wall of foliage. "Better hope there isn't a whole pack of 'em coming here to the river."

"It's nearly dark," Garner said. "We can't do much more here tonight. Secure the hatches on all the pods and carry as much as you can back to the tents."

He hated leaving the job of unloading the pods before it was done, but he'd already pushed his crew beyond reasonable expectations. They were exhausted, famished, and ravaged by thirst, some of them staring at the murky river with undisguised longing.

"We'll have a good meal and drink our fill back at camp," Garner added. "Don't try drinking river water until we have the purification equipment working. You don't want alien parasites in your gullets," he warned.

Garner was the last to leave the landing site, now dotted with six of the seven pods that had landed safely. The seventh was somewhere downriver, lost when one of the lines broke and the men holding the other rope couldn't hang on. At least the passengers who'd landed in it were safe. He wanted to believe they could retrieve it later, but for now they had more pressing needs: food, water, and shelter. He regretted the loss of supplies, but his greatest problem was to get people to work together for survival, especially since higher castes believed themselves exempt from manual labor.

The tents were set up on dryer ground closer to the jungle, but their usefulness was dependent on good weather conditions. It was late summer on Brona and, thanks to information sent back to Prima by probes, he knew what to expect when winter began: excessive rainfall, possibly with torrential storms and flooding.

For now they could exist on food and water carried on the pods, but the supplies wouldn't last long. They had to start hunting for game and edible plants; that meant setting traps and mastering primitive methods of survival. Each pod had a small store of guns and ammunition, but the shrill screams that accompanied them as they walked back to camp only confirmed what he already knew: Firearms could only be used for defense. They had to save every shot for emergencies.

They didn't have a zoologist among the passengers because their original destination, the moon Bedir, had no native life forms. The manifest did include several botanists on their way to staff the vegetation domes. Erasma Dee was the senior scientist among them, and Garner hoped he'd be an asset when they began their quest for food sources. He was a likable little man, in spite of his addiction to chitchat.

Were those shrieking creatures coming closer? He had every reason to worry if they were. They could be carnivores large enough to prey on humans, and he had no way of knowing whether their camp was vulnerable to attack.

He'd never been so weary, not even at the Academy, where a Prola recruit was fair game for every sadistic upper-form cadet who wanted to inflict misery. Garner was carrying the heaviest load back to camp: pistols, knives, and small tools from Pod Number Ten, the one that had brought Alena and him to the planet's surface.

When he thought of her, anxiety gnawed at him,

making his burden seem even heavier. After a few minutes of short-lived elation at being among the first Primans to walk on an alien planet, he'd accepted the gravity of their situation. He didn't share the captain's belief in imminent rescue. When the first manned vessel came to Brona, it might not have the capacity to take all the survivors back to Prima. That was assuming it would come while they were still alive. Space expeditions were planned years in advance of actual liftoffs, and he didn't believe the captain was privy to inside information, even if he was the highest-ranking Bellicosa on Prima. Blaz expected an immediate response when—if—he managed to contact the control center. Garner would be happy if he lived to see another ship from his own world at any time in the future.

At the camp, people were milling around outside the seven dark green synthetic cloth tents set roughly in a circle. They spoke only in brief, hushed sentences, as though the fearsome creatures shrieking in the jungle might hear them. Garner looked first for Alena, a habit he could neither break nor excuse. She wasn't his personal responsibility. As executive officer, he had to consider the welfare of all the survivors, yet he was uneasy whenever she was out of sight. He felt like a man assigned to guard the wind: forever grasping at the intangible.

"Where's the captain?" he asked Velma Pitt, waylaying her as she hurried from one tent to another.

She gestured over her shoulder. "He has Officer Col in there with the communications equipment, but poor Vane is in agony. I'm worried about his leg, Garner. I may have to amputate it."

She'd never before called Garner by his given

name. He was sensitive enough to know she was trying to establish a bond between them—one that would allow her to save Vane Col's life, over the captain's objection if necessary. Why hadn't he noticed before? Vane was more than a patient to her. She might even be in love with him, and he felt a twinge of envy, knowing that no caste restrictions stood between them.

"What about the passengers? Isn't there a technician among them who can help operate the radio?"

"I suppose most of them could in ordinary circumstances, but something's wrong. Vane says a magnetic field surrounding Brona is blocking the transmission."

"The captain hasn't made radio contact with Prima?"

"No, but he won't accept failure. He won't agree that it's impossible without more specialized equipment than the pods carried." She brushed away a strand of dark hair that escaped from the coil around her head.

"The unmanned probes sent back signals for several years," he said, trying to sound optimistic.

"They had special high-frequency radios. We don't. Vane can't convince the captain that it's hopeless to keep trying."

She sounded as weary as he felt, and he awkwardly patted her shoulder, wishing he could give her some kind of reassurance.

"This planet has everything we need to survive," he said, forcing himself to sound optimistic.

"And a few things we don't need, if those beasts are as big as their voices," she said wryly.

He forced himself to smile for her sake, then wearily trudged over to the tent where Catton Sur was self-importantly supervising the two passengers in charge of handing out rations. Garner's mouth was so dry his tongue stuck to the roof of his mouth, and his stomach gnawed with hunger under the sweat-soaked, muddy undersuit that clung to his body.

He drank part of his water ration standing in front of the food tent, carefully replacing the cap on the collapsible water sack. Then he found a deserted spot between two tents and dropped to the ground to consume his meal. The protein paste was gritty, but he squeezed it into his mouth without water to wash it down, then munched on the dried fruit cubes, saving the water for last.

As tempted as he was to sink into oblivion where he sat, he still had much to do. First he stepped behind the tent and peeled off his sweat-and-mud soaked garment, using handfuls of dry sand to cleanse and dry his body. He knew the dangers of fungus: Human skin could literally rot away under wet, contaminated cloth. What he didn't know was how to convince the others, beginning with Captain Blaz, that nudity was more hygienic and safer than wearing damp garments.

He stood and stretched, his head and shoulders higher than the tent that shielded him, grateful for the whisper of cooler air that dried his hair and refreshed his flesh.

Brona's three little moons were visible, but the light from the pale blue orbs was scarcely sufficient to see his hand in front of his face. One emergency lantern glowed by the food tent, giving an illusion of security in the dark void of the night, but he couldn't risk authorizing the use of it all night. Soon the camp would be totally dark until the natural light of dawn. Each power pack had to last as long as possible, especially if the captain continued to use one in the radio tent without any thought of conserving it.

He wrapped the soiled garment around his waist and stepped back into the circle of tents to speak to the people there.

"I know how tired you are," he said, losing his thought for a moment when he saw Alena standing by the lantern, her hair streaming over her shoulders like rays of sun bundled together to light the night.

"Tired," he repeated, unable to tear his eyes away from her.

When their garments rotted to shreds and they were forced to do without clothing, she couldn't possibly look more provocative than she did now in the pale blue undersuit that clung to her more seductively than a joy-girl's sheath of golden cloth.

Their eyes met, and he quickly looked away, but not before he saw the way her nipples pushed against the soft cloth and her love nest rose in a small mound under her sleek belly.

"I need volunteers to stand guard." He looked at the timekeeper on his wrist, straining to make out the luminous numerals under the fogged glass. "We'll divide the night into two-hour watches until we become accustomed to Brona's cycle of time. We'll need two men for each shift. I'll take the first with one other man."

He expected reluctance from the exhausted men, but several spoke up, among them Roar and Gullaner, whom he put in charge of the shifts that followed his. He couldn't help but notice that the Scientifica caste, with the exception of Erasma, held themselves aloof as much as possible, but the Bellicosa and Guilders seemed resigned to sharing the work. He was satisfied to have an electrical tech named Appon Zee stand watch with him, although the man showed no inclination to socialize with others of the party. Two greasers volunteered to fill out the other shifts, but he warned that every man would have to take a turn in the nights to come.

Garner had two more duties requiring immediate attention: instruct the men on watch in the use of the pistols and make his report to the captain. The volunteer guards were overly eager to be armed, and Garner issued stern warnings not to use the weapons except in a dire emergency.

"A wasted shot might mean a lost life at some later date. Any man who fires without extreme provocation will be denied the use of all weapons—permanently."

Even Gullaner mumbled a protest, but Garner forced himself to ignore the general disapproval.

Leaving his volunteers, he stooped to enter the captain's tent, and went down on his knees inside it because the ceiling was too low for him to stand. Vane Col and the captain were both occupied with an array of equipment salvaged from the pods.

"Sir, I've set guards for the night. I'm taking the first watch myself."

The captain's face was putrid yellow in the light from the emergency lantern, but Vane's was more unwholesome, blanched white with pain, his eyes dark hollows. His expression was a silent appeal to Garner to help him find release from the hopeless duty of trying to contact Prima, but they both knew there was nothing he could do.

"Mister Rie, what do you think you're doing, crawling into a Space Service Commander's headquarters like a naked savage?"

"Sir, my clothing was soaked."

"I don't care if it's riddled with skin ticks. You're an officer in the Space Service now, not some

Prola hooligan. If you ever report to me again without decent covering, I'll evoke Code 182."

"Sir!" It was Vane who gasped in shock. "Code 182 hasn't been used in over a hundred years, and even in archaic times it was unthinkable for a captain to use corporal punishment on his executive officer."

"It was also unthinkable to appoint a Prola as an officer," Blaz said angrily.

Garner stared past the captain, focusing his eyes on a dark tent wall while he struggled to control his rage. His instinct and his reason increasingly suggested that Blaz was unfit to serve as their leader, but it would be nearly impossible to replace him. Even if Garner wanted Blaz's blood on his hands, he would only make himself an outlaw by killing him. The passengers would condemn him as a murderer, even if he acted for their own welfare. He was a Prola, and no higher-caste member would even accept him as leader.

Could he find support among the crew members? Vane was too weak from his injury to intervene, and Garner had had a serious enemy in Tacka since denying him a promotion to chief. Even though most of the greasers would be sympathetic if he tried to assume leadership, they were too thoroughly conditioned not to look on other castes as their betters. As for Lon Weal, he was the poorest specimen of an officer Garner had ever met.

As he knelt in the captain's tent, trying not to let Blaz's venomous words pierce his mental armor, Garner was too exhausted and disheartened to care whether he lived to see another dawn on Brona. Maybe he should rid the survivors of their incompetent leader. As for himself, death at the hands of the passengers might be a more merciful way to end his life than dying gradually on this pesthole of a planet. He hated the stench of decay in the air, the piercing shrieks of unseen creatures, and the hopelessness of their situation.

"Garner." Vane was saying his name over and over, trying to get his attention, as though the communications officer could read the murderous thought in his mind. "Garner, we need you."

This quiet statement calmed Garner, and he looked at Vane with gratitude. If he killed the captain, there was no question about his own fate. Passengers like Catton Sur would demand his death. Even if he managed to escape, his survival chances alone in the wilderness without supplies were poor to nonexistent.

He watched Blaz for a moment, but the captain was back at the radio, totally oblivious to his near-miss with death.

Another chilling thought made Garner eager to get away from his commanding officer: It looked as if the man was on the verge of mental collapse. His obsession with the useless radios, his neglect of all other survival concerns, and his blind faith in the workability of the caste system in this situation made him an unstable leader at best, but the look in his eyes reminded Garner of patients he'd once seen in a mental rehabilitation facility.

Garner backed out of the tent, shaken by his encounter with lunacy. He still ached to strike out at the captain, but Vane's quiet intervention had done more than remind him of his own precarious position. If both he and Blaz were dead, Lon Weal would be in command. What chance would anyone have of surviving under the leadership of the cowardly second officer?

What chance would Alena have?

He went outside the circle of tents and angrily

pulled off the garment wrapped around his waist, defying the captain with his nakedness. His boots were still where he'd left them to dry, and he spread his undersuit on top of the nearest tent, hoping the night air would make it wearable by morning.

Shrill sounds still rang out from the jungle behind him, but they sounded more distant and less frantic. Perhaps the creatures had finished hunting and were feasting on their kills. Or perhaps he was being fanciful, imagining predatory beasts when the shrieks came from harmless airborne creatures.

He wasn't imagining that he was the only one patrolling the circumference of the camp. He circled the dark tents, carefully picking his way over dry sandy soil, loose and comfortable under his bare feet. Apparently Appon Zee had decided to creep off to sleep instead of standing watch. It was too dark to tell whether he was sleeping out in the open as many were, or sheltering in one of the tents, but Garner knew enough about handling men to know he couldn't let a sentry desert his post. He found the emergency lantern outside the food tent and activated it, then carried it with him as he searched for the derelict guard.

He found him curled up outside a tent, his rhythmic snoring blending with that of other noisy sleepers. Garner stood over him, contemptuous of a man who volunteered for an urgent duty, then didn't perform it. He brought his foot back and kicked hard, no doubt hurting his own bare toes more than the man's rump, but accomplishing his purpose by waking him. He kicked again so Appon Zee would know it wasn't an accident.

"You low-bred lout! Prola Scum!" the man

roared, jumping to his feet and theatrically grabbing his backside. "You have no right to attack your betters!"

By now most of the camp was awake and listening, and Garner shouted because he wanted others to hear.

"You're supposed to be on guard duty, Mister Zee. You took the Space Service Oath, and that means you follow any order given by a superior officer."

"You're not my superior," he said belligerently. "I don't take orders from a bastard Prola. I decided sentry duty isn't necessary. Those cries are too far away to worry about."

"You decided!" Garner grabbed the front of the man's undersuit and yanked him closer. "If it's so safe, you go sleep out there!" He spun him around and pushed him forward with his foot on his backside. "Go on!"

"I'll have you—"

"Go!" Garner roared, so angry he forgot to be self-conscious about his nudity.

"You can't make—"

"Go!"

Appon tripped over his own feet and fell forward, but Garner knew he couldn't relent, not unless he wanted the passengers deciding which orders they wanted to follow.

"I'll stand guard," Zee gasped, lying on his belly in the sand.

"You'll what?"

"I'll patrol the circumference, but I'm not leaving the camp," he said belligerently.

"You'll patrol a double shift," Garner said, prodding him with his foot until he scrambled to his feet, "and if you pull anything like this again, I'll punish you according to Code 182." He was self-possessed enough to see the irony of using the same threat the captain had made against him.

"What's that?"

"Corporal punishment for failure to obey a direct order."

"The Space Service doesn't do things like that!"

"The code is still on the books." He disliked himself for threatening the man, but a distant shriek reminded him they hadn't began to discover all the dangers on the planet.

"Is that what you learned at the Academy—at public expense, Rie?"

The man wasn't humbled, but Garner didn't think he would neglect his assignments again.

As soon as Appon scrambled for his weapon and began his foot patrol around the tents, Garner announced his intention of scouting a broader area. He pulled on his boots, wary of obstacles underfoot, but defiantly left his undersuit to finish drying.

Several times he heard the scurry of small creatures getting out of his way, a good sign that game might be plentiful, but the area between the river and the jungle seemed relatively safe—for the moment. He returned to camp to find Appon still on patrol duty, joined by the two men assigned to the second watch.

Garner found a spot behind one of the tents and stretched out on sand still warm from baking in the sun during the day. When boots wore out, as they soon would, protective footwear would be another pressing need. He fell asleep trying to list all the urgent things he needed to see about immediately.

"Garner!" A soft hand prodded his shoulder, and a distinctly feminine voice repeated his name. "Garner, get dressed!"

He awoke expecting to see Alena, but only because she was so often in his dreams. Instead, Velma was kneeling beside him, pushing a bundle of clothing under his chin.

"Vane told me about the captain's threat. For all our sakes, get dressed before he sees you. I don't know what we'd do without you!"

He grabbed the bundle and held it over his groin, but Velma only laughed.

"I'm a medical officer, and bodies mean no more to me than another piece of meat to the butcher," she teased. "Although as men go—no, I won't inflate your ego. We'll all be naked soon enough. I for one will refuse to wear padded clothing when my undersuit rots away."

Garner smiled lazily, glad he could still be entertained by the thought of Pitt's sturdy body naked as the day she was born. Perhaps if she let her hair fall loose . . .

He sighed and sat up, wondering if a time would ever come when he could think of hair without imagining Alena's golden-red locks cascading down her back.

The moment for pleasing fantasies quickly passed. As soon as he stepped into the camp circle, he was besieged with requests for suggestions and decisions. He glanced toward the captain's tent, disgusted by Blaz's single-minded efforts to do the impossible.

"Rie, the women delegated me to make a request," Catton Sur said self-importantly. "It's all well and good for low-caste men to relieve themselves in the open, but facilities that give more privacy are urgently—"

"I agree. It's essential, and I need a man who's totally trustworthy to oversee the project. As ranking Scientifica, you're best qualified to serve as sanitary engineer. You'll find shovels in the supply tent, and I'll rely on your judgment to recruit helpers and choose sites."

Garner turned his back so Catton wouldn't see him smile at the thought of a Scientifica on latrine duty. He didn't doubt the job would get done, now that everyone understood what it meant to be enrolled in the Space Service. Appon Zee had done him a favor by neglecting his duty.

Chapter Seven

Alena awoke the next morning to find herself alone in the tent she shared with the other women. The other female passengers were assigned to distribute rations of food and water, and Velma no doubt had many duties that caused her to rise early. Alena felt guilty for sleeping when there were so many tasks to perform, but in truth, all her offers to help had been courteously refused the previous day.

She understood why no one would allow her to work. The caste system would lose much of its significance if a high-status female Scientifica worked side by side with a Guilder or, unspeakable impropriety, a Prola. Willing or not, she was a figurehead, a symbol of the culture they'd left behind on Prima.

Brushing vigorously to remove grains of sand sticking to her clothing and face, she tried as best she could to ready herself for the day. Like all passengers, she had a small kit of personal items from the stores in the pod: an implement to clean her teeth, a small rubbery comb, a tube of healing ointment for small abrasions, a drinking cup, and a chunky bar of soap. She used the soap on her teeth, hating the taste, and worked the comb through her uncoiled hair, then tied it at the nape of her neck with a thread she unraveled from the ankle cuff of her undersuit.

In her father's house, servants prepared a deep font of perfumed water for her daily bath and brushed her hair until it gleamed like polished bronze. They laid out freshly laundered garments to wear after they anointed her body with scented lotion. This morning she would gladly trade a year of such pampering for a basin of hot water, but it wasn't the grubby state of her person that made her long for the unattainable. It was Garner Rie.

Last night, hidden from sight behind the tent flap, she'd peeked out while he berated the negligent sentry. Garner had stood only a few feet from her place of concealment, and she still couldn't believe how splendid he was, unfettered by clothing, his naked flesh illuminated by the handheld lantern. Her breath came in short gasps and her thighs trembled as she remembered details. She imagined running her hands over his muscular arms and back, caressing his broad chest, patting his round, compact buttocks, locking her legs around his powerful thighs and calves.

She tried to tell herself this frenzied fantasizing was only the result of seeing a totally unclothed male for the first time. Of course, she'd seen statues in the Cultural Museum and pictures in her science texts, but cold stone and line drawings had done little to prepare her for the reality of a man like Garner. Nor had she suspected that a mere glimpse could be so unsettling.

Even his anger was exciting—when it wasn't directed at her. He'd had good reason to rebuke the guard; it frightened her to speculate on what might happen if men deserted their posts at will. They had no way of knowing what night creatures might invade their camp unnoticed if no one stayed awake to watch. Her father was often severe with servants who displeased him for much more trivial reasons. She couldn't fault Garner for penalizing a man who put them all in jeopardy. She certainly didn't want those shrieking creatures to sneak into camp when everyone was sleeping. It was Garner's job to see that the people from the *Moon Courier* were safe, and after last night, she had even more faith in him.

She only wished she could help him in some way besides supporting him in his disagreements with the captain.

Captain Blaz: She frowned when she thought of him. It was admirable for a commander to try to save his passengers and crew, but Velma had assured her none of the radios from the pods could get through the magnetic field to establish contact with the control center. They'd been designed to contact Prima or Bedir if the pods ejected within range of the home planet or the moon. Until the first manned expedition landed on Brona, the Space Service was only concerned with flight to the moon and back. The man who should have understood this best, Captain Blaz, had spent the whole day in his tent, forcing Vane Col to work with him on the equipment. Didn't he realize their survival depended on adequate food, safe drinking water, and better shelters, not on help from Prima that might never come?

The problems facing the small band of Primans

were almost overwhelming, yet she sat idle. There had to be a way for her to help. She went out into the camp circle determined to be useful.

Garner spent the day by the pods directing the salvage operation. The muddy chutes could be washed later and fashioned into clothing, blankets, and bandages as the need arose, but they had to be cut free and folded into manageable pieces. Every last removable object had to be hauled back to camp. He wanted to save the pods themselves, seeing them as perfect emergency shelters, but the boggy land was working against it, slowly sucking down the metal shells.

He made one attempt to pull a pod to firmer ground, using all the available ropes and men, but the exhausting labor failed to move the craft after it was beached.

He sent a party of scientists under Erasma Dee to search for fresh water and possible food sources in the immediate vicinity, but safety was his most nagging concern. Prima was home to many large predators capable of tearing apart a tent and killing its occupants; he had to believe a primitive planet like Brona had its share of savage beasts too. If they had to defend themselves, he didn't know what to expect from the crew or passengers; only the officers and a few greasers had any experience with firearms. He didn't have ammunition or time to spare for lessons or practice sessions. Even with his Academy training in armaments, he knew his skills were rusty.

While he labored knee-deep in mud with his crew, he thought of the one person he most wanted to protect from harm: Highness Alena Yor. He chafed at his responsibilities in the salvage operation, knowing his time could be better spent exploring for a more advantageous campsite before the rainy season began, but Weal was the only officer available to help direct it. Garner had already learned the second officer was as useless at grueling labor as he was cowardly in times of crisis. He did a minimum amount of work, skirting a fine line between reluctant obedience and punishable insolence whenever Garner gave him orders. After a few hours of salvage work, Garner decided Weal's attitude was detrimental to the men's morale. He sent him downriver alone to look for the pod that had drifted off when the rope broke. Not surprisingly, Weal returned late in the day reporting no success, but looking as refreshed as a man who'd enjoyed an afternoon nap.

The next day Garner awoke at dawn, still fatigued from long hours of arduous labor but uneasy because the previous day had passed without a glimpse of Alena. True, he'd returned to camp after dark the night before, so filthy he scrubbed himself with untrampled sand before approaching the tents. Then he'd wearily gone to get his evening ration by the light of a single lantern. His duty included reporting to the captain at the end of every day, never a pleasant task. Last night Blaz had roundly berated him for his lack of technical skills because he'd had no suggestions on adapting the pod radios to contact Prima. Garner had smarted under the unjust criticism, but long practice had taught him how to disassociate himself from unwarranted abuse. After his report, the only ones awake were the two sentries, so it wasn't surprising he hadn't seen Alena. Still he worried.

Garner was pleased with the way the passengers were allotting the rations. They were conscientious and fair, allowing each person two adequate, if not filling, meals per day. They'd calculated how long the supplies from the pods would last: 20 days or less.

He was less pleased with the progress they were making on shelter. It was patently obvious the current site was unsuitable, but the captain wouldn't listen when Garner tried to bring up the subject. Blaz seemed to think they only had to wait a few days, and a ship would come from Prima to rescue them.

Garner assigned Weal to finish the salvage operation; the supply compartments were nearly empty, and his lazy ways could do less harm. All the second officer had to do was help Tacka and one of the Guilders tear down or cut out any material, from seat harnesses to hatch doors, that might later prove useful. This freed enough men to form two scouting parties, one to search upstream and one downstream.

Garner led the upstream party, returning before dark with discouraging news. The river widened into an impassable marsh that blocked their way less than half a day's march from the camp. There was no possibility of finding a better campsite to the north. Worse, they'd seen murky depressions in the mud that confirmed his belief that large beasts of some type roamed in the area.

Returning to camp, he first looked for Alena, then asked where she was.

"I haven't seen her all day," Velma said, her eyes deeply shadowed by exhaustion. "We've had an outbreak of skin infections, mostly among the men who were wet all day working in the mud. I'm treating it with a fungicide powder, but we'll soon run out. The quickest way to eradicate it would be to shed their soggy clothes and let the sun beat down on their hides."

"You'll have to clear that with the captain," he

said, managing an ironic smile. "Would you please see if Highness Yor is in her tent?"

"She isn't. I just came from there."

"Where then?" He tried to hide his anxiety.

"Let me think. Maybe she went for a walk."

"Where would she go?"

"She mentioned how beautiful those specks of color looked scattered all over the foliage," Pitt said, pointing at the distant mass of greenery.

"In the jungle?"

"If that's what you're calling it, yes."

His heart thundered in his chest as he ran toward the wall of foliage. He covered the half mile or so as quickly as possible in loose sand, following a trail of depressions made by other survivors. He hoped she hadn't gone alone. He'd strongly urged everyone to leave camp in parties of three or more, but he'd been reluctant to make it an order. Without the captain's support, he had his hands full getting work done without trying to regulate every move the passengers made.

The trail veered off, skirting the jungle instead of entering it, but farther to the north, beside a particularly colorful plant, its branches heavy-laden with trumpet-shaped blooms, he found evidence that a single person had gone through the wall of foliage.

He'd been too busy to explore the jungle, so he wasn't prepared for the strange world he entered. Pushing aside some low-hanging branches with leaves shaped like huge flat ears, he began forcing his way through vegetation so thick it engulfed him. For a hundred paces or so, he staggered blindly through exotic plants higher than his head; then they gradually thinned, and he stepped into a clearing shaded by tall tree-like growths with rough-textured green trunks. He stopped to get his bearings, aware of how easy it would be to get hopelessly lost in the dense vegetation.

He'd picked up a hitchhiker; a many-legged creature the size of his thumbnail scurried down his arm. He was fascinated by the glistening purple fluorescence of the fast-moving insect, but he quickly shook it off, glad his tattered long-sleeved garment gave him some protection from minor pests he might encounter.

"Highness Yor!"

His voice sounded eerie in this primeval forest, but he called out again and again as he carefully picked his way over ground made slippery by a yellow mossy growth. Creeping tendrils caught on his feet, almost as though they were reaching out to ensnare him, and more than once he had to take out the small knife he'd appropriated from the weapons cache to cut himself free. If Alena was exploring in this morass, she could be in serious trouble.

"Alena!" His voice was hoarse with apprehension, and he was acutely aware of how alien this planet was. In the corner of his eye, he caught a flicker of bright orange slithering through the undergrowth. He instinctively froze, but the serpent, if that was what it was, was apparently shy of intruders. He didn't see the bright, ropy creature again, but he became even more wary of where he placed his feet.

Blooming plants were everywhere, with fire-red, garish purple, and violet-blue flowers that gave off a scent like putrid fruit. He was finding it harder and harder to breathe, stopping often to gasp for a lungful of the cloying air. He'd never seen such vivid but repelling colors, and he recalled a childhood fable about a garden of evil.

"Alena!" He knew he'd have to turn back soon

while it was still light enough to see the marks of his own passage. He couldn't be sure she was anywhere near, but he called out desperately, unwilling to abandon his search.

"I'm here."

Her answering cry was faint, but it went through him like an electric current.

"Alena! Keep calling! I'll come to you."

"No, I'll find you. Let me hear your voice again."

"Here! I'm here!" he bellowed in his eagerness to see that she was all right.

Sound was deceptive in the dense rain forest, and she found him in only moments. He was so relieved to see her, he forgot himself and rushed to meet her, putting his arm around her shoulders in a sheltering gesture.

"Garner, look what I've found!" She held out a bundle wrapped in a single huge leaf and uncovered a waxy yellow chunk riddled with comb-like holes.

"What is it?"

"Taste it!" She dipped her finger into the mass and licked away the stickiness. "It's wonderfully sweet."

He grabbed her hand to stop her from ingesting more, terrified she might be poisoning herself.

"This hasn't been tested! Our botanists have to pass on everything before anyone eats it."

"This has passed my test," she said with a disarming smile. "I saw a flock of small winged creatures feasting on it in the stump of a fallen tree. They were kind enough to fly away and let me have this sample. Here, try it. Nothing this sweet could be harmful."

She dipped her finger and brought it to his lips covered with a thick golden syrup. At first he resisted, but she softly teased his lower lip until he took her sticky fingertip between his teeth and gently sucked it.

The substance she offered was strangely delicious, but not as sweet as the pad of her finger on his tongue. He held it in his mouth, gently suckling even after the sticky offering was gone.

"Would you like more?"

"Yes," he said, speaking with his heart, not his head.

She dipped her finger again and brought it to him, losing a tiny drop on his chin, then parting his lips.

He took her whole finger this time, feeling it tickle the base of his tongue. He'd never tasted a more delectable substance; he was spellbound by the pleasure she was giving him.

"Isn't it wonderful?" She pulled her finger down the length of his tongue, hooking it for a moment on the sharp ridge of his lower teeth.

She dug into her treasure again, this time sucking her own finger between puckered lips. She looked as pleased as a child with a sugared fruit, and he smiled broadly, imprinting her image on his mind to savor later. Her hair was in disarray, streaming over her shoulders in a golden tangle, and she'd torn the pale blue garment, allowing him to see the satiny skin of her shoulder.

"I'll share with everyone when we get back to camp," she assured him, again offering him a dab on her finger. "Am I wicked to eat my fill first?"

"Not as wicked as I am for accepting a share from you," he said, taking her hand in his and guiding it to his mouth.

He knew he had to stop. Sucking her finger was more arousing than anything he'd ever done with a joy-girl's breast, and he'd already gone beyond the limits of his self-control. Could she really be so naive—so innocent—that she didn't see what she was doing to him?

"Another—"

"No!" He spoke as sharply as he could, hating the way her smile dissolved and her eyes clouded. "Stop this nonsense!"

He couldn't have been more brutal if he'd slapped her, yet he did it for her well-being. At that moment he would gladly have sacrificed his life to realize one perfect moment of sexual congress with her, but he couldn't ask her to pay the terrible price of a union between them.

His eyes strayed to the thin platinum bracelet that was as much a part of her as luminous brown eyes and soft pink lips. She'd already dishonored herself in the judgment of her peers by touching his lips, by speaking softly with that compelling sparkle in her eyes. He couldn't forever blight any life she might have beyond this primitive jungle clearing. He didn't share the captain's faith in imminent rescue, but he did believe High Minister Yor would move heaven and earth to retrieve his daughter. If there was a vessel ready for manned flight . . .

He couldn't think of it now. For a moment he wavered, obsessed by the need to take her in his arms and ravish her sweet pink mouth, but a shrill, piercing sound brought him back to reality—and to an overwhelming sense of danger.

"It's nearly dark," he said. "They're starting to shriek." He grabbed her hand and started to pull her.

"This way. It's quicker!" she breathlessly gasped.

He looked at her dubiously.

"I have a perfect sense of direction. That's why my father had me trained as a cartographer."

He knew she spoke the truth. He followed her through the thick, menacing jungle.

When they emerged, the sky above was gray with dusk, but not dark enough to conceal their return to camp.

"Never go in there again!" he warned, drawing her into the shelter of a high shrub. "It's not safe for you to leave the camp alone."

"And it's not proper for me to go with any of the other passengers! Do you expect me to be a prisoner in my tent?"

She sounded so forlorn he was hard put to admonish her as severely as necessary.

"Stay within the circle, at least. We don't begin to know how dangerous this planet is. You could get lost. . . ."

"You're the one who might have gotten lost without me to guide you out of the jungle."

"I only entered because you were missing."

"Are you my keeper now?"

"I'm responsible for the safety of all the survivors. That includes you."

She meant more to him than any other living being, but admitting it to himself made him speak even more harshly.

"I have neither the time nor the patience to be your guardian," he went on. "I wasted valuable time searching for you, neglecting a myriad of duties that have to get done before I can sleep."

"I can look after myself."

As she spoke, the shrieks began, this time a spat of shrill cries echoing the first.

"What will you use to subdue the beasts making that noise?" he asked. "Do you think you can intimidate them by flashing your pretty bracelet?"

Her lower lip trembled, but she didn't give way to tears. "No man has ever spoken to me like that!"

He didn't like inflicting pain, but her haughty pride was dangerous if it led her to believe she could do as she pleased.

"When you raised your hand and repeated the Space Service Oath, you made yourself subject to military discipline. As an officer, I order you not to endanger your life or that of others by wandering away from the camp without an authorized escort. Is that clear, Highness Yor?"

"Yea, sir," she said with a trace of mockery. "I'll be as obedient as the most docile Prola. You won't have cause to chastise me as you would a female of your own caste."

She'd done the one thing that could make him truly angry: thrown his caste at him.

"Go first. I'll follow in a while so no one sees us return together," he said gruffly.

She walked quickly, staggering a little in sand too slippery for an aristocratic swagger. He watched her go, touched by her vulnerability but still smarting from her cutting remark.

He silently renewed his pledge to preserve her life at the cost of his own, if necessary, but he didn't know if he was strong enough to protect her from himself. Even when she angered him, he wanted to be alone with her for the rest of his life.

Alena felt Garner's eyes on her back until she reached the circle of tents. She'd behaved badly again, but she didn't regret her trek into the jungle. She gave her leaf-wrapped bundle to the woman distributing the evening meal, but declined to accept anything but her ration of water.

She quickly sought the shelter of the tent, grateful to find it empty. Sitting with her legs folded, she tried to calm herself by meditating, but every image she called forth reminded her of Garner.

She imagined the clear stream that meandered through her father's gardens, and Garner intruded, stepping naked into the sparkling water and stooping to splash it over his back and shoulders. When she tried to recall the bright colors of the jungle blossoms, he stepped into her vision and plucked a fiery red one, tucking it behind her ear.

Tears filled her eyes, and she railed at her fate, not bemoaning her exile on Brona but regretting the loss of her heart. She'd lived 22 years without knowing what it meant to fall in love, and now she was hopelessly, miserably enchanted by the strongest, most attractive man she'd ever met. Yet if she had the power to turn sand into gold or moonbeams into a magic highway home, she still couldn't hope to be Garner's beloved mate.

She tried to imagine living the rest of her life on this strange planet. Garner could make her his woman, and together they could begin a new generation. They would love each other as man and woman were meant to, and their children wouldn't know what a caste was.

She knew how wicked she'd been to tempt him! She could still feel the exciting pressure of his mouth sucking her finger. Just the thought of it was enough to make her secret place pulsate.

She was worse than wicked! She'd tested her feminine powers on Garner, wanting him to hold her in his arms and kiss her, needing him to touch her in ways she'd only imagined.

She was a failure as a temptress, but this only made her heart swell with tenderness and gratitude. He could have possessed her, and she would gladly have carried their secret beyond the doors of death. Instead he'd been strong enough for both of them, chiding her for wandering into the jungle alone, instead of using the opportunity she'd given him.

Her tears dried, but her heart still ached. Garner had saved her life, and a tradition more ancient than the caste system dictated that she reward him. Yet he'd refused the only precious gift she had to give: herself.

She slept at long last, lost in dreams, awakened by an insistent voice that wouldn't go away.

"Highness Yor, I'm sorry, but the captain insists."

"Insists on what?" She sat and stared sleepily into Velma's face.

"He wanted me to invite you to join him for breakfast."

Alena laughed, struck by the ridiculous idea of issuing an invitation to eat unappetizing dried rations in a makeshift camp on a savage planet.

"Please tell him Highness Yor would be honored to join him—after she gets the sand out of her hair."

Velma laughed with her, both of them doubling over from the sheer joy of enjoying a joke after all that had happened.

"I needed that!" The medical officer wiped tears from her eyes.

"I like you," Alena said impulsively, hoping she might actually have a friend on this planet.

"I like you too—enough to tell you a secret. The captain's only coming out of that stinky little tent because he's in misery from a skin infection. He's raw in places I won't even mention, but he's too stubborn to throw away his moldy undersuit and let the sun bake away the rash. I have a dozen or more men suffering from the itch but afraid to strip down because of what the captain told Officer Rie."

"What's that?" She was only beginning to realize how little she knew of what was happening around her.

"He said if Garner didn't wear a proper garment—fancy calling an undersuit 'proper'—he'd evoke Code 182."

"Code 182?"

"It allows a commanding officer to beat a disobedient subordinate until he loses consciousness."

"I can't believe the Space Service would allow that!"

"I've never heard of it being done, but no one had the foresight to revise the code," Velma said.

"It's too barbaric!" The thought of anyone harming Garner . . .

"Archaic too. Code 182 hasn't been used in a century or more. I'm worried, Highness."

"Please, call me Alena."

"Alena then, when we're alone. I'm worried about the captain's peculiar behavior and the way it's affecting others. Vane Col's leg isn't healing properly. There's not much I can do for him until the captain releases him from duty. They sit hunched over that useless equipment all day, even though there's no hope of sending a signal to Prima. It makes no sense to me. Are you sure you wouldn't like me to invent an excuse so you won't have to eat with the captain?"

"It's something I have to do," she said grimly.

Captain Blaz repulsed her in the best of circumstances. When she joined him for breakfast, his skin looked as pale as one of the bloated slugs the servants sometimes found in her father's gardens. A stench hung over him, as though his very person was decaying, and she sat as far from him as possible on the opposite side of a square of fluorescent yellow cut from a chute and spread in front of his tent like a picnic cloth.

"I understand we have you to thank for this delicacy," Blaz said, pressing a hard cracker against a small chunk of the sweet substance she'd found.

He handed her the morsel, and she forced herself to eat it, even though she disliked taking food from his unsavory fingers.

"I'm eager to contribute something to our survival," she said.

"Highness Yor, entertain yourself as you wish. It's unthinkable for a woman of your status to labor like a Prola."

"My life is tedious, Captain, for want of anything to do." She idly fingered the edge of the chute cloth. "I do have a proposal. There must be reams of this material. I'm sure there must be needles or punches in the stores from the pods. I could fashion more suitable garments from it, loose-fitting to allow air to circulate. I understand some poor unfortunates are suffering from a skin condition that could be cured by less confining clothing."

"I'm not sure that's a fitting occupation, Highness."

He gave lip service to propriety, but she could see how avidly he wanted relief for himself.

"Naturally I'll bring the first example to you for your approval," she said. "I can enlist others to do the hard labor. It won't be too difficult cutting the fabric with knives. And I may need to search for a substitute for thread—perhaps some plant fiber might work."

"You don't need my permission, Highness. You're free to engage in any project that amuses you."

Blaz didn't linger over their scanty meal, much

to her relief. He had a new idea about establishing communications with Prima, but he didn't want to weary her with the details.

"I understand Officer Col may need more surgery on his leg," she ventured to say.

"Impossible right now. He's the only expert on this planet. I can't possibly spare him when all our lives are at stake."

She wanted to point out that a tent full of transmitters would be valueless if the shrieking beasts made a foray into the camp, but she was sure the captain wouldn't grant any more concessions that day.

Chapter Eight

On the eleventh day Alena tasted wild game for the first time. A party of hunters led by Tacka provided meat by learning to trap small animals in the jungle. They dug pits and covered them with giant leaves, using a bit of the sweet substance Alena had discovered as bait. Her find proved to be abundant, at least at this time of year when bustling orange insects were busy storing it in their nests. A squat, hairy, snout-nosed mammal the hunters called a porcine was particularly fond of it, and almost everyone in camp had tried roasted portions of this easily trapped, relatively small beast. But she'd resisted, repelled by the process of skinning and butchering.

"You must eat the meat," Velma admonished her. "Garner said to save the rest of the pod rations for emergency use. In another day or two we'll be living entirely on what the planet provides."

"I can survive on wild fruits and seeds," Alena insisted.

"Those are seasonal foods. The botanists haven't found enough safe plants to stockpile through the rainy season."

Alena reluctantly accepted her portion of hot meat roasted on a long stick over a pit. The outer rim was black with charcoal from the fire, but she bit into the well-cooked flesh, finding it strong-flavored but not as repugnant as she'd expected. She tried not to think of the meats that graced her father's table: plump domestic fowl with tender white-meat breasts or fish so succulent it flaked apart before it got to the plate. She managed to finish her portion except for the burnt part, and licked the grease from her fingers as the others did.

Lon Weal, whose chief responsibility in the camp seemed to be cutting notches in a thick branch to keep track of the days, sat near her but not too close. He was still wearing his filthy undersuit; the river was too murky from the swamp that drained into it to use for any human purposes, even laundering clothing. Erasma Dee had warned against eating any living creatures that inhabited it. With so much water so close, it was irksome to fetch enough for their use from a pure stream nearly a half hour's walk away. People complained far more about water rationing than about the quality and quantity of their food.

Nearly half of the company now wore the knee-length garments Alena and her helpers had fashioned from the chutes. They proved surprisingly easy to make, since they were little more than sacks with holes for the head and arms. Her only problem was thread. The strands unraveled from the chute material were constantly breaking, and after the seams were sewn down the sides, they ripped apart easily.

The next morning she joined a party led by the botanists for a trek north into a part of the jungle no one had explored. She hoped the abundant vegetation would yield some fibers she could twist together for her purposes.

"I heard you're going with Erasma," Garner said, approaching her as she stood waiting to leave.

It was the first time he'd spoken to her since she'd tempted him with her sweets in the jungle.

"I need plant fibers for sewing," she explained.

He was still wearing his tattered black undersuit, although he'd ripped off the sleeves and cut the legs off above his knees. Those suffering from skin infections had received the first chute sacks; she was glad he hadn't needed one, although she wondered how his sun-bronzed arms would look against the vibrant yellow fabric of the makeshift garments.

"Tell Erasma what you want," Garner said. "He's the best searcher in the camp. He'll find it for you."

"I won't know what I want until I see it," she replied, snapping at him to cover the girlish confusion she felt just speaking to him.

"No, let Erasma handle it. The farther a party goes from camp, the greater the risk."

"Mister Rie!" The captain came striding toward them.

Blaz should have looked ludicrous with pale hairless arms and legs sticking out of his sack-garment, but his eyes had a cold, reptilian cast that overshadowed his physical inadequacies. Alena never saw him without a vague dread of what he might say or do.

"I want you to find the best climber among the greasers," he said to Garner. "I need some wire strung in the tallest tree on the fringe of the jungle."

"I believe that would be Roar." Garner hesitated before continuing. "Sir, I don't think it's wise for Highness Yor to go into the jungle."

The captain pursed his lips thoughtfully. "It's proper if one or more Scientifica accompany her. We have to adapt caste rules to our temporary circumstances."

"I'm concerned about her physical safety, not meaningless conventions," Garner said.

"You'd better be more concerned with Space Service conventions, mister! You stand at attention when you address your commanding officer, and I expect full military courtesy. Is that clear, Mister Rie?"

"Yes, sir."

Garner stiffened, but Alena was sure it was more in anger than respect.

"Captain Blaz, it's not essential that I go," she said, trying to smooth things over.

"You have my permission to explore as you like, Highness Yor, as long as you have proper chaperones. It's unthinkable that a Prola interfere with your freedom of movement. Mister Rie, give yourself an hour of parade penalty to help you remember your place. I'll appoint Weal as timekeeper."

"Oh, no," Alena protested, not sure what Blaz meant.

"Yes, sir," Garner said stiffly as the captain walked away.

The camp circle was largely deserted, but Garner still seethed with rage and humiliation as he stood his hour of parade penalty. This was an indignity reserved for cadets at the Academy: to stand at rigid attention until the stance became a torture. He'd never thought it could happen to an executive officer in the Space Service.

Alena moved out of his range of vision, but he could hear the group departing, perhaps half a dozen scientists from among the passengers. If she had to explore, a group was safer than solitary wandering, but he was afraid she'd stray from the others, trusting her uncanny sense of direction to bring her back to camp.

By the time their voices faded in the distance, his legs ached and his shoulders felt the strain of motionlessness. He relaxed slightly, struck by the captain's lunacy in punishing him for trying to protect a female Scientifica.

"Tighten up there, mister!"

He nearly broke stance when a hard blow resounded across his buttocks, but he remembered just in time to save himself a double-time penalty. The same stick prodded his shoulder, reminding him of torments at the Academy.

"Do that again, Weal, and I'll choke the life out of you," he said between clenched teeth.

"Don't blame me, Rie! The captain sent me to be a monitor. It wasn't my idea. Don't take it out on me!"

There was no satisfaction in hearing Weal whine. Garner silently raged at the captain, so preoccupied with his radios and caste conventions he didn't even acknowledge the chilling shrieks that disturbed their sleep and kept all the rational survivors on edge. Every evening Garner made his report to the captain, and every evening he urged, argued, and even begged the captain to authorize a move to a better site. They needed walls for protection, a roof for shelter when the rains came, and a convenient source of fresh water. Every day they lingered there without taking action put the whole group in greater peril. Yet he was forced to stand like a delinquent schoolboy when he should be supervising work details and planning a fortress.

It still wouldn't be easy to wrest the command away from Blaz. He was seldom alone in his tent, and at night he'd taken the precaution of having a personal sentry on guard, usually Tacka and several others taking watches. Garner might be able to place the captain under restraint based on Code 79, which gave an executive officer emergency powers when a commander was physically or mentally incompetent, but without the support of crew and passengers, it would never work.

Even the pampered, high-caste passengers, unaccustomed to grueling labor and physical discomforts, were not yet murmuring against Blaz's leadership. No one was alarmed enough to see disaster ahead if they didn't make preparations for the rainy season.

He knew the situation was hopeless. Not even the most vocal malcontents would accept a Prola as commander. They brought their problems to him and expected solutions, but the accursed bracelet on his arm made him little more than a servant in their eyes.

He finished his penalty because any other course would be mutiny, then limped off aching from his shoulders to his ankles to accomplish two days' work in what was left of one.

At dusk Garner returned to camp, following his own strict rule that everyone return to the circle of tents by then. It was Weal's duty to take a count, and he was conscientious, no doubt because it was an easy duty he didn't want to exchange it for a more demanding one.

The curfew hour came, and Garner didn't need the second officer's report to know the party of botanists, including Alena, hadn't returned. He didn't waste time consulting with the captain.

"Roar, issue arms. Patrol One, come with me; Patrol Two, go on alert around the circumference of the camp."

No one took the alert lightly. Erasma was obsessively punctual. He never returned late, and he didn't tolerate stragglers who lagged behind on the excursions he led.

Garner led his handpicked men, all the greasers except Tacka and four trustworthy Bellicosa passengers, urging them into a brisk trot. They carried two lanterns, the bearers lighting the way and bringing up the rear.

In the distance, the shrieking had begun. Garner fervently wished one of the beasts would show itself. No man could defend himself against the unknown, and even his bravest greasers were terrified of the invisible menace. Was he only imagining that the screams were louder tonight?

They were less than a hundred paces from the jungle when one figure, then another, stumbled through the wall of foliage screaming in terror, pain, or both.

Garner was the first to reach the men, both carrying a pale, oval, speckled object as large as a human head.

"In there!" one of them screamed so hysterically the whole patrol crashed through the brush, smashing and trampling their way into the primeval forest.

Garner lost his lead, then regained it, driven by human screams as well as bestial ones.

He fought his way through the thickest foliage, then covered the ground with running leaps, leading the men who were swinging lanterns into a scene of carnage so horrible he fired his pistol before he knew he was doing it.

One of the passengers was being ripped apart by three birdlike creatures attacking with bloody beaks and appendages more like claws than wings. Garner's first shot missed, but another struck one of the monstrous entities just below its long green-plumed neck. Other men took aim, several firing at the retreating creatures, but even the wounded one managed to escape into the dark depths of the jungle.

The men of the patrol stood in stunned silence, too horrified by the bloody carnage to act. One passenger lay dead, so brutalized by the savage attack he could no longer be recognized. The other collapsed beside him. Several of the large speckled objects lay near the dying man's feet.

"Eggs," Garner said, struggling to believe that ferocious creatures who stood as high as his shoulder and were powerful enough to tear men to shreds could begin life within the speckled shells.

He was afraid to look beyond the victims, terrified he might see a third mangled passenger with golden-red hair.

"Garner!"

She rushed into his arms, and the terrible disaster became more bearable, if not less shocking.

"They were green," she said. "Green birds. How can beautiful creatures do this?"

The shriekers had seemed anything but beautiful to Garner. They were covered with pale green plumage, shading to dark jade over their breasts, but their razor-sharp claws and vicious beaks were the most savage weapons he'd ever seen.

And there could be more nearby, possibly hundreds even now being summoned by the attackers.

"Get out of here!" he yelled to the lone survivor beside Alena and to his patrol. "Get going!"

"The bodies," someone said.

No one could doubt the second victim was dead too.

"We can send a burial party in the morning."

The whole party plunged through the underbrush, heedless of other dangers, following the lead of a faint lantern.

Garner kept Alena beside him, holding her close with his arm around her shoulders until they were safely beyond the wall of foliage. He feared she'd gone into shock, but she kept pace with him, only her labored breathing revealing what she'd been through.

"My fault, all my fault." A man was weeping with bitter, forlorn sobs that caused the stunned patrol to shy away from him.

Taking Alena by the hand, Garner went up to the man who'd survived the attack of the shriekers and left the woods with them. It was Erasma, the thin little botanist who'd worked tirelessly to find safe sources of food.

Garner remembered the man's high caste but didn't care. He put out his arm and pulled him against his chest, letting Erasma's tears soak the front of his garment.

"I knew we were running late," Erasma said. "Time is my responsibility. I shouldn't have let them investigate those nests."

"Erasma, listen to me," Garner told him sternly, speaking as his own father had spoken to him as a boy. "This planet is more dangerous than any of us wants to believe. All we can do is live and learn.

You've done more to help the group survive than any ten men. I'm your military superior, and I order you not to blame yourself. We don't have time for regrets."

"I thank you, Garner Rie," the little man said, straightening and walking ahead to join the patrol trekking back to camp.

"I can't thank you enough either," Alena said in a soft voice, walking an arm's length from him now.

"Just tell me how you survived the attack," he said gruffly, still shaken to his core by the vicious creatures that could so easily have killed her too.

"I don't think their senses work like ours. I stood still as a statue, but the first man tried to run. When he was attacked, all but Erasma bolted. The second victim never had a chance. If there'd been more shriekers . . . if they hadn't been so intent on killing . . . I don't think any of the runners would have survived. But they didn't seem to notice the two of us who didn't move." She spoke in a confused, rambling way, but her account seemed accurate to Garner.

"I've heard there are creatures on Prima that see well but only notice moving things. The shriekers' hearing may be poor—certainly the noise they make is unbearably loud to us. We'll learn if they have a keen sense of smell if . . ." He didn't want to spread new alarm, so he didn't mention the possibility of the creatures tracking them to their camp.

"I owe you my life again." She sounded so contrite, he had to dredge up his earlier anger to keep from taking her in his arms within sight of the camp.

"I promised not to let you die. I intend to keep that promise." He spoke in stiff, clipped sentences, determined not to let her see how he really felt. "I would appreciate it, Highness Yor, if you would help me. Try to use good sense and avoid dangerous situations from now on."

When they got back to camp, Alena went to her tent and sat reliving the horror of the attack over and over in her mind. Could she have done anything to prevent it? Would those poor men be alive if she'd insisted on starting back to camp earlier?

Erasma had urged them to go back without investigating the cluster of nests they'd found around a stagnant green jungle pool. The others had called him an old woman and said they were tired of plucking leaves and digging roots. Alena could still hear Elt Fay gloating over the huge egg he planned to take back to cook for his dinner.

She remembered how Elt Fay had died. The shriekers had attacked his eyes first. . . .

She shook in spite of her determination not to give in to the horrors she'd witnessed. They were trying to live on a new world, and they still didn't know the rules for survival. If they didn't learn soon . . .

Velma woke up, and listened intently while Alena told her what'd happened in short, clipped sentences. They shared a cup of water, and Alena was grateful for the medic's concern. When there was nothing more to say, Alena sent the medic to her sleeping mat and made a vain attempt to sleep herself.

She knew the watch had been doubled. The circumference of the camp would be patrolled by twice the usual number of armed men for the rest of the night, but she didn't think any of those who'd seen the attack would be able to sleep. Velma was a good listener, but Alena needed to talk with someone who understood what was out there.

She needed Garner.

He was still on watch, as she'd known he would be. The other men stood watching the jungle, listening to the anguished shrieks of the creatures. She tried to think of them as parents weeping for lost children, but she couldn't imagine emotions like love or grief behind those dark, bulging, lidless, alien eyes.

She waylaid Garner on the river side of the camp, far enough away from the other guards not to be heard or seen.

"I . . . I couldn't sleep," she softly murmured.

"Nor could I, even if I didn't want to stay on patrol."

"It's not just what happened. I feel so . . ." She took a deep breath, more afraid of his scorn than the possibility of a night attack by the shriekers. "I should have done something to prevent it."

"What could you have done?"

He sounded bemused; the gentleness of his question encouraged her to speak what was in her heart.

"Erasma didn't want the men to go near the eggs," she replied. "He made an issue over returning to camp on time, but I think he had a premonition. . . ."

"Or the good sense not to take rash chances," Garner said dryly.

"I could have added my voice to his, insisted. . . ."

"Insisted they pass up on the eggs? Remind them that you're a high-caste woman? Do you really think it would have made a difference?"

"I . . . I don't know."

"If you have the authority to tell men when to

come and when to go, then you should be the commander of this group."

Was he mocking her? She wasn't sure, but his gentle chiding was better than scorn or anger.

"If I were, I would make everyone hurry away from this place at first light," she said.

"Then you're wiser than our captain," he said bitterly. "We must build a fortified camp, and we need to be closer to fresh water."

"And farther away from the shriekers!" She shuddered and wrapped her arms across her bosom. "Garner, don't spare my feelings. Do you think a ship will come for us?"

He was silent for a long moment. "I don't know. It's possible, but we have to live as though this is all we'll ever have."

"Yes. That's how I feel."

She stepped closer, aware of the breadth of his shoulders and the way his strong chin was high enough to rest on the top of her head. His hair was dark and shaggy, untrimmed since the collision that had eventually brought them to Brona, but she liked the way it waved on top of his head and curled over his forehead and ears. He must have been a beautiful child, an imp with a headful of ringlets, the kind of babe she longed to call her own.

"I'm keeping you from your patrol," she said without moving away.

"No, it's not my watch."

"You couldn't sleep while others were in danger?"

"Not while you were in danger," he whispered so softly she had to strain to hear.

"Garner, I'm sorry. . . . "

"Sorry because you were born to wear a platinum bracelet?"

"A slave bracelet! It keeps me from what I most want!"

"Sometimes we want too much. The price is too high."

"No! If we're here forever . . ."

"Don't, Alena!"

He touched her shoulder, his fingers caressing the skin where her undersuit was ripped. Her spine turned to water and she swayed against him, her whole body an uncontrollable mass of yearning. His arm was bare under her hand, and she gripped it to keep from collapsing.

"Alena!"

He wrapped his arms around her and held her against his chest.

"I would go back into the jungle this minute to be with you," she said, clinging to his neck with his face only inches from hers.

"I wouldn't let you! Alena . . . Alena." He bent his head, pressing his lips against her forehead with a heat that made her feel branded. "This can't be!"

"It already is! I know you're not indifferent to me!"

"Indifferent! You haunt me, you entice me, you fill my spirit with a longing that could be the ruin of both of us!"

"I'm only a woman. . . . "

"Alena, stop! Go away!" He gripped her shoulders and put distance between them.

"We may be here forever!" she said. "We can't be banished to a wild, savage region as punishment for our love. The Outlands on Prima may be horrible beyond imagination, but this is a new place. How can the old rules be important on a new world?"

"Don't you understand? We've brought our

world with us. There's no place for us to be together here either."

She did understand. She turned and ran, rushing to her tent even though its flimsy walls couldn't protect her from the menaces of the planet and her own wild desires.

Chapter Nine

Garner assigned men to the burial party and prepared to leave with them right after the morning meal. He didn't pick the two men who'd saved their lives by plunging through the wall of foliage, nor did he require any of the greasers to return to the scene of carnage with the exception of Roar. He wanted one armed man he could trust at his back.

He didn't expect to find many remains to bury; jungle scavengers would see to that. He did want every member of their party to understand what they were up against, especially the timid among them, and the best way was to take different men to the site.

"I see no reason why I should go," Catton Sur protested. "You can't expect me to dig graves!"

"Not with your own hands, sir," Garner said, trying to be tactful. "But as sanitary engineer, you need to see things are done properly."

"I'm going with you," Erasma told Garner.

"It's not necessary. . . ."

"No, but I'm a trained scientist. I might see something. . . ."

Garner readily acquiesced, although he wouldn't have demanded it of Erasma. The little botanist seemed to be the only one besides himself who understood the truth: Brona was still too dangerous and primitive for a tame civilization to exist. They were the aliens on this world, and all the odds were stacked against their ultimate survival.

They started off, 12 men walking in the defensive square Garner had learned at the Academy. He was beginning to appreciate the worth of military training, all the grueling time-consuming drills that had little to do with life aboard a space vessel.

He kept Weal at his left, glad the second officer was too terrified to do more than whine occasionally, and Erasma on his right. They'd covered only half the distance to the jungle when the botanist made his first find.

"Look at this," he said, holding a bright green feather gingerly between his thumb and first finger.

"So the shriekers do leave the jungle," Garner said. "I wish we knew how they move. Are those feathery appendages good for anything besides killing?"

"Usually when winged creatures evolve with such long legs, they stop relying on flight. But it would be dangerous to assume anything. I'm worried about their sense of smell too."

"It may not be keen. We do know you and Highness Yor saved yourselves by not moving."

"That only tells us their vision is keyed to detect motion." Erasma lowered his voice to a barely audible whisper. "Garner, we're in deep shit here."

"Yes, sir, we are." He smiled in spite of their grisly reason for proceeding toward the jungle. Most of the greasers respected him, and Velma Pitt seemed to like him, but Erasma was the only survivor who spoke man-to-man, treating him as a person of equal worth.

"We don't know where the shriekers stand in the food chain." Erasma mopped his lined forehead with the back of his hand. "There could be any number of larger beasts that prey on them, especially since they're here on the fringe of deep jungle. They could be avoiding their enemies. I'd hate to meet a creature large and fierce enough to prey on *them*!"

"And on us! Our kind had a hard enough time evolving on Prima, we're such tasty morsels," Garner joked in a loud voice, finding release from the grimness of their trek in humor.

"Are you mad?" Weal finally found his voice. "You make it sound like we'll be the next meal for some ghastly creature."

"Don't worry. The beast that tries to digest you will have a belly full of bile," Garner said.

"I'll tell the captain!" Weal's voice squeaked in outrage, and several men laughed.

"Watch yourself, Mister Rie," a voice from the rear called out. "The captain will say bad things about you in his next imaginary conversation with the Space Control Center."

"He won't let you board his rescue ship—when it gets here a thousand years from now."

Garner hadn't heard such spirited ribbing since before he boarded the *Moon Courier*. He knew it didn't change the fact that he was a Prola, but it helped him make a decision. He knew what he had to do when they returned to camp.

If they returned . . .

Garner led the men through the wall of foliage, over the slippery moss-covered floor of the jungle, following a trail of trampled plants and broken branches toward the clearing where the shriekers had attacked.

"How much farther to the pool with the nests?" he whispered.

"Not far enough for my peace of mind." Erasma shuddered and pointed to the left. "Maybe two hundred paces from that linneas acropos."

"Linneas acropos?"

"The tree with lumpy yellow fruit. To amuse myself, I've been naming plants—trying to begin a primitive system of classification. Keeping track of their properties. For instance, don't eat the little green berries on that lacy-leafed bush unless you want a thorough purging." He lowered his voice so only Garner could hear him. "I haven't told anyone yet, but the seeds from linneas acropos produce erotic visions. I have to be more careful about experimenting on myself."

Garner laughed, wishing he could share his own secrets with Erasma. He didn't need a hallucinogen, tempting as the linneas acropos seeds might be. All he had to do was think of Alena, and he ignited a need that burned like a white-hot flame. He carried her image like a precious icon, bringing it out for sacred contemplation in the dark hours of the night when sleep eluded him. At times he thought the force of his passion would push him into madness, but he held on to his sanity for her sake. She needed him here on Brona as she never would on their own planet, and he lived to keep her safe. She could seduce him with a flicker of her lashes, but the thought of anything harming her unmanned him.

He glanced at the botanist, wishing he could lighten the burden on his spirit by confiding in him, but it wasn't to be. Erasma was reaching out to him in friendship, but his arm was banded with platinum. Nothing could change that.

"Here. They should be here." Erasma froze, and all the men with him held their breaths. "I remember those three trees. See, they seem to share a single root system."

"There's blood." Weal's voice sounded as shrill as a girl-child's.

Garner saw it too: a large stain on a green trunk. Hundreds of tiny green insects almost obscured the reddish-brown smear.

"There has to be more," he said. "Fan out by two's, but don't go more than a hundred paces." He had to gulp for breath to force the fetid jungle air into his lungs.

They didn't search long, but what they found sent several men running into the bushes to be sick. In the end, they dug one small hole in the jungle floor and consigned the pitiful remnants of the two men to the soil of Brona. Garner recited an abbreviated version of the Space Service Burial Rite, and no one wanted to stay longer to add personal words to the eulogy.

There was no joking on the trek back to camp. They'd lost nearly a third of their original number in distant, fiery crashes, but this was the first time most of them had seen close-up evidence of violent death.

Garner's mood was as black as any man's. He understood the odds against long-term survival.

The whole company was waiting within the circle of tents, and even Captain Blaz stepped out into the sunlight when the burial party returned.

Garner knew this was the moment to act, whatever the consequences.

"Sir," he said, going through all the formalities demanded by the Space Code. "I request an immediate meeting of the Officers' Council."

"You're out of line, Mister Rie. We aren't in space. What you're suggesting is mutiny. There's no provision for a Council in this situation."

"Sir, the Code doesn't cover being marooned on an alien planet," Garner agreed. "But it doesn't make any exceptions based on the location of the command. I have the right to request a Council in emergency situations. The death of two high-caste members of this party qualifies as a serious crisis. I want the Council to approve the building of a fortified shelter on a site to be determined immediately."

"That again!" Blaz's face had no more warmth and animation than cold stone. It could have been a death mask carved by some primitive artisan. Only his eyes were animated, and Garner could feel the hatred that flared up in the icy depths.

"Very well. Come into my tent," the captain said impatiently.

"I request a public Council," Garner insisted. "This is a life-or-death decision involving every person here."

A dozen voices shouted agreement, with not a single negative comment coming from the onlookers.

"Very well. If you want to air our differences in public, I hope you realize what you're doing to your career, Rie. There's not a captain on Prima who will have you on his vessel when I get through with you." He'd spoken softly for Garner's ears only. Then he barked an order: "Weal, call the roll of eligible participants."

The second officer stepped forward and began calling out the names of the officers. "Captain Blaz, Executive Officer Rie, Second Officer Weal, Communications Officer Col." He paused while Vane limped forward on makeshift crutches. "Medical Officer Pitt, Chief Engineer Roar."

"I object!" the captain shouted. "Greaser Roar doesn't belong on the Council."

"Sir, the Code specifically says the chief engineer should be included, even if it means appointing a person to that position especially for the Council," Garner said. Then he stood, legs apart, bracing himself for the captain's protest.

Before Blaz could speak, Catton Sur elbowed his way to the front of the circle of watchers. "Captain Blaz, your subordinate, Mister Rie, appointed me sanitary engineer. I've discharged that duty in good faith, knowing the health and comfort of this group is a concern that shouldn't keep you from your rescue efforts. I thereby request to be included on the Officers' Council."

"There's no precedent," Garner began.

"There is now. Catton Sur may vote as a member of the Council," Blaz said with a triumphant nod.

The small group assembled, sitting on the ground in the camp circle, surrounded by the other survivors. There was little debate on the need for fortifications, not after word spread of what they'd seen in the jungle that morning. Six of the seven Council members, including Catton Sur, voted to leave immediately and begin building a fortress on a better site.

"The first rule of survival is to stay on the site where you landed," Blaz raged. "Do you think the rescue team will search the whole planet if we leave the place where the pods went down?"

"Sir, the pods are at least half buried in mud," Garner explained. "They may disappear completely after the heavy rains begin. Staying here doesn't increase our chance of being rescued, only our chance of dying."

"Silence, Rie! If you think your insubordination will go unpunished when we get back to Prima, you're a bigger fool than you appear to be. Even a Prola should have enough sense to look out for his own hide."

"Captain Blaz, I believe the next order of business is to decide where to go," Catton Sur said, puffing up his chest in the shapeless tunic made of chute fabric that they all wore now. "As sanitary engineer, I recommend a site beside the freshwater stream we've been using. It's possible we may be able to divert it to provide running water within the fortress walls."

"That's a good proposal, Catton Sur," Garner said, "but the ground there is too soft. We don't know how saturated it will be when the rains begin. I suggest we move south and send a scouting party ahead to look for firmer, higher ground. We've only seen a tiny portion of the area."

"Next you'll be suggesting we inflate one of the rafts and try to cross that damned river," Catton said, "if you can call something that wide and foul a river."

Garner caught a glimpse of Alena, her face pale under the halo of hair she'd swept up on her head. For her sake, he didn't give up, instead vehemently insisting they search for a better site.

The captain grudgingly voted for the familiar site near their water supply.

"At least we can use those hills behind it to enhance the effectiveness of our transmitters," he said.

Catton Sur and Lon Weal agreed without waiting for a formal vote. Garner opposed them, supported by Roar and Vane Col.

Everyone looked at the medical officer; her vote was the tiebreaker. Garner almost allowed himself to relax. Velma had common sense, and she should be the first to understand why a low-lying site could be a serious health hazard in the rainy season.

"We're waiting for your vote, Officer Pitt," the captain said in his most intimidating tone.

Velma didn't even glance at Blaz. Her eyes were riveted on Vane Col, and something passed between them, an expression that disturbed Garner. She wasn't thinking of the welfare of the group; whatever decision she made, it would be based on her feelings for the injured officer.

"I vote for the site near our present water supply," she said woodenly.

The decision was made. The camp became organized chaos. The tents, foodstuffs, arms, and essential tools had to be carried to the new site immediately. The fastest walkers and strongest haulers would make more than one trip that day, but everyone had to leave the old camp at least two hours before dark. Anything left behind would have to wait for foraging parties to retrieve it the next day.

Erasma showed the feather to everyone who wanted to look. The shriekers had left the jungle, and no one wanted to be at the old site when the nocturnal creatures started to howl again.

Alena found Garner in the process of instructing four men who would serve as armed guards during the trek to the new site. She waited until he dismissed them, then motioned him to step behind one of the two tents still standing.

"Velma Pitt asked me to speak to you," she said shyly.

"I don't have time." He didn't look at her.

"She knows you're angry, but please, Garner, she had a good reason. Vane Col will have a terrible time getting as far as the stream. He can't possibly travel any farther, and she won't have him left behind."

"So she's willing to risk everyone's welfare for the sake of one man."

His gruff tone hurt Alena. Even though the decision hadn't been hers to make, she could understand why Velma acted out of love for Vane Col.

"Why are you so stubborn? You don't know anything about love!" She ran from him, fighting back tears because she didn't want him to see her weakness.

The whole party trudged to the new site, most of them wearing their tattered undersuits again to protect their skin as much as possible. Alena volunteered to return with those going back for a second load, and her offer wasn't refused. No one, not even Lon Weal, was shirking work, and caste meant little compared to the urgency of protecting themselves from the shriekers.

By the time she returned from the second trip, she had needles of pain shooting through her shoulders from pulling a load fastened to two long poles. She ached from her neck to the soles of her feet, but she had the satisfaction of knowing she was useful.

Already the men had felled several dozen tall, green-trunked plants that were the closest thing they could find to the trees on their planet. They were working on the north wall of the stockade, digging holes and setting stripped poles twice the height of a man upright in them. The stockade, as people were calling it, faced the mud banks of the great river on the west, and the only entrance was planned for that side. A long ridge of hills on the east sheltered them from the jungle that lay beyond them.

The freshwater stream was on the south side of the site, and having it close would save the water carriers a long daily trek. Catton Sur, officious and annoying but fairly competent, was already trying to devise a plan to divert water into the stockade, although Alena suspected he was just as interested in avoiding the grueling work of felling logs and hauling them to the site. The hills were only sparsely covered with grass, but a forest of the trees they needed shaded the freshwater stream. Erasma was supervising the cutting, trying to insure that their needs didn't devastate the area and destroy possible food sources. Someone found peculiar blue hard-shelled creatures in the stream, and everyone was hoping they would prove edible.

Spirits were high among most of the survivors, but Garner was morose, speaking only to give orders. Alena knew he was unhappy about the site, but she couldn't help sharing in the general feeling of relief; she couldn't forget what was behind that ominous wall of foliage, but it lifted her spirits to know they wouldn't be living within sight of it. In spite of her exhaustion, she felt new hope as she saw men slaving to erect a section of the wall before dark.

Five days later they had a crude stockade enclosing almost as much space as they'd had in the circle of tents. Platforms were built so sentries could keep watch from within the log walls. Sleeping space was increased by using the tents and chute material to build crude lean-to shelters, and for the first time since leaving the *Moon Courier,* Alena lay down to sleep in a small space that was hers alone.

When the outer walls were done, Garner gave the people a day of rest to let blistered hands and sore muscles heal. Their frenetic activity had cost more than minor aches: One greaser had a deep ax wound on his calf, and the Guilder responsible for lashing the support beams together with tough jungle vines was suffering from a fractured arm after falling from a makeshift ladder.

The captain rarely commented on the work. Instead of helping, he spent all his time in his lean-to with the useless radio equipment. Garner reported to him once daily, but more often than not, Blaz scarcely listened. He sat for hours sending distress signals that no one would ever receive, stopping only to rant against the folly of building when they would soon be rescued. Vane Col joined him when he was able, but he was suffering from severe bouts of fever and chills.

"This is a miserable place," Vane said when Garner visited him in his lean-to. "Velma won't admit it, but I have a sickness we've never seen on Prima. If it spreads . . ."

When Garner repeated Vane Col's fears to Erasma, the botanist was gravely concerned.

"Insist that people boil all their drinking water, and keep a smoky fire going at night to drive away the insects," he advised.

Garner followed the scientist's advice, wishing he dared speak to him about Alena. She was working as hard as any greaser, even though the others still deferred to her whenever she allowed it. This gave him too many opportunities to see her. Even though they dared not speak, they locked eyes too often. He was afraid they might be betrayed by emotions too powerful to conceal. He could only hope the others were too busy to notice.

She frequently supped with the captain at his request, and Garner hated seeing her smile at the loathsome, bleached-out face of his commander. Could she possibly take any pleasure in being with the swine?

On the free day Blaz left his radios and dogged Alena like a lovesick youth. Garner seethed with anger, hating it when the captain presented her with a nosegay of tiny blue and yellow blooms that she tucked into her coiled hair.

He suffered in silence while she chatted with the captain, but jealousy over a woman was so new and strange to his nature, he didn't recognize it as the reason for his foul mood.

The site pleased him even less as work progressed. They had to dig through many feet of sandy soil to erect the poles in solid ground, and even then they weren't as firmly planted as he would have liked. A more obvious fault was the stink of the swamp that carried to the stockade when the wind came from the north.

They were nearly as vulnerable here as at the old camp, and late at night following the free day, Garner wasn't surprised when the stockade was attacked.

"Sir, there's something banging on the wall!"

Garner awoke instantly to find Gullaner, a sentry on duty, anxiously shaking his shoulder. He was on his feet and running toward the nearest platform before the stocky young greaser could say more.

Garner beamed the sentry's lantern over the top

of the wall. A flock of six or seven long-legged shriekers were hurling themselves at the north fortification, pecking at the logs with their lethal beaks.

"Get in position to fire if any come within range," he yelled to the sentries on the other three corner platforms.

He didn't hear Alena climb the ladder to stand beside him, and he didn't want her to see what had to be done.

"Go back to your bed," he ordered, taking aim with the loaded pistol he kept beside him in the night. "Fire when you're sure of your aim," he told Gullaner.

The creatures attacked with running leaps, hitting the wall so hard it shook. The impact stunned them for an instant, but they recovered quickly and kept up the assault.

"Now we know they can't fly," Garner muttered, taking careful aim with the short-barreled pistol at one of the creatures who'd just charged.

His shot hit home, but the horrifying death shriek made his hand less steady for the second shot. He cursed himself when he missed.

Gullaner shot twice in quick succession, and the other sentry on the north wall added his firepower. The whole flock was shrieking, and the din was so horrendous Garner lost count of the number of gunshots.

"Take careful aim!" Even as Garner shouted the command, he knew this skirmish was won. The shriekers were fleeing.

"I'd like to get a close look at a dead one," Erasma said, joining Alena, who'd chosen to ignore Garner's order.

"I'm pretty sure I shot one," Garner said. "I'll go out and see."

"No, you can't leave the stockade at night. It's the rule!" Alena said.

"It's my rule, Highness Yor, and it doesn't apply to the sentries in emergencies."

He had the barricade removed from the narrow entryway and stepped out with Gullaner and Erasma at his back. They searched the length of the north wall, then the whole circumference of the stockade.

"Are you sure you downed it?" Erasma asked.

"Yes."

"It fell down dead and didn't get up again. I saw it," Gullaner attested.

"Then we're dealing with a creature that carries away its dead after an attack," Erasma said solemnly.

"Farther up the evolutionary scale than we thought," Garner said.

"More intelligent—and more dangerous."

They hurried back inside the stockade, but the shriekers didn't return. All night long they could be heard in the distance, and it wasn't hard to imagine rage and grief in the distant howls.

In the morning, the survivors began caulking the walls.

The plan called for sleeping huts built against the inner walls of the stockade, plus one large common room, an adjoining kitchen, and smaller storage rooms. The best log cutters and builders worked putting up the structures to provide dry shelter before the rainy season began. Others were assigned to fill baskets and wooden buckets with thick, sticky mud from the river's edge and haul it to the walls. Catton Sur was directing the caulkers without dipping his own hands in clammy mud. Every chink between the logs had to be filled to weatherproof their shelter, but first he was having them fill in the gouges left by the shriekers' beaks.

Alena volunteered to collect mud from the bank of the river, although she wasn't proud of her reason for avoiding work on the wall. She couldn't bear to put her hands on the raw scars left by the murderous creatures. As odious as the mud was, she preferred scooping it into buckets to chalking over the evidence of attack.

There was a trick to finding mud of just the right consistency, she found. If it was too thin and watery, it would make poor caulking. She broke a fingernail learning that too-dry mud was difficult to scoop into her two buckets made of hollowed chunks of log with ropey vine handles.

She wandered downstream, ridiculously pleased when she found a stretch of perfect mud. If only her father could see his pampered daughter excited by a find of disgusting brown mud! His world seemed so far away she felt fragmented into two different people.

Using both hands, she scooped up a big chunk and squeezed to wring out excess water.

"You look like a little girl making mud pies."

She stood, startled by Garner's sudden appearance, but miracle of miracles, he was smiling at her.

"Do you enjoy watching me wallow in this goo?" She wiggled her bare toes, enjoying the cool mud that oozed between them.

"You're beautiful even with dirt on your face."

She automatically touched her cheek, leaving a much bigger mud smear.

"Let me," he said, stepping onto the muddy bank wearing only the tattered bottom of his black garment.

He touched her cheek with his fingertips, gently trying to wipe away the mud.

"Did you follow me?" she asked, keeping her eyes focused on his toes half-buried in the muck.

"I hate it when you're out of my sight," he said, not exactly answering her question.

"The mud is better here."

He laughed, a wonderful throaty sound that made her heart tingle with happiness.

"Highness Yor, a connoisseur of muck!"

"Are you making fun of me?"

"Yes, definitely yes." He looked younger when he allowed himself a moment of happiness.

"Then see how you like a mask of mud!"

She reached out and caught his face between her muddy hands.

"Now you have a beard," she teased, loving the smooth-shaven feel of his face. "Do you scrape away your whiskers because the captain demands it?"

He frowned, and she regretted saying something that might destroy his mood.

"No, because I'm more comfortable," he said, grinning mischievously before he retaliated, swiftly scooping up a dab of mud and painting the tip of her nose.

"You beast!" She ran a few paces away and hurled a handful at him, missing his face but plastering his broad, silky-haired chest.

"Is it war you want?" He yelped like a schoolboy playing war games and sent a fistful of the muck in her direction. It landed harmlessly on her shoulder, but she tried to back away, losing her footing in the slippery mud.

She sat with a noisy plop, damaging only her pride as the wet mud seeped under her short hand-sewn tunic.

For a moment her innate dignity warred with her sense of humor. She tried to pull herself up, but her hands slid and she plopped down a second time.

He laughed uproariously, and she would gladly have wallowed in mud up to her neck to see him without the scowl that had seemed to be permanently etched on his comely features.

"Let me help you." He stepped close, towering over her clad only in his makeshift knee-length britches, his powerful legs even more shapely from her new vantage point. She looked up slowly, letting her eyes roam over his groin and belly, up his torso to the smirk on his lips.

"Aren't you afraid you'll soil your elegant outfit?" she asked.

"If I pound these rags against a rock one more time to launder them, I might as well go about as nature intended."

"If you're trying to embarrass me, you won't succeed so easily," she challenged, reaching out to grab the hand he offered.

She used her weight, slight as it was compared to his, and yanked with all her might, catching him off balance. He slipped, tried to right himself, then plunged forward, toppling as she'd planned but landing on top of her.

He knocked her flat, soaking her hair and back in the gooey mud. She squealed and fought with breathless pleasure as his body crushed hers. His thighs pinned her body, and his legs were pushing hers deeper into the mud. Most surprising of all, she could feel a change happening to his body, and something hard prodded her groin, almost making her forget their murky bed.

She tried to push a mud-caked strand of hair away from her eyes, but he caught her arm.

"Your platinum shines even in this muck," he said in a soft, sad voice. "I must be mad, rutting in the mud with a high-caste woman."

She put her arms around his neck trying to hold him close, but her hands were slippery. He easily rolled away, rising to his feet, his true feelings betrayed by his ragged breathing.

He didn't offer his hand again. She was too agitated to think of requesting it.

He plunged into the water, splashing and scrubbing as he ran, his frantic retreat telling her he was trying to wash away more than the mud that coated his body.

She ran after him, intimidated less by the brown depths of the river than by the prospect of returning to the stockade coated with mud. The water was warm but not pleasing to her nostrils, and she gingerly stopped when it was no higher than her waist. The bottom was soft and covered with vegetation that whipped around her legs and clung to her toes. She quickly bent forward and wet her hair, scrubbing with both hands to remove the worst of the mud, then dipping down to wash her shoulders and back. It was a poor bath at best, but she hated the creepy vegetation sticking to her legs and the way she sank to her ankles in the loose muck on the river bottom.

Garner was 20 paces farther into the river when she heard a sudden strangled cry.

"My leg!" he called out in agony, making her forget her aversion to the river bottom.

"Garner—what . . ."

She started toward him, swimming even though she was afraid of swallowing the swamp-polluted water. When she looked again, he'd disappeared.

"Garner!" She screamed his name and strained to see him across water so murky it scarcely reflected the sunlight.

His head bobbed up, closer to her now, and she

raced toward him, staying near while he struggled to swim to shore.

"Let me help you."

"Get out of here!"

She followed him, hovering like a mother waterfowl watching its offspring. When he reached shallow water, he seemed unable to continue, standing on one leg but doubled over in pain.

She stood and slipped under his arm, taking as much of his weight as she could, helping him stagger up the bank, through the mud flats, beyond to dryer ground.

"I've never felt such pain," he gasped, collapsing and clutching his left leg.

"Let me see what's wrong!"

"There's something in my leg. I . . . I can't see clearly."

She bent beside him, examining the ugly purple wound on his calf.

"Stung me," he said brokenly. "Shooting pain."

She saw the puncture mark, but the foreign object that caused it was buried in a puffy mass of swollen flesh.

"It needs to be cut," she said, trying to remember everything she knew about extracting foreign objects.

Garner muttered incoherently. Terror for his sake gave her the courage to do the only thing she could think of. She pushed hard with both thumbs on either side of the puncture mark, nearly faltering when he screamed in agony. Loathsome green fluid flowed from the wound, but she saw the cause of his suffering: a needle-thin spine protruding from the puncture. She pulled carefully and extracted it.

"Careful," he moaned. "Don't prick yourself."

"It's from a water plant. I'll save it for Erasma."

She ran and dropped it in her muck bucket, leaving it for later, then rushed back to Garner.

"I can run back for men to carry you."

"No, I'll walk."

She helped him to his one good foot, urging him to put his weight on her as he struggled to move forward.

"I'm too heavy . . . let me. . . . " he said, but without her support, he would have toppled over.

"Did you say a plant stung you?" She shuddered, remembering the creepy vegetation that had clung to her legs in the water.

"Attacked me." He mumbled like a man intoxicated by strong drink.

He fell twice on the way back to the stockade, each time rising with greater difficulty, complaining that he had no feeling in his arms. When they finally came within sight of the walls, she eased him to the ground and shouted until help came. Two strong greasers ran out and carried him to Velma Pitt's lean-to. They laid him on a makeshift bed and hovered over his unconscious form until the medic came and sent them to find Erasma Dee.

Alena held his hand between both of hers, willing her own life current to flow into him.

Chapter Ten

"Please don't die."

Garner heard Alena, but she seemed to be speaking from some distant place he couldn't see. The fear and anxiety in her voice made his heart ache, but when he tried to go to her, he couldn't move.

"Darling Garner, if you die, I don't know what I'll do. Please don't leave me." She was holding his hand, pressing it against her cheek.

He tried to speak, but words wouldn't come. His vocal chords were frozen; his lips and tongue wouldn't move.

"You promised not to let me die," she said. "How can you keep your promise if you're not here?"

Alena! He called out to her in his mind, but no sound came from his mouth.

He desperately wanted to comfort her, but he didn't know how to make her hear him.

My darling, I'm alive, he called out in his mind, struggling to give her a sign he heard her.

"I know it's supposed to be wrong to love you," she said, kissing the tips of his fingers, "but my heart tells me differently. Oh, Garner, come back and love me. I need you! Please hear me!"

I hear you! I love you, Alena! You're all that matters to me in this universe!

In his mind he was screaming, but he couldn't speak, couldn't see, couldn't move. He was desperately straining to show he could hear her.

She dropped his hand, and he heard small sounds that made him believe someone else had come.

"Velma, he's so ill," Alena said. "Can't you do something to help him?"

"There's nothing more I can do." The medical officer had never sounded so weary and defeated. "Did I tell you to keep him cool and change the hot compress on his wound once an hour?"

"Yes, I'll do that and keep his mouth and throat moist. Maybe I can spoon some broth into him. He seems able to swallow. It's the only hopeful sign so far."

"Yes, do that," Velma agreed sluggishly.

"There's still a chance he'll regain consciousness, isn't there?"

"I've told you all I can, Alena. If he does come back, there's no guarantee he'll be all right."

Was she saying he was doomed to be a vege table, of no use to himself or anyone else? What cruel fate had imprisoned his spirit in a useless body? He couldn't allow himself to believe he wouldn't recover!

"Don't believe her, darling," Alena whispered when they were alone again. "When the poison wears off, you'll be fine. You have to be!"

He strained to reach out to her with every molecule in his body. He could remember what had happened: A vicious spine from an aquatic plant had stabbed him. He vaguely recalled a rubbery frond slapping his thigh, wrapping itself around him before the spine penetrated his calf. It was as if the plant had captured him, then injected the near-lethal poison. He wanted to tell Alena about this bizarre underwater hunter. If he'd been a smaller creature, would the plant have made a meal of him?

He slept again, and when he awoke, Alena was beside him talking to Velma.

"Forgive me," Alena said. "I'm selfish to expect comfort from you when Vane Col is so ill."

"He's dying," Velma replied.

Garner was grief-stricken by this news, and frustrated beyond endurance by not being able to help.

"There must be some hope. . . . " Alena sounded young and vulnerable, nothing like the haughty woman he'd first seen on the *Moon Courier*.

"Not in this forsaken place," Velma said bitterly. "He's refusing drugs as well as food and water. Brona has broken his spirit. He can't face being a cripple. He thinks he's hindered our survival efforts. He blames himself for letting us build the stockade where it's so dangerous."

Garner's residue of anger against Velma dissolved. She was paying a terrible price for voting to build on this site: She was losing the man she'd tried to save.

"Garner's life is in your hands now, Alena," the medical officer said. "Keep giving him the injections until the medication is gone. I'll be with Vane."

"Your life is in my hands," Alena said when they

were alone again, her mouth so close to his ear he could feel the tickle of her breath. "Garner, you're locked away inside yourself with only me to call you back. I feel so inadequate! All I can offer is my love."

He felt a trickle of water pass his lips. No matter how hard he strained, he couldn't see her or give any sign that he was aware of her. He thought his brain would explode from the effort of trying to speak. He loved her with all his heart and soul, and nothing seemed more important than telling her that.

"Velma drained the poison from your wound as best she could. You'll have a scar where she cut your leg." She laid her hand on his forehead, and he felt her cool touch.

"Oh, my darling, you're still so feverish!"

What exquisite torture it was to hear her voice and feel her fingers gently massaging his brow without being able to see or respond.

"I'll be by your side as long as you need me," she promised fervently. "Velma told the captain I have a contagious fever and mustn't be disturbed. She's the only one who knows we're together. Imagine what would happen if they knew! Catton Sur would want to return to Prima just for the pleasure of having us banished. And the captain would be livid! That horrible man thinks he honors me when he insists I take my meals with him. How I loathe him! Oh, Garner, please come back to me. You're my only reason to go on living in this wretched place."

She stretched out beside him, resting her head on his chest, her hair tickling the skin over his ribs. Aware now of his nakedness, he was embarrassed, hating the way he lay like a babe fresh from the womb.

"I never thought of men as beautiful," she said, stroking his chest, letting her fingers linger on the nipple nearest his heart. "But you are."

And you're a naughty girl, he thought with a surprising flicker of amusement as he felt her hands shyly roam over his torso, bedeviling his navel with a fingertip.

"There's nothing I wouldn't do to bring you back," she cried out fervently, and he could feel the dampness of her lips matting the hair on his chest.

It was sheer torment to have Alena close and be unable to take her in his arms and love her as no man had ever loved a woman: completely, fully, with tenderness and unparalleled joy.

"I know you're alive in there," she said in a passionate tone more angry than mournful. "You've been avoiding me—trying to pretend we don't belong together. Don't you know we were fashioned by a divine hand to complete each other? Would a loving deity bring us to this desolate planet for any reason but to unite us for all eternity? Oh, men understand nothing! I want to live and bring forth life! Is that so wrong? Is it evil to love you even though I'm enslaved by this infernal bracelet and all that it stands for? Why should other people have the right to brand our love as evil, when I know it's the greatest good in my life?"

She pressed the hard metal band against his lips.

"Someday you'll take this slave band from my arm and consign it to the depths of the sea," she vowed. "If you could hear and answer me, you would assault my ears with a hundred reasons why it will never happen, but I believe we'll be together, Garner Rie. I believe you'll live, and you'll accept our destiny together! I loathe those who would punish us for breaking caste rules!"

Alena! Alena! he cried out in silent misery. Did she know how she was torturing him? Since they'd landed on this planet, he'd spent every waking moment yearning to be with her; when she wasn't nearby, he felt like a walking dead man: numb and dispirited. But he knew more of their world than she did. She didn't understand what it meant to be banished for defying caste laws. Her family would hold a death service in her memory; her possessions would be incinerated and her father disgraced. She would be sent to the most desolate place on Prima, the dreaded Outlands, tormented by the knowledge that she'd brought ruin to her parent and her kin. And Garner's family would fare even worse. They were poor and at the mercy of vengeful employers. Their friends and neighbors would shun them and make their lives a perpetual torment. There was no mercy on Prima for anyone who defied caste laws. The most horrendous sin on the planet was love between an elite-caste woman and a lowly Prola.

All I've tried to do is save you from a living hell, he cried out in the dark prison of his mind.

"Oh, Garner, please come back!"

She left his side for a moment; then he felt a hot compress scald the raw wound on his calf. Excruciating pain shot through his leg, and the agony was unbearable. He slipped away from her into deeper blackness.

When he became aware of his own existence again, the pain had subsided but he was cold, chilled to his bones.

"Your teeth are chattering," Alena said, drawing a covering over him.

Warm me, he silently cried out.

As though she'd heard, she lay beside him, holding him in her arms, covering his uninjured leg with hers until her body heat brought him a warm sense of well-being.

He slept again, awaking the next time to a strange sensation.

"What have I done? Oh, I hope Velma doesn't come now! I'm wicked, unforgivable! How could I! I was wrong to be so curious." She was whispering urgently near his ear. "I didn't understand—when you pinned me in the mud—I felt—and now you're so huge and hard again. Oh, if Velma comes, I'll die!"

Had she touched him—fondled him? His groin was pulsating, adding new torment to his helpless state. This was too bizarre to believe, and yet he knew what was distressing her: He had an erection.

Somewhere deep in his brain, he digested the irony of his involuntary state, and bitter laughter welled up in his throat.

"You laughed! I heard it! You laughed!" She knelt over him and showered kisses on his face, pressing her lips on his eyelids, his cheeks, his chin, his mouth.

"You . . . are . . . a . . . yorita."

"You talked! Garner, you talked! I was so afraid—what's a yorita?"

"Witch." He forced words though his raw throat. "Seduces men. In their sleep."

"Oh, no, I didn't—I couldn't. . . . "

"Come here."

She did, pressing her face against his throat.

"How long . . ."

"You've been unconscious for nine days. Garner, I was so terrified. First Vane Col . . ."

"Dead?"

"Yes, some hours ago. How do you know?"

"Heard. Some. Sorry."

He slept and woke, taking small amounts of nourishment when he was able, his sight gradually returning. Sometimes Velma fed him broth from a carved wooden spoon; other times Erasma grinned down at him and offered soft bits of tangy fruit. By the third day he was able to sit with assistance and chew whatever was offered.

He was alone more often now, but he heard the pounding of stone hammers and the shouts of builders racing to complete the roofed shelters before the rains came.

Alena sneaked in to see him when she wasn't gathering mud or caulking the newly constructed huts within the walls of the stockade. Garner was still in a lean-to, but she assured him that soon they'd all sleep in the new shelters.

He didn't tell her how much he'd heard while he was paralyzed and unable to speak. She seemed embarrassed when he tried to thank her for her tender care, and her visits grew shorter and less frequent. Some days he wondered it he'd imagined her impassioned words, but in his heart he was sure he hadn't.

The shriekers had come several times while he was comatose, sometimes as many as 20 battering the north wall until the sentries' shots drove them off. Lately, though, as dark clouds formed on the distant horizon and frequent small showers soaked the stockade at midday, their howls and attacks no longer broke the peace of the night.

Garner relied on Erasma to report on what had happened.

"My guess is those shrieking devils migrate before the rainy season begins in earnest," the botanist said. He pulled on the sparse white beard that had grown since landing on Brona and sniffed the air. "I don't think it will be long now. I smell a storm building up."

Velma checked on Garner twice daily, but she was silent and morose, mourning Vane Col. She supervised others who helped Garner learn to walk again, but she took no real interest in his progress or in anything else. Garner felt as though he'd lost two good friends, and he had few enough among the edgy, short-tempered survivors.

The captain looked in on him the day after he moved into the roofed hut he was to share with Roar and Gullaner.

"Now they tell me you'll live," Blaz said, looking down at Garner, who sat resting after a hard period of exercise on the mat of reeds that served as a bed. "I appointed Weal as acting executive officer until you're ready to resume your duties." He was carrying one of the slender portable antennas from the pod radios, nervously slapping his palm with the silver rod.

"I'm ready now, sir."

"Very well, but don't think I won't include this latest episode in your fitness report."

"What episode?" Did this lunatic intend to cite him for neglecting his duties while he was comatose?

"Approaching a high-caste woman when she wasn't properly chaperoned! I know you were alone with Highness Yor before your accident. I will not permit a Prola to flaunt caste rules. You're still under my command, mister, and I won't tolerate it. I've warned you enough times!"

He lashed out furiously with the antenna, using it as a whip on Garner's naked back. He struck a second time and a third, breathing hard and making strange moaning noises.

Garner clamped his teeth together to keep from

crying out as the captain's blows crisscrossed his back with burning welts. He used every bit of the strength he'd regained in recent days to keep himself from throttling his tormentor. He wouldn't give Blaz an excuse to have him executed!

"My ancestors yoked your kind to carts and used them like animals! Now our timid politicians are so afraid of mobs, they pander to the Prolas and try to make a space officer out of the likes of you!"

He landed another blow, but it lacked the force of the others. Garner realized his stoic attitude was robbing Blaz of a bully's pleasure in inflicting pain.

"You'll live with greasers, eat with greasers, and work with greasers, Rie. I swear by the Space Service Code, I won't allow an arrogant Prola to corrupt those entrusted to my care. You flaunt one more rule—one caste tradition—and you'll wish the bitch who gave you life had strangled you at birth!"

Garner stared straight ahead at the log wall long after Blaz left. His back was on fire, but the pain was easier to deal with than his rage. All his life he'd been frightened, coerced, conditioned, and indoctrinated into accepting the caste system as righteous and just. No longer! He couldn't respect a social order that elevated men like Blaz and Weal into positions of authority.

When he finally stood, he trembled with weakness and pain, but he'd never felt more at peace with who he was. The captain had demeaned himself by lashing out like a maniac; it had nothing to do with Garner's worth as a man. He pulled on a makeshift tunic, one Alena had made for him, and went out to resume his duties.

* * *

Alena yearned to be with Garner. She constantly thought of the long days and nights she'd spent by his side, telling him all the things locked in her heart. Even though he could neither hear nor answer, she'd felt closer to him than she ever had to anyone.

Now she didn't dare go near him. She couldn't pretend to be sick again, not without Velma to maintain the fiction. The medical officer rarely spoke to anyone, and more often than not, she wasn't able to preform her duties. Her hair was a tangled mess, and she didn't take the trouble to bathe or wash her tunic. Once strong and robust, she was rail-thin and withdrawn.

When Garner came out of his hut for the first time without Gullaner or Roar by his side, she hurried to a vantage point between the common room and the lean-to kitchen where she could watch him without attracting notice.

He was thinner too, but not wasted like Velma. In fact, his cheeks were flushed above the dark, heavy stubble that had grown while he lay paralyzed. His soft dark hair, the same locks she'd touched so lovingly without his knowledge, were ruffled by the wind that swept through the stockade.

If she could be with him forever, she would gladly live out her life on Brona. But even here she was watched, her every move monitored by the odious captain.

"Oh, here you are, Highness Yor," Blaz said, finding her beside the kitchen.

She was beginning to believe he spent his days keeping track of her. Certainly he was as indifferent as ever to the needs of their group, and with Lon Weal in charge, Erasma was beside himself trying to stockpile enough food to get them through a rainy season that could last 20 or more days, according to information sent back by early unmanned probes.

"Excuse me, please, Captain. I feel a headache coming on." She couldn't look at him. He looked so much like a plucked fowl in the short makeshift tunic, she might forget herself and mock him.

"No wonder, after such a long bout with fever." He looked at her the way scientists examine a specimen. Did he suspect her of feigning illness to stay with Garner? If he did, what would he do about it?

She looked beyond him and saw Garner covertly watching her. Blaz would never strike out at her directly, but he could hurt her beyond measure through Garner. She shuddered, cold for the first time on Brona. She longed for the predictable seasons of Prima, but not for the life she'd left behind there. If they were rescued, her father had her future mapped out for her. He would be shocked, outraged, and vindictive if he even suspected she'd lost her heart to a Prola. Captain Blaz knew this, and he had a way of making even casual conversation sound like a veiled threat.

She didn't fear her father for her own sake, but High Yor would be merciless in avenging his family honor if the captain carried reports linking her with Garner. The people of Garner's caste were powerless against a First Minister, and she went cold with dread when she thought of what her father could do to him.

When she looked again, Garner was gone.

The first heavy rains came that night, pounding on the peaked roofs fashioned from long poles and covered with bundles of water reeds to repel the water. When morning came, the sun seemed as brilliant as ever, but the air was chilly. The stockade was a mud-clogged, sorry place, and people seemed stunned by the sudden assault by the weather. At least half of the roofs had suffered some damage, and makeshift lines had to be strung everywhere to dry soaked bedding and clothing. They built the largest fire ever within the walls and drank hot broth for breakfast to warm themselves.

Garner was in charge again. The whole company seemed to sigh with relief when he made work assignments, sending out parties to gather bundles of the huge jungle leaves to be put on the roofs in place of the inadequate reeds.

Alena worked as hard as anyone, trying to waterproof their stores by wrapping food in the rubbery leaves. They'd had a sample of a Brona storm. Everyone was taking the coming season seriously.

Alena had a secret agenda of her own. Once the rains began in earnest, they might be confined in the stockade for long periods. Her chance of stealing a moment alone with Garner would be nonexistent. One way or another, she was going to speak with him before then.

The next day she climbed to the lookout platform facing the hills to eat her evening meal in solitude. She had little enough appetite for stew made with bits of dried meat, greens, and roots dug from the jungle floor without having to eat under Blaz's watchful eyes. She ate all the food allotted to her, even a seedy green fruit that reminded her of the skin lotion she'd used on Prima, because it was her duty not to waste precious stores. When her baked-mud bowl was empty, she set it aside and stared moodily out at the hills that bordered the stockade on the east. They began no more than ten paces from the wall and rose in some places to the height of low mountains. A few intrepid explorers had climbed them, including the greaser delegated to string a wire and put one of the captain's antennas in place on the summit of the highest slope, but it was an unrewarding trek not worth the expenditure of energy.

The slopes were little more than hard-packed mud, sprinkled with sharp-bladed grass that cut the feet and legs of climbers. Even small ground animals and winged creatures seemed to avoid them, and so did the Primans after they proved valueless in the search for foodstuffs.

No one worked or wandered along the east wall, and since the shriekers' attacks had stopped, the lone sentry always used the platform facing north or west.

By her reckoning, they had less than two hours left of daylight. Lon Weal would take a count to be sure everyone was inside, then report to Garner, who was responsible for ordering the door closed. After that the only entrance to the stockade would be blocked by the door and secured by a heavy crossbar.

After the evening meal, people hurried to do personal tasks: bathing in water hauled from the stream, washing or repairing garments, and doing what could be done to make the rude huts habitable.

The door was on the west; the stream flowed just beyond the southern wall, and that was where people congregated, since Catton Sur's plan to pipe water into the compound hadn't worked out.

She forced herself not to rush, not to attract attention. Once she could have trusted Velma to carry a message to Garner. Now she had to rely on a greaser, but approaching one of them was almost as risky as speaking directly to Garner.

Fortune smiled on her; Blaz himself solved her problem by sending Gullaner to request her presence in the common room.

"I know you respect Garner Rie," she said in a hurried undertone. "Are you loyal to him? Would you do anything you could to save him from harm?"

"Yea, Highness, even if it meant my life." He scratched his sun-bleached mane of hair and eyed her warily.

"Then tell him to meet me outside the east wall as soon as he can. Tell him it's urgent!"

The young man frowned, no doubt as disapproving as the captain in his own way, but to his credit, he hurried off to deliver her message without asking questions.

Alena hurried to the common room, not pleased to find Blaz there alone.

"I'm presuming on your good nature, Highness, to ask you to join me in a small indulgence. Tacka discovered, quite by accident, that one of those fleshy red fruits ferments into quite a potent drink."

He handed her one of the cups from the pods half filled with a clear reddish liquid. She sniffed cautiously, then took a tiny sip and feigned a cough.

"Captain, I'm afraid it's too potent for me." She choked as convincingly as she could. "Thank you for offering it, but I'm afraid it's a drink for strong men."

"I'm so sorry, Highness Yor. I only thought . . . let me get some water for you."

"No, I'm on my way to the stream." She coughed again for emphasis. "Excuse me, please."

She rushed away, coughing until she was beyond his hearing, and passed unnoticed through the entryway. Most people drew water where the stream was widest and deepest, but she rushed upstream until she could safely get behind the eastern wall without being seen. Erasma had insisted they leave some trees and bushes near the site, and she was thankful to him for the concealment they provided.

Garner was standing close to the wall, scowling up at the barren hills. Like many of the survivors, he'd changed into his silvery trousers and a heavy black tunic as protection against the cold winds of the rainy season. Alena had donned her insulated trousers, but still wore the hand-sewn tunic that left her arms bare. She shivered, and remembered the heat of his fever and the warmth of his flesh when she'd embraced his unconscious form.

"Garner Rie." She whispered even though there was no chance of being heard by anyone within the stockade.

"You shouldn't try to see me," he said, his eyes telling her something entirely different.

"I don't want to cause trouble for you."

His laugh was short and bitter, but his features softened when he looked into her face.

"I want to thank you," he said. "for tending me when I was ill. I owe my life to you."

"Oh, no, Velma Pitt . . ."

"Alena, I know you were by my side day and night. You took a terrible risk."

"The captain thought I had a fever—something nasty and contagious. How do you know I stayed with you? Did Velma tell you?"

"She's said little since I revived."

"Then how . . ."

"I heard you. You called me back from a dark and lonely place."

He spoke so tenderly, she wanted to weep. But

even more, she wanted to feel his arms around her.

"We can't deny it anymore," she whispered, afraid to look up into his face.

"No, we can't. I love you, Alena, more than I ever thought it was possible to love."

"Did you hear me speak of my love?"

"Yes, but tell me again."

"I love you, Garner!"

He pulled her close and pressed his lips against hers, kissing her with tender passion until she forgot where she was.

"I love you, Alena. No matter what happens, remember that."

"Don't talk that way. I can't lose you!"

She pressed against him, trying to meld their bodies and their souls together. He groaned and kissed her more roughly, burying his fingers in her hair and parting her lips with his tongue.

She was dizzy, breathless, burning, aware of nothing but his smooth face where he'd scraped off his beard and the wild beating of her own heart.

"You don't know what you're doing," he gently chided, pulling away, then relenting and holding her close and touching her closed lids with his lips.

"I know you're all that matters to me."

"My darling . . . Oh, Alena, how can I find the words to say what I must tell you?"

"Don't talk. Kiss me again."

"I may not be able to stop a second time."

"Then don't! We'll run away together and live for each other!"

"Darling, don't you think I've longed to do just that since the first day we stepped foot on this planet?"

"I'm not afraid of anything when I'm with you. Let's do it, Garner. We can leave now and never look back!"

"Alena." He said her name with agonizing regret. "Without food, shelter, weapons, we wouldn't have a chance. I won't take you away to die!"

"If I'm with you, I'll die happy!"

"No! Don't you see? They won't let us. How far would we get before Blaz tracked us down? There's not a single person here who wouldn't rather see us both dead than together. Our love violates their sacred caste traditions, and nothing we can do will persuade them that we have a right to be together."

"The greasers . . ."

"As bad as the Scientifica! Even poor Gullaner was shocked to the core by your message. He could never believe I'm willing to risk everything I've accomplished for your sake."

"I can't let you! That isn't what I want for you! Oh, Garner, forget me! Leave me before I ruin you! No, I'm not strong enough to send you away." She knew she was babbling, but she still ached for his touch.

"I can't destroy your life, Alena, and that's what I would be doing if I let this continue. Go inside the stockade. Look at the sky! It's nearly time to barricade the entrance. Go now, and never try to see me alone again."

"No!" She couldn't accept what he was saying. "Don't tell me that! You don't mean it!"

"No, I don't. I hate sending you away. It's tearing me apart!"

She'd never heard such pain in a man's voice, and she realized his life was in more jeopardy than hers. He would pay a much higher price for their love if they were caught. True, her father wouldn't rest until he got her back, but he most likely would find a way to save her from banishment. She might be cloistered in his home for the rest of her life; certainly no man of her own caste would want her, but she would rather be a prisoner than accept any man but Garner. She would gladly take this risk for him, but she couldn't destroy him with her selfish need for him.

"Be strong for me, Garner! I don't want to be the cause of your banishment if we're rescued. I've heard about the Outlands of Prima. It's a horrible, barren, bleak place where the Uncasted live like animals! Your family would be disgraced. You'd come to hate me for making you suffer so much."

"Never!"

He kissed her again, a desperate, hasty attempt to drain the despair from her mind.

"I've heard that Prolas turn against their own when a caste law is broken," she said. "They do brutal things to offenders—even worse punishment than the banishment."

"Quickly, Alena, listen to me." He held her at arm's length and spoke urgently, making her more aware of the gray shroud of clouds hanging over them. "Go inside as though you've just finished your evening tasks. Compose your face; walk slowly. Don't speak unless you can't avoid it, and on no account weep for my sake. I'm going to say good-bye, and you must promise this will never happen again. Mourn for me; pretend I'm dead."

"I can't!"

"Alena, you must!"

"Kiss me one last time."

He gathered her in his arms, holding his mouth against hers as though memorizing the taste and texture, then roughly pushed her away.

"Go now," he said harshly.

"Garner . . ."

"No!" He gripped her shoulder and shoved her in the direction she had to go, swatting her backside to propel her forward.

"It's not finished!" she said angrily, rubbing her stinging buttocks. "You can't get rid of me so easily, Mister Rie."

She heard him moan as she hurried away, but she wasn't going to feel sorry for him—or herself. Their lives were illuminated by the love they shared. Somehow, on this planet or another, they would be together. It was their destiny! When she stopped believing that, she would lose her reason for living.

Chapter Eleven

The rains came, surprising even Garner with the volume of water that fell in driving, windblown sheets. Some days the survivors had a few hours of respite; more commonly, the downpour lashed at the stockade all day and all night, making it impossible to keep up with repairs on the roofs.

The temperature plummeted, and it was a continual battle to keep dry and warm. Cooking became impossible after the lean-to kitchen was blown down, and people had to be content with dried meat and fruit, a diet that caused stomach cramps without fully appeasing their hunger.

Garner did his best to keep order, but forced idleness made his job more difficult. A few survivors made the best of the circumstances. Erasma and a few others kept busy teaching each other, sharing knowledge of their specialized fields in small study groups. Others devised games of chance, wagering money and possessions they might never see again on Prima, and sometimes the executive officer was called upon to arbitrate disputes. A few artisans among the Guilders put their skills to work, carving useful objects from wood scraps, making baskets and sandals from reeds gathered earlier for that purpose, or fashioning bowls and pots from sticky mud they baked in pits that also helped keep the common room warmer. Alena and the other young woman, Melga, sewed tirelessly, trying to keep garments in repair.

Unfortunately not everyone found useful pursuits to fill the long, dismal hours of confinement. Garner discovered Tacka and two other greasers intoxicated in their hut. He made them stand in the rain to sober up and confiscated their secret cache of potent drink, intending to put it with the medical supplies in case a time came when there was nothing else to relieve pain. For a change the captain supported him in disciplining the men, but he insisted on taking their beverage to his own dwelling place.

Several times Garner found Blaz drinking in his hut, and he regretted finding the cache. Tacka was more sullen than ever, and Garner slept with a pistol by his mat, even though the rain was giving him temporary peace of mind about jungle predators.

As irksome as the confinement was, Garner suffered much more whenever he caught a glimpse of Alena. His arms ached to hold her; his mouth hungered for the taste of her. He'd never been so desperate for a woman, yet a bevy of joy-girls with all their tricks wouldn't have satisfied him the way a smile from Alena could. He awoke, when he'd been able to sleep, aching for her physical presence, but the pain of being near her and not able to speak was even worse.

The days passed as one long, dreary ordeal, and without Weal's notched log, Garner would have lost all track of time. The second officer was on his second makeshift calendar; the first, with a hundred days marked by raw slashes in the wood, was stored in the captain's tent as a permanent record of their sojourn on Brona. If a space vessel came too late and found no living Primans from the *Moon Courier,* the crude calendar would show how long they had managed to survive.

On the 16th day of the wet season, the sky lightened and the rain lessened to a sprinkle. Garner, accompanied by Roar and Erasma, made an inspection outside the stockade, and all three were distressed to see the south wall listing. The stream had overflowed and washed away much of the sandy soil holding it in place. Worse, the high mud hill near the southeast corner had been stripped of vegetation in the continual downpours and loomed over them like a great mud cone flattened on the top.

"I hope the rainy season is winding down," Erasma said. "I don't want to be standing at the bottom of this mud pile if it starts to slide."

Later Garner spoke to the people in the common room when they gathered for the evening distribution of food. With several people too feverish to leave their mats, there were less than 40 gathered in the musty room where the roof leaked into wooden buckets in half a dozen spots.

"I don't want to alarm you," he said, "but a lot of debris has washed down the hill behind the southeast corner. We should be all right if the rains keep diminishing, but as a precaution, everyone with huts in that section of the stockade should sleep in the common room."

"Surely you're not afraid of a little mud," Lon Weal taunted.

"I saw a whole village buried in a mud slide in the equatorial zone on Prima. Seven people died," Erasma said, his mild but factual tone effectively bringing home the danger.

"Should we leave the stockade?" Catton Sur asked.

"We should," Garner said, glancing at the captain, who stood silently at the back of the room. "But where would we go?"

Blaz was sullen but silent, as he had been since appropriating Tacka's cache of drink. Surely he'd consumed all of that by now, Garner thought, suddenly afraid the greaser was keeping him supplied from a fresh batch. Much as he hated playing detective, he had to put a stop to it. People were on edge without having to deal with drunkenness within the stockade.

"This is old women's talk," Blaz called out, enunciating each word carefully in a vain attempt to conceal his condition. He swaggered outside, and people scattered into the drizzle that had continued all day.

"Is there any point in posting a watch?" Garner asked Erasma, the only one among them who'd seen a mud slide.

"No, there wouldn't be time to do anything. You warned them. Now all we can do is hope to see the last of this wretched wet season soon."

Garner fell asleep to the soft slap of raindrops on the leaf-covered roof and Gullaner's noisy snoring. He dreamed of a beast so large that all he could see was its shadow turning day into night. Alena stepped forward, her body glowing with luminous gold paint. He was terrified that the wet lacquer would suffocate her when it dried. He tried to wipe her breasts clean with a handful of her long red-gold hair, but she took his hand and guided it to her love nest.

"The beast requires a sacrifice," the dream-version of Alena said, dropping to her knees and pulling him down with her.

He took her in the beast's shadow, shuddering as he came into her.

The earth shook, and the beast roared. Alena dissolved into a pool of glistening gold paint, and he was drowning in it. He thrashed and screamed, trying to wake himself, but sleep had him in a deathlike grasp. He tried to throw his body from one side to the other, knowing he had to wake up, but he was paralyzed again, a prisoner in his own mind.

Gullaner was screaming. Garner awoke and sprang to his feet, abruptly leaving one nightmare for another.

Cosmic thunder drowned out his screams, and white lightning illuminated the hut. A storm like none they'd experienced before roared through the night, and the ground shook. He was deafened by the din and blinded by the glare, but adrenalin raced through him, shocking him into full awareness of reality.

He ran to the cloth-covered entryway and ripped aside the curtain, stopping himself just as a lightning bolt sliced through the mantle of rain and crackled across the compound.

Roar was by his side, pulling him back, but he didn't need urging. All that stood between them and death were the flimsy walls of the hut. Overhead the wind ripped away a portion of the roof, but he hardly noticed the icy rain that drenched him.

Alena was alone and unprotected! Was she safe? Could he do anything if she wasn't? He started to run headlong into the storm, but Roar's iron grip restrained him.

"You can't do anything!" Roar screamed, but Garner broke away and dashed into the storm, racing across the compound ahead of the next lightning bolt. He ran into Alena's hut just ahead of certain death, knowing he was a fool to tempt the forces of the universe, but so relieved to see her unscathed he took her in his arms and soaked her with his wet, frenzied embrace.

She clung to him as the ground rumbled and the wind smashed the poles on the roof and carried them away like fluff from a pond weed.

He backed her into a corner and tried to shield her body from the driving rain, but in an instant she was as soaked as he was. They were two shivering creatures clinging together in the face of nature gone mad.

The storm blew itself out with the same explosive suddenness, and cries of distress tore them apart. They went out into the dark night, guided by the voices of anxious survivors.

Someone managed to light a lantern, carrying it into the yard of the ravaged stockade, but even without light to see all the damage, everyone felt the numbing dread that follows a major disaster.

The south end of the compound was engulfed in mud, a half-dozen huts buried under a great mound where the wall had stood. The east wall was gone, knocked flat and partially buried, and there wasn't a sound roof left in the stockade.

Garner called out for Weal, their census-keeper, the counter of heads, expecting to find him cowering in the ruins of the common room. Instead he found the captain there, shocked out of his drunken state but mewling like a schoolboy called to account for his transgressions.

"What happened, Rie? I order you to explain this, mister!"

"Look for yourself, Captain Blaz. A mountain of mud has come calling!" he said with biting sarcasm, rushing back to those more deserving of solace.

Dawn came with the amazing return of the sun on the distant horizon, but none of the survivors rejoiced seeing the long-absent golden orb. Death had dwindled their numbers again.

For the first time in his cowardly life, Lon Weal hadn't taken precautions to protect his own skin. He was lost under the primeval mud, along with Melga, who'd been slipping out to Weal's hut while her husband, Atan Nash, slept.

Feverish and emaciated from the same illness that had claimed Vane Col, Atan dug at the mud with his hands, screaming curses at Lon Weal and weeping for his wife. Garner had Velma Pitt sedate him, hoping she would rally some of her old spirit and help him in this new crisis.

The survivors huddled under tents and remnants of cloth, trying to come to terms with the latest disaster. For a while the return of the sun gave them some hope. The worst of the storm had passed on, but later in the day a cold, driving rain turned their roofless shelters into quagmires. When dawn lightened the sky for the second time after the mud slide, Alena dropped all pretense of sleeping and went to see what could be done in the ruins of the stockade.

Garner was already busy with several men, so even in these circumstances she didn't dare approach him openly. Her heart still ached when she remembered how he'd tried to discourage her from speaking to him, but if this wretched planet parted under their feet and swallowed them like a beast consumes its prey, she would die loving him.

The rains had finally stopped and, like all the other men, Garner was naked to the waist, preferring the chill morning air on his skin to the sodden weight of a soaked tunic. She watched him discussing the damage, frequently shaking his head and saying words she couldn't hear. She had a lump in her throat, and it took all her resolve to keep her tears at bay. She wanted to weep for the people of the *Moon Courier* and all that they'd lost on this world, but even more she was grief-stricken by the hopelessness of her love for Garner. They belonged together. She should be standing by his side instead of watching him from a secluded vantage point beside a roofless hut.

People were leaving their makeshift shelters, and she knew this was no time to dwell on her aching heart. The wet days had taken a heavy toll on the health of many survivors: Small wounds became infected easily, minor ailments caused major distress, and the trauma of the mud slide had left nearly half their number in need of some medical attention.

Velma was a medic in name only, and Alena knew she could best help by seeking out Erasma. Between them they salvaged as many of his herbs and homemade remedies as possible and gathered together the people most in need of attention. She helped start a small fire, and together they brewed a strong tea with soothing properties and rubbed a pungent ointment made of porcine grease and plant extracts on inflamed wounds.

She was weary but satisfied with her day's work

when she saw Garner again. He came for tea to take away some of his weariness, touching her fingers when she handed him a full clay bowl.

"I'm proud of you," he said softly, sipping on the cloudy brew and facing her across the small fire pit. "You have a healing touch. People feel better just because you minister to them."

Her heart swelled with happiness, but there was nothing she could say with other survivors milling around the makeshift aid station.

He finished his tea quickly and turned away from her, still naked from the waist up. She recoiled in shock when she saw a crisscross pattern of marks on his back. Someone had whipped him!

"No!" she cried aloud, remembering how the captain had threatened him with corporal punishment.

No one else could have done that to the executive officer. What crime had he committed to deserve the pain and humiliation of a beating? When had it happened? Had it been done secretly so no one could protest, or was she the only one who didn't know about it?

Was she the cause of it? Were others more aware of the attraction between them than she thought? Had the captain discovered her ruse: faking illness to care for Garner? She followed him, sinking to her ankles in a watery depression that was deeper than she thought, then floundering forward, driven to make amends even though she had no idea what she could do.

Blaz came up to the group of men, and for the first time in her life she was maddened by hatred. The whey-faced, posturing, incompetent coward had failed them as a captain and abused the man she loved.

"This is all your doing, Blaz!" she said, loudly

accusing him in front of the dumbfounded men. "Instead of leading us to a safer site, you sacrificed our safety while you played with a useless radio. You don't deserve to be a commander! You're a disgrace to the Space Service, to your caste, and to our species!"

"Highness Yor, this incident has clouded your mind. Go to your hut and stay there until you come to your senses."

He spoke softly, but the venom in his voice chilled her blood. She'd never been so frightened of a man, but she was determined to expose him as a fraud.

"What will you do if I disobey? Resurrect some ancient law to justify torturing me?" she challenged.

"Alena!" Garner cried out in shock, overhearing all she was saying from a few paces away.

"Your father can't protect you from military justice here, Alena Yor," Blaz said, dropping all pretense of courtesy.

"Justice! You don't know the meaning of the word! You're a petty tyrant without the courage to leave this wretched site. Thanks to your ineptness, two more people are dead."

"Escort Highness Yor to her quarters!" Blaz ordered, but no one moved to obey.

"You can't silence me! I'm only saying what everyone is thinking! All this is your fault!" She made a broad sweep of the stockade with her arms.

"You high-caste meddler!" he snarled. "How dare you question my decision? The first rule for survivors is to stay near the crash site."

"Only if there's hope of rescue! Vane Col knew the truth! The radios from the pods can't get through the magnetic field! You've been sending signals that no one will ever receive!"

"You lie!" His face was ashen, contorted by hatred and rage into an evil caricature. "You'll obey me, or I'll discipline you like I did that Prola scum you lust after! We'll see if you're so haughty under the lash!"

"Captain! I protest!" Catton Sur stepped forward from the group of people who'd gathered to hear them. "You can't speak that way to a woman of the Scientifica. To even suggest such . . . such . . ."

He sputtered helplessly, unable to repeat the captain's threat, but Alena knew he was speaking for every person there. Her caste gave her immunity from the captain's wrath, but she trembled when she realized the terrible thing she'd done to Garner. He had no protection from the captain's anger. The other survivors wouldn't rally to the defense of a Prola, no matter how unjust the captain was.

"What matters now," Garner spoke up, "is how we're going to survive."

The angry muttering subsided as people responded to his calm, reasonable statement, and Alena thought her heart would burst with love and admiration. A lesser man would have been incapacitated by the rage she could see in his eyes.

"I'll see to that," Blaz said. "We'll rebuild the wall."

"That's no solution," Erasma said. "The shriekers will be back soon, and the rains will come again. The next bout of fever could be much worse. I'm convinced this area is too close to the swamp to be a healthy environment."

"It's not likely we'll be here for another rainy season," the captain said coldly. "Staying here gives us the best chance to be rescued. Nothing else matters."

"People matter," Erasma said mildly. "We must rebuild on higher ground."

"We'll rebuild here. The Space Service doesn't abandon its own!" Blaz insisted.

"I'll find a safer site," Garner said with quiet determination.

"Captain, I think Officer Rie should be allowed to scout the area," Catton Sur said.

Judging by the murmurs of agreement, he spoke for all of them.

"If Mister Rie wants to wander around looking at mud banks and swampland, it doesn't matter to me," Blaz said. "If a vessel comes in his absence, he's the one who'll miss his ride back to Prima. But I still give the orders here. Rie, before you leave, escort Highness Yor to her quarters and confine her there for insubordination. She took the oath with everyone else. Her freedom of movement is hereby curtailed; she's to be under guard at all times. She may leave her hut only for hygienic purposes. Arrange for meals to be sent to her."

"You can't make me a prisoner!" she cried out, trying to break free of Garner's grip on her arm.

"Come with me, Highness Yor," he urged.

She tried to resist, but her feet slipped on wet ground. He saved her from falling, but left her no option but to move toward her miserable little hut.

"Take me away with you!" she pleaded as he gently shoved her past the bedraggled curtain that still covered the entryway.

"I can't."

"You don't want to!" She threw herself at him, wrapping her arms around him.

"Alena, don't do this! It's too dangerous! Blaz may have ordered me to bring you here in order to trap us in an indiscretion."

"You swore to be responsible for my life! If I can't go with you, you can't leave."

"That's why I can't take you with me. I have to find high ground, and that means new dangers—ones I might not be able to overcome."

"Do you think we'll ever be rescued?"

He shook his head. "We have to live as though we'll be here forever. Rescue is out of our hands, but survival isn't."

"In my heart, I don't know if I can to return to my old life, but I'm afraid to stay here with Blaz." She caught his arm as he moved her aside and tried to leave.

"Don't be! I'll make Roar and Gullaner your guardians. The captain won't dare harm you. The others wouldn't stand for it."

"When are you leaving?"

"Immediately. I've stayed here too long already," he said, misery in every word.

"No!" She didn't want to cry, but tears ran down her cheeks. "I'll follow you!"

"Darling Alena." He melted her resistance with a tender kiss on her forehead. "Roar and Gullaner won't let you."

"Don't leave me here!" She clung, burying one hand in his hair and circling his shoulders with the other.

"I have no choice!"

He kissed her, forcing her lips apart and roughly silencing the rest of her arguments with his tongue.

She tried to break away, desperate to make him hear her plea and change his mind, but he kissed her harder, holding her so tightly she didn't have breath to argue further.

His kisses grew more brutal, but she reveled in them, wanting him with an urgent passion that made her forget everything else.

"This may be what Blaz wants," he gasped. "To tempt me into violating you. He wants an excuse to execute me!"

"No!"

She broke free and backed away in horror, frightened to the core at the thought of causing his death.

"I have to leave. Trust me, Alena, it's best."

"Take me. . . . "

But he was gone.

Something in her died when he left. She stood in the wet ruins of the wretched hovel and stared inward, seeing a bleak and purposeless future without him.

She lost all track of time, but Roar called her back to harsh reality when he came to guard her door.

"Highness Yor," he said without pulling aside the door hanging. "You're not to be afraid. Gullaner and I will never leave you unprotected."

"It doesn't matter," she said listlessly.

"He'll find what he's looking for, and he'll be back," the chief engineer said. "You can be sure of that."

Chapter Twelve

What had she hoped to accomplish by confronting Blaz?

Garner was so upset with Alena, he scarcely took note of his surroundings during the first few hours of travel. Partly he was awed by her courage, but she'd made a dangerous enemy. He hated leaving her behind, but the alternative was much more perilous. Even if he could protect her from natural hazards, he couldn't predict what the other survivors might do. Even gentle, tolerant Erasma might turn against them and want to drag them back if they flaunted laws that prohibited a Prola from intimacy with a high-caste woman.

Now he had to worry about the captain avenging himself on Alena. He wouldn't harm her person; the others of her caste wouldn't allow it. But Blaz was as cunning as he was demented. Sooner or later he would find a way to make her suffer bitterly for her verbal attack. Confining her in the ruins of her hut was only the beginning. Garner hoped he could get back before the captain dared to torture her in other ways. Meanwhile, Roar and Gullaner had sworn to keep her safe at any cost.

He knew approximately where he wanted to explore. The great river ran through a wide valley between two mountain ranges. The jagged peaks in the west had demolished three of the *Moon Courier's* pods. To reach them he would have to cross a river inhabited by savage plants that hunted with poisonous spines.

The eastern range loomed up behind the jungle and the mud hills. He hoped to find an easier route to high ground by going south along the riverbank. It was a gamble at best, but the alternative was to rebuild the stockade where it was, forage in the jungle for food, fight off shriekers, and hope they would be able to survive another rainy season in the pestilent lowlands.

He was traveling light, bringing his pistol with a dozen rounds of ammunition, a knife, his survival kit from the pod, water, and a small store of food from the nearly exhausted supplies. He carried everything in a makeshift backpack, using a section of chute material that could double as a ground cover.

The first night he slept in the open, awaking at dawn to find a hard-shelled river creature exploring his battered boot. He roasted his catch over slow-burning sticks he found on the bank, glad he had a piece of flint to start fires. The meat was white and succulent, and for the first time in many days he digested a meal without painful cramps.

The next day he wasn't fortunate enough to find food; by the third day his rations were exhausted, and the unfamiliar territory seemed more threatening. He passed several long gray-black sea serpents sunning themselves on the mud bank along the river. They slithered into the water when he approached, but not before he'd seen their razor-sharp teeth and incredible speed. Hungry and weary as he was, he elected not to bed down close to the shore.

Alena! He hardly took a step without recalling her confrontation with Blaz. What had prompted her to goad him that way?

His mood was as bleak as their prospects of rescue. He knew the immensity of space, and he was learning how gigantic and savage Brona was. No matter where they were on the surface of the planet, there was little chance of being found. Did he even want it? Could he return to Prima and resume his old life, knowing he would never see Alena again?

He shook his head ruefully. Their prospects were no better on Brona. As long as a single high-caste male was alive to thwart them, they wouldn't be permitted to live as man and wife. Their love was doomed on either planet, but without Alena, he cared nothing about his own future. How could he return to life in the Space Service while his heart was held hostage by a woman he could never have?

The terrain was changing. The trees inland were larger, and the dense jungle gave way to verdant woodland. The current in the river was swift, and the banks were dotted with bushes of purple and red blooms. Eager to leave the valley, he walked half the night, and began to hear a distant roar. When he was too tired to go on, he climbed into the lowest branches of a huge tree and slept as best he could straddling a branch with his back against the trunk.

His anger at Alena gradually subsided. She had

a right to protest to the captain, even though it wasn't wise to berate a lunatic in public. He still entertained thoughts of upending her and smacking her bottom, but only because her rashness had put her in greater danger. She had much to learn about the harshness of their homeworld and the evil of some of its inhabitants. She was a woman of great beauty, charm, and sensitivity, but she still had a child's understanding of the realities of life. For the first time in her life, she couldn't rely on her father's high position to protect her. He himself wanted to be her protector, her teacher, and her guardian, but most of all, he yearned to be her lover. He found himself talking aloud to her, explaining his fears for her safety and declaring his undying love. The days passed quickly because he carried her with him in his heart.

On the fifth day he saw the waterfall. As far across as he could see, the great river dropped down hundreds of feet with a deafening roar. He watched it for several hours, trying to pick out the safest way to descend the rocky cliff beside it. He finally decided on a natural pathway some distance from the falls, and spent many hours climbing downward, at times hanging onto sheer rock or dislodging dangerous boulders.

Exhausted and famished, he finally stood near the lower river, able to marvel at the great falls from a spectacular vantage point.

It was there he found the lost pod.

The escape vehicle was severely battered, the original shape almost unrecognizable, but it had sailed over the falls without splitting open and lodged on the shore, partially buried but intact.

The hatch was covered with dirt, but the day he spent digging it out with his hands, using a sharp-edged rock to loosen the soil, wasn't wasted. The latch on the supply compartment had held, and he was able to salvage many emergency supplies, including food packets. What he couldn't carry easily, he left in the pod, securing the hatch to keep the rest safe until he returned.

Once past the falls, he began moving toward higher ground. The valley and the river narrowed, and he could see high mountains on either side, their peaks shrouded by misty clouds. The days were getting longer and hotter, but the air was fresh, untainted by winds blowing off the swamp.

He bathed in small streams, and by the eighth day he rolled his flight clothing into a bundle and continued the trek as naked as his species had been when they'd first walked upright on Prima. He'd never felt so free, unfettered by any of the trappings of civilization. After a day of traveling naked, he smarted in places untouched by sunlight since his boyhood days when he disobeyed his parents to swim in a river with friends. But his hide toughened quickly, burnished to a coppery tan by white-hot solar rays, and the soles of his feet grew leathery.

The elevation rose gradually, and he reveled in being the first from his planet to climb the rugged slopes. The air was cooler, and he found joy in observing the flora and fauna of the highlands. Some plants were familiar, including the one Erasma had named linneas acropos, which seemed to flourish everywhere on Brona. No shriekers howled in the night, but that didn't make him less wary. He saw the spore of larger creatures, and once he caught a glimpse of a yellow and green dragon-creature that stood as high as his head. It scurried away, but he began taking extra precautions at night.

On the 11th day he reached the summit of the

foothills. The dark, savage peaks of the mountain range loomed up in the east, but he wouldn't challenge them this trip. He found a small valley where vegetation flourished and fresh water was readily available in a sparkling, boulder-strewn stream. This was where they should build a new settlement.

His food supplies were getting low, so he picked a familiar lumpy yellow fruit from the linneas acropos, wolfing it down, skin, seeds, and all, to dull his hunger.

He found a natural depression in the side of a hill, checked it for unfriendly life-forms, and spread his blanket for the night. This was his favorite time of day, when, exhausted by long hours of travel, he could lie back and think of nothing but Alena.

She came to him in that drowsy state between wakefulness and sleep, but this time she was no shy maiden to be wooed with words of love and soft caresses. She uncoiled her silky red-gold hair, then slowly disrobed, tossing aside a sheath of golden fabric. When she was naked, so beautiful it hurt him to breathe, she touched herself to entice him, beckoning to him with damp fingers.

He'd never before dreamed of such an encounter. She exhausted him time and time again, rising over him and taunting him, alternating between sensual tenderness and small erotic cruelties to bring him to new heights of arousal.

He heard his own cries as he thrashed in the arms of a demon temptress. He shuddered, shook, and came, but she continued to torture him with blood-red nails, a curling tongue, and sharp pearly teeth.

He awoke at dawn with a raging thirst. His torso was slippery from his own perspiration, and his legs were so weak they trembled when he tried to stand upright. He staggered to the stream, lay down on his belly, and gulped the cold mountain water.

He splashed his face and head, too lethargic to plunge into the stream for a thorough dunking. The sandy streambed was littered with water-polished rocks that had lain there undisturbed for eons, and he found it soothing to search for small gemlike stones. He liked the idea of stone walls and stone cottages. With so much sand, Erasma would be able to invent a cement to serve as mortar. Garner daydreamed about a mountain refuge, the beginning of a new world, until he felt something sharp. He winced and withdrew his hand, glad to see the skin unbroken but curious enough to fish for the sharp object until he found it.

What he saw made him bolt to his feet. He studied a black chunk and quickly stooped to search for others, finding an even larger piece in a few minutes.

He knew what he'd found: blackened ceramic shards. He smashed the rough edge of one with a heavy boulder to be sure he wasn't being fooled by a volcanic cinder. There was no doubt in his mind. He'd found debris from a protective shield designed to withstand heat during planetary reentry.

Maybe he was still hallucinating! He belatedly remembered Erasma's warning that the seeds of the linneas acropos produced erotic visions. He recalled enough to know he'd carelessly eaten some with the rest of the fruit. He flushed just thinking about Alena as she'd appeared in his visions: wildly seductive, wickedly erotic, maddeningly desirable. Remembering her that way was torment! He missed the real Alena desperately; the woman in his vision was all that any man could desire and much more, but he'd drive himself crazy if he didn't let go of those feverish fantasies.

The blackened shard wasn't part of his fantasy, and he remembered the pods exploding as vividly as if it had just happened. All three had come down in mountains far to the west, perhaps two or three hundred kilometers from where he stood. There was no way debris from the pods could have scattered this far.

Unless the planet had had visitors from far-distant worlds, a concept he dismissed as highly unlikely, he was holding debris from one of the unmanned probes sent to record data about Brona.

He'd never experienced such compelling curiosity mixed with a trace of fear and dread. His vision of stone cottages in the idyllic valley came from his doubt that they would ever be rescued. But somewhere on Brona there was a probe that might change everything. If it was still capable of sending signals back to Prima, then rescue was possible. Garner had never seriously considered trying to find one of the probes; a man could search his whole life and cover less than a hundredth of the vast wilderness planet.

He tried not to think of the consequences of going back to Prima, but the captain's threats couldn't be ignored. At best, there would be a board of inquiry and long hearings to determine his fitness for further service. As soon as a rescue vessel made contact, Alena would be lost to him forever.

He brooded. In his heart he knew Alena would never share a stone cottage with him on Brona, not as long as other Primans lived to prevent it.

They were as much prisoners of the caste system here as on their home world. Their love was doomed, but he could still keep his promise to keep her alive by making rescue possible.

Late that afternoon, when he was almost ready to give up for the day, he saw the shroud embedded on a mountain ridge far above him. The rounded metal cone was used to protect on-site probes when they entered the heat of a planet's atmosphere. Once ejected, the shroud uncovered the landing legs. Theoretically, the probe could function for centuries, but it worked automatically. It was useless to the survivors unless he could interface with it.

He knew the probe had a keyboard jack used to program it before launch. All he had to do was salvage a keyboard from one of the pods, and he could sent out a distress signal that would circumvent the magnetic field around Brona.

The probe couldn't be moved without mechanical help; the keyboard could. He itched to scale the steep mountain and see the probe up close, but it would be wasted effort until he had a keyboard.

He left at dawn the next day, returning to the pod below the falls. The hatch was still secured, but he was bitterly disappointed when he retrieved the keyboard and examined it in the sunlight. The case had cracked in a dozen places and the mechanism was smashed. He had no choice; he had to return to the stockade for a functional keyboard.

On the tedious return trip, he decided not to tell the survivors about the probe until he was sure it was sending signals. False hope could be devastating after all they'd been through. Somehow he had to steal a keyboard without being detected.

His best hope was to make contact with Roar or Gullaner outside the stockade.

When he was a few miles downstream from the stockade, he dressed for civilization, reluctantly donning his silver flight pants and boots but leaving his chest bare. Was he reverting to a savage? How would he adjust to the constrained, overly regulated world of Prima where he was denied both status and respect?

More importantly, how would Alena fare if this place had to be her permanent home? No matter how tempted he was to pretend he'd never found the probe, he couldn't sentence her to life on Brona if there was an alternative.

Luck was with him: The first person he saw after his absence of more than 20 days was Erasma. The old man was alone, casting a line into the river.

"Are you so hungry you'll eat the noxious bottom-feeders in this pestilent river?" Garner asked.

"Thank the fates! You're safe!" The botanist abandoned his line and ran to embrace him.

"Is there famine in the stockade?" Garner asked anxiously.

"No, no. We're all right for now. I'm trying to catch a sea creature. I've devised a microscope of sorts from Atan Nash's spectacles—oh, you don't know he died."

"The fever?"

"Yes. I'm hoping to compare specimens from Atan with bacteria carried in river life. It seems I'm not much of a fisherman, though."

"Forget your pole and bait. Let's try another way."

While Garner tied his knife to the fishing line and waded in the muck near the shore, being careful not to let water go over the tops of his boots, he told Erasma what he'd found.

By the time he speared a fleshy blob, a nasty puce-colored creature shaped like a round, fat pancake with hundreds of wire-thin legs, Garner had answered as many of Erasma's questions as he could.

"I agree about the secrecy," Erasma said. "Don't let the captain know what you've found. He's seldom sober these days; we know Tacka supplies him with a fermented fruit drink, but no one's been able to catch or stop him."

"Can you get a keyboard for me?"

"Easily. Blaz spends most of his time in the common room cursing Prolas, women, and this planet, not necessarily in that order," Erasma said dryly, tightening his lips in disapproval. "I'll get the best one and bring it to you after dark. No one bothers to secure the entrance at night anymore, but at least Roar has appointed a watch rotation to look out for those damnable shriekers."

"They're back?"

"We hear them regularly, but they haven't attacked yet. I'm hoping they have short memories."

"Maybe everybody should leave now." He didn't know if he could make himself abandon Alena a second time.

"They won't follow you, Garner. I'm sorry, but most of them are delusional, still believing they'll be rescued if they sit tight. If you weren't . . ."

"A Prola?" he asked bitterly.

"Yes, it's the only thing that disqualifies you. I've never met a finer man, but the caste system has had a stranglehold on our mentality for thousands of years. I'm not condoning it, but I'm not a rebel either. I live with it."

"Come with me," Garner suggested, realizing how much he'd missed talking to the botanist.

"Don't tempt me!" the older man groaned. "These people will starve waiting for servants to deliver their meals unless I'm here to prod them. And the greasers are unruly without you to keep them in line. Except for Roar and Gullaner, they hunt in packs and roast their kills on the spot instead of bringing meat back to share. When they do return to the stockade, they get drunk on Tacka's rotgut and spend the night playing games of chance."

"The walls?"

"Rebuilt as best we could. No one wants to dig out the mud and recover the bodies. I suppose there's no real point. Highness Yor is still a prisoner of sorts, although the captain doesn't enforce it. She comes and goes as she pleases, but Roar or Gullaner are always nearby armed with a pistol. I'll breathe easier when those renegade greasers run out of ammunition. They will soon, using it to hunt."

"If I stay awhile . . ."

"No, hurry back to the probe and see what you can do. I'll bring the keyboard to you tonight. Meet me behind the east wall when the three moons are over the river. With luck Blaz will fall asleep before then, and the greasers won't come back to the stockade. Meanwhile, keep out of sight. And thanks for catching this fellow."

Erasma plunked the odd sea creature into a basket he carried on his back and smiled broadly."I missed you, Garner Rie."

Alena evaded her guard the way she always did: by slipping out between the loose poles in the wall of her hut. Nothing had been properly repaired. The reeds on the roof would blow away in the first good storm, and even the stout outer walls were rotting along the base from the damp earth that held them. She was making plans of her own, hoarding her food and secretly drying fruit and seeds in a secluded place on the side of a hill. If Garner didn't return soon, she was going to find him. She still had her greatest gift: a phenomenal sense of direction.

She wouldn't let herself believe he'd come to any harm.

When the stockade was quiet and Gullaner was gently snoring on the other side of her entryway, she crept out to gather the fruit she was drying and add it to the small store she was hiding in a stout basket with a cover. She kept it hidden under brush near the east wall, and so far it hadn't been discovered by pests or other survivors.

She was drying some small, tasty red fruits hung by the stems on a long string, and she nibbled a few, pleased by the chewy consistency. They were ready to store in the carefully sewn cloth packet she'd salvaged from garment-making remnants.

At first the dark form of a man frightened her, but the moons were at their fullest, giving off enough light for her to recognize the slight form of Erasma. She nearly went up to him, knowing he wouldn't betray her, but a second dark form materialized. She quickly hid behind a full-branched tree and strained to hear.

It was Garner! Her heart raced furiously, and wet tears of happiness streamed down her cheeks. But why was he here, behind the wall in the darkness? Did anyone besides Erasma know he was back?

". . . a packet of spare parts," Erasma was saying. "The best."

"I'll never be able to thank you enough," Garner

said, his voice carrying better than the older man's.

"Good fortune go with you—for all our sakes," the botanist said fervently.

Alena made her decision instantly; it was as if she'd known her opportunity would come. This time Garner wasn't going to go off without her!

As soon as the two men parted and went their separate ways, she rushed forward to confirm her suspicions. Erasma returned to the stockade, but Garner was leaving again without a word to her.

She got her basket and hurried after him, keeping her distance because he wasn't likely to leave the riverbank for some time.

He traveled all night at a pace she was hard put to maintain, even though her feet were comfortable in reed sandals one of the Guilders had made. By dawn she was exhausted from following him, but still not willing to let him see her. They were too close to the stockade; he still might make her return.

She dozed uneasily, concealed by a few trees that grew on the fringe of the hills. When she awoke, parched and weary, he was gone, but he'd left an unmistakable trail. The tracks she followed were made by a man's bare feet, and she saw the wisdom of conserving her sandals while the ground was sandy and soft.

His trail was easy to follow, but she didn't dare stop for rest. She munched the hard, strong-flavored bread Erasma had taught them to make, and tried to fight her thirst with the freshly dried berries. Several times she crossed shallow streams and stopped to drink, noting marks in the soil that showed Garner had done the same.

She passed a mud flat where ugly sea serpents were sunning their long, shiny gray-black bodies, and for a few anxious moments she thought one of them was going to pursue her. She froze, and the horrible red-eyed creature slithered away, but that night she didn't dare lie down to sleep.

She stumbled on his campsite at dawn, watching awestruck when he dropped down from a tree as naked as a man could be.

"Alena! How . . ."

"I saw you meet Erasma. I followed."

"Have you lost your senses? Go back now, or you'll never be able to return."

"Will I be tainted for life because I followed the man I love?" she asked with disarming directness.

"Yes, you will," he said with such quiet sadness that her love welled up and choked back all the arguments she'd meant to use.

"Why did you sneak back at night, then leave without letting me know you're still alive? If you knew how worried I was . . ."

"Alena." He sounded touched by her anxiety, but she could tell he wouldn't change his mind. "I found a probe, but it's useless without a keyboard. I only came back to get one."

"That means you can signal Prima?"

She'd long ago stopped believing in rescue, and now that she was with Garner, she wasn't ready to return to her old life.

"Possibly."

"That's the only reason you were with Erasma?"

"My darling . . ." he whispered gently, but backed away as though just remembering his nudity, worrying that it might shock her. "Let me dress."

"No! I mean, not on my account. We'll all be naked soon enough. Cloth wears out so quickly here."

"Unless a ship comes."

"I'm not sure I want to be rescued," she said.

"It's only a possibility. The probe may be damaged. Now you must go back."

"No."

"Were you under guard?"

"Gullaner was sleeping outside my entryway."

"He'll be in trouble."

"I'm sorry, but going back now won't help him."

"There will be hell to pay if we find the probe, then go back together."

"If we go back."

"We will. I can't condemn you to a life here if there's any chance at all of returning to Prima. This planet isn't ready for our species." He was digging in his pack, taking out his trousers and slipping into them with his back turned.

She stifled a giggle, irrationally wondering how any woman could take a man seriously while admiring his bare backside.

"You can't stop me," she said matter-of-factly. "Drag me back, and I'll follow you again. I can help, you know. There may be a quicker way to reach the probe. I have a feeling—my father calls it a sixth sense—for directions."

"Alena, please . . ."

"I'm coming with you."

"I can't let you!"

"What will you do to stop me? Tie me? Beat me?"

"Don't be ridiculous!" He stood, hands on hips, towering over her, but not quite able to hide the smile that stretched the corner of his mouth.

"I'm anything but ridiculous!" She stood as tall as she could, tensing her jaw to give him a haughty stare.

He shook his head, and she relaxed, rejoicing in

her victory even though she knew as well as he did what the cost would be.

They rested when the sun was hottest, then traveled through the dark night, skirting a stretch of jungle with primitive night sounds chilling their blood. They heard distant shrieks, and her jaw trembled, making her teeth chatter. Without talking about it they put more distance between themselves and the dense foliage.

Pale light washed across the early morning sky, but Alena hardly noticed. She was so exhausted Garner had to grab her arm to stop her from walking into the midst of a covey of brilliantly plumed creatures. She saw the emerald bodies and grotesquely swaying necks and froze.

"Don't move," Garner whispered urgently. "No matter what they do."

The shriekers were weirdly beautiful in the soft light of dawn. If she hadn't seen the brutal killings, she would have admired their startling grace and gorgeous plumes, but she stared at the bobbing, strutting creatures expecting to see blood on their beaks and claws.

Her legs ached, and she couldn't control the trembling in her arms, but at long last the largest shrieker led the others back toward the jungle in a stately procession.

"A male with his harem," Garner speculated. "I think the males shriek to warn off rivals."

"They made a terrible racket the night their eggs were stolen. I thought the females were outraged over lost offspring."

"We could both be wrong," he said. "Erasma thinks they shriek when they mate."

She tried to imagine the ungainly creatures in the act of mating, but she was far more curious about the male of her own species. Would Garner make love to her now that they were alone together? She wanted him to . . . desperately. Yet he was so . . . she quivered nervously . . . large . . . sometimes. Not when she'd found him . . . was it only yesterday? Her thoughts were jumbled. How long had it been since she'd slept? Her feet were still moving, but she didn't seem to be controlling them.

"Poor Alena," he murmured close to her ear. "You're sleepwalking."

He took her hand and led her up a gentle incline to the shade of a massive tree.

Chapter Thirteen

The branches gave an illusion of safety and seclusion, but Garner was doubly wary now that he was responsible for Alena. He spread a ground cloth and let her collapse on it. Before he could suggest they eat, she was soundly sleeping, her soft rhythmic breathing reminding him of how vulnerable she was.

Instead of dropping down beside her as he wholeheartedly desired, he circled the green-trunked tree, checking the branches for wildlife that might drop down on them. He saw a nest of sticks, but the small gray and white winged creatures hovering around it didn't seem to pose a danger. Their soft chirps were reassuring, as though the tiny sentries would warn them of approaching danger.

He walked the circumference of the tree several times, each time making a larger circle. He didn't see any warning signs, no emerald feathers or large beast's spore. A hundred paces or so from where Alena slept, there was a mirror-surfaced pool that reflected the blue of the sky, but again the inhabitants were non-threatening: small yellow and white waterfowl that had more to fear from a hungry Priman than he had from them. If such vulnerable creatures were content in the area, it should be safe for him to rest awhile by Alena's side.

Her hair was spread over her slender shoulders like a silky shawl, and he was hard put to resist touching it. He'd never noticed how small and delicate her feet were, or how white her shapely ankles were. Every moment he spent with Alena was like a voyage of discovery. He didn't think one lifetime would be enough to appreciate her wonderful uniqueness, but fear of losing her was like a heavy weight pressing against his heart. He had to learn to live for each day, each moment they shared. He had to store up memories for the inevitable time when they would be torn apart.

He had to allow himself to experience joy, to love her to the fullest without being haunted by the specter of separation.

"I love you, Alena," he said aloud to her sleeping form. "And before we reach the probe, you'll know what it means to be loved."

He lay beside her, filling his nostrils with the sweet, warm scent of her body. He desired her, but for now he was content just having her close, knowing he could reach out at any moment and enfold her in his arms.

He was wary, but his body craved the regeneration only sleep could bring. At last not even his fascination with the woman beside him kept him from dropping off to sleep.

His dreams weren't peaceful, and he awoke in

torment, clutching at his itching chin. He flicked something off his face, only to find himself under attack in dozens of places. He scrambled to his feet, trying to brush away an army of small brown insects crawling on his skin, but they seemed to be everywhere, bedeviling his flesh with tiny nipping mouths too small to see.

"Alena!"

She was still sleeping, but he could see the tiny invaders on her bare leg and flank, relentlessly crawling upward.

The ground around them was alive with the small creatures, and he quickly saw the futility of trying to brush them away. The ground cloth was spread in the midst of a huge colony, and he saw only one way to defeat them.

He scooped her up and ran toward the pool, dropping her into the clear water and diving after her.

She flailed and splashed, twice disappearing under the surface before she came up sputtering and coughing. He caught her in his arms, but she pushed him away and soundly berated him.

"You're drowning me! You beast! Are you this eager to get rid of me? Couldn't you just desert me? Must you send me to a watery grave?"

She kicked out, inflicting no small amount of pain when her foot connected with his groin, then swam out of reach.

"Oh, what's this?" She plucked a half-drowned but still biting insect from between her breasts, then knocked another from her shoulder.

"Take off your clothes! You'll have to wash them anyway," he called out.

He was following his own advice, stripping off his trousers in the shallows by the shore, scrubbing at his body to be sure the last of the invaders had been washed away.

She hesitated for an instant, then waded a short distance and turned her back, peeling off her tunic and splashing furiously to rid herself of the crawling insects.

She seemed small and vulnerable, standing in water to her knees and furiously swishing her tunic. Wet hair, darkened by the water but still coppery against her honey-gold skin, clung to her shapely shoulders and back. Her waist was so slender he thought he could span it with his fingers. Her buttocks were pertly rounded, fleshy in the way a woman's should be, and he ached to cup them in his hands. Her slightly parted thighs were lean and luscious, making him forget the hundreds of tiny bites tormenting him from his ankles to his armpits.

She turned and covered her breasts with the wet garment, but not before he'd seen their creamy fullness and rosy-brown tips. Her love nest was as coppery as the hair streaming down her back, and he ached to take her as she stood there.

He thought he knew about women; he could make a cynical joy-girl weep with happiness in the throes of sexual congress, but he didn't know how to approach the only woman he'd ever loved. How did he begin? Would he hurt her? Frighten her? Could he bear it if he did?

He didn't doubt her innocence or purity; it was unthinkable for a daughter of the Scientifica to be with a man until her father chose a husband for her. She was watching him now, her mouth rounded in a startled O, fingers pressed against her lower lip. He could impale her as she stood and carry her to heights she'd never dreamed of, but was it worth the risk of frightening her, of bruising her body or her spirit?

He would be her first lover. The responsibility sat heavily on his conscience. He would rather sacrifice his manhood to a temple castrator's knife and doom himself to a life as a eunuch fawning on the superiors in a religious order than to make her loathe him for crudeness or brutality.

He sighed deeply and turned away from the temptation of her flesh. Their time would come, but not on ground occupied by a colony of devilish insects. He absentmindedly scratched his hip and side and tried not to succumb to feeling sorry for himself.

He was attacked again while retrieving their scanty belongings, but it was almost worth it to hear her rippling laughter when he plunged a second time into the pool. They had to clean the insects from everything, and the food she'd carefully hoarded had provided a feast for the tiny beasts. They abandoned her basket, since carrying it had chafed her arms and hands, and set off with two makeshift backpacks and the garments on their bodies.

Was she disappointed? She wasn't sure. Seeing Garner in the pool had made her feel like a different woman—a reckless, wild savage who belonged on this primitive world. She wanted all restraints to fall away; she yearned to follow the dictates of her heart without considering consequences. His face had softened with passion; his eyes had devoured her, telling more about his desires than words ever could. For a few suspenseful moments she'd expected him to come to her.

Was such a thing possible, for a man to make love to a woman standing in a pool? The things she didn't know tormented her. She didn't want to be ignorant of the ways of men with women. She burned to know how Garner felt, what he thought, whether he denied his own needs for fear of hurting her.

Just knowing him as Garner Rie, executive officer of the *Moon Courier* and an extraordinary Prola, wasn't enough. She wanted to learn about the inner man and understand the life that had made him what he was. She needed to know how deep his love for her was, and whether he would be disappointed by her ignorance in the ways of lovemaking.

They traveled fast, her load light now that the basket had been abandoned. If the weight of the keyboard was burdensome to him, he didn't show it. She thought of hundreds of questions to ask him now that they could speak freely, but she was reluctant to push him to talk. Several times they heard faint rustling in the foliage, and she realized how important it was to listen for danger signals.

The air was hot, but fresher than it had been in the stockade, and Garner seemed to relax as they got closer to the great falls he'd described to her.

That evening he suggested they begin sleeping at night and traveling in the light. Once they got to the top of the falls, they had to travel over rougher terrain.

As soon as it was dark, they roasted tiny eggs he'd found along the way and ate their fill of the lumpy yellow fruit that was so plentiful on Brona. She carefully picked out the seeds, as Erasma had taught them all to do, and ate the slightly tangy, melon-like flesh with relish. She bit down on a seed she'd missed and took it out of her mouth.

"What do you suppose would happen if I accidentally ate one?" she asked Garner.

He grinned, but only said, "Trust Erasma on this."

She meant to savor these minutes of rest together, planning to uncoil her hair and ask him to comb it with his fingers. Then perhaps . . .

Quickly covering her mouth to hide a yawn, she watched him spread the ground cloth and unpack the keyboard, removing the casing to check for wayward insects that might cause damage.

Lying on her stomach to watch and cradling her head on her arms, she was acutely aware of her breasts flattened against the earth and so sensitive they tingled. She felt like a person who'd just entered a strange new body, tensing each part from her shoulders to her toes to experience new sensations. If only she weren't so weary . . .

Garner watched her fight drowsiness, amused by the childlike way she used her arm as a pillow. He'd thought of this moment all day, the time when they could settle down beside a slow-burning fire that, hopefully, would keep them safe from predators and let them savor their hard-won intimacy.

He wasn't surprised when she fell asleep, nor did he resent a further delay in celebrating their love. She'd kept pace, even though he'd pushed her hard to get beyond the dangerous jungle region. He longed for the clean, crisp air of the highlands and the verdant valley where he'd found the shards. Maybe when they reached it, he could pretend for a while they were meant to be together.

The fire gave her skin a ruddy glow and made her hair as vibrant as a setting sun. She was ravishing, so beautiful and desirable it hurt his throat to think of what she'd sacrificed to be with him:

her status, her privileges, and the only way of life she understood.

He cursed his own birthright, hating his inability to give her the life she was born to live. She was a goddess among mortals, a princess among commoners. She was his woman, and he loved her so much it devastated him to know he might bring her to harm.

He slept fitfully, frequently waking to check that Alena was safe. He mocked himself, knowing he was like a fretful mother keeping watch over a newborn babe. He wondered if excessive love could drive a man to lunacy, but in his heart he knew loving her brought out the best in him. He hadn't been a whole person before he met her. His ambition, striving to rise above the limitations of his caste, had no more significance than a game played out among schoolboys. In his whole life, only two things had significance: his fascination with the far reaches of space and his love for Alena.

Alena awoke suddenly, forgetting for a moment where she was. The fire had burned down to cinders, but the stars overhead sparkled with heavenly radiance. She'd never seen such a beautiful midnight-blue sky, and she sensed it was the final magnificent display before gray dawn streaked the horizon.

Garner was sleeping on his side, wearing his ragged space trousers, no doubt for her sake. An impulse as ancient as her species made her stand and peel off her sleeveless tunic. The breeze coming across the great river was warm and sluggish, but it carried the fragrance of the exotic purple and red blooms that flourished along its banks in this season. Erasma called them florio persimmeas, and warned the survivors against inhaling their golden pollen. He was as vague about this taboo as he was in his warning not to eat the seeds of the linneas acropos. She suspected it had to do with arousing passions best left at rest in a small community with a scarcity of women.

She slipped into her sandals and wandered a short distance from the ground cloth, remembering a bush with especially beautiful fire-red blooms. When she found it, she plucked a large velvet-petaled flower and tucked it behind her ear.

On the way back to Garner, she deliberately broke off a branch and made a rustling noise to disturb his sleep, smiling to herself when he frantically called her name.

"I'm here," she said softly, touching the flower and shivering with excitement.

"What possessed you to wander away in the dark?"

He sounded angry, but she only smiled more broadly.

"Maybe I'm testing you," she said. "Do Prolas really beat their women when they disobey?"

"Come here!" He grabbed her arm and pulled her close, his sharp intake of breath telling her he was aware of her nakedness. "I made up a false tale, and I regret it. Prolas don't make a practice of abusing their females, at least no more than men of other castes. Perhaps less, because our women work beside their husbands and share equally in many decisions."

"How will you punish me if I'm very, very bad?" She took the bloom from behind her ear and tickled his nose with it.

"Like this."

He took her in his arms and gently teased her

lips, not quite kissing her but making her wish he would.

She circled his neck with her arms and caressed his cheek with the flower until he took it from her.

"What is this? One of Erasma's passion flowers?" He laughed loudly and tossed it aside. "Do you think I need an aphrodisiac to make me desire you?"

"I wondered. . . . "

He caressed her shoulders and back, running his fingers down her spine and tickling the hollow where her cheeks began to part.

"All I need is to hear your voice or see you swing your head to push your hair aside, and I burn to make love to you," he said.

He kneaded her backside, making her squirm until she was pressed against him, hanging on his neck, locked against him in an embrace that robbed her of breath.

"I wanted you when I first saw you. I want you now. I'll always want you. . . . " He kissed the corner of her mouth, making her eyes water with love.

"I've been waiting . . ."

"I know." He kissed her softly, trailing his lips to her earlobe.

". . . so long."

"We can never go back to the way things were," he said gravely.

"You tried so hard to save me from myself," she said, loving him so much her heart ached.

"From me."

"I only have one life. I want to share it with you."

"We have so little time," he said sorrowfully. "The others won't rest when they realize—"

"Then we can't waste another precious second." She dropped to her knees and reached up to release the closure on his trousers.

"No—not on your knees."

"Because Highness Yor shouldn't kneel for a Prola?"

"It's not the way I want to love you!" He dropped down beside her.

"I want to be your woman, Garner. I would rather be chastised by a man who loves me for myself than adored and cherished for my caste."

"I loathe your caste," he said fervently. "I want you to be mine, body and soul, for all eternity. I love you because you're kind and good and nurturing. Because you light up my heart when you smile and hold my happiness in your soft hands. I love you because I think you love me for the person I want to be."

"I love the person you are!"

He finished what she'd started, shedding his trousers and lying beside her to take her in his arms.

Nothing had ever felt as wonderful as lying naked in Garner's arms, rubbing her leg against his deliciously hairy calf, pressing her nipples against his hard chest, joining her mouth to his for a kiss so sweet and loving she never wanted it to end.

"Touch me," he said, and she understood how anxious he was about her first time.

Seeing was nothing like touching. She loved the velvety softness and the ramrod hardness under it. She was hardly able to believe she would at last learn about this thing men did to women.

He kissed her until her lips were swollen, stinging in a way that only made her yearn more desperately for release from the pulsating tension that rippled through her. He lavished attention on her breasts, gently suckling her nipples until she cried out in pleasure and surprise, but still she burned with curiosity and something more.

Dawn crept up on them, heightening her pleasure because she could see his beloved face, his eyes murky with passion and his mouth as swollen as hers. She adored his minuscule nipples, dark knobs that hardened under her tongue, and his lean, hard body, overwhelmingly masculine but beautiful in her eyes.

When he rose above her on his knees, straddling her hips, she thought the time had come when the mystery would be revealed to her. She braced herself, determined to give him pleasure no matter what the cost to her in pain, but he spoke soft words of love and kissed her closed lids, caressing her breasts with such a light touch she pressed his hands against them to make him knead them harder.

Whatever she'd expected, it wasn't the gentle way he spread her thighs apart and moistened his fingers with his tongue. She'd never been touched between her legs, never known a man's hand could send lightning bolts coursing through her. She heard herself crying out, but she clutched his wrist to keep him there, panicked that he might mistake her ecstasy for pain.

"Now, now. Now!" She couldn't feel this way and not share it with the man who owned her soul.

"If I hurt you, tell me and I'll stop."

She could only guess how hard it would be for him to keep this promise, but she would never hold him to it. She wanted him inside her, and if pain was the price, she would bite through her tongue before she asked him to stop.

"Alena, don't let me hurt you!"

He guided himself, continuing the magic with his fingers until she thought she'd die of sheer joy.

He moved slowly at first, bending his head to kiss her shoulders and breasts, bringing her hand to his lips and sucking each finger to distract her from the pain that had to come.

A sudden, sharp stab surprised her more than it hurt, and she bit down on her lower lip, lifting her hips to meet his slow thrusts.

She thought the stars of night had returned. Brilliant colors flashed inside her closed lids.

Garner said her name again and again, but she could only clutch at his back, digging into his flesh with her nails and wrapping her legs around his hips to brace herself for the final spontaneous burst of bliss.

"Alena, darling Alena." He was hovering over her, anxiously whispering her name and brushing strands of damp hair from her face.

"I've never been so happy," she murmured.

He kissed her, slowly and deeply, then collapsed beside her and pulled her against him, cradling her head on his chest.

"Neither have I," he said. "Neither have I, my love."

She didn't know which of them fell asleep first.

When she woke up, the sun was hot on her backside, and she wiggled against him until her lips brushed his.

"Wake up, sleepyhead," she said.

"I think I am awake, unless I'm dreaming there's a beautiful woman in my arms."

"I want to be your wife, Garner Rie."

"You're my woman, darling. The only one I've ever loved or ever will." He tried to kiss her, but she evaded him.

"You don't understand. I want to be your real wife so no one can separate us. Ever!"

He sat up and pulled her onto his lap.

"Do you see a temple? Do you see a priest?"

"No, but we don't need either. We only need each other."

"No marriage is valid without filing an intent, then registering the contract."

"Ours will be. We're on a new world. We'll go by the laws of Brona."

"The laws of Brona!" He laughed and kissed her soundly. "Survival is all that matters here, but I don't want to live without you, Alena Yor."

"If you call me wife in your heart, that's what I'll be."

"I do," he said solemnly.

"You'll always be my husband, the only man I've ever loved or ever will."

"Alena . . ." He started to say something, but she put her fingers over his lips, not wanting to hear anything that would cast shadows on their future.

Garner leaned back on his elbow and watched Alena wander away to pluck a lumpy yellow fruit and split it in two on the edge of a rock. All his senses were especially acute this morning. He could smell the perfumed flowers that grew in clusters along the river, hear tiny buzzes and chirps of unseen creatures, and feel the heat of the day building around them.

Being here with Alena was so perfect he was afraid it was only another hallucination. His heart swelled with love, and he was enchanted by the way she offered him the fruit, kneeling and holding bits to his lips, letting him lick the juice from her fingers.

They were both as naked as primitive savages, but the love he felt for her was pure and serene, untainted by self-serving lust. For the first time since childhood, he allowed himself to live for the moment, reveling in the contentment it brought. He wanted to give her a gift, but his only possession was the despicable caste band on his wrist.

She laughed when he pretended to capture her fingers in his mouth, and he realized one gift was his to give: a perfect day together, one so memorable it would sustain them both no matter what the future held.

The other survivors would know she was gone, but they had at least a day before the fastest pursuit could overtake them. Then, once he led Alena past the great falls, it would take a clever tracker to find them. He couldn't predict what Blaz would do, but he was sure this day was theirs to spend giving each other pleasure.

He found a seed in a fleshy bit of fruit she gave him and pushed it between his teeth, waiting for her to take it from his mouth.

"What would happen if I ate this?" she asked, snatching it away.

"You would have . . ." He groped for words. "Disturbing dreams."

"Tell me truly, have you eaten one, or are you only reinforcing Erasma's warning?"

"I probably ate several at once—foolishly forgetting what he said about them."

"What did you dream?"

"I hallucinated about a she-devil."

"Was she beautiful?"

"She was you! Even in my dreams, I can't love anyone but you!"

He lay back and pulled her on top of him, so drowsy and content he didn't think deeper happiness was possible.

She snuggled against him, wiggling to find a perfect fit for their bodies, squirming against his torso and raining tiny kisses on his neck and shoulders.

He made a game of being impassive, trying not to respond to her gentle caresses and sweet little kisses, watching wide-eyed because he wanted to remember the way her warm brown eyes grew murky with passion and her lips trembled against his.

"Don't you want me again—that way?" she asked with an embarrassed little smile when he didn't show any reaction to her teasing.

"I want you more than you can imagine," he said gently.

He made love to her slowly, as though he had all eternity to discover what made her quiver with expectation and shiver with desire. Excitement raced through him like a powerful stimulant. He ached from the intensity of his arousal, but more than anything, he wanted his beloved Alena to experience the mystery of love in all its dimensions.

"Now, now," she gasped, but he'd only begun their sensual adventure.

He massaged her arms, her legs and feet, her belly and breasts, not wanting the slightest residue of tension to impair her senses.

She went as limp as a cloth doll stuffed with pond weed fluff, and he rolled her over, massaging her shoulders and back. He knew the secrets of a spinal rub, and used his knuckles to make her moan with pleasure. He fondled the flesh of her buttocks in his palms, then kneaded hard, not stopping until her skin was rosy.

"Why are you doing this?" she moaned, not resisting when he bent her leg and caressed the back of first one knee, then the other.

She giggled when he massaged her toes, separating each one, then rubbing the balls of her feet until she tried to escape.

They laughed and teased and came together like practiced lovers, but being inside Alena was like nothing he'd ever experienced. She'd captured his heart with her beauty and grace. Now she was claiming his manhood, enriching his understanding of what it meant to be male.

They slept in each other's arms, awoke to make love again, and finally, driven by hunger, packed up their possessions and began to move toward the great falls and their destiny.

They found a tree with soft-shelled nuts that Erasma especially liked as a protein source and ate their fill, packing extra for the days of leaner pickings when they were trekking in the foothills.

"Tell me," she said, mischief sparkling in her eyes as she walked naked beside him, as comfortable reverting to nature's ways as he was. "I've heard that men of the Space Service seldom marry."

"We're gone too much," he said, not sure he liked the drift of her conversation.

"Instead they visit women who make love for money."

"Joy-girls," he said, pointing to a shrub heavy with tiny purple berries. "Do you think we dare try some of those?"

"Have you done that?" she asked, not distracted by the fruit, one they both knew should be avoided.

"Alena . . ."

"I won't censure you if you have. My life began when we left the *Moon Courier,* and I think you're not the same man either. I just want to know. . . ."

"It won't add to your happiness to know all

about my past." Or my happiness either, he thought frowning.

"Then tell me, are all men so wonderful, or were you schooled by your—experience?"

"Wives shouldn't ask such questions," he said, playfully swatting her bottom.

"Do you want me to believe one man is much like another—that you're not the only male who could made me burn and tingle and—"

"Alena! Women don't speak this way to men!"

"Do you mean it's all right to lie in your arms and hold you inside my body, but not proper to talk about it?" She stopped walking and faced him with her hands on her sleek hips, challenging and inviting him at the same time.

"I don't know how things are when a man and woman of your caste wed," he admitted, not sure whether to be angry at her or himself for the uncomfortable feeling he had. "My parents were too busy earning enough to feed and house their family to banter about anything."

"My father talked to me about philosophy and government and advances in the sciences," she said thoughtfully, "but I can't remember him saying anything about feelings. Except, of course, to tell me what pleased and displeased him in my deportment."

"I love talking with you," he admitted, "but some things are better unsaid."

She laughed uproariously, startling him with her outburst.

"I love you, Garner." She threw her arms around his neck and kissed him with gusto. "I don't care if you learned all the tricks a joy-girl can teach, as long as you swear you only love me."

"I swear it," he said, hugging her in relief.

They waded through waist-high water in a

broad stream, the waters murky but not evil-smelling like the great river. The bottom felt sandy and clean, and Alena urged him to rest on the far bank.

"I'm so warm," she said. "I'd love to swim awhile."

His first impulse was to say no, but he'd bathed in countless streams on his trek to the foothills and back. He didn't want to deny her a refreshing swim.

"All right, but stay close."

"I'll only go as far as that log floating on the surface," she said.

He sat on the shore, watching her naked form glide through the water with strong, even strokes. He couldn't stop thinking of the glorious moments when their bodies were joined in lovemaking. He'd never been happier, never felt more free. She made him forget about the probe and the deranged captain. His apprehensions receded, and all that mattered was a passion that, at least for now, could be satisfied.

The sun was a fireball low in the sky, and her tresses flowed behind her like a flaming banner. Watching her ignited the heat in his groin yet another time, and he wanted to take her standing as she stepped from the stream.

He chided himself, knowing they had to find a safer resting place before dark. Even though he hadn't heard shriekers in the area, he couldn't assume they were the only hostile predators. Having Alena with him made him doubly wary of potential dangers.

"Alena, come back now!" he called loudly, feeling more uneasy as the sun sank lower.

"Come join me!" she called back gaily, playfully splashing water in his direction.

He was tempted, but suddenly his worst nightmare was real. The log moved, and a broad, blunt snout broke the tranquil surface of the stream. His first impulse was to leap in after her, but in the fraction of a second before he acted, he detected movement with the corner of his eye.

"Alena! Don't move! The log! Stay still! Don't attract attention!"

He called out as loudly as he could, rooted to the spot by the menace approaching on the ground from the far left. He didn't want to take his eyes from her, but he had to see what was moving toward him. If he were injured or killed . . .

Ignoring the knot of terror in his stomach, he slowly turned his head enough to see a rough-skinned reptile nearly four times his own height crawling along the shore less than 500 meters away. The creature was four-legged with a heavy tail as long as its bark-green body, and its snout was wide and blunted. Its yellow eyes were small and glassy, and Garner prayed it would have trouble detecting prey that didn't move.

There was no doubt: The same kind of giant reptile was menacing Alena in the water.

He didn't need to see her face clearly to recognize the look of horror etched on her patrician features. His first instinct was to rush into the water to save her, but any movement he made might cause the creature to attack and drag her under. The giant reptile was too close to an easy prey to be diverted by anything he could do.

Then a second snout broke the surface of the water, and he took a desperate gamble, running into the stream with as much noise and splashing as possible, hoping against hope the two beasts would bypass her and attack him.

Without warning, the second smashed into the

first, opening its alien snout and attacking its competitor with small but lethal-looking teeth.

Garner subconsciously realized that two bulls were fighting over prey. He rushed to Alena, who was frantically swimming toward shore, and pulled her into his arms and onto the bank.

The beasts fought furiously, tails thrashing and jaws snapping. Garner caught a glimpse of red staining the turbulent waters; then Alena's scream warned him of deadly danger. The reptile on shore was making a mad dash, its deadly speed giving them no hope of outdistancing it. He pushed Alena away, shouting at her to run and save herself.

He stared at death and felt adrenalin flowing to his weaponless hands. He felt an instant of self-hatred for being so befuddled by love he'd left his pistol and knife in the backpack.

Alena froze, and they both watched as the reptile suddenly lost speed, slowing down but still lumbering toward them, its massive jaws threatening attack.

Garner did the only thing he could. He leaped to the right of the charging beast and threw himself at the beast's snout, putting all his weight on the head and forcing the great jaw to close. The giant's tail flailed on the ground, every swish a potential death blow, but he was able to hold the snout shut.

"Run!" he shouted at Alena, knowing his victory was only temporary. He and the beast were deadlocked, but the instant he released his pressure, the reptile would kill him. He couldn't see what was happening in the water, but he didn't doubt the victor would try to claim her as its prize.

Alena wasn't running. He screamed desperately, but she was moving toward the reptile, holding a piece of deadwood that had washed ashore.

He watched in horror as she brought the stick crashing down, sure it wouldn't faze the monster.

One instant he was screaming at her; the next the beast went limp, thrashing its tail weakly in its death throes.

He stood and saw what she'd done. The beast had a soft spot, a blowhole, on the top of its skull. She'd rammed her stick into the only vulnerable place on the giant reptile.

She was trembling with fear, her face so white he thought she might faint, but he couldn't comfort her—not yet. He grabbed her hand and raced to their packs, scooping them up and handing her the small one, taking the precious keyboard with him.

With a frantic backward glance, he saw the victorious bull lumbering out of the stream. They ran, not stopping until they'd gone many times the distance the dead reptile had charged.

His gift of one perfect day had ended with fear and horror. They stopped and dressed, putting on footgear for a trek through the night.

He longed to disappear with her forever on the vast planet. He would gladly risk hardships and dangers to live out his life alone with her, but he had to face the impossibility of this dream. If something happened to him, she would be alone to face great dangers and incredible loneliness. She was stronger and braver than he'd ever dared believe, but he couldn't risk leaving her to face this savage world by herself.

They trudged through the night, and he knew their love was doomed.

Chapter Fourteen

Alena walked by Garner's side through the dark night. In her mind, she killed the beast again and again and again, feeling its death shudders when she rammed the stick into the blowhole.

"You were very brave. I'm proud of you," Garner said when they were well away from the dangerous stream.

"I'm still frightened."

"I know. You have reason to be."

He stopped and held her in his arms, murmuring endearments until she finally relieved her tension in tears.

"I don't want to cry. . . . "

"It's all right." He kissed her damp face, brushing away tears with the backs of his fingers until she grabbed his hand and pressed urgent kisses on it.

"I might have lost you," she said, confessing her worst fear.

"We're alive; we're together. That's all that matters now."

"It's all that will ever matter to me! Throw away the keyboard. We can go into the mountains, and no one will ever find us!"

"Darling, don't you know how much I want to? But if something happened—if I were to die—you would be alone."

"I'll be alone wherever I am, if you're not with me!"

They walked on in silence, their hands locked, and she knew he was grieving as much as she was. All her life, she'd dreamed of perfect love, unselfish and uplifting, never suspecting the cost.

At dawn they bedded down, sleeping in each other's arms and awaking to make love with silent urgency.

The next day they came to the great falls. She tried to describe the stupendous rush of water, but words were inadequate. As far as she could see, a great wall of water cascaded down a sheer drop.

"The descent is treacherous," he said. "I have a length of cord Erasma gave me. Let me tie it around your waist and mine."

She enjoyed the tricky downward climb, preferring to negotiate the boulder-strewn drop-off with bare feet even though she bruised her toe.

"Where are we going from here?" she asked when they reached the bottom.

They stood side by side, so close to the churning white water they were soon soaked by the perpetual mist.

He pointed at the mountains in the east. "We're not quite halfway."

They climbed over rock shelves and boulders, moving to a better vantage point, then stripped off their clothing to let it dry and basked in the sun.

"The lost pod is down there," he said, pointing downriver. "I dug it out on the last trek, so we should be able to get more supplies fairly easily."

"I want to take everything with us," she said, but his only answer was a long, deep kiss.

They made love standing, his backside braced against the side of a huge boulder. She responded to his driving urgency, her cry at the moment of climax muffled by the roar of the falls.

She was drowsy and would have napped, but he looked upward, telling her without words they were no longer safe from pursuit.

The supplies in the pod delighted her, but she was still reluctant to be confined in such a close space. She stood outside while Garner picked out what they would be able to carry, handing foodstuffs, a blanket, and small items to her through the hatch.

They made two heavy packs, including the keyboard in his, and used lengths of cord to secure them on their backs.

"Yours is too heavy," he decided, but she wouldn't let him lighten her load.

"Being with you makes it seem light," she said.

Garner described the valley where they were going, and she was able to discern several shortcuts. Even without her calipers and compass, she worked out the best route, relying on her innate sense of direction.

"I can't believe I'm here," she said, looking back for a last glimpse at the falls before they traveled through a narrow pass between two foothills.

She touched his arm, needing to feel the solid reality of his flesh. Her life had taken a widely different direction from the one mapped out for her since childhood. When she looked into his sapphire-blue eyes fringed by a mane of windswept black hair, she felt blessed beyond measure. He was still scraping away his bristles every few days, and she wondered how he would look with a magnificent black beard. Someday his blade would grow too dull to use, and he would give up the last custom that tied him to the old world. She wanted to be with him when that happened.

They pushed themselves, but not so hard there wasn't time for lovemaking under the stars. Her legs cramped from climbing, and her back ached from the heavy pack, but she didn't let herself dwell on transitory pain. The thought of bedding down at night with Garner gave her energy and resolve.

"You're amazing, darling," he said. "You never complain, and you keep pace no matter how difficult the climb."

She smiled demurely, deciding to save the truth for another time. She hurried, not for the reason he thought, but because she was always eager to lie in his arms.

When they reached their destination, it was just as he'd described it to her: a peaceful setting with lush vegetation and sparkling water in the stream. They picked a downstream spot to bathe so there would always be fresh water upstream, and spent an idyllic hour scrubbing each other with a precious cake of soap from the pod. She loved having him run foamy hands over her slippery skin, and afterward he took her on the grassy bank with such renewed vigor her cries of ecstasy echoed through the valley.

Later, after virtually feasting on packets of food from the pod, seafood with root vegetables and dried eggs with bits of cheese and meat, they retrieved the shards from under a pile of stones he'd stacked to mark their location.

"It is a shard." She gave up her last hope of never being rescued. The blackened piece of ceramic was unmistakable. It must have scattered when the probe landed or been carried to the valley by a water run. They might never know which, but it meant they couldn't be too far from the probe.

That night their lovemaking was bittersweet with the knowledge that rescue might be within their grasp. Later, when he was sleeping, she carried the keyboard to the stream and reached into the cold, swift water to find a boulder to smash it.

"There are others," he said, coming up to her before she could carry out her plan. "I would have to go back and get one."

"You of all people belong here," she said, looking up at his lean, muscular body tanned and hardened by his treks, knowing he was a man who could make the savage planet his home.

"I don't want this harsh life for you," he said.

She'd never heard him speak so sternly, but his words only challenged her.

"On Prima my life will be planned by my father, dictated by my caste. I can't go back to being what I was! I won't!"

"We're not alone, Alena. The others will find us eventually. There are three women on this planet now—one past her prime and the other, poor Velma Pitt, addled in her wits. How long do you think it will be before I have to kill to keep you?"

"But my caste . . ."

"Means nothing here. The greasers are out of control, hunting in a band and not bringing meat to the others. If more of the men left in the stockade die from fever, Tacka and his followers can easily take control. The old ways we brought with us are meaningless."

"You're their leader. They wouldn't be doing this if you were there. They respect you!"

"Some, perhaps—not Tacka. And if it comes to war against them, do you think the high-caste passengers will follow me?"

"Are things really so terrible here? This is such a huge planet. There should be room for all of us. We could begin a new settlement. Erasma is clever, and Roar is faithful to you."

He pulled her into his arms and kissed her tenderly, but she couldn't be comforted. She had a vision of a better life, and he was the last person she expected to shatter it.

In the morning Garner awoke at dawn and found Alena already up.

"Are you so eager to begin searching?" he asked, wondering if he would ever know her mind.

"The probe can't be too far from the shroud," she said optimistically. "We won't take long to find it."

"Not far if you have wings and can search from the air," he said.

"Mister Rie, must you always see the gloomy side?" she teased.

"I can't believe you're eager to send a distress signal. Yesterday you sorely regretted the possibility of rescue and were ready to smash the keyboard."

"Today I see how much better it would be for us if all the others were rescued. If we hide, the Space Service won't spend much time searching. We could live here for years—generations—before another vessel comes."

He shook his head and smiled sadly, wishing he could believe in her fantasies. Their ties to Prima were like strands of a net ensnaring them. He couldn't bring himself to believe they had a future together.

When he pointed out the remains of the shroud, visible on the mountainside from where they stood, she spoke confidently about the best route to follow. When they were ready to go, she led the way with her hair in a single red-gold braid that fell down her slender back. His fingers itched to untangle the plaits and see it flow freely around her shoulders, but he had to be content with watching the way her backside and thighs flexed as she climbed ahead of him in her short tunic.

They found the shroud before the sun reached its zenith. Alena was in her element, measuring angles, studying the terrain, and speculating on the way it had separated from the probe. He was restless watching her; it wasn't his way to stand by in idleness while another worked.

"What have you learned?" he asked.

"That patience isn't one of your attributes, my love. Sit and rest. I'm only trying to save us time when we begin to search."

He sat and felt the weariness of many days of travel creep over him. Alena was revitalized by the challenge of finding the probe, but he couldn't share her enthusiasm. It might be in their best interests if the probe was too damaged to send a distress signal. If so, they could plan from there, but he knew neither of them could leave the site before they exhausted all possibilities of finding it.

He sat and leaned against a tree trunk on the wooded slope, sleepily warning her to stay where he could see her. He didn't intend to sleep, but his eyelids were heavy and his brain was hazy with fatigue.

He awoke with a start, angry at himself for napping, and called out to her.

"Alena!" He stood and looked in all directions, shouting her name again and again.

He was so afraid for her that his chest tightened and his throat constricted. He couldn't see her, and she didn't answer his calls.

Desperately, he began to search in ever-widening concentric circles so he wouldn't lose the shroud in the process of trying to find her. To his great relief, he spotted her flaming braid among the green foliage in only a few minutes, but he was furious at her for wandering off.

"I asked you not to leave my sight," he said, not hiding his anger.

"I'm not a child, Garner. You were sleeping, and I had work to do."

"Didn't you hear me calling?" He stood, hands on hips, still so agitated he could feel a pulse hammering in his forehead.

"I heard and answered. It's not my fault my voice didn't carry up the slope."

"Last night you were ready to smash the keyboard. Today you're so eager to find the probe you defy my order."

"Your order! I'm not one of your greasers! You can't dictate to me!"

"Of course not! High Yor's daughter holds herself above ordinary common-sense rules like participating in pod drills. Far be it for you to obey a Prola!"

"You're being hateful! Just because you fell asleep, you're making it sound like I'm flaunting my caste!"

"Aren't you? You want to call me husband, but you obey your own whims!"

"Finding the probe is no whim! Have I bruised

your male pride by being a better tracker than you?"

He'd never seen her angry like this, her face flushed and contorted. Her beauty took on an ominous cast, and he'd never seen such a stubborn expression. He was hard put to restrain from shaking her!

"I haven't done anything to justify that accusation!" he said. "It's not unreasonable to ask you to stay close."

"I'm going after the probe. You can stay close to me—if you can keep up!"

"If you wander off again, I'll bind you with a cord and lead you where I please!"

She stood legs apart, hands on her hips imitating his stance. She was defying him like a willful child, adding fuel to the flame of his anger.

"The sooner I find the probe, the better," she said with soft-spoken fury. "Then we can be rid of each other!"

She flounced off, leaving him to scramble after her. She returned to the shroud and took up her backpack without a word, leaving him to retrieve the keyboard and follow in haste.

They were wearing tunics, trousers, and footgear, but it was inadequate protection on the densely wooded mountain slope. Branches scraped their arms and faces, and loose stones made walking hazardous. He wanted her to climb more cautiously, but he was too angry to suggest she slow her pace.

She kept the lead, spending her energy recklessly and making him angrier with each step. He regretted some of what he'd said, but she deserved a sound scolding and more for disappearing on him.

He followed her on a zigzag of switchbacks,

climbing upward over increasingly difficult terrain. His legs ached, and he knew she must be hurting too, even though she stubbornly kept on. He trusted her sense of direction implicitly, but not her judgment in rushing up a mountain never before trod by Primans.

He wasn't angry because her talent in exploring overshadowed his. It wasn't his ego that suffered because of her impressive talent. What he felt was deep sorrow that he might ruin her life by loving her.

She hadn't spoken a word, and he began to wonder if she ever would. The longer she stayed silent, the more her anger goaded him. He felt like tumbling her on a bed of mountain brush and teaching her what dominance was. He watched her back, so straight and proud under her pack, and he envied true savages who could cuff their females into submission without suffering pangs of conscience.

One element of his passion was the awe he felt just looking at her, knowing she was finer and better than he could ever deserve. Respect was part and parcel of his love, and yet her anger rankled him. Was it always so complicated to love a woman? How could he curb her recklessness without subduing her spirit? He longed to hear sweet words from her mouth, even as he fantasized about ripping away her garments, spreading her legs, and making her cry out in ecstasy.

One moment his eyes were riveted on her taut thighs, thinking of the secret place between them, and the next he lost his footing, put off balance by loose dirt and stones that gave way under his step. He fell forward and groped for a handhold to stop his downward slide, but his feet went over a precipice before he could stop himself.

He grasped at loose dirt and caught a sapling growing into the side of the mountain, clutching it desperately to stop his fall. The rope holding the keyboard on his back shifted, and he felt the pack hanging from one shoulder in danger of dropping off into nothingness.

He cried out for help, but Alena was already on her belly in the dirt above him, reaching down to him.

"Get the keyboard!" he cried out.

"Let it fall! It doesn't matter. Take my hand!" She strained but couldn't quite reach him.

"Take it!" he insisted. "Then I can drag myself up."

"Garner . . ."

"Just do it!"

He held his breath while she crawled to the very edge of the dropoff and stretched down to take the board.

"Don't fall!" he said, knowing how futile his words were.

She put the pack, keyboard and all, safely behind her and reached for him, but he knew it was too dangerous to take the hand she offered. He would rather fall himself than risk having her topple over the edge helping him.

"Take my hand!" she cried frantically.

"No . . . too dangerous. Tie yourself to something first."

"I'll use the cord!"

He could hear her gasping, and loose gravel rained down on him when she crawled away from the edge to secure herself to a tree.

When she reached down again, he was still afraid of endangering her.

"Maybe it would be better . . . just throw the rope to me."

"It's not long enough!"

He was straining for a toehold, his foot slipping again and again on the crumbling side of the mountain.

"No time! Take my hand," she begged. "Garner, if you fall, I swear I'll follow you!"

She reached down, straining to catch his hand. He clung to the sapling with one hand and groped for her with the other. Again and again their fingers touched, but perilous inches separated their palms. The rope that held her secure was too short. It kept her from getting close enough to the edge to help him.

He became more frightened for her sake with each passing second. Even if they did lock hands, she couldn't possibly pull his weight over the edge.

He tested the whiplike strength of the sapling and knew he had at best one chance to propel himself upward before it snapped under his weight.

"Get back!" he screamed urgently, not daring to look up to see if she obeyed him.

He swung his legs and pulled them up, bracing his feet just below the sapling, and lunged upward, praying his acrobatic scramble wouldn't send him to his death. He let go of the sapling, literally diving upward, blindly reaching for a solid handhold. He dug his fingers into loose gravel, grasping in vain for something to stop his backward slide.

It was hopeless. The harder he scrambled, the more he lost ground.

Then he stopped sliding. Alena had caught his arm with both hands and was holding on with strength born of desperation.

Slowly, laboriously, he wiggled forward on his belly, gradually gaining purchase, acutely aware of her nails digging into his arm.

He took her in his arms as soon as he was on firm ground, hugging her with all his strength as she trembled against his chest.

"Are you sorry for saving me?" he teased softly. "Sweet Alena, I owe you my life!"

"You're a beast to punish me this way!"

"What . . ."

"I was furious at you, and you deserved it! Now you've frightened me so badly, I can't remember the reason!"

He laughed and covered her face with hungry little kisses.

"I'm the one who deserved to be punished!" he said "I was so angry I wanted to take you against your will."

"You couldn't! The time will never come when I don't want you!"

"You don't understand. I wanted to hurt you," he said with shame.

"Your angry words hurt more than blows."

"I know." He smiled ruefully. "I'm still smarting myself."

"We mustn't quarrel again." She smiled, and he understood a little more about the awesome power she had over him.

"I would rather suffer a tongue-lashing than have you grow to hate me." He surprised himself with this revelation.

"I'll never hate you—but I don't like it when you treat me like a child."

"A child?" He arched his brows, wondering if she would ever run out of surprising things to say.

"Yes! You tell me where I may go and what I should do, as though I'm irresponsible. Do you think I would risk losing a single moment of precious time with you?"

"I was too anxious about keeping you safe," he admitted.

"When I'm with you, I am safe."

They held each other for a few more precious moments, but both were eager to move upward before nightfall. So far they'd only seen small creatures eager to avoid them, but they needed a secure campsite before they could lie in each other's arms again.

Garner called a halt with only a few hours' climb left to reach the summit.

"We could make it by dark," she said, although he suspected it was more to test his reaction than from eagerness to go on.

"Yes," he agreed, "but this is a perfect refuge for the night." He pointed at water trickling down smooth rocks and a natural hollow in the rock wall.

That night their lovemaking was doubly sweet. He was tender and tireless, wanting her to feel how much he regretted the bad feelings between them. She admitted it was hard for her to let go of anger, then showered her love on him.

She fell asleep in his arms, but he was awake for a long time, wondering if Alena was unique in her ability to puzzle and intrigue. Or were all women mysterious to men who loved them? Either way, he wanted nothing more than the chance to know the secret recesses of her mind.

In the morning they hurried to begin the final ascent. The air was cooler than any they'd experienced since the rainy season, but on this tropical planet, it was a blessing.

Garner followed her lead, even though the vegetation was scanty near the summit and it wasn't as challenging to find the easiest way. Mist swirled around them in the early hours, but the sun burnt it away by late morning. Unlike the jagged peaks to the west that had destroyed the three pods, this mountain was an ancient one, the top worn down and rounded by eons of wind and rain.

The probe lay on the eastern edge, as well placed as though a giant hand had laid it there for their convenience.

"The shroud must have plunged down the mountain sometime after the landing," Garner speculated.

"Possibly it was hit by lightning, or a boulder shifted and dislodged it," Alena said. "I hate to think there are any creatures in the mountains large enough to move it."

"The Space Service can be proud of this." He touched the burnished surface of the conical probe. "It passed through the atmosphere and is still as solid and shiny as the day it was launched."

He walked around it, fascinated as always by space hardware but heartsick at the prospect of activating it. If it still functioned, the link to Prima could blight their lives.

"The eye is smashed," he said.

"Does that mean it won't work?" She sat back on her haunches, eying it warily.

"No, it only means we can't send our pictures back to Space Control."

"But it could be dead," she said hopefully.

"The antennas are intact. It's too soon to tell what it can still do."

He touched it, resting his hand on the sun-warmed surface, awed by the trip it had made through space. He knew how to trigger the mechanism to reach the inner control panel, but he felt like a man assigned to dig his own grave.

"Bring the keyboard," he said curtly, afraid he

would never bring himself to do it if he didn't act immediately.

She hesitated long enough to show him how difficult this was for her, then took the board from his makeshift backpack and handed it to him.

He connected the jack without difficulty, ignoring the tremors that made his hands unsteady and his fingers clumsy. He thought of Erasma and all the botanist was doing to keep the survivors alive. He remembered Roar and Gullaner, good-hearted men who deserved a chance to be rescued.

He couldn't think about Alena, even though she hovered close to his elbow. It hurt too much knowing the old world might intrude on their new one if he succeeded in sending a signal.

Without a conscious effort to remember, he punched in the distress code drilled into him at the Academy a lifetime ago.

"Is it working?" He could hear the catch in her voice.

"Listen."

They both heard the tiny whine that indicated the distress signal was going out into space, beamed at an alien planet they'd once called home.

"We've made Blaz's fantasy come true," she said bitterly. "Do you think he'll find a way to take credit?"

"Does it matter?" he asked sadly.

She shook her head and turned away from him.

He understood the meaning of damnation as he watched her, unable to say anything that would comfort her.

Chapter Fifteen

When they came down from the mountain, they rested for three days, trying to pretend the tranquil valley would always be their home.

"We should name this place," Alena said.

"If we don't, how will we receive communications?" Garner teased, putting aside the sharpened stick he was using to spear small finned creatures in the stream.

"Paradise Valley. What do you think of that?" she asked.

He scooped up his catch, holding by their tails the three silvery-blue water creatures he intended to roast for their supper. "It sounds like a name a storyteller would invent. I prefer to call it Alena's Valley."

"No, you discovered it. Garner Valley would be better." She watched him making sparks with his flints to ignite the pile of sticks she'd gathered.

"No, it's never been my ambition to leave my

name on maps. Call it Moon Valley to remember the way the night sky looks when I hold you in my arms."

"Moon Valley." She tested the name and smiled. "I like it. What *are* your ambitions, darling?"

He looked at her in surprise. "No one has ever asked me that."

"No one has ever loved you as I do. So tell me, when did you first set your sights on space?"

"Maybe I was born wanting to explore the heavens. Anyway, I saved every coin that came my way—there were precious few—to enter a training program for greasers. It was a long shot. For every hundred trained, one man might be fortunate enough to serve on a space freighter. But I was determined to someday work on a flight to Bedir."

"And you were chosen."

"No, I never served as a greaser. The government began a program to admit a few Prolas to the Academy. It was only a gesture to quiet unrest in the Prola ghettos, but I qualified. When I finished third in my class, they had to commission me in the Space Service or admit the program was a sham."

"I'm very proud of you." She wrapped her arms around his waist, and he loved the way it felt having her cuddle against his naked backside.

"Don't be. I'm not a good officer. I loathe having an incompetent like Blaz as my superior. One reason I'm going back—"

"Don't say it!"

"Alena." He turned and took her in his arms. "Even if I did decide to disappear in the mountains, I couldn't take you with me. The chance of surviving more than a few seasons is slight, and I can't stand the thought of leaving you here alone if something should happen to me."

"I'm willing to risk it."

"And if we should have a child? Imagine the solitary life he would have to endure when we're gone."

"Someday Prima may colonize Brona."

"And our offspring would be a curiosity, a specimen to take to a laboratory and study."

"We could have dozens to keep each other company."

"And would they mate with siblings? Imagine generation after generation from the same gene pool. Do you want to be the mother of a race of freaks?"

Tears were running down her cheeks, but she didn't try to refute the truth in what he said. "I guess it's not simple to populate a new world. Oh, Garner, I love you so much it's a torment!"

"There's another reason why I have to get back, darling. I can't disgrace my family and caste by becoming a renegade. Not only would my parents and siblings grieve for me, they would be scapegoats, vulnerable to government persecution."

"But why?"

"To save face for those who set up the program taking Prolas into the Academy. Remember, I'm a token low-caste cadet. If I fail to live up to government expectations, someone has to suffer. The program can't be faulty; my parents will be punished for raising an unstable son."

"That's so unfair!"

"There's no fairness in the caste system."

"We have to leave here, don't we."

"Yes. If rescue comes—and I believe your father has enough power to see that it does—they'll expect to find survivors near the probe. We have to bring the others here."

"To our valley."

"To Moon Valley, my love."

She smiled through her tears. "This will be our last night alone here, won't it?"

He felt an unmanly tightening in his throat, and there was nothing he could say to comfort her. "We've delayed as long as we can. We have to bring the others here to wait for rescue."

He roasted the mild-flavored, flaky flesh of the stream creatures and fed it to her with his fingers, every gesture a prelude to love.

Alena took the last bite from his fingers, then walked to the stream to wash her hands. He followed, as she knew he would, wading into the shallow water and splashing her until she retaliated. She laughed at his antics and doubled over when he pretended to tickle her ribs, but inside she was devastated, dreading the morning when they had to leave their spiritual home.

They made love under the star-studded canopy of the sky, coming together with fierce intensity until the ground under them seemed to shake in the throes of their mystic union. He was more than a man and more than a lover, filling her again and again with the fluid of life, and she loved him desperately, wholly, completely.

"Have I hurt you?" he asked as they lay watching the stars disappear in the coming of dawn.

When I'm with you, even pain is ecstasy," she said, wrapping her arms around him and wishing she could make time stop so this moment would never end.

He ministered to her tender love nest with his tongue, carrying her to a whole new dimension of well-being, and she fell asleep with her cheek cradled on his belly.

* * *

In the morning they began the trek back to the stockade.

She didn't keep pace as well as previously, frequently finding excuses to rest: Her toe was bruised; her legs were cramping; the fast pace made her breathless; the sun made her dizzy.

"I know what you're doing," he said on the fourth day of their journey. "We've scarcely covered the distance possible in three days of easy walking. You're dawdling on purpose."

"Is it my fault your legs are longer and stronger than mine?" she asked, pretending to pout.

"Not only that, this shortcut you suggested will cost us an extra day of travel."

"I'm sure you'll find a way to punish me," she teased, annoyed when he only shook his head and walked on, pretending to leave her behind.

Once they'd left the foothills and scrambled up the cliff beside the falls, the sun became their enemy. The river valley was a steaming cauldron at the peak of the hot season, denying them any relief by day. Her skin reddened and burned, and even his tougher hide suffered from exposure. Yet clothing was a worse torment, sticking to their skin like wet fruit peels left to rot on a sandy shore.

They began traveling at night, which was more hazardous but less debilitating. By day they stretched out on their ground cloth, sleeping when they could, making lazy love, or just lying in a stupor. Alena wanted to know all that had ever happened to him; she longed to store away his every thought and word. But the heat defeated her; sometimes she lay for hours, her damp palm in his, too exhausted to ask questions.

Several times he tried to soothe her troubled

spirit with platitudes, but only succeeded in annoying her.

"Things may work out for the best when we get back to Prima," he said one afternoon when they were lying side by side on their bellies in the shade of a gnarled green-trunked tree.

"Not likely, and you know it!" she said, her temper frayed by unrelenting heat. "You're horrid to even suggest any good can come of returning to that wretched planet! Or maybe you're pining for a space ship like a naughty boy scheming to get a new toy. I've lost all patience with you!" She reached over and swatted his hot, glistening buttocks until he retaliated with a burst of energetic tickling.

"I surrender!" she cried out, and she did.

When the sun sank low and a faint breeze cooled their overheated hides, they set off again, sluggish and heavyhearted.

One day they found safe but separate perches in a massive, low-branched tree, remembering the sharp-tooth serpents that sunned on the mud banks in the area. Before long she ached from sitting in a cramped position, but not having Garner beside her was a worse torment. She resolutely pushed thoughts of a long—and perhaps permanent—separation from her mind, but even in sleep she suffered from an overwhelming fear of losing him. How could she go on without her savage lover, without feeling his hot breath on her neck and his questing hands on her breasts? Could either of them survive apart after living as two halves of a couple joined by deepest passion and truest love?

An 11-day trek stretched into 15, and Garner knew he was as guilty as she was in prolonging it.

Sometimes he was afraid to make love to her, terrified he might lose control in his urgency and hurt her when desire clouded his mind and possessed his body. The closer he came to losing her, the greater his obsession with every facet of her intriguing nature and every part of her sensuous body.

He knew the die was cast. Rescue would come, and the vessel wouldn't return without High Yor's daughter. He thought of plans to feign their deaths and remain behind, but in his saner moments he knew he'd never condemn her to life on the primitive planet. Already foodstuffs from the last pod were nearly gone, and she'd never quite succeeded in masking her distaste for the red-blooded flesh they would need to survive if they stayed on Brona.

How could he care for her if the rains came and fever rotted their bodies and addled their minds?

They were so close to the stockade and the end of their life together, he felt like a man walking through quicksand, sucked down by every step, continuing only through hellish exertion.

"Give me the gift of one more night in your arms," she said when they were only hours from the stockade.

He didn't refuse. He couldn't.

They spread the ground cloth at dusk, hearing the distant howls of shriekers for the first time in many nights. Oddly, the eerie screams didn't affect him, and Alena laughed off her earlier fears.

The first time they made love it was primeval and savage, without tender words or soft caresses. She was hot and moist, as eager as he was to consummate their love in unforgettable ways. She raked his buttocks with her nails and arched her back to revel in his demonic assault. Their climax was searing, as shattering as the explosion of a star, and for an instant he thought he would never be able to move again.

"I love you, I love you, I love you," she cried out, thrashing and moaning in his arms while he anointed her spirit with passionate words and gentle kisses.

"This can't be our last night together," she said, sobbing dry-eyed until his efforts to comfort her carried them to new heights, less erotic but tender and deeply satisfying: the lovemaking of a world-weary pair reconfirming their faith in each other.

She dozed, and then he did, but never both together. They fought the oblivion of sleep, not wanting to waste a precious moment of their time alone together. The night was as dark as their despair, and they clung to each other, sometimes whispering wild plans to escape their bleak, separate destinies. He gave her the gift of words, telling her all the ways he loved her. She gave him the gift of silence, not begging him to do the unthinkable and escape into the mountains with her.

At dawn his sense of foreboding was overwhelming, making him so lethargic he had to struggle to lift his head from the ground. He wanted to make love again, to leave her with memories of his tenderness and caring, but he felt weak and drained, as though a water plant had driven a poisonous spine into his flesh again.

"Lie still," she said, and he smiled at the irony of her command.

He didn't know which gave him more pleasure: seeing her hover over him, the tip of her tongue caught between her lips in concentration and her breasts swaying like lush, ripe fruit, or feeling her hands creep down his belly and make a shy assault on his groin.

He thought he'd long ago passed beyond shyness or embarrassment on the bed of love, but the guileless pleasure she took in fondling his parts made him cover his face with his arms.

"I still don't understand how a tree trunk can sprout from a bush," she teased to cover the sadness they both felt. "I must be poorly schooled in the ways of living beings."

He couldn't speak for fear of showing weakness with tears, but he signed deeply when she spread her thighs and took him into her body.

Their mating was pure love. He'd never been more deeply satisfied.

The next day at dawn Alena woke first and sat watching Garner sleep. She loved this man more than life itself, and being without him was unthinkable. She put her fingers under his nostrils to feel the warmth of his breath, and stroked ringlets of dark hair spilling over his forehead. She couldn't endure an everlasting separation! Somehow there had to be a way for them to live out their lives together.

A strange broad-winged creature swooped down and dove into the murky waters of the river. It emerged in a few seconds, holding a squirming gray-black sea serpent in its beak. She watched with horrified fascination as the russet-red and brown predator settled on the bank and devoured its prey, then flew off toward the jungle. She'd never seen a sea serpent this close to the stockade. What instinct made them avoid this shore and gather on the distant mud flats to sun with many others of their kind? All her life she'd been praised for her intellect, yet she'd understood little of life until love for Garner had opened her eyes to the wonders of this primitive new world.

She didn't want to leave Brona. There had to be a way to survive here. Perhaps if another woman and her choice of mate or mates stayed too . . .

"What are you thinking, darling?" He sat up sleepily and pulled her into his arms.

"About you."

"And that's why you were frowning?" He nuzzled below her ear, took her lobe between his teeth, then filled her ear with his tongue, making her giggle and pull away.

"If you must know, I saw a hideous winged creature catch a sea serpent and swallow it alive."

"The way the fates are consuming us. There's no way to make this easy," he said, holding her against his chest, not letting her see his face. "I want you to leave for the stockade now. I'll follow in a few days."

"What use is it to go back separately? Everyone will know the truth!"

"They'll know we've been together, but they won't have to deal with it if we don't flaunt it."

"It's no use! Blaz won't let it pass!"

"Alena, listen to me." He put his hand under her chin and looked into her teary eyes. "You have the highest status on this planet. Who would dare accuse you of consorting with a Prola if there are no eyewitnesses to see us together?"

"But when you do come . . ."

"They'll be too excited about the probe to take any action against us."

"I want people to know I love you!"

"No good can come of it," he said miserably, kissing her eyelids to comfort her. "The quicker you go, the sooner I can follow. I'll be watching you from a distance, staying concealed until I'm sure you're safely in the stockade."

"You will come? This isn't a ruse? You're not

going back to the mountains alone?"

"I swear I'm not." He sealed his promise with a gentle kiss on her brow.

She walked toward the stockade, prepared to tell an elaborate tale of how she'd tried and failed to find Garner Rie, never for an instant expecting to be believed.

Her return was nothing like she'd expected. The survivors in the stockade were so demoralized, they scarcely took note of her return. No one asked questions, and Blaz only gave her a surly, hate-filled stare and stalked away.

When she began counting heads, she was dismayed to find only 26 of their number still living there. Of the women, only Velma Pitt was left. There had been 70 passengers and crew on the *Moon Courier*; 45 had landed safely on Brona.

She cornered Erasma alone as soon as she could. His beard was bushy white, and his eyes were darkly shadowed, whether from illness or fatigue she couldn't tell.

"Seven greasers are gone, probably for good. Roar is still here—he helps me all he can—but most have given up."

"Gullaner?"

"I'm sorry, Alena." He spoke in a kindly voice. "The captain beat him with an antenna for letting you get away."

"Oh, no! Is he . . ."

"No, no, he's young and strong. No doubt he's healed by now, but he went off with the other greasers the last time they raided the stockade."

"Raided?"

"No better way to put it. They took all the guns and knives, even Blaz's. You can bet he ranted and raved for days afterward! They stole what little food we had too. Worst of all, they had their way with poor Velma. Some wanted to take her across the river with them on the rafts from the pods, but that scoundrel Tacka has some superstition about crazy people being bad luck. Thank the fates you weren't here when they came!"

He shook his head, pursing pink lips that seemed too large for the rest of his shrunken face.

"The rest . . ."

"Fever. I think it's finally run its course for now. We've been here nearly half a year, you know, not that anyone bothers to notch a stick anymore."

"Where are you going?" She'd followed him outside the listing walls. "I have news only you can hear."

"I've been watching some pond grass. When it ripens, we may get enough grain of sorts to stockpile some for the rainy season. But I won't lie to you, Alena Yor. If fever comes again, not many of us will be strong enough to resist the infection, and so far none of the victims have recovered."

"Erasma, listen! I know you won't betray me. I've been with Garner Rie."

"I can't approve of that," he said dryly, "but I never doubted it."

"That's not the important thing! He found the probe and activated it. It's sending out distress signals even as we speak. There's a chance we'll be rescued!"

"Ah, I was afraid to hope. You're sure the signal is working?"

"Positive! Garner will be here in a few days to tell everyone else."

"I'll keep it to myself and let him have his moment," the old botanist said. "Prola or not, he deserves better than what's in store for him if we are rescued. I don't think Blaz will forget or forgive his executive officer for being a better man than he is. He's been like a man sitting in a bed of thistles since you defied him and ran off with Garner."

"Erasma, have you ever thought of staying here—beginning a new civilization on a new world?"

He shook his head solemnly. "It's true I don't have a family to go back to, but this world is still too savage for our kind. Most of them . . ." He gestured contemptuously toward the stockade. "Most are too traumatized to go any further than the banks of the stream, even though I desperately need hands for gathering food."

"But a few strong people could build a new world. . . ."

"I'm tired, Alena. I want to go home."

"You will!" She hugged the old man. "Garner is coming to lead us to a beautiful mountain valley near the probe, so we'll be easy to find if a ship comes."

"If you're right about the probe, a vessel will come. The first manned exploration of Brona was less than a year from readiness when we left Prima." He smiled for the first time since her return. "There are going to be bruised egos in the Space Service. We've robbed the first expedition of their moment in history by being the first of our species to land on an alien planet."

"Why does that seem so unimportant now?" she asked wearily.

Moments seemed like hours, and the slowness made her wait seem like an eternity. She tried to talk to Velma, but the medic was too withdrawn to reach, living in a private world of torment.

Three days passed, and they were the longest in Alena's life. She managed to struggle through them by throwing herself wholeheartedly into Erasma's food-gathering forays. Even with their number greatly diminished, they needed to carry a good supply of food on the trek to Moon Valley. The botanist had never given up his search for edible plants, and Alena was sure the others would be starving by now if it weren't for his efforts.

She woke on the morning of the fourth day, so anxious for Garner's return that she couldn't swallow the watery gruel cooked in a clay pot for their breakfast. She wouldn't let herself believe he'd broken his promise and gone back to the mountains alone. What could possibly delay him when he was so near the stockade? She thought of the sea serpents, and worried that they might be as poisonous as the plants in river.

She found excuses to search for food south of the stockade, hoping for a glimpse of Garner when he returned. By late afternoon she had a heavy basket full of edible berries that would be sweet and chewy when they dried, but she was frantic over Garner's continued absence.

Catton Sur supervised the meal preparation, as officious as ever even though he scarcely dared rush to the stream and back once daily. He had a team of three Guilders, Jonet, Fain, and Diez, who did the work, and Alena wasn't proud of her own caste, some of whom contributed nothing to the group's survival.

She ate mechanically, so disheartened she had to fight back tears. Just as she finished her ration of a cooked root Erasma called guma, Garner walked into the stockade carrying two large winged creatures like the one she'd seen catch and devour a sea serpent.

"I haven't returned empty-handed," he said to Catton Sur, handing him the dead game he'd roped together by their feet. "I haven't tasted their flesh, but it should give us a feast to celebrate our rescue."

"Rescue? What are you talking about, mister?" Blaz asked, stalking forward from the corner where he'd eaten his meal alone.

"I found a functional probe and started sending distress signals."

"That's a lie! It's not possible! You can't send signals on a probe without a keyboard."

"I gave him one," Erasma said, stepping forward and facing the captain.

"By whose authority? I didn't give you permission to take a keyboard, old man. You won't get away with this!"

"I think he will," Catton Sur said. "I want to hear about this."

Several other survivors shook off their lethargy and urged Garner to tell them more.

Alena hung on every word Garner said as though she hadn't shared in the quest for the probe. She was relieved to the depths of her soul to see him safe and sound.

"Our best chance is to be as close to the probe as possible," he concluded. "Based on distance alone, the soonest a vessel can get here is about twenty days from now. We can't know how long it will take to ready for launch, but we should start traveling to a valley near the probe as soon as possible. It's an eleven-day trek at a good pace." He glanced at the avid faces around him. "With a large group stopping to hunt for food, we should allow at least sixteen."

Was he remembering all the wonderful delays on their treks? He didn't meet her eyes, but the warmth in his voice told her how vivid his memories were.

"Survivors should never leave the pod site.

That's a basic Space Service rule," Blaz said angrily, his pale face cadaverous above his filthy tunic.

"The pods can't send transmissions through the electromagnetic shield, so the rescue ship's sensors won't detect us here. We need to be near the probe. I'll be leaving at dawn the day after tomorrow. All those who want to join me should be ready then."

"You're not in charge of these people!" Blaz said angrily, the hatred in his eyes alarming Alena more than his words.

"You could meet the rescue vessel and send them here," Catton Sur suggested.

"Surface vessels have limited cruising capacity," Erasma said. "None of us should chance being left behind by staying here. And remember, the shriekers were most dangerous just before the rainy season. I suspect they become more aggressive when they're mating and establishing nests, although most of what they do is still a mystery."

"We'll all go then," Catton Sur said, his face puckered as though he'd just swallowed a sour elixir.

"I knew a rescue ship would come," Blaz said to those assembled in front of the common hut. "There will be hell to pay for low-caste scum who don't know their place when it gets here." He gave Garner a malevolent look, and went into his makeshift shelter against one rickety wall of the stockade.

No one had thought to link her absence with Garner's. She wanted to proclaim her love publicly and be done with the artificial restrictions of the caste system, but she looked into his eyes and saw him begging for her discretion. Somehow, on this world or their home planet, she was determined they were going to be together. She would have to be patient, difficult as it was to be apart from him for any time at all.

That night she lay down in the ruins of a small hut she shared with Velma. Knowing Garner was near but forbidden to her, she felt even more lonely than she had before his arrival.

When she dozed, her dreams were so disturbing they woke her, although she couldn't remember the content. At last, even before she could see the first faint signs of dawn through an unrepaired section of the roof, she rose and went to the stream, stripping off her ragged tunic and scrubbing herself in water made tepid by the long, hot days.

She walked slowly back to the stockade, trying to steel herself not to seek out Garner. Oh, how she wanted to feel his arms around her! How she longed to feel his lips, alternating between tenderness and demand, pressing hot kisses on hers. She'd grown so accustomed to his lovemaking that just the thought of his body made her pulsate with desire.

"Please, darling, be strong for both of us," she whispered as she walked through the unsecured entrance to the stockade.

She wasn't the only restless sleeper. She nearly collided with a dark form that materialized in her path. The first gray streaks of dawn helped her see his face, and her heart thudded erratically as Garner held her away at arm's length.

"I couldn't sleep for thinking of you," he whispered.

"Nor could I. These past days have been a torment."

"The beginning of lifelong torture," he said sadly.

"Oh, Garner, I love you!"

She didn't plan it, but she dove into his arms, pulling his face down to meet hers in a kiss so sweet and passionate it clouded her mind.

"We can't. . . . " He pushed her away, his hard hands punishing her shoulders.

She heard the misery in his voice and turned to hurry to her own hut.

"I have you this time! You're a disgrace to your caste, Highness Yor!" Blaz said, stepping out of the shadows. "Sneaking out to couple with a Prola swine!"

He was thumping his palm with a silver rod she recognized as an antenna.

"You can't talk to me like that," she said without conviction.

"Your lover will beg for death before I'm through with him!"

"Stop there, Blaz," Garner said. "I won't let you make these accusations!"

"You won't let me!" Blaz shrieked, his face contorted by hatred. "This female has polluted her caste, rutting with a degenerate Prola!"

"You don't know what you're saying!" Garner argued, speaking reasonably in a low voice but watching with wary intentness.

"Are you carrying his bastard?" Blaz asked her. "Did he plant sub-human scum in the high and exalted daughter of High Yor? You don't deserve to be called Highness! You're walking filth, lower than joy-girls who spread their legs for pay!"

Alena was vaguely aware of others coming out of the huts, roused by Blaz's high-pitched accusations.

"Stop your tirade!" Garner demanded furiously. "You don't know what you're saying. You're a lunatic! You're imagining things because your own mind is a cesspool!"

"Think whatever you like. I'm a Space Service captain and your commander. It's my responsibility to enforce the laws all decent Primans embrace. You're guilty of defiling a high minister's daughter, Garner Rie. I hereby pass a military sentence of death on you!"

Alena stood paralyzed, too shocked to appeal to anyone for help in thwarting the berserk captain.

"It is my order that you execute yourself for the high crime of sexual congress with a high-caste female!"

"You're crazy!" Garner backed away while the watchers looked on in stunned silence.

"You are to carry out your own death sentence by piercing your jugular with this!" He waved the rod, and Alena was horrified to see he'd sharpened the end into a wicked point.

"You can't do this!" Roar protested, restrained from rushing forth by Erasma's urgent tug on his arm.

"This isn't a matter to settle here!" the botanist said.

"There's every precedent necessary to order the execution of a Prola who defiles a Scientifica while under military jurisdiction," Blaz declared. "As an executive officer bound by Space Service rules of conduct, Mister Rie, you stand condemned for the vile sin of fornicating with a high-caste woman. Execute my sentence immediately."

"Never!"

Garner had steadily backed up, with Alena staying by his side. Now a good 50 paces separated them from the captain.

"Blaz, this is an intolerable abuse of your power!" Erasma grabbed his arm, but Blaz turned on him, striking down the old man.

"You'll obey my orders now, Mister Rie, or I'll beat you senseless before I let you die!"

"You're insane!"

"Are you too cowardly for an honorable death?"

Blaz ran toward Garner and Alena, slashing at the air with his lethal antenna. He lunged, spittle running from the sides of his mouth and lunacy blazing in his pale eyes. Alena was horrified by his final descent into madness, but all she cared about was Garner. She stepped in front of him, but he pushed her away so hard she literally fell into Velma Pitt's arms. Blaz was within striking distance, armed with his sharply honed weapon, and for an instant she thought Garner would die. Then Garner suddenly sidestepped and knocked into Blaz with his shoulder to avoid his lethal thrust.

Blaz toppled over like a marionette suddenly cut from its strings, falling on the rod and driving it through the thin skin of his throat, straight into his jugular. He flopped—whether voluntarily or not, she didn't know—and lay on his side, clutching the rod embedded in his throat as his lifeblood spurted out.

Alena pushed the medic toward him, but Velma stood helplessly over him, all her medical training lost along with her will to live. Alena fell to her knees beside the captain and tried to staunch the flow, his blood spattering her until she recognized his death throes and moved back in horror.

Blaz was dead. Lon Weal and Vane Col were gone; Velma was as useless as an officer as she was an a medic. There was no one to speak out for Garner, no one to explain what really had happened. She looked into the faces surrounding her, terrified for Garner's sake.

"He was insane!" she cried out, standing and

trying to wipe her hand on her blood-soaked tunic. "You all know it!"

"Garner Rie acted mutinously," Catton Sur said, his voice raspy with fear. "He killed the captain."

"An insane, lunatic captain, who was a threat to us all!" she vehemently insisted.

"He can't assume command," Catton Sur said, "not when he's guilty of mutiny."

"Then Roar must!" she said, grasping at straws. "The chief engineer must assume command."

"I won't follow a Prola!" a voice called out.

"Nor I!"

It was like a rallying call, the high-caste survivors clinging to tradition instead of dealing with the horror of a lunatic captain dying by his own insanity.

"Stop this!" she said, standing before them and raising hands still red with Blaz's blood.

To her wonder, they grew quiet.

"I have the highest status of anyone on this world. I hereby take command of Brona. If anyone disputes my right to lead, let them speak now or later be subject to military discipline under the Space Service Code which we all swore to honor."

"Alena, are you sure you want to do this?" Erasma asked mildly. "We could meet in Council. . . ."

"No, only one thing matters now. Rescue! Everything else can be decided on Prima."

She heard nothing but relief and agreement, not a single voice disputing the right of a high-caste female to assume leadership.

"There's an order of execution on Garner Rie," Catton Sur reminded her.

"We need him to take us to the probe!" she insisted. "Roar, Jonet, Fain, and Diez, you're to guard him with your lives. No one is to harm Garner Rie. He will not be judged on this planet. Again I ask, does anyone dispute my authority to give this order?"

"It's your right," Catton Sur grudgingly agreed.

"Take him to Blaz's hut," she said to Garner's appointed guardians. "Everyone must be ready to leave at dawn tomorrow or be left behind."

"What about the greasers?" someone asked.

"They made their choice by turning against all of you and doing grievous harm to Officer Pitt. They've forfeited their chance to be rescued."

Murmurs of approval followed her as she rushed to the stream to scrub away the odious blood of Captain Hurex Blaz.

Chapter Sixteen

Garner had never loved Alena more than when she proclaimed herself commander of the survivors on Brona. In his eyes, she realized her own majesty at that moment and used her status with full understanding of the responsibilities it entailed. She became the leader her high caste entitled her to be.

He'd also never wanted to chastise her more than when she appointed guardians to watch his every move. He paced like a caged beast in the tiny hut, the entryway blocked by two Guilders who might better spend their time preparing for the trek. Awe for what she'd done tempered his anger, but he sorely wanted to make her repent for making him a prisoner.

Even more than that, he wanted her with him.

"I don't know who I am without her," he murmured under his breath, realizing he loved her not just for herself, but because she inspired him to be more than he was.

He could see stars in the night sky through open spaces in the roof when Roar came with food for his evening meal.

"I'll stand watch now," the chief engineer told the two Guilders, handing over a bowl of watery gruel with morsels of fruit.

"What's happening out there?" Garner asked, noticing his friend's uneasiness as he stood against the flimsy wall pulling on a strand of his rusty beard.

"She has those high-caste bastards working like field hands," Roar said. "I never thought to see the day when Catton Sur would get down on his knees to bundle supplies."

"I should be helping."

"There's nothing I can do about that," he said, his blunt, open face troubled. "Highness Yor is coming to see you."

"And you disapprove," Garner said, stung by the censure in his friend's voice.

"It would be safer for you to keep a bloody shrieker as a pet. It never turns out good, mucking with a high-caste bitch. If you want to cut out, I'll go with you."

"Thank you, Chief Roar," Garner said, clasping the other man's arms in a gesture of friendship. "I'm tempted, but . . ."

"Don't be hasty in saying no. Most of the renegades are good fellows. Tacka turned them against the passengers, but you could win them back, especially if you brought both women with you. None of those smug high-caste parasites has guts enough to stop you," he said contemptuously.

"I can't leave," Garner said sadly, knowing that more than his promise to Alena kept him from escaping into the wilderness.

Roar was silent for several minutes, then said, "I understand. The government would use it as an excuse to ban all Prolas from the Space Service. But I don't trust what they might do if you go back to Prima."

"Blaz was mentally unfit to command. Every person here can testify to that. If the witnesses tell the truth, I have nothing to fear."

"If they do," Roar said skeptically. "But I respect your decision."

Garner didn't hear Alena approach, but when she quietly told Roar to leave them for a few minutes, he was hard put to keep from rushing to her.

"So you've come to gawk at your prisoner," he said gruffly when she came into the hut.

"No, I've come to have words with my lover."

She sounded so contrite, he wanted to sweep her into his arms, but Highness Alena Yor was now his commanding officer—and his jailer.

"Free me, and perhaps your lover will have words for you."

"Darling, please!"

She touched his arm, making his flesh tingle and eroding his resistance. But he couldn't let himself forget she was holding him captive.

"I was afraid what the others might do. This was the only way I could keep you safe," she said.

"Safe! The others expect you to drag me back to Prima in chains. What crime have I committed in your eyes, Highness Yor?"

"Maybe you enchanted me! I must be under the influence of some magical potion to love a lout like you!"

"At last the truth! You think I'm a lout—not refined enough for a minister's pampered daughter!"

He was thankful for the darkness. If he had to look into her warm brown eyes, he couldn't hold onto the last remnants of his anger.

"Do stop this, Garner Rie! If you need proof of my feelings, then run away with me this instant. I have bundles of food and supplies in my hut. We can be far from here before anyone suspects us."

"Roar will know."

"I'm sure he won't do anything to betray you. He might follow us, but he won't betray us to the others."

"I can't hide you away on Brona," he said regretfully. "If the renegades find us and kill me . . ."

"It's a huge planet!"

"And we're unlike any other creatures inhabiting it. We can't hide from anyone who really wants to track us. We leave a trail wherever we go. Tacka and his followers are ahead of us in developing wilderness skills, and they have most of the weapons. Eventually they'll find us, no matter what we do to evade them."

"Garner, I don't care about all this! I won't be separated from you!"

"Do you think I want to go on living without you?"

His anger forgotten, he crushed her against him, punishing her lips as though he could brand them with his kisses.

"A short number of days with you is better than eons apart!" she cried.

"No, Alena, no! I activated the probe for your sake. I won't jeopardize your chance for rescue!"

"Garner, I'm afraid. . . . "

"You have more courage than anyone I've ever known!"

"That's not true! I fear so many things!"

"You face your fears and overcome them one by one. That's what courage is!"

"If you won't run away with me . . ."

"I won't, my darling. I can't be swayed on this."

"Then run away and save yourself! Blaz sentenced you to death!"

"Blaz was insane!"

"Yes, but Catton Sur is saying the captain's judgment against you should be carried out. As long as we're here, I think the other survivors will obey me. They're still afraid of offending a minister's daughter, but once we're back on Prima . . ."

"I'll have to take my chances with a Board of Review."

"You can't rely on the Space Service! The Bellicosa who serve in it are too entrenched in the evils of the caste system! I won't have you judged by people still deluded by false values."

"Alena." He held her away from him, feeling her slender shoulders trembling under his touch. "It's no use. If I desert now, my caste will pay a terrible price. I'll be used as an example to prove the folly of advancing Prolas into responsible positions. The Space Service might ban all Prolas from space flights and train only Guilders to serve as greasers. Tacka's and the other greasers' defection is blow enough to my caste, and I have to consider my family as hostages. I won't have them suffering for my desertion."

"Then we have nothing more to say to each other," she told him sadly, turning from him and leaving the squalid hut.

He felt as if his heart were being clawed apart within his chest cavity. Tears, screams, even vile curses would have been easier to bear than the profound sorrow in her voice.

Hot tears welled up behind his eyes, and he sank to his knees, covering his face in agony, knowing he had to accept their separation, however painful and bitter. Not only did his honor demand it, he had to be sure Alena would return to the world where she belonged.

The trek began the next morning. Numb with misery, Garner gave his oath not to escape. He swore he would lead them to the probe, and in return he was allowed to move unrestrained among the survivors. He preferred to keep aloof as much as possible, walking 20 paces ahead of the others. He was willing to show them the way, but in his solitude he relived every precious moment of his time alone with Alena.

Catton Sur whined and made them drive away the sea serpents with flaming torches before he would pass the mud bank where they sunned. He whimpered and had to be lowered on a rope to the bottom of the great falls. Garner didn't speak directly to him or smile at his ludicrous behavior, but he sensed Catton was blaming him for his loss of esteem with the group.

Alena was a true leader. She gave orders for rations to be distributed, arbitrated disputes, and set the pace for each day's travel.

Several times Garner saw her pacing restlessly while all but the lone sentry slept. He longed to go to her with all his heart, but he suffered untold agonies rather than approach her. They'd said their final good-byes.

By the time they reached Moon Valley, supplies were nearly exhausted and tempers were frayed. Stockade life had weakened them; even Roar and Erasma were exhausted by the 17-day trek. The small-finned creatures in the stream made meager meals when divided among all the survivors, and even the abundant fruit of the linneas acropos was becoming scarce.

Several times Alena approached him and seemed ready to speak, then hastily retreated as though she couldn't bring herself to confront him. By the tenth day of waiting for rescue in Moon Valley, she'd organized hunting parties, setting an example by eating whatever meat they brought back to roast.

Was she trying to prove she would do anything to survive alone with him on Brona? He admired her so much his heart swelled with pride, but he knew the planet would kill all of them if rescue didn't come soon. He saw the spore of larger breasts, and made it his responsibility to be sure fires burned all night. It was only a matter of time before predators learned how weak they were and started picking them off.

Meanwhile, he made a spear by peeling bark from a straight branch and chipping at a rock until it had a sharp point. Roar and several Guilders came to him for help in making weapons of their own, but there was little talk of anything but rescue among the others.

Sometimes he let himself dream of a new society on Brona. Alena was a natural leader now that she'd found her true self, and he had confidence in his own survival skills. But he had serious doubts that many of the others could adjust to a lifelong sojourn on the primitive planet. When Erasma warned them to prepare for the rainy season, they ignored him, calling him an overly cautious old man, and did little except watch and hope for the arrival of a space vessel.

* * *

Alena watched the sky with dread: Rescue would make it far more difficult to see her beloved. Even though they seldom spoke, she lived for the moments when his eyes met hers. Every glimpse of his well-loved face was like balm on a festering wound. How could she continue to live if they were separated by the old life they'd left behind on Prima?

The days grew shorter, and the nights were so cold the survivors huddled together for warmth, using every scrap of fabric as ground covers and blankets.

"Feathers are warm, and the skins of beasts repel water," Erasma dourly suggested, "but you'll have to hunt now. No telling what this valley will be like when the rainy season begins."

Some days Alena thought she'd go mad trying to keep the survivors alive. Even the Guilders, usually hard workers, were so focused on watching for a rescue ship, she had to compel them to hunt for food and work on building a rude shelter of stones and mortar under Erasma's direction.

She wouldn't let anyone fire the lone gun they possessed, the one confiscated from Garner. She'd seen the beasts in the stream and the spore of other monsters, and it was only a matter of time before they would have to defend themselves again. Each night sentries kept large fires burning, even though the high-caste survivors complained unceasingly about the necessity of gathering branches to use as fuel.

Garner warded off starvation for all of them by hunting with his spear and knife, taking no one but Roar on his expeditions. Erasma dried and preserved the scanty leftovers, becoming more impatient with his fellow survivors with each passing day.

Alena lost all track of time, but it seemed like a hundred days since they'd trekked to Moon Valley. Had they miscalculated the time it took to travel from Prima to Brona? Had the ship come and left before they were close enough to the probe to be found?

Had the idyllic days and nights she'd spent with Garner made them miss the rescue vessel? Her spirit lightened with each passing day. If the ship didn't come, her obligation to the other survivors would end. She could be with Garner, freely and openly. The restrictions and traditions of Prima would be meaningless.

She slept little and rose at dawn one cold morning, hoping for a glimpse of her beloved while he was still asleep. Instead she found him by the stream, staring upward at the gray sky.

He turned when he heard her, and his face made her want to weep.

"It's here," he said solemnly.

"You must be mistaken! I see nothing but hazy gray sky."

"I've been watching for several hours, my darling," he said softly. "I can tell the difference between a ship and the stars."

"No, you're wrong, Garner! We missed the rescue ship! I'm sure of it!"

"Would that we had." He looked away, but not before she saw his deep blue eyes glistening with moisture.

"This is our last chance, Garner! We can run to high ground, lose ourselves in the mountains forever!"

He shook his head and wouldn't look at her.

"I'm not afraid of anything when I'm with you!" she told him.

"I won't watch you starve. I won't put your life in jeopardy."

"You'll find food! We'll hide!"

"We would become food ourselves sooner or later. I've seen evidence."

"What evidence?" she asked.

"I found Gullaner's caste bracelet while I was hunting."

"He took it off. It doesn't mean anything!"

"He wouldn't take it off unless he planned to be an outlaw for the rest of his life. You know what it means to remove the bracelet. It's a serious crime, one that means total banishment from the society of all Primans."

"He just happened to come this way and tossed it where you found it."

"No, he tried to follow us. He must have regretted going with Tacka. He was attacked and savaged by some kind of beast with teeth. I found remains."

"Poor Gullaner!"

"He was young, strong, and armed with a loaded pistol he didn't have a chance to use. This planet is still too savage for our kind."

"For me, you mean! You don't for one moment doubt your ability to survive here."

"Look." He pointed upward.

At first all she saw was a faint silver sliver. Then she realized what was happening. A mother ship, a vessel not unlike the *Moon Courier,* had launched one landing craft and then another.

She ran into Garner's arms and clung to him with all her strength, pressing frantic kisses on his throat and standing on the tops of his feet to cling to his rigid shoulders.

"They're coming," a hoarse female voice said, tugging on Alena's arm.

She stared in wonder at Velma Pitt, amazed to hear her speak after countless days of trance-like silence.

"Don't be found together," Velma warned, her voice raspy from disuse.

"She's right," Garner said, moving away from Alena and stalking off without another word.

Alena stood frozen for what seemed an eternity, only dimly aware of Velma's arm on her shoulders. The survivors were hysterical with joy, waving and shouting at the slowly descending landing vessels, cheering when bright yellow chutes billowed out to slow their descent. Part of her mind recorded the moment when the first craft touched down, its large shock-absorbing legs like those of the *Moon Courier*'s pods but much larger and more sturdy. She saw the rocket motors on the bottom, the power sources that would return them to the mother ship, taking her back to the stifling, loveless life she dreaded.

Survivors surrounded the first landing craft, and the hatch opened. A tall, slender male dressed in a black flight suit and helmet emerged.

She watched, hardly daring to breathe, while the man took off his helmet and revealed a lean, stern face with piercing blue eyes and a thick mane of silver hair. First Minister Stanko Yor set foot on Brona; her father had come for her.

From that moment on, everything that happened seemed like part of one long nightmare. The crew of the rescue ship was authorized to spend ten days on the planet, and each one was a torment to Alena. Even after seeing her father, she desperately wanted to run away with Garner, but she rarely caught a glimpse of him in the temporary city of tents. When she finally went aboard for the trip back to Prima, she wasn't even sure he was on the ship.

The *Space Courier,* sister ship of the *Moon Courier,* was larger than the lost vessel and had been built to accommodate three landing craft and sufficient fuel to return to Prima, as well as ample supplies for a long sojourn on Brona. But in spite of its enormous size, Alena's stateroom was a tiny cubicle where she had to fight back feelings of claustrophobia whenever the door was shut.

Her father's attitude changed once they were headed home. On Brona, he'd embraced her with concern, then beamed his approval because she'd taken command. Once aboard the vessel with the terrain of the primitive planet fading from sight, he became an interrogator, determined to debrief her on every aspect of her "adventure."

"Tell me," he said, "why do you think two Prolas stayed with their betters instead of running off and saving their hides?"

"They had no reason to run away," she said, irritated by her father's tone and words. "Mister Rie and Chief Roar aren't guilty of any crime."

"Catton Sur tells me otherwise in Rie's case. He said Garner Rie cold-bloodedly killed his commanding officer. Catton witnessed it, as did all the survivors."

"Blaz was a lunatic! If Garner—Mister Rie—hadn't left the stockade and found the probe, we wouldn't have been rescued. Blaz resented his success."

Her father made her go over every detail so many times she wanted to scream, but still he had more questions about the events on Brona. Worse, he insisted on confining Garner in a lower-deck cubicle, treating him as a prisoner on Catton Sur's say-so.

"Catton Sur was so cowardly, he disgraced his caste and his gender. Why don't you believe your daughter instead of him?" she pleaded.

High Yor frowned. She knew he was unaccustomed to arguments presented by his daughter. He was too solicitous of her well-being to rebuke her harshly, but she saw doubt and suspicion in his eyes.

She wasn't well. Food repelled her, and she lost the contents of her stomach with distressing regularity. There was no pleasant lounge for passengers to enjoy the heavens on this more utilitarian ship, and her only diversion was wandering the cheerless corridors, hoping for a glimpse of Garner. His door was always closed; he was lost to her as surely as if he'd elected to stay behind on Brona.

The voyage lasted an eternity, and by the time they boarded the landing craft to go down to Prima's Space Control Center, she couldn't remember how it felt not to be nauseous, heartsick, and miserable.

She had the firm concrete landing strip under her feet when she finally saw Garner. He was being led from the hatch of the second landing craft, his dark hair in wild disarray and his lower face dark with bristles. She swayed and felt her stomach churn. Then the ground come up to meet her. She blacked out in a vortex of furiously swirling dots of light.

She awoke coughing and pushed away the hand holding a vial with wicked-smelling fumes under her nose.

"Are you all right?" Her father's voice seemed to come from a great distance.

She couldn't answer. Her mind was locked on the awful vision of Garner emerging from the hatch, his hands and feet shackled with the flexible but unbreakable metal cable used to restrain criminals.

"You can't arrest him!" she finally cried out.

"My daughter has been ill," High Yor was saying to someone she couldn't see. "I'm afraid she's delirious. I want her transported to my home immediately. I'll bring in private consultants to see to her welfare."

She felt a sharp prick in her hip and realized they were sedating her. She tried to protest, but a mantle of darkness pushed her into oblivion.

The next time she awoke, she recognized the pale blue ceiling with its starry motif; she was lying in her own bed, but there was nothing familiar about the face hovering over her or the pain in her hand where a tube was putting yellow liquid into her vein.

"How many fingers am I holding up, Highness Yor?"

She looked beyond the chunky digits hovering over her nose into a round, moist face with thick lenses.

"You seem to have the proper number for our species," she said, beginning to remember the rude treatment she'd received after landing.

"High Yor wants her to have total rest," an authoritarian voice said. "Is the sedative ready?"

"No! Wait!" she protested loudly, but to no avail. She felt a hard jab on her exposed backside and fought frantically against oblivion, knowing she would lose.

Chapter Seventeen

Alena awoke hungry for sensations, needing to see, hear, and feel evidence she was still alive. The ceiling-high windows in her bedchamber allowed sunlight to stream over the shimmering white canopy above the bed. The soft rustle of the window hangings as the wind stirred them and the satiny softness of the bed sheets against her bare legs were reassuringly familiar, but she was still too groggy to understand what had happened to her.

Slowly she began to remember. The tube was gone, but a big purple bruise on her hand was proof she hadn't imagined the solution dripping into her vein. She pulled herself up, and was painfully reminded of the injections that had robbed her of consciousness.

She sat and swung her legs over the edge of the bed, surprised for a moment by the contrast between the plush white rug and her golden brown feet.

"Oh!"

She had to lie back on the mound of pillows, too dizzy to follow her instincts and rush from the room. She closed her eyes to wait for her head to stop spinning, wondering if her whole body was still bronze from Brona's sun. Had she lain there long enough for her tanned skin to fade?

Garner, where are you? she thought in panic, remembering him shackled like a common criminal. She had to speak to the authorities! Catton Sur was a spiteful coward for speaking against the man who saved them all from almost certain death.

Her father came into the room and smiled at her. "My dear, I'm happy to see you looking so much better."

"Why did you keep me sedated?" she asked angrily.

"You weren't yourself when we landed. I feared for your mental health." He was wearing a robe of pale blue brocade that hung from his shoulders to his sandal-clad feet, and she was struck by the contrast between the warm color of the cloth and the coldness in his eyes.

"I don't believe that! You can't possibly think I'm a lunatic."

"Your actions were questionable," he said sternly, reminding her of the many times when his frown had reduced her to abject repentance for trivial misdemeanors. "I thought it would be best for your reputation—"

"For yours, you mean!"

"Best if you were allowed to rest until you had some perspective on what happened on Brona."

"I know the truth! That's all that matters!"

"Alena, listen to me," he said harshly. "It's unthinkable for you to become involved in the trial of a Prola."

"Garner Rie is going to be tried?"

"Assuredly so, but it's no concern of yours. You've had a terrible experience."

"No! No, I haven't! I was the acting commander on Brona. Everything that happened there is important to me!"

"Alena, you surprise me. You're making a difficult situation worse. I forbid you to involve yourself in the trial of Garner Rie. That is my final word."

Alena met his icy blue eyes, so unlike her own warm brown ones inherited from her mother. Once she'd loved this man dearly, showering affection on her only living parent. Now all she felt was pain and disappointment because he cared nothing about the fate of an innocent man.

"I think you should occupy your mind by pursuing advanced studies," he said. "When you're stronger and more yourself, we'll decide how to channel your intellect into a new field."

"I have a calling. I'm a cartographer," she protested, astonished that her father was suggesting she pursue another career.

"I blame myself for letting you become involved in an unsuitable discipline."

"Unsuitable—"

"Hear me out," he interrupted, walking over to the huge globe hanging on chains from the ceiling. "Look at our planet." He laid his hands on the single huge continent that accounted for much of the land mass on Prima. "The civilized world has been mapped for centuries. So much sea, so little land," he said, speaking for all Primans who regretted the scarcity of habitable land.

"The Outlands . . ." she started to say.

"A worthless chain of islands with hellish climate and disease-ridden savages." He laid his hands on territory that stretched from the equatorial region to the southern pole. "Useful only as a place for the Uncasted to die in misery."

"The largest island is a third the size of our continent. It must have some useful resources," Alena said, amazed she was contradicting her father without a qualm of guilt.

"Irrelevant!" He whacked the flat of his hand on the globe and set it into motion, swinging on its chains in a blur of dark blue, the color of the sea. "I should never have let you travel in space. Others can map Bedir."

"I'll make my own plans," she said, even though she acknowledged to herself how little her old ambitions mattered. Let her father talk about her future if it distracted him. She had no interest in a life that didn't include Garner.

He left in anger, telling her the servant Boota would see to her needs. The woman must have been right outside the door, because she presented herself immediately. The dour, sandy-haired Prola never smiled and seldom spoke more than a few words; she was the last person Alena wanted as her personal servant.

"Where is Nita?" she asked, missing the cheerful young woman who'd been her number-one attendant before the moon flight.

"Married."

"To whom?"

"Pesta Falm."

"The head gardener's son? The one who works at the Hall of Justice? I thought Nita loathed him!"

"Her father said she had to," Boota said, squinting through her tiny eyes and nodding with satisfaction as though obedience to a male parent was the pinnacle of virtue. "Now she works at the prison."

Alena understood why her father had chosen Boota to serve her. She wasn't a sympathetic listener and would never be a friend as Nita had been. But it would take more than a glum servant for her father to break Alena's spirit.

She recovered quickly in the next few days, furious when she realized she'd been sedated for eight long days and nights. The nausea that helped make life on the *Space Courier* a living hell was gone, and she did everything possible to regain her strength.

Her father had removed the tela-machine from her room, and when she searched the spacious house, she found all the others were nonfunctioning. She couldn't activate a single screen to bring her news of the world outside her father's mansion.

She walked in the meticulously landscaped gardens to strengthen her legs, taking little pleasure in the orderly plots of pastel flowers or the geometrically trimmed hedges. She missed the lush wilderness of Brona, but mostly she yearned for the wonderfully unfettered life she'd shared with Garner.

The luxuries of her home seemed pretentious. She took no interest in the spacious closets full of elaborate gowns, remembering instead the crude garments she'd stitched with her own hands. She had no appetite for the elegantly prepared food served in her chamber. Everything in her father's white stone dwelling seemed like a stage setting: thick plush carpets in shades of white, ivory, and pale blue; walls covered with classical paintings glorifying Prima's past mounted in heavy gold frames; delicate furniture made of rare woods and polished daily to maintain their sheen; chairs and reclining seats upholstered in embroidered floral patterns. The beauty surrounding her mocked the turmoil in her soul.

She had to find out what was happening to Garner. As she regained her health, she couldn't ignore certain signs. She might be carrying a babe, a child that would forever link her fate to his.

She seldom saw her father, and their brief encounters were no more cordial than formal exchanges between strangers. He spent his days at the ministry, the majestic hub of political life in the capital city of Danica.

As a member of the Scientifica, Alena could summon a private conveyance to take her to the center of the city at any time, but she didn't want to ride through the crowded ghettos surrounding the city in one of the conspicuous bullet-shaped land crafts. Instead she walked for 30 minutes and waited to board the trama, a public conveyance that operated on an electrified ribbon of steel recessed between concrete guardrails. The long passenger tube was nearly empty when she entered it, but its rear sections quickly filled with lower-caste riders swarming into the inner city from their respective districts.

Closest to the city and poorest of all, the Prola ghettos were a maze of crooked, unpaved streets and haphazardly built dwellings in danger of collapse whenever there was an earth tremor. Today the poverty and decay she viewed through the window of the trama affected her like a whip lashing at her conscience. A naked babe, so dirty she longed to scoop him up and bathe him, was playing in an alleyway, contesting with a furry creature for a meatless bone. For the first time in her life, she felt ashamed of her father. How could First Minister Stanko Yor justify owning ornamental gardens so spacious it took the better part of two hours to circle them when children were scrapping in the dirt with animals for bits of food?

Garner, dearest love, is this what you couldn't bring yourself to explain to me? Her eyes grew misty as she thought of a feisty, dark-haired child fighting to put ghetto life behind him.

With a final burst of speed, the trama climbed the slope to the heart of the city, a complex of gleaming white buildings constructed of great blocks of stone. It stopped in a low-roofed terminal, and she walked with others to the central square.

The great white columns and majestic statues no longer awed her. She scarcely noticed the polished green tiles underfoot or the many sparkling fountains with water spilling from the mouths of mythical creatures carved in granite. Garner was a prisoner somewhere in the sprawl of public buildings, and she had to find a way to learn what was happening to him.

The Ministry of Information occupied a lofty building with a pyramid of steps leading to the entrance. She stopped at the top and looked back. A burly man in a gray tunic and dark trousers paused halfway up the steps, and she realized he'd left the trama just after she had. She quickly reversed her course, hurried back down the steps, and dashed across the open square. She was wearing a long-sleeved blue tunic over white trousers, her hair covered by a filmy black scarf tied under her chin. She'd hoped to pass as a lower-caste laborer, since high-caste women seldom wandered the inner city unattended. Now it seemed her masquerade was pointless. The burly man followed, keeping his distance but never letting her outdistance him.

Her father had her under surveillance!

She slowed her pace, but inside she was frantic. How much did her father know about Garner? Did he suspect she loved him? Had she spoken in her drug-induced state? Had he questioned other survivors and learned about her long absence at the same time Garner was away from the stockade?

How could she make contact with Garner without being restrained by her father? He'd already shown a ruthless side that shocked her, keeping her sedated and cutting off communications into the house. What means would he use to keep his daughter from disgracing him for the sake of a Prola lover?

Just when she was ready to accept the hopelessness of her quest, she thought of poor Nita, married to a man she despised. Boota said she worked at the prison. Alena's heart ached for her former servant and companion, yanked from a congenial position to work with a brutish husband. What was she doing in the prison? Cleaning? Cooking? As a Prola, no doubt she'd been assigned some lowly task.

What was more natural than searching out a well-loved former servant to be sure she was all right?

Alena felt a stab of guilt: She'd been too anxious about Garner to think of Nita, even though they'd been together since childhood when Nita's mother was a kitchen servant in High Yor's house.

Now Alena had a legitimate mission. She walked boldly up the steps to the Hall of Justice, a lofty white-pillared structure set on the highest of six hills holding public buildings.

She uncovered her hair, pulling out the pins to let it fan out over her back. Now it was urgent she be recognized.

"I'm Highness Alena Yor. I want to know the whereabouts of my former servant, Nita Tan, wife of Pesta Falm," she said to a somber-faced civil servant at the reception desk.

The man took off his eyeglasses, wiped them on his sleeve, and replaced them before answering.

"Now, please," she said impatiently. "I'm not accustomed to waiting for a Guilder to wipe his spectacles."

"A thousand pardons, Highness Yor. You took me by surprise. I thought you were an illusion."

"I'm no illusion, nor will your chastisement be imaginary if you keep me waiting any longer." She'd never spoken so rudely to a member of a lower caste, and she was ashamed, in spite of her great need to intimidate him into cooperating. She turned slightly, just enough to confirm the burly man was still nearby, lounging by the door and pretending to look beyond her.

The man behind the desk punched a keyboard, smiling with relief when he found the information she wanted.

"Nita Tan-Falm is on duty as a custodian in the prison."

"I wish to see her. Immediately."

"I'll have to consult with the prison master and—"

"Just do it!" she snapped, glancing once again at her pursuer. Now that she was this close to seeing Nita, she didn't want him to do anything that would interfere. Nita was her only hope: Who would know more about the inmates in a prison than one of the custodians?

Finally it was arranged. The civil servant escorted her to a small room two levels down and opened the door with a courtly gesture.

She smiled warmly and touched his arm as she entered the room. "Thank you, friend."

"Highness!" Nita cried out in joy, and flung herself into Alena's arms. "I thought I'd never see you again!"

"And I thought I'd see you the moment I returned!" She hugged her, feeling a surge of joy for the first time since returning to Prima. "Tell me, Nita, how did this happen?"

"My father . . ." She spread her arms helplessly. "I tried to resist. He—hurt me."

"Oh, my poor girl. If only I'd been here!"

"You couldn't have done anything. It was his right to agree to a marriage contract. I'm just so glad to see you!"

"You're so pale. And your hair. Why is it so short?" She stroked the pale blond curls, unable to believe even a lout like Pesta would rob Nita of her long, beautiful mane.

"It's a prison rule, so inmates can't use long hair to drag custodians close to the bars when we're mopping corridors."

"You don't belong here!"

"Pesta wants me to work where he does."

"Are you . . ." She couldn't bring herself to ask if the wan-faced girl was happy. "Are you all right, Nita? Is there anything I can do for you?"

She shook her head sadly. "I'll never love him, but he doesn't beat me unless I disobey."

"I'll help you get an order of separation."

"I've thought of that, but I wouldn't be free of him without a legal divorce. It would cost more than I earn in three years, and Pesta takes all my earnings."

"There has to be a way. . . ." But even as she

said it, she knew Nita's situation was as desperate as her own. High Yor would never agree to pay for a former servant's divorce, and Alena didn't have funds of her own.

"Just seeing you again is wonderful!" Nita said.

"I need your help, Nita. My father doesn't want me to know about the trial of Garner Rie, but I desperately want to know what's happening to him. Have you seen him?"

"No, he's in a solitary detention cell, but none of the custodians believe he's guilty of murder."

"Murder!" Alena staggered back and sat on one of the metal chairs to keep from collapsing. "He can't be charged with murder!"

"They say he killed his superior officer," Nita said, kneeling in front of Alena and rubbing her wrists. "Captain Hurex Blaz."

Somehow Alena got home, not caring whether she was followed or not.

Garner needed her, but she didn't know how to help. If she testified that Blaz's death was an accident, survivors like Catton Sur could accuse her of consorting with a Prola, a crime some thought more heinous than murder. No one would believe what she said if it came out Garner was her lover. He would be blamed for having sexual congress with a high-caste woman, and this could be construed as another motive for killing Blaz: to avoid the captain's punishment for flaunting caste law. There was no way Alena could explain their long absence at the same time, not with witnesses like Catton Sur to damn her.

From what Nita had told her, she realized the trial would be a national sensation. A Prola officer was accused of causing the death of his commander. It didn't matter that his hand hadn't inflicted the death blow. His refusal to obey Blaz by killing himself had led to the final confrontation and Blaz's death.

No matter how twisted and prejudiced the testimony of Catton Sur and others might be, there was no way for Garner to refute it without witnesses on his behalf. Who would step forward for his sake? Roar? Even if he were allowed to testify, no one would take the word of another Prola. Erasma respected Garner as a man, but he'd disapproved of their love. His lone voice wouldn't be enough to save Garner, but he could be compelled to give a damaging account of the time they'd spent together. She couldn't pin any hope on the aging botanist.

Garner could be executed. She lived with this dark horror every day after visiting Nita, and suffered from terrifying nightmares at night. She would gladly die in his place; she preferred dying by his side to going on without him, but this choice was denied her. There was no longer any doubt: She was carrying his child in her womb.

Thirty days passed, then 40, and she gleaned what news she could from servants' gossip. Her father avoided her, easy for him to do under the guise of urgent state business. She could come and go as she pleased, but never without being followed.

At last a date was set for the trial. Because it was a court-martial, the military denied access to the public and to the information-purveyors of the city. She started going every day to the Hall of Justice, standing outside with the crowds waiting for scraps of news doled out by a Space Service spokesman.

Each day the spokesman came out on the steps

and summarized the events of that day's part of the trial.

"Testimony today indicated the mother of Captain Hurex Blaz was officially banished by her family for consorting with a male of the Prola caste," the spokesman said one day, his voice droning on without a shred of emotion.

Alena felt a glimmer of hope: Surely the Tribunal of Seven who were judging Garner would see that Blaz was prejudiced against him from the beginning.

"Prola scum!" a voice near her cried out.

"That's what comes of not keeping them in their place," a gray-haired matron said, her face contorted by hatred.

Alena couldn't believe it! She was hearing a groundswell of approval for Blaz, as though his mother's tragic love affair excused his lunatic behavior.

"My darling Garner," she cried out as she rushed away from the mob congregating outside the Hall of Justice. "How can I help you?"

She paced her room for hours when she got home, finally so exhausted she lay on her bed in a stupor. She could feel the gentle swell of her belly; she couldn't keep her condition a secret much longer. She would have to tell her father, much as she hated the thought of a confrontation with him.

The next day she went again to stand outside the Hall of Justice, waiting for crumbs of news from the Space Service spokesman. She watched from the crowd when the heavy doors swung open and a witness was rushed in under heavy guard. Velma Pitt was supported by two Space Service guards in black tunics and trousers, both wearing the thick gold bracelets of the Bellicosa. Velma looked frail and wasted, a mere shadow of the robust medic who'd served on the *Moon Courier*. Alena wanted to rush forward and beg her for news of Garner, but the two guards angrily repelled several people who tried to approach her.

Alena realized she had stood outside too long, dying inch-by-inch, waiting for reassuring news which never came. She had to see Garner. Somehow she had to gain access to the prison, and it had to be done secretly so her father wouldn't hear of it and take measures against Garner.

That night, after all the servants were in their own quarters, she dressed in black and covered her head with a hood, arming herself with a sharp knife from the cook's utensils. She'd never walked alone at night on Prima; she'd never entered the Prola ghetto on foot with or without an escort. She boarded the last trama to run before the curfew, getting off at a location Boota had reluctantly described. She didn't trust her—or any of her father's servants—but hopefully Boota believed Alena's bluff that she would have her sent away if she said a word to anyone.

She hadn't been prepared for the pungent odors of the ghetto, the smell of rotting garbage, raw sewage, and desperate poverty. No matter how hard she tried, she couldn't shake off the fear that made her quiver at every sound. She'd survived encounters with shriekers and water monsters, but they were mindless killers, acting on instinct. The dangers of the ghetto were just as frightening, and she knew there were hate-crazed Prolas who would gladly risk death for the chance to avenge themselves on her caste by raping and murdering her.

Yet she had to find Nita.

She tried to conceal her shock when she saw the tar-paper shack where Pesta had brought his bride. It was the worst dwelling on a rutted dirt street that stank of rotting flesh. She knocked softly on the graying wood of the door, holding her breath until Nita opened it a crack, held up a light, and looked out warily.

"Highness Yor! Come in! Oh, it's madness for you to come here. Don't you realize—"

"I'm desperate, Nita! Only you can help me!"

"I can't even help myself," she wailed, setting down the small oil lamp she'd brought to the door.

Alena tried not to see the abject poverty in the shabby single room. She tried to pretend the sleeping mat on the floor wasn't rumpled from many nights of restless slumber—or worse.

"Where's Pesta?" she asked urgently.

"He has another woman!" Nita started weeping as though her heart was broken.

"You said you despise him. Why are you crying?"

"I loathe him! He knocked me down and kicked me black and blue!"

"Then why . . ."

"He wanted me to go to you and beg enough money for a divorce. He's found a widow who inherited her husband's franchise for cleaning the public fountains. She'll marry him if he can free himself of me."

"Is that what you want?"

"Oh, yes! I want to go live with my brother's family in the rural sector. My sister-by-marriage has a cousin . . . but I won't beg money from you!"

"You won't need to. I'll find the amount you need if you'll help me see Garner Rie. Nita, I have to sneak into the prison. Will Pesta help if I give you enough for a divorce?"

"He will," she said bitterly. "And if he tries to betray you, I'll see he's no use to the widow."

Just before dawn Alena followed Nita through a maze of streets littered with rubbish and foul alleys where the homeless slept huddled against walls. When they emerged from the ghetto near a trama station, she hugged her friend and boarded the first conveyance, hoping to get home before the servants awoke and discovered her absence.

She slept a few hours before Boota arrived with a tray of food: tiny eggs in a creamy sauce, toasted wedges of bread with sweet, fruity preserves, a platter of seasonal fruit from the gardens, and an herbal beverage in a steaming pot.

After eating enough to ward off Boota's curiosity, she bathed herself in tepid water and dressed in a shimmering blue robe with a golden sash and sandals. She no longer had the patience for hedonistic rituals: scented baths, massages with perfumed lotions, or elaborate grooming. She quickly dressed herself and prepared to leave the mansion.

She met her father on the front veranda.

"It's early to leave your chamber," he said. "If you're hurrying so you can loiter outside the Hall of Justice, your effort is wasted. The tribunal won't be meeting. Have you forgotten today is the day the sacred fire is taken through the city on the prophet's ancient chariot? It's a holiday from official business."

"Are you so sure I don't intend to follow the procession?"

"Is that your plan?" He raised one eyebrow, a sign of skepticism. "You haven't been near the temple since your return."

"My plan is to visit the bazaar. I need some scented oil."

"Surely Boota could go for you."

"If I allow her to choose my scents, I'll reek like cleaning polish!"

"Very well," he said. "I haven't deposited funds in your account of late. Let me provide a small sum. Buy yourself a gift." He handed her several pieces of paper currency, and she swallowed her pride to accept them. She desperately needed all she could scrape together.

"Thank you, Father." She bowed her head submissively, although it stung her pride to honor the man who had her watched and followed through all her waking hours. "With your permission, I'd like to attend a lecture this evening on the philosophy of Luta Chin."

"You have my permission and my approval. I'm glad to see you take an interest in cultural matters. I'll see that you have an appropriate escort."

"I could take Boota."

"She can't protect you. I've kept you out of touch to give you time to recover from your horrendous experience, Alena, but you need to know these are troubled times. I've hired guards to watch you and our home for good reason. The Prolas are restless. That infernal trial has stirred up trouble in the ghettos. There have been several violent incidents of late."

"I understand, Father," she said to cut short his lecture.

An hour later she arrived at the bazaar, held daily in a huge field set aside for merchants who set up brightly colored tents and hawked their wares under awnings set on poles. She knew one of her usual burly guards was following some 50 paces behind her, but this was the easiest place in the city to lose an unwanted escort. She pretended to browse by a table of toiletries, buying a small vial of oil in case her father wanted to see her selection. Then, while her guard was bored and inattentive, she quickly slipped around the side of a multicolored striped tent and raced away, weaving and ducking until she found a large packing case to conceal her until her escort ran by.

Her mission had nothing to do with scented oil. Every piece of jewelry she owned was secreted away in a cloth bag tied around her waist under her robe. She only hoped it would raise the sum needed to pay for Nita's divorce.

She found the man she was seeking: Ovat Tap, a buyer of gems and precious metals. Nita, who possessed amazing knowledge about the workings of the city, had said this merchant could be trusted to buy her jewelry and sell it far from the city. Alena found him just where Nita had said he would be.

He invited her into his tent, securing the flap behind them and lighting a large, brightly glowing oil lamp to examine her offerings. Ovat Tap had an extraordinary black mustache, the ends drooping down below his chin in oiled points, but there wasn't a single hair on his head or his brows. He spoke with an unfamiliar accent, and Alena had to listen carefully to understand what he was saying.

They haggled over every piece, and she had to steel herself against sentiment, especially when he agreed to pay a handsome price for a golden necklace set with dark blue stones that had been her mother's.

When she left Ovat Tap's tent, she had more than enough currency for Nita's divorce secreted away under her robe. She hurriedly made her other purchases in this place where everything could be bought, then strolled casually, buying a small bag of her father's favorite sugared nuts to further allay his suspicions. She didn't know how she would explain the loss of all her jewelry, but nothing mattered now except feeling Garner's arms around her again. All her hope rested on the belief that he could tell her how to help him.

Chapter Eighteen

The night air was so cold her Bellicosa guards wore heavy black coats and fur hats with flaps to warm their ears. It was unseasonable for the icy breezes from the eastern sea to strike so early, but Alena took it as a sign that the fates favored her plan to see Garner. Now she had a legitimate excuse for wearing a green hooded cloak and a white velvet eye mask to protect the sensitive skin under her eyes from chilling winds.

Her apparel was more appropriate for a costume ball than a lecture on philosophy, but the unimaginative Bellicosa didn't seem to notice.

The plan was simple: Before she took her place in the lecture hall, leaving the guards to watch her from the arched entryway behind the seats, she went to the sanitary facility for women. Thankfully it was deserted, and she met Nita unobserved. They changed outfits quickly, giggling nervously when Nita adjusted the red-gold wig

Alena had bought at the bazaar.

Alena left the facility behind the woman elegantly garbed in her emerald cloak; Nita could pass as her double to all but intimate acquaintances. In the exchange Alena had donned a heavy, drab blue hooded cloak and Nita's uniform for work, a roughly woven mustard-colored jumpsuit with numbers embroidered over the breast pocket. With her hair twisted into a severe topknot and wrapped turban-style with a kerchief, Alena looked like one of the many Prola custodians who cleaned public buildings. As a final precaution, she wrapped a plain scarf tightly around her face, leaving only her eyes exposed.

Nita told her how to enter through the back entrance to the prison, and Alena had never been more grateful for her sense of direction than when she raced through dark alleyways from the lecture hall to the Hall of Justice. She ran the whole distance, anxious to arrive when the work shift was changing. She felt the thin metal identification card in her breast pocket, praying that Pesta had secured one that wouldn't be questioned. From now on everything depended on Nita's husband, and Alena hated having to trust a brute who abused his wife and fornicated with another woman.

Garner was dozing on the thin mattress covering the hard metal bed bolted to the wall of his cell when the door clanged open and rough hands roused him to his feet. He hadn't been interrogated since the trial began, and he felt more anger than fear at the prospect of being harassed again. Although torture was officially banned, he'd suffered every kind of deprivation while his captors were trying to wring a confession from him. Food, sleep, water, even sanitary facilities had been denied in the unsuccessful effort to break his will.

"What are you doing?" he asked furiously, knowing no physical torture could compare to the mental anguish of missing Alena.

Instead of an interrogator, a female in custodian garb came in as the man who'd roused him left and pushed the solid door shut behind him. She paused an instant, then ripped off her head covering.

"It can't be. . . ."

"Garner, darling, dearest!" She rushed into his arms, raining kisses on his face and mouth until he stopped her wandering lips with a kiss so hungry and hard she gasped for air.

"My love, my love!" He held her against him, feeling her heart beat like an echo of his own. "I thought I would never see you again!"

"I can't live without you!"

Her hands were under his rough prison tunic, covering the skin on his back with frantic caresses.

"Have they hurt you? Do they feed you enough? Are you well? Oh, my darling, I don't have words to tell you how much I miss you," she said in one breath.

"My precious." He touched her face with both hands, trying to convince himself she wasn't a dream image.

He laced his fingers in her topknot until her hair tumbled to her shoulders, then buried his face in the sweet-smelling mass of curls.

"You're trembling!" he exclaimed, feeling her shoulders quake under his hands.

"Excitement! And I had to ride inside a horrible cart that holds cleaning supplies. I nearly passed out when the cover came down shutting out all the light and air."

"My love, whatever possessed you to come here? The risk—the danger! If they find you . . ."

"No, don't!" She covered his mouth with her fingertips. "Don't waste these few moments rebuking me. I couldn't go on without seeing you. Garner, tell me what I can do to save you. I don't care what the cost is. I'll die if it will free you from this terrible place!"

"Don't talk that way!" He held her so tight he began to worry he might hurt her.

"I'll tell the truth at your trial—that Blaz tormented you and whipped you for no reason. You don't deserve this treatment! You were the one who found the probe. You made the rescue possible. That has to count for something!"

"Alena, the one thing you absolutely must not do is testify on my behalf." He held her away and looked into the shimmering depths of her dark eyes, so afraid for her sake that he was in agony.

"But I was the acting commander!"

"Darling, if the Tribunal of Seven learns about our love—our absence at the same time—not even your father will be able to save you from being Uncasted."

"I'm not afraid!"

"You should be! The Outlands are every bit as savage as Brona, only the most dangerous predator is the male of our own species. If you were banished, sent there alone . . ." He couldn't control the trembling that shook his limbs. "If you survived rape or torture, you could be enslaved, forced to . . ."

He couldn't bear think of what might happen to her. "Promise me you won't call attention to our love in any way!"

"How can I when—"

"Alena, please don't add to my torment. I can bear anything but the guilt of knowing I caused you to be Uncasted."

"Garner, they might execute you!"

"I prefer that to a lifetime in a steel box." He gestured at his cell, devoid of all but the most basic furnishings. "Accept the inevitable, my dearest darling. We've had more love in our short time together than most people know in a lifetime. I wouldn't trade a single moment with you for anything."

"We mustn't waste these precious moments quarreling! Oh, Garner, how can I go on without you? There has to be a way to save you! Isn't there one grateful survivor to speak on your behalf?"

"Velma Pitt tried, but I don't think she impressed the Tribunal favorably. Erasma said good things about me, but they badgered him until he lost his temper and called the high-caste survivors lazy bastards." He smiled wryly. "At least no one mentioned your name; no one linked us together. I wonder if your father . . ."

"He could save you, Garner, if only he would!"

"Beloved Alena, High Yor wants me convicted. I'm sure of it, even though my appointed defender is afraid to admit it. Your father must suspect. . . ."

"I've given him no reason to!"

"Perhaps not intentionally."

"Oh, Garner, I don't know. After we landed, my father kept me sedated for days! My backside was covered with needle marks when I finally regained consciousness. I might have said something and not remembered."

"It's done, darling. Kiss me so I'll never forget

your sweet taste!" He ravished her lips and covered her mouth with his.

"Have we time. . . . " he started to ask as three sharp raps made the door vibrate.

"I'll stay the night," she said. "I can leave when the night shift goes home!"

"The daughter of High Yor can't disappear! Where does your father think you are?"

"At a philosophy lecture," she said with a trace of a smile. "As though I care about elaborate codes of ethics! Love is all that matters, and I love you more than anyone has ever loved!"

Three more raps resounded through the cell.

"Go, darling, go," he begged, so anxious about her safety he couldn't help sounding angry.

"I'll find a way to come again!"

"No, never! Swear you won't even try." He gripped her arms so hard she cried out.

"How can I—"

"Alena, this is the last thing you'll ever be able to do for me. Give me peace of mind. Promise you'll never risk your life again by coming anywhere near me."

"You're too cruel to ask. . . . "

"Not because I want to be. Swear, Alena!"

"I'll never come here again," she said, tears running down her face. "I swear it."

He kissed her once more, a bittersweet meeting of their lips that seared his soul; then he turned his back, clenching his fists to keep himself from weakening. If he took her in his arms one more time, he might not be strong enough to release her until they were forced apart by jailers.

He heard her heartbroken weeping, then the harsh clang of the door as it closed behind her.

"By all that's holy," he said, lifting his face to the

cold steel ceiling, "was love created to be a torment?"

He slumped down on his knees in agony, knowing that no punishment, not even death, could be as cruel as never seeing Alena again.

Somehow Pesta managed to help Alena back to the lecture hall where the Bellicosa were waiting to escort her home. She dully noted Nita's gratitude and her husband's greed when she handed over the payment for their divorce, but her heart was back in the bleak cell with her beloved.

She didn't sleep that night. A thousand plans to rescue Garner raced through her mind, each more desperate and hopeless than the one before it. When morning came, she felt as though her world had exploded into a million sharp pieces that lodged in her heart. She sat on the edge of her bed, too weary and defeated to care about Boota's brusque exhortations to bathe and dress for the day. She imagined how comforting it would be to slip under the water in her bath and cease to be.

Boota was speaking, but Alena didn't hear her words, intrusive as they were. She was consumed by pain, immobilized by despair.

She might have sat that way forever, frozen by her sense of loss, but she felt a tiny flutter in her midsection, a stir of life. The child she carried suddenly seemed real, a living reminder of the love she'd shared with Garner. She clutched her belly, willing the tiny being to make itself felt again, and tears streamed down her face when she felt another movement.

She couldn't sink into a mire of self-pity. She had to be strong for the sake of the precious child she was carrying. No babe was ever conceived in greater love! She was responsible for another life, and she had to do all she could for Garner's offspring.

She couldn't put off the inevitable any longer. Stanko Yor had to know his daughter was carrying a child.

Her inertia fell away, replaced by frenetic energy. She rushed about the household, instructing the cooks to prepare her father's favorite meal, as though delicacies for the palate could help him ingest the bitter truth: His grandchild was the babe of a Prola.

In her chamber, she searched through gowns, aware of her swollen breasts and thickened waist. Even if she didn't confess, her father would soon notice her condition. She pressed her hands against the gentle swell of her belly, trying to imagine the miniature human in her womb. Was it fair to bring this child into a world where worth was ordained by birth, where a father's caste meant more than talent, intellect, or virtue?

An hour before the time her father had told the servants to expect him, she coiled her hair into a topknot. Her mirror image seemed like that of a stranger: Her dark eyes were deeply shadowed, and her face was pinched with anxiety. She remembered Garner burying his face in her flowing locks, and the memory brought fresh pain. She loathed herself for not helping him escape from that damnable prison! She would gladly give up everything, even her life, to be beside him, but she had to be strong for the sake of his child.

Her father was in a mellow mood at dinner, pleased because she'd taken pains to look elegant for the meal.

"You didn't go out today," he said. "That's good. It isn't seemly for a high minister's daughter to stand in the throng outside the Hall of Justice. It could be dangerous too. Every day there are reports of unrest in the Prola quarters. Security around the capitol has been doubled."

"Father, there's something I must tell you," she said when the last platter of food had been cleared from the long oval table where they dined at opposite ends, and the servants had left them alone.

Her throat was so dry, she had to sip water to continue. Her father's cold blue eyes watched intently, waiting for her to speak.

"I'm carrying a child," she blurted out, forgetting all her carefully rehearsed words intended to soften the impact of her news.

He didn't say a word, but scorn was etched on his face.

"You don't know what it was like on Brona," she continued, desperate to make him understand. "Until Garner found the probe, there didn't seem to be any hope of rescue. I fell in love thinking the rest of our lives would be spent on that primitive planet. We faced death every day. I saw horrible shriekers kill strong men. If Garner hadn't saved me, I would've been a meal for a monster who hid in the depths of a stream."

"So it was gratitude that made you give yourself to him." His voice was low but harsh.

"No, it was love!"

"You allowed that lout to seduce you."

"I wasn't seduced. I gave myself eagerly. I followed him because I didn't want to live without him."

"How dare you let this happen?" Her father shouted, raising his voice in a way she'd never heard. "Do you know what this could mean to my career?"

"I love Garner Rie," she said proudly, as angry as her father.

"Leave this table. Go to your room and stay there."

His voice was so hate-laden and menacing, she didn't think of disobeying.

But before she left his presence, she had to know what he intended to do.

"Please, Father!" She got down on her knees in front of him. Her hands fluttered in the air until she clasped them together. She was afraid to touch the man who'd given her life. "It's my own fault. I . . . I seduced Garner Rie. He's an honorable man. He would never have overstepped caste traditions if I hadn't encouraged him. Please! Don't make him suffer for my actions!"

He stood and walked away, leaving her to weep with rage and frustration.

She retreated to her room, desperately wanting to run away from her father, but there was no refuge for the errant daughter of a high minister. No members of their own caste would risk his wrath by taking her into their home. Even if she ran to a Prola ghetto for sanctuary, she couldn't be sure Nita would still be there to take her in. Divorce was a quick business for those who could pay, and her former servant could have left for her brother's home already.

Confronting her father had been even worse than she'd imagined, and in the days that followed, he tortured her with his silence. The messages she sent through Boota were never answered, and whenever she tried to leave her room, she was stopped by a Bellicosa guard outside her door.

She was confined to her room like a naughty child, and she resented it more with each passing day. She had a right to know her fate and that of her unborn child, but seven days passed without word from her father.

She thought of Garner in his dismal cell, and knew her confinement was an easy burden compared to his. Still, she suffered the agonies of the damned, not knowing what was happening to the man she loved. Was his trial over? Had he been condemned to death? Was her father keeping her prisoner until her child's father was executed?

She raged at the silent Boota, but she couldn't break through the servant's stubborn refusal to speak of anything happening in the capital city.

Late in the afternoon of the eighth day, she received a summons to dine with her father. Boota laid out her gown, picking the same one she'd worn at their last meeting. Did the servant know she was with child? Was it obvious to anyone who saw her now?

Alena stood naked in front of the full-length mirror on the door of one of her closets. The swell of her belly was amazing and frightening. She wanted Garner's child desperately, but she was terrified of the fate that awaited it. How could she protect her babe when it emerged into the cruel world?

She wanted to rage at her father, to accuse him of being an unnatural monster devoid of love for his own offspring. But defiance would be futile. She would only fuel his anger, and now two others were vulnerable to the consequences: Garner and their child.

At the appointed hour, she entered the richly appointed dining chamber, bowing low to her father, who was already seated.

He acknowledged her with a curt nod, and she trembled from the effort of playing the part of a meek daughter.

She took her place, waiting in silence while the table servant, a graying male Prola with deep creases on either side of his mouth, served clear broth for the first course.

She was burning with questions. Was the trial over? Was Garner dead? What lay in store for her child? She wanted to scream in frustration! It was sheer torture not to have control over her own fate.

Swallowing the slightly salty broth was almost impossible; her throat was constricted by anxiety. When she had her nearly full bowl cleared away, her father glared in her direction but said nothing.

Everything brought to the table was a reminder of the pampered life of luxury she'd once enjoyed: succulent morsels of seafood in a thick, creamy sauce; tender green legumes so tiny it took a servant an hour to strip enough from pods for a single serving; hot bread only moments from the oven; a choice of pastries filled with fruit preserves.

She forced herself to swallow a few bites, not sure her stomach would accept food. The babe fluttered continually, as though aware of her anxiety.

Her father ate with maddening slowness, not speaking a word until a servant cleared away the last of the serving pieces.

"Tell me about the trial," she begged at last, unable to stand the excruciating suspense another moment.

"A hiatus was declared," he said, feigning indifference. "A member of the Tribunal of Seven is ill. It should resume in a day or two. Of course, the rest of the proceedings are just a formality. Garner Rie will be convicted of causing the death of Captain Hurex Blaz. The only possible sentence is execution."

"Oh, no!" She'd steeled herself for days to hear the worst, but she reeled under the impact of her father's cruel words. "He's not guilty!"

"He deserves the most painful death possible!" her father said with quiet fury.

"I must go before the Tribunal of Seven. I know my testimony could save him!"

"Don't be a stupid child! If you interfere, you'll condemn him for a far worse crime."

"He doesn't deserve to die!"

"Keep silent. I've come to a decision about the bastard you're carrying."

She flinched as though he'd slapped her face.

"I have the authority to ensure leniency for the father of your bastard."

She hated him for slandering her child, but she knew he had the power to back his words. The government was corrupt; as a high minister, one of three who virtually controlled the planet, he could call in favors, even from the members of a Space Service tribunal.

"Will you do it?" she asked in a husky voice, terrified he was only toying with her, raising her hopes to dash them.

"I'm offering a bargain. It's the only alternative you have, and I'll require your sworn oath immediately."

"What are the terms?" She was so frightened for Garner's sake, her voice was a hoarse whisper.

"You must relinquish your child when it's born and pretend the disgraceful, illegal liaison never happened."

"Oh, no!" She fought back tears.

"You must vow never to see Garner Rie again, never to mention his name, never to reveal the existence of a child. I won't have my name sullied and my career blighted because my daughter has behaved like the worst kind of whore, consorting with a Prola!"

"That's not the way it was!"

"I don't want to hear excuses, and I never want you to mention the incident again. Is that understood?"

"Yes, but what will happen to my child?"

"I'll arrange for a Prola wet nurse to care for him in the ghetto. He'll be raised as a Prola without knowledge of his origins. Garner Rie must never know he has a son. Do you agree to these terms?"

"What will happen to Garner?"

"He'll be stripped of rank. I can't expect the Space Service to reinstate him as an officer, not even to keep peace in the ghettos and rid myself of a bastard. But he can continue in the service in a job more fitting for a Prola."

She felt trapped, but there was no option but to accept her father's conditions. She loathed him with all her heart and soul, but there was no other way to save her beloved from death.

Alena gave him her oath, but in her heart she vowed to be a part of her baby's life. Not even Stanko Yor could keep her from being with her child.

In the months that followed, she watched her body swell as her spirit withered. The trial dragged on, delay after delay prolonging her torment and reinforcing her father's insistence that she honor her vow. He swore that Garner would be released from prison as soon as the bastard child was born and out of his house. Alena was forbidden to leave his property until that day.

Her babe didn't keep her waiting. Alena gave

birth to Garner's son a few days before the date she'd anticipated. Boota, her only attendant, was little comfort during the 27 hours of torment.

"All first babies take a long time," Boota said matter-of-factly.

The babe howled when he entered the world, and Alena fought to hold him in her arms, expending her last reserves of strength in a futile attempt to wrest him away from Boota, who had orders to spirit him away immediately.

That night, after she'd wept until her tear ducts ran dry, her father allowed her to see a communication sent to him. Officer Rie's trial had ended with a not-guilty verdict. He lost rank and was given a reprimand for insubordination, but the tribunal declined to explain their reasons for this punishment. Garner was assigned to duty as a greaser on a space freighter leaving within days.

Chapter Nineteen

Garner had long ago lost hope. He'd expected to end his days in the place known among prisoners as the Bottom Level, the lowest cellar under the Hall of Justice. The method of executing condemned felons was a carefully guarded secret. In the distant past, the leaders of Prima had decreed that no details be revealed, on pain of death. Not knowing the form death would take was the ultimate form of mental torture.

After countless days of contemplating death in its most horrifying forms, Garner suddenly, unexpectedly, found himself free, standing outside the prison wing where he'd been confined since stepping foot on Prima.

The cold, fresh air made him giddy, and he shivered in the lightweight tunic and trousers he'd been issued to wear during his trial.

He was free.

The sun was blinding after his long sojourn in

artificial light, and he wondered if his legs still held the strength and elasticity for running. He'd tried to keep his body strong and fit in prison, exercising as best he could in his cell because there was little else to do. On rare occasions a few comrades from the Space Service had visited, but he'd discouraged it for their own sakes. A man's career could be tainted by associating with a criminal, especially a Prola felon.

He'd written begging his family not to come to Danica, and his parents had reluctantly complied, discouraging his siblings from making the trip. As soon as Garner had begun receiving wages that were princely by Prola standards, he'd moved his family to a rural district and bought them jobs in a small food-preserving business so they would be assured of work. Whatever happened to him, he wanted his 12 nieces and nephews to grow up far from the ghettos. He wouldn't permit his family to give up their employment and jeopardize their futures to share in his dark hours.

Nor did he want them to learn of his involvement with a high-caste woman. He felt no shame in loving Alena, but his parents would never be able to understand why he'd risked so much to possess her for such a short time.

Day by day, through delays, postponements, and rescheduling, he'd waited for one of the high-caste survivors to accuse him of consorting with a Scientifica. Yet not even Catton Sur, who painted him as the blackest of scoundrels, linked his name with Alena's.

Now, miraculously, he'd been found guiltless in Blaz's death and lightly disciplined on the charge of insubordination. He must be the first man in Space Service history to be demoted for refusing to execute himself. Losing his rank was painful, but he hadn't been cashiered from the Space Service. He was assigned to a freighter leaving almost immediately.

In spite of his amazement, he wasn't joyful about his release. He was mystified by the tribunal's decision and unsure whether a sinister power had influenced it. There'd been little testimony on his behalf, and the prosecutor in charge of his case had thoroughly discredited his two best witnesses: Erasma and Velma. Did someone conspire to have him released, only to make him available for private vengeance?

The only thing he wanted was to hold Alena in his arms again, but she was farther from him than if she'd stayed on Brona. He couldn't contact her. Even if it were possible, he wouldn't risk her well-being.

He wandered the streets of Danica, going into the ghetto where he'd spent his boyhood, but he didn't know what he wanted to do with the rest of his life. He desperately needed the solace of a female, but he was repelled by the thought of visiting a joy-girl. Only Alena could satisfy his longing. He yearned to hear her voice, to see her hair flowing down her naked back, to part her lips and savor the sweetness of her mouth.

His newfound freedom was a sham. He would be a prisoner of unfulfilled love to the end of his days.

When he was exhausted from his long trek through the city, he returned to the sparsely furnished room in the Space Service residential compound that served as his quarters between flights. When the lunar tug left on its run to haul supplies to Bedir and return with minerals, he would be aboard as a greaser in the engine room. It was a terrible demotion, a blow to his pride and a career reversal he could never outlive. But he'd brought enough disgrace to his caste. He would serve out the years of his enlistment rather than face desertion charges.

He went through the motions of preparing for the flight, purchasing the uniforms and gear required for a greaser. Writing to his family was his most difficult task, but he tried to conceal his bitterness. He'd forbidden Alena ever to come to him again, but his life was empty without her. He tried to harden his heart, but death still seemed preferable to never seeing her again.

He steeled himself to report for duty on the freighter, but he could see nothing but misery ahead of him in a life without Alena.

Alena wished for death in the long days that followed the birth of her son, but her robust good health prevailed. She recovered from the delivery of her child, but not from the horror of losing him.

"I'll name you Bron, after the world where you were conceived in love," she said, pretending to speak to her absent child when she was alone in the gardens.

She tried to convince herself that her father's strategy was best for the baby. It was better to be a Prola than to be banished with an Uncasted mother. But she'd seen the terrible hovel where Nita had lived, and she ached with anxiety over her son's fate.

The only good to come of her oath was the freedom to come and go as she wished without escorts. She'd sworn never to attempt to see Garner, but her heart ached with love for him.

For many days after the birth, she pumped milk from her breasts to keep it flowing, trying to believe her father would relent and let her nurse her own child. But he barely spoke to her, spurning her overtures and refusing to discuss anything with her. She was forced to accept that he would never rescind his order to banish the child to the ghetto.

She became accustomed to solitary meals, and her request for a more congenial servant to replace Boota was denied by Phin Yen, the chief steward of the household, who was, of course, following her father's orders.

At last her milk dried up in spite of her best efforts, but the gnawing hunger to hold her son in her arms was stronger than ever. She ached to be with him and tried to find a way to learn where he was. With little else to do, she studied the servants, watching their comings and goings to determine if there was a pattern in their activities. Her son was being kept in a ghetto, and someone had to pay the wet nurse caring for him. Her father had little respect for the trustworthiness of Prolas, except those ruled by his iron hand. She surmised he wouldn't pay large sums in advance, but would dole out small amounts at regular intervals.

She wasn't surprised to realize Boota was always absent after her morning duties were done on the fifth day of every nine-day cycle. Alena sewed a drab gray tunic cut from rags set aside to be used as polishing cloths and practiced disguising herself as a Prola. Who but Boota would her father trust with the secret location of his grandson? She was the only witness to the birth, and it couldn't be coincidence that she frequently wore jewelry and bits of finery not usually seen on servants.

Alena followed the next time Boota went on a mysterious errand. It was easier than she'd anticipated. Boota was reliable but not overly clever, and she ambled toward the trama completely indifferent to her surroundings.

Heart pounding with excitement, Alena followed when the servant got off near a Prola ghetto. Trailing Boota through the maze of streets and alleys without being seen was difficult, but it helped immensely that the woman didn't have enough imagination to check behind her for possible assailants.

Boota took a complicated route with many twists and turns, but Alena took careful note of the way, committing each turn to memory. The servant stooped at a small wooden-sided hut no larger than others on a narrow dirt street, but the place had an air of prosperity lacking in nearby homes. Fresh white paint covered the outside walls, and a row of small green plants were budding in front, coaxed to open by the seasonal warming.

Alena hid while Boota made her visit, entering without knocking on the door. It wasn't long before the servant left, walking away without looking in any direction.

When she was sure no one was in sight, Alena knocked softly, her heart pounding louder than her knuckles on the wood.

"What is it?" The woman who opened the door was the least-favored female Alena had ever seen. She was tall and gawky, towering over Alena, and her ponderous breasts made look her top-heavy on spindly, scrawny legs encased in frayed blue trousers. Her face was marred by a long scar from the tip of her left eyebrow to the side of her mouth, as though a knife had sliced it open leaving a bright pink worm of scar tissue. Her nose was a bulbous lump, and her lips were so thin they didn't quite cover her chipped front teeth. But when Alena looked into her ruined face, she saw great, luminous brown eyes, the pupils radiating warmth and, at this moment, fear.

"Please, may I come in? I know you have my babe."

"Oh, no, I'm not to show him to anyone! Oh, dear, I don't know what to do! Oh . . ."

Alena made the decision for her, slipping into a surprisingly neat, cozy room with a door leading to another chamber at the rear.

"It's much better if we don't speak on the street," she said apologetically, touching the woman's arms in a gesture of friendship. "I'm Alena. What are you called?"

"Sena Gome, widow of Rige." She was pale with fear, her disfiguring scar even redder in contrast to her pale face.

"You're wet nurse to my babe. Please trust me, Sena. I'm not here to bring you trouble. I'm dying for the sight of him. I'll do anything for the chance to hold him in my arms at least once. I've lost his father. I can't lose him too."

The woman's face seemed to crumple, and tears moistened her cheeks. "My own dear man died from lung sickness just before the cold set in, and our babe was too tiny—too weak—to survive."

"I understand." Alena put her arms around the weeping woman. "It's a wonderful thing you're doing, giving nourishment to my son. Please, no one will know I'm here. Let me see him."

"No mother should be deprived of her babe. Oh, he is a fine one. He came to me without a name, so I call him Love." She led Alena to the back room, a tiny bedchamber with a narrow cot and a sturdy wooden crib where a dark-haired babe was sleeping.

"Bron, I call him Bron," Alena whispered, almost overcome by the love that welled up at the sight of her child.

The babe opened his eyes and wailed. Sena stepped back, letting Alena take her precious babe in her arms.

She hadn't felt such a surge of joy since she'd last lain in Garner's arms. Her child was perfect: round-cheeked with fine dark hair and such rich-brown eyes she was startled. Garner's eyes were blue like the waters of a deep sea, but this babe's were the same shade Alena had inherited from her own mother.

Her only sorrow was that she couldn't share this moment with her beloved.

"Come whenever you dare," Sena said when it became urgent that Alena leave. "But take care. There've been some nasty clashes of late. The Prolas are in an ugly mood, restless because jobs are scarce and reform comes so slowly. Your topknot is a giveaway. No woman who belongs here wears her hair that way."

Alena thanked her profusely, realizing as she hurried home that she had a purpose for living again: to love her son. She retrieved her gown from a secluded glade on the walk from the trama line to her father's mansion, donning it as she planned little gifts to carry to Bron on her next visit. The danger meant nothing if she could hold her child and coax him into smiling at her.

Garner returned to Prima because his 100-day stint of service mandated a furlough, but he didn't welcome the 20-day rest period. He wasn't suffering from space fatigue. He was mentally depleted, his soul ravaged by the unending hopelessness of his love for Alena. Leisure time to dwell on thoughts of their love would only fuel his despair.

The only solace he'd found during his 100 days of service had come when he climbed into his narrow bunk, the uppermost in a tier of three in the greasers' sleeping compartment, closed his eyes, and allowed himself to remember making love to Alena. But sometimes his memories brought such pain and sense of loss, he left his bed and asked the engineer on duty for the roughest, dirtiest jobs to keep his mind occupied. Once he'd volunteered for an outside engine check, not caring if the lifeline broke and left him abandoned in space to float away and die.

The other greasers had been wary of his notoriety at first, testing him in the crude ways men reserved for newcomers, but when he quietly accepted their hazing and performed the most menial tasks without complaint, they slowly came to accept him as one of them.

He returned from space to go to the sparsely furnished room that was the closest thing he had to a home. He had neither time nor funds to visit his family, and seeing his robust young nieces and nephews would only increase his sense of loss. Without Alena, he would never have children of his own.

He ached for the release only a female could provide. The joy-girls were quartered near the Space Control Center for the exclusive pleasure of Space Service men. Garner knew his place; he didn't go to the luxurious suites where officers were entertained, and where he'd once been a favorite visitor. Instead he stood outside the blocky wooden house where greasers were welcome. He thought of losing himself between the soft thighs of a professional joy-giver. He needed to fondle female breasts and squeeze a plump backside to reassure himself that he was still a virile male.

He walked up and down the walkway to the house, thinking of the uninhibited pleasures offered by the women within, but he couldn't make himself enter, not even for the therapeutic good a few days there would provide. Only one woman could quiet the turmoil in his soul, and he loved Alena too much to try to see her.

He walked the great distance to the inner city, welcoming the ache in his legs as he got used to the planet's gravity again. He thought of dulling his perpetual sense of loss with strong drink, but he didn't want to blunt the sharp edge of his love for Alena. He would rather live with pain than risk losing any part of what she meant to him.

In the Ministry of Information, he bought a metal token and inserted it in one of the telamachines, then reclined on a comfortable lounger to watch the screen. He set the controls on the arm rest to get a summary of recent happenings in the city, desperately needing something to distract his mind.

Much of the news was alarming. There'd been a recent uprising in the ghetto he'd once called home over the beating death of a Prola boy by some upper-caste youths. Apparently the Bellicosa youths had gone into the ghetto looking for trouble. When they were tried for the crime and declared not guilty by reason of self-defense, rioting broke out.

The news summary only angered Garner. He remembered from his own youth that Bellicosa boys liked to test their manhood by making forays into the ghetto. Once he'd had to fight three of the bullyboys to protect his sister from molestation, and for many days afterward he'd lived in fear of being dragged before a tribunal to be punished for thoroughly pummeling them.

He left the screen before his time was up, wandering without purpose into the Prola ghetto because there was nothing else he wanted to do. He had no desire to renew old acquaintances, and he was grateful his checkered career had allowed his family to escape the grinding poverty of their life in the capital city.

The wind was up, cold blasts whipping through the crowded ghetto, battering ramshackle huts and carrying dust and debris. The thoroughfares were crowded, as though people were too restless to go to their beds after their day's labor was over. All the faces he saw were troubled, some reflecting anger and others fear. He didn't know what new incident had stirred the ire of the Prolas, but he was too weary to care. He was ready to return to his quarters when the crowd grew more dense, pushing him against the barred door of a food seller's building. He heard a woman's voice raised in fearful protest, and a second later he caught a glimpse of flame-gold hair whipping about in the wind. He elbowed his way though the crowd, curious to see the owner of such a wondrous mane.

The woman was being menaced by two ruffians. Her hood had fallen off, and she was backed against a wall, trying to ward off their advances, while others pressed close, curious but too cautious to interfere. Garner saw a flash of gold and pegged the would-be assailants as Bellicosa youth made bold by the recent acquittal of the murderers who'd killed a Prola boy.

The woman shrieked in fear and fought them with kicks and blows, but she was certain to be dragged away and raped. He pushed close and froze in shock.

"Alena!"

Without stopping to think, he threw himself at the first assailant, felling him with a single bone-crushing blow on his chin. He reined in his anger for a moment, not wanting to cause a crisis by killing a Bellicosa in the ghetto, then purposefully approached the second bullyboy, who turned to confront him.

The boy was powerful but still ungainly, charging in a way that made him an easy target. Garner caught him off balance and gave him a sharp rap on the back of his neck, knocking him flat, his face in the dirt of the street.

"Do you want to leave here alive?" Garner asked, holding the youth down with his foot on the small of his back.

The Bellicosa sputtered and spat dirt.

"You have a count of ten to pick up your friend and be gone, or you'll suffer a beating like you've never imagined."

The youth fled, half-carrying and half-dragging his companion. Garner didn't think they would be quick to tell anyone about their ignominious row.

He turned and caught a glimpse of Alena's red hair disappearing down an alley. He chased after her, breathless from the shock of seeing her in danger.

He easily caught up and pulled her into the sheltered doorway of a commercial building that was shut for the night.

"What in blazes are you doing here?" He was so horrified by what had nearly happened, he wanted to shake the truth from her.

She shook her head, either unwilling or unable to answer.

"Tell me!" he demanded. "Don't you know how dangerous the ghetto is? Were you slumming, entertaining yourself by seeing how the less fortunate live?"

She still didn't answer, and her silence maddened him. His hopeless love had eaten at his soul too long, and he lashed out at the woman who obsessed him.

"Speak to me! Give me a reason why you're risking your life here!"

"Garner, I . . ."

Hearing his name on her lips only made him more agitated. "Are you here to meet a man? Do you have a new lover, Alena? Are you going to destroy another Prola? Do you shatter men's lives for sport, Highness Yor? Did our love mean nothing?"

Once started, he wasn't able to stop. He burned to know if her love for him had endured hardships and separation. Did she still love him as he loved her?

"Tell me, Alena, why are you here?" He grabbed her arm without remembering his strength. "Did you ever really love me?"

She slapped him, the soft hand he knew so well resounding against his cheek, stinging like a blow from a strap. He was too dumbfounded to react.

She broke from his punishing hold, her eyes deep cauldrons of anger. "I never loved you! I don't love you now! Leave me, and never come near me again, not even if I'm being torn apart by savage beasts!"

Her words hurt more than anything he'd ever felt. He released her and grasped his cheek, but the real pain was in his heart. He watched her flee into the murky depths of the ghetto, too stunned to think of following.

Too late he tried to find where she'd gone, but she'd disappeared as surely as if the earth had swallowed her.

For hours he searched, prowling the streets, frightening strangers with his frantic questions. Alena didn't want to be found, and no one knew better how to hide in places where he could never find her.

At dawn he gave up, returning to his quarters to collapse and sleep like a man in a coma. He awoke many hours later, rubbing his cheek, sorry the sting was gone because it would have been tangible proof he really had seen the woman who was always in his thoughts.

He remembered his wild accusations and regretted every word. Seeing her again had snapped his reason; knowing how close she'd come to grievous harm had made him behave like a lunatic. Would she have said those damning things if he hadn't provoked her? He wouldn't know a moment's peace of mind until he knew for sure.

He remembered details of their encounter: the poor quality of the cloak she was wearing, the scuffy boots on her feet. She was trying to pass as a Prola woman, even though her beauty would attract attention no matter where she went.

He left his quarters, sure of one thing: Alena had a reason for being in the ghetto. One way or another, he was going to discover what it was, even if his worst accusation was true and she did have a new lover.

The crowds were thinner, and the last hour of daylight had passed, when he finally found a ragged street urchin who was willing to answer questions for the sake of the currency Garner dangled in front of him.

"I seen 'er before," the lad boasted. "She comes regular to the ugly woman's place."

"Who is the ugly woman?"

"Sena Gome, her that lost her husband. She'll

never find another. Her face is right scary, I can tell you."

"Does Sena Gome live alone?"

"Far as anyone knows. She has berry bushes behind her hut. Don't even scream when we pick a few, so I guess she's not so bad."

Garner followed the boy through a maze of alleys until he pointed at a well-kept hovel, more prosperous than those around it. How did a woman without a husband rise above the poverty of her neighbors?

He hated his first thought: that she kept a room where lovers could meet secretly for a price.

He knocked, afraid of what he might find. The woman who cracked the door was fierce-faced, but her expression was more fearful than fearsome when she saw him standing there in the tunic worn by off-duty Space Service greasers.

"You have a frequent visitor," he said. "A comely woman with red-gold hair."

"No sir, not I. You must be in the wrong place."

"I think not." He was debating whether to force his way in when he heard a sound that made the back of his neck prickle.

"What was that?"

"My child!" the woman cried out. "You're keeping me from my babe!"

"Let me see it." He pushed his way inside and closed the door behind him, following the lusty cries into a small back chamber illuminated only by the light coming through the door.

"Bring your lamp," he ordered. "I don't want to frighten the child."

The woman was timid now, silently holding the lamp close to the crib where the babe was loudly wailing.

The child was young, certainly far short of his

first natal anniversary, but his head was covered by thick black curls. Garner leaned close and saw warm brown eyes, wide and sparkling and so distinctive his throat constricted with emotion.

"You don't need to tell me lies," he said softly to the anxiously hovering woman. "I know this babe."

He reached out and picked up his son. The child quieted, and Garner thought his heart would burst with love.

Chapter Twenty

Garner watched in fascination while Sena Gome sat down with the babe and lifted her tunic. The child needed no urging. He took her dark nipple into his mouth, clutching the swollen white breast with one small hand while he suckled.

One tit didn't begin to satisfy his hunger. When Sena switched him, his head bobbed impatiently until he fastened his mouth on the other nipple.

Garner felt neither embarrassment nor lust watching this intimate procedure. Instead his heart swelled with love, and he couldn't stop marveling over the miracle of his son.

"How does it feel to nurse? Does it cause discomfort?" he asked, curious about anything that concerned his child.

"No, it's a great relief to have him take some. I swear I have enough milk for two babes. Of course, it may be different when Bron's teeth break through."

"Bron. Who gave him that name?" He knew the answer, but he wanted to hear that Alena had chosen it.

"His mother, but I shouldn't be telling you things." Sena looked toward the door, as though she feared someone would catch her talking to him.

"I already know enough to have you banished. You're harboring a mixed-caste babe."

"You won't betray me?" She blotted milk from the babe's chin, much to Bron's annoyance.

"Bron is my son. I'll never do anything to interfere with his care, but please, don't torture me with secrecy. I need to know how he came to be with you. Did his mother bring him?"

"Oh, no, sir! She found him by following the woman who comes to pay me."

"What woman is that?"

"A servant by the looks of her. I don't know who her master is. I've only dealt with her. My poor dead husband's brother made the arrangements. The woman who comes here never asks about the child, only hands over what's coming to me and takes her leave. The mother, though, wants to know everything he does. It's a terrible thing to be deprived of your newborn."

"How often does the mother come?"

"As often as she can, I suspect. It's unusual for more than two or three days to pass between visits. She brings lovely things for little Bron. Look at his toys, would you! They're overflowing my marketing basket! But it doesn't matter because I never leave here. My brother-by-marriage takes the payment and buys all we need."

"Does the mother come by day or night?" he asked, trying to make his questions sound casual even though he felt as if his life depended on the wet nurse's answers.

"She usually slips in before the supper hour. I think she picks the busy time when people are returning from work, hoping she'll be less conspicuous. Sometimes she only stays a few minutes. Others visits she'll stay all evening and leave under cover of darkness, but I worry about her being out so late. These are bad times. I've offered her my bed so she could leave at dawn, but she always seems anxious to be gone."

Garver held his son and patted his back, rewarded by a noisy burp and a smile that made his heart constrict. He stayed to see Sena bathe him, enchanted when he kicked and flailed with strong, plump limbs. Surely there had never been such a perfect son or one who enjoyed splashing in a pan of water more than little Bron.

When Garner could tear himself away from his child, he returned to his lonely quarters more heavyhearted than ever. What could he do for his son? Obviously Bron had been sent to the ghetto to be raised as a Prola, but who would care for him, teach him, sustain him through the difficult growing years?

He wanted to claim his son as his own, to have his birth legally registered, and provide a real home, but how could he do it without raising ugly questions about the boy's parentage? Since the trial, the name of Garner Rie was familiar to everyone in the city, and even his visit to Sena's home was risky. If someone recognized him, he might find himself under investigation again. He didn't delude himself: He had an unknown but powerful enemy, and High Yor was the man with the most to lose if Garner's love for Alena ever became public knowledge.

He knew the wisest course was to stay away from his son, but he was drawn to him like metal filings to a magnet. Every day of his furlough was precious now, because it was one more day to bask in his son's delightful company.

He wanted to shower Bron with gifts as Alena had, but he didn't want to reveal himself that way. Instead he pressed currency into Sena's hands, begging her to hide it until the day came when his son needed something.

Every day he went to Sena's, learning to appreciate the love she showered on his son. But how long would she be allowed to keep him? It troubled her too, because she'd grown to love Bron as she would have loved the child she lost. Garner's stomach knotted with anxiety at the thought of losing contact with Bron. No doubt he would be taken from his wet nurse when he was weaned. Where would he be sent to keep his true identity a secret? Would Alena try to stop it and bring great trouble upon herself?

He watched his son play and longed for Alena to come. He'd spent four days at Sena's, hoping against hope she couldn't resist seeing her son, when finally a soft knock made his heart leap.

He stepped into the back room, not wanting to frighten her away. Just hearing her precious voice when she came into the outer room made him ache with longing.

"How is he? Is he well? Oh, I hope he's not sleeping! I have less than an hour to spend with him today."

"You're just in time to see how he's crawling," Sena exclaimed. "He loves to scramble after that ball you gave him."

"What a strong boy, to crawl so soon," Alena cooed, bending over to better watch him. "I went to the Ministry of Information to learn what babies should be doing, and you, darling Bron, are far ahead of ordinary children."

She got down on her knees to kiss him, and Garner couldn't stay hidden any longer. He stepped into the room, overcome by the sight of Alena with his child.

"Garner! Oh, no!" She jumped to her feet in dismay.

"Did you think you could hide my son from me forever?" he asked softly.

"You must leave here! Pretend you've never seen me! Oh, this is terrible!"

"Seeing me again is terrible? Knowing I have a son is terrible?"

"You don't understand!"

"Make me understand!" He grabbed her by the arms, forgetting Bron and Sena were in the room.

"I promised never to see you. You don't know the consequences!" she cried out.

"Let me guess. You struck a bargain to save my life."

"You were acquitted by the tribunal!"

"My case was hopeless. All the testimony weighed against me, even that of well-intentioned witnesses. Then miraculously, I was free."

"My father . . ."

"He suppressed all mention of you at the trial, didn't he?"

"Yes, I'm sure he did."

"What did he demand of you in exchange for my life?"

She hung her head, avoiding his eyes. "Never to see you."

"And my son?"

"You can see." Her hands fluttered helplessly. "He's to be raised as a Prola."

"Does your father know you visit?"

"Oh, no! He mustn't find out!"

"What you said about not loving me . . ."

"A lie! A hateful, awful lie!"

She came into his arms, and he vaguely noticed that Sena scooped up Bron and took him into the other room.

He'd dreamed of kissing her so many times, he couldn't believe her mouth was locked on his, hot and wet and urgent, demanding more than she had ever asked of him before: a memory that would never fade.

"I have to go!" she cried out frantically, pulling away in panic.

"You can't leave now. We have too much to settle."

"Garner, it is settled! I made a pact: your life in return for becoming the dutiful daughter again!"

"You shouldn't have sacrificed our son's life to save me!"

"I didn't sacrifice it. I'm giving him the only life possible in our society. The only alternative was to become Uncasted, to let him be banished with me. Would you want that?"

"No, no, of course I wouldn't. We could go into the rural area. My family would help us hide."

"No!"

"You won't become a Prola wife for my sake—for the sake of our son?"

"Gladly! There's nothing I want more! But my father would never permit it. Never! He'd rather see me dead!"

"We'll take false names and live in obscurity!"

"His arm is too long! He can cast a net over the whole of Prima. He only has to give the word, and we would cease to be—not just you and me, but Bron too."

"Would he have his own grandson killed?"

"Bron means nothing to him! All he cares about is his career, his power, his status. I loathe him!" She burst into tears, sobbing against the front of Garner's tunic, her shoulders shaking and her hands icy to his touch.

He tried to comfort her with words and caresses, but inside he was weeping too.

The door suddenly flew inward, the bolt ripped loose from the tremendous impact. Four Bellicosa stormed into the small room, seizing Garner before he could think of fleeing.

"Now I know how little your oath means!" a fifth man said, striding into the room and pushing shut the ruined door.

"Father!"

Garner recognized High Stanko Yor, although no one had ever been willing to identify him when Garner had been a defendant on trial for his life. Several times the lean, sharp-featured man had stood at the back of the room while the Tribunal of Seven heard testimony about his alleged crimes.

"You were at my trial," he angrily accused the minister, straining in vain against the burly Bellicosa, two holding him and two struggling to secure his arms behind him with metal wrist bands linked by a chain.

"Occasionally. I had to be sure the witnesses were behaving as instructed. That botanist was a stubborn old man. Fortunately, my assistants were able to persuade him that any mention of Alena would harmful to both of you as well as him." He turned to his daughter. "Regretfully, you've broken your vow."

"I didn't! Garner saw me by chance and learned the reason why I come here. This is the first time he's caught me visiting my babe."

"Whether or not it's the first, it will certainly be the last. That child is no longer yours. You have no right to visit him. We agreed he was to be raised as a Prola."

"You coerced me into agreeing!"

Even though he felt the cold hand of doom, Garner's heart swelled with pride. Alena didn't cower or back down, though in truth, the high minister's eyes were cold enough to make a strong man tremble in terror.

"I made the best possible arrangements in the circumstances," Yor said. "Now you're forcing me to alter them."

"No!" She ran into the other room and came back with Bron, holding him at arm's length under the gaze of her father.

"Look at this child! Those aren't his father's eyes! You weren't so cold and cruel when my mother was with you. Look, he has your own beloved wife's warm brown eyes! Don't tell me there's no love for her left in you. How can you cast off the flesh of her flesh?"

"He's tainted with Prola blood!" Yor protested angrily.

"Take him! Hold him in your arms! Tell me your grandson doesn't deserve your love!"

She thrust the babe into her father's arms, and for a terrible moment Garner feared Yor would let Bron fall to the hard stone floor. Instead he held him, and for a moment Garner thought the stern face softened. Then the high minister forcefully handed him back to Alena.

"You can't believe I'll flaunt the laws and traditions of our caste for the sake of a Prola bastard."

"Please, Father, let me go away with Garner and

our son," Alena pleaded. "What harm can that do to you?"

"I've been a kind and lenient father," he said solemnly. "Now I'm being punished for indulging your whims and giving you too much freedom. I tried to use reason, when perhaps a rod would have served my purposes better."

"Let Garner go!" she begged, dropping to her knees, pleading with tears running down her face. "Don't kill him!"

"I don't intend to. I don't want you mourning for a martyred lover, but I can't trust you not to arrange clandestine meetings. Stand up and hear me out."

She rose, so pale Garner thought she might faint. He struggled against his guards, but Stanko Yor had brought men of extraordinary strength, perhaps fearing for his own life in the ghetto.

"Garner Rie is hereby declared Uncasted. He'll be banished to the Outlands, and you'll never be tempted to break your vow again."

"What of my family?" Garner asked.

"They'll be told you died honorably in space, your remains sent into the great void. As long as they believe it, their wretched lives will go on as before. I don't want the scandal of banishing a whole family."

"I thank you for that," Garner said, realizing how little it mattered whether he was banished in space or in the Outlands if he couldn't have Alena by his side.

"As for you, daughter, I'm going to arrange for a period of study at a temple retreat. I think a few years of the contemplative life will do much to discipline your unruly ways."

"I want to be near my child."

"Impossible. By the time you return, he'll be

weaned and permanently placed in a Prola home. This is the last time you're to see him. Do not disobey me again, or the consequences will be more painful than you can imagine."

"You're inhuman," she cried out, but he paid her no further heed.

"As for you, nurse, I don't know if you conspired to help my daughter defy me, nor do I care. You may keep the babe until it's time to wean him, but if you ever breathe a word of what happened here, you'll suffer beyond the scope of your imagination."

"I never will," Sena said, trembling with terror.

"We've been here too long," he said to the Bellicosa. "Inject him now."

Garner was roughly knocked to the floor and held there, his trousers forced down. He felt a vicious jab in his buttock, then he started sinking in a vortex of whirling pinpricks. There was no way to fight. . . .

Alena watched the burly Bellicosa carry Garner away, joking among themselves, amused because a Prola had been brought low. She hated them and the caste system that allowed them to behave as arrogant bullies. Even more, she loathed her father and wanted to hurt him as he'd hurt her.

"You never loved me—or my mother!"

He grabbed her arm and held it in a painful grip, rushing her out of the hovel before he spoke.

"I loved her well enough when she was an obedient bride," he said angrily. "But she was headstrong and intractable, just as you are now. If fate hadn't taken her away, I would have had to put her aside."

"I feel sorry for you, Stanko Yor," she said with

deep sorrow. "You'll die alone, knowing you killed my love for you."

That night Boota became her jailer. When Alena tried to leave her room, she found the servant sleeping outside the door, blocking her way and awakening before she could climb over her.

"High Yor said I'm to see to all your needs, Highness."

"I wish to walk in the gardens."

"It's dangerous at night. He won't permit it." The solidly built servant still blocked her way, and Alena knew Boota well enough to know she would make a noisy outcry if necessary to carry out High Yor's orders.

Before this day, Alena had had Bellicosa guards. Now her father knew Garner was no longer a threat. He wasn't wasting funds by paying expensive guards to keep watch over his errant daughter.

"I told the master your jewelry is gone," Boota said spitefully. "You think you're beautiful and wonderful, but now you're poorer than me."

Alena was shocked by the triumphant glee in the servant's voice. "What have I done to make you hate me so?"

"Just because you're you," Boota said, both stupid and wise in her answer. "I hate your caste. I hate your pretty clothes and long hair."

"Why are you saying all this now?"

"You won't be here much longer. Then I have High Yor's permission to go. I've saved enough from what he's paid for my silence to buy a job making gloves."

Alena had no love for Boota, but she'd never mistreated a servant, much less the woman who drew her bath and tended her clothes. Her cruel words hurt, making Alena wonder how many others loathed her because she lived in her father's mansion and ate his food without laboring for it?

Two days later a packet came for Alena. A ruffian delivered it, and she knew the sender when she saw Garner's timekeeper on the man's wrist.

She took the crudely wrapped packet to her room, away from the curious eyes of the servants, her hands trembling as she opened it.

It was a Prola caste bracelet, the heavy bronze discolored where it had hugged the wrist of her beloved. On Brona she'd longed to have him remove it. To do so then would have meant a final break with the odious system keeping them apart; it would have meant staying on Brona. Now she held it in her hands, knowing he'd sent it as a love token, the only thing he could give her to remember him. The Uncasted were banished with only the clothes on their backs and the small personal possessions with them when they were seized. Everything else was confiscated by the government.

She knew he'd sent it at great risk, and she slipped it over her banded wrist, pushing it up to the fullest part of her arm. She would wear it there, under her sleeve, so some small part of Garner would be with her always.

That same day her father gave Boota funds to purchase several black robes, the garb required for those studying at a religious retreat. When Alena learned of it from the boastful servant, she saw it as a precious opportunity to leave the mansion where she was imprisoned while waiting to go to the highly disciplined religious order. She swallowed her pride and went to her father.

"Will you let me go with her to pick out the

robes?" she asked. "Boota hasn't sense enough to buy my size. Do you want me to disgrace you in robes that show my ankles?"

"Go with her," he said dismissively.

She hurried away to join Boota, elated because she could finally see a way to escape the constraints society had placed on her. It took all the acting skill she possessed to assume the sour demeanor of one condemned to the bleak life at a retreat.

Alena had evaded her guard once before in the mass of brightly colored tents at the bazaar, and Boota was easily distracted by the trinkets on display.

Less than two hours later Alena arrived at Sena Gome's, dressed in the rough garb of a Prola with a tunic that tied at her wrists. Under it, her wrist was bare.

Garner no longer bothered to count the days since he'd been brought by boat to the port of Dismay in the Outlands. The voyage had been uncommonly rough, with seas mercilessly battering the old wooden vessel, but he'd made himself useful to the captain when many of the crew, even seasoned seamen, were sick from the roiling and tossing of the waves. In return, the captain had given him the names of two honest Uncasted men who were willing to take on a third partner. Garner went to them and became a prospector, learning there were alternatives to living as a savage even though he'd been banished.

He'd brought them luck, they told him. After less than a hundred days of searching, they found a promising valley strewn with rich deposits of highly prized gems.

Working at their find one day, Garner wound

his scarf more securely around the lower part of his head, then raised his pickax above his head, bringing it down on a boulder with shattering force. The great rock split, revealing a virtual nest of colorless but chalky gemstones, highly valued when they were polished.

"I've made a strike," he called to his two companions.

He would share equally with Birk and Sebago, the partners who had taught him how to extract the resources of the rugged mountains that ran through the chain of large islands that made up the Outlands.

Much to Garner's surprise, Uncasted men rarely fought each other or tried to cheat those who banded with them. Those who did were driven far south to the Lawless Islands and forbidden to share in the lucrative trade of mining gems and precious metals to be smuggled to the continent of Prima.

"Well done," Birk said, hurrying over to see Garner's find. "Those beauties will buy an arsenal of the weapons we'll someday need."

"They might better be used to stock a room in the public building with books," his partner said. "It's knowledge, not force, that will someday make the Outlands a powerful, righteous nation."

"What do you think, Garner Rie?"

Garner laughed at both of them, knowing how much they enjoyed their constant bickering. In truth, they both agreed the future of their world lay in the rugged Outlands, where a new kind of society was slowly and painfully evolving. Birk reminded him of Roar, as much for his loyalty and worth as for his ruddy hair. It saddened him that he knew nothing of Roar's fate; he had never been brought to testify. He wondered if he might someday find him among the Uncasted for defying Stanko Yor and refusing to be a false witness.

Birk's partner, Sebago, had a razor-sharp mind and an excessively lean body, and he took great pleasure in baiting both his old partner and his new. Garner would have been satisfied with his new life in the company of good men like these if he could forget his longing for Alena and his son. But that would never happen.

Life was difficult in the Outlands. Food was scarce, dwellings were primitive, and necessities like medicine and weapons had to be smuggled in by the greedy seafarers who took more than their share of the wealth found in the mountains. At least the government of Prima took no interest in the illicit trade, believing as their forefathers had generations ago that the Outlands were only a dumping ground for the dregs of their society. In truth, Garner had never felt closer to his comrades or more a part of a community. The rulers of Prima didn't exaggerate the hardships when they threatened banishment as the ultimate punishment, but they were ignorant of the true nature of life on the vast chain of islands.

Most of the people Garner met were intelligent and responsible, dedicated to building a better life without the outmoded, crippling restraints of caste, which would someday be the undoing of Prima's government. The Outlanders weren't criminals or the offspring of criminals. They'd become Uncasted for breaking caste laws, not for committing felonies against others. Garner found them dedicated to building a new society.

This new way of living suited Garner. He was young and strong enough to survive extremes of temperature, raging storms, poverty, and primitive living conditions. He heartily approved of schooling all the children and nurturing those among them with a scholarly bent. Leaders, both men and women, were chosen by their peers at regular intervals, no individual allowed to serve for more than three consecutive periods.

Outwardly, Garner was thriving, but he yearned to see Alena and Bron with a hunger bordering on madness. Gradually he realized that banishment wasn't imprisonment. The more daring among them could and did make forays to the main continent, bringing back supplies, information, and even loved ones.

As soon as he had wealth enough to hire a boat, he was going back to find his woman and his son. He knew the penalty for being caught: death. He feared it less than a lifetime without them, and he earnestly believed the future of the planet lay in the Outlands. Eventually their just and equal society would prevail over Prima's archaic caste-ridden system—perhaps not in his lifetime or Bron's, but their descendants would see it.

That evening, while the three men were celebrating the rich find by passing around a flask of strong drink, they had a visitor: Dante Foy, a grizzled old miner who worked the mountains alone in search of gems and nuggets in the streams.

"There's a flame-haired lady asking about you in Dismay, Garner Rie," the old man said.

"Did you tell her where I am?" He was excited but fearful. What catastrophe had brought Alena to the Outlands?

"Not I. I'm not a man to meddle in another's affairs."

Garner suddenly worried he might be imagining things: the fire blazing in an open pit, the dark peaks around them, the fey messenger talking about a woman from another lifetime. Was it possible he wanted her so badly his mind was creating an illusion to trick him into believing she was within reach?

"What is she doing there?" he asked, afraid the messenger would dissolve in front of him like the smoke being whisked away by the wind.

"Working as a serving wench. The boys are flocking round her like scavengers at a kill. No doubt even the ugly one who lives with her will pick a mate before I lose another tooth, women being as scarce as they are hereabouts. It's a blessing to me I can do without 'em. Had me a mean old lady back in Danica. Got meself banished just to get away from her nagging."

Garner was too eager to confirm the existence of the flame-haired woman to listen to the saga of Dante's marital woes. Even if the old man was an illusion conjured up by his own loneliness, Garner had to act on what he'd said. Darkness or not, he had traveling to do.

Each night Alena returned exhausted to the small hovel on a cliff overlooking the sea. Part of each day she served a strong drink called diza in a public house near Dismay's lone dock. She'd used the last of the funds from selling her platinum caste bracelet to rent the two-room shack, so she had to work to feed Bron, Sena, and herself. What would she do without the wet nurse? Alena thanked the fates Sena loved Bron so much she'd insisted on coming with them. Otherwise, how could she work and search for news of Garner?

This place was every bit as primitive as she'd expected, but even Sena, whose face bore the horrible scar once inflicted by Bellicosa bullyboys taunting her for sport, felt safe here. People treated them with respect, not because she was

Highness Yor, but because it was the way of the Uncasted. Unruly behavior wasn't tolerated, although Alena could do without the hoards of lonely men who courted her favors with kind words and unwanted gifts. Women, it seemed, were in short supply. Sena too had suitors, and Alena hoped the scarcity of women meant Garner hadn't turned to another, believing as he did that they would never see each other again. No, he wouldn't do that! Love like theirs couldn't be put aside so quickly! Still, in the dark hours alone on her thin pallet, she tortured herself with doubts and longings. What would she do if Garner was lost to her forever?

Alena found solace in Bron's happy face and Sena's friendship, but she hungered for the sight of Garner. Was he well? Would she ever find him? How could she search for him when she had to work to keep them fed?

When her work was over every day, she walked the waterfront, asking about the man known as Garner Rie. He was famous, even here, for being the first Prola officer in space, and she never heard a word of condemnation for his actions on Brona.

"I 'spect he did what any true man would've," a weather-beaten old man had said.

Even when she spoke with a hundred people in a single day, she was painfully lonely, searching every face in hope of finding him.

A gale was whipping up the wind as she returned late one night to the hovel clinging to the side of a cliff in a cluster with others like it. There was no safety on the coast during the wet season. Soon she would have to move Bron and Sena inland where living quarters were more costly. Her wages barely kept them fed, and she had only one thing left to sell: herself. She shivered with dread, her need for Garner a physical ache whenever she thought of trying to go on without him.

Light showed through the only window, a small square covered with greased paper. She hoped Bron wasn't sleeping, but she was late tonight, held in town by a prospector who claimed to know where Garner was working. He'd told her nothing that would help find him, and this wasn't the first time a man had given her false hope for the sake of her company.

She opened the door, so weary she wouldn't be disappointed if Bron and Sena had both dropped off to sleep in the small back room curtained off by a remnant of torn sail she'd bought from a seafarer so Bron could have a quiet place to nap. Her own bed was a mat on the floor, so like the one Nita had shared with her abusive husband that Alena often thought of her, hoping she'd found a better future.

The light was dim, not reaching the corner where her mat was.

"You're late, my darling."

"Garner!"

He rose from her pallet, naked to his waist.

She flew to him and circled his waist with her arms, so overwhelmed by happiness she was afraid to look into his face and discover her eyes were playing tricks. She hugged him desperately, finding his broad chest a haven and resting place for her tear-streaked face.

"I love you! Oh, I love you so much!" She wept for joy, hungrily kissing his dark nipples even as her tears dampened his chest.

He lifted her against him, frantically kissing her mouth, devouring her lips with such joyful urgency all her hesitation dissolved in a rush of deep desire.

He held her away for a moment, his face soft with passion in the dim light, and loosened her topknot, unwinding her hair until it cascaded down her back.

"You can't be real!" he said with wonder in his voice. "You're not really here. I've conjured you in my mind because I want you so desperately."

"I'm real, I'm flesh and blood, and I've been dying to find you. Without you, my spirit will wither and die."

"Your father's infamous net—will he snare you in it and force you to return?"

"He can't!" She threw off her cloak and pushed up the sleeve of her tunic. "I sold my platinum bracelet and used the funds to bring us here. I'm Uncasted, and no power on Prima can restore my high-caste status. When I took off my bracelet, I broke with my father and his ways forever. He'll never forgive me, nor does it matter if he does. Not even his power can overturn banishment for such a serious crime, and in his eyes I'm dead."

"You can never go back?"

She shook her head, looked up at him, and then glanced at the curtained opening.

"They're sleeping," he said. "Sena knows I'm here."

"I can't believe you are!"

"If you hadn't come, I was going back."

"How could you? It would mean death."

"Only if I were caught. Many have done it and returned safely. I only had to accumulate enough gemstones to pay for passage and hire those who could help me find Bron. I want him to grow up here."

"Were you going to bring me back too?"

"If you wanted to go."

"Did you doubt it?"

"I know how much power your father has. If you stopped loving me . . ."

"Stay right there," she said in the haughty voice of Highness Yor, backing away from him.

"No one gives orders here," he said. "It's the custom among the Uncasted to speak with courtesy." He advanced a single step.

"Stay there!" she ordered even more arrogantly, hard pressed not to smile as she pulled her tunic over her head and kicked off thick rope sandals.

"I've had seventeen proposals of marriage since coming here," she said, turning her back and pulling down her trousers with deliberate provocation, then facing him again.

"Have you accepted any?" His voice was strained, and he looked more darkly handsome than ever with a thick black beard covering his lower face.

"I know exactly what kind of man I want." She stood naked before him, tears of joy drying on her face, savoring their reunion, even though she wanted him so badly her groin was on fire. She'd imagined this wonderful moment a thousand times, and she wanted to prolong it until it was special beyond her wildest imaginings.

He slowly shed the rest of his clothing, his trousers and boots, and stepped so close the tip of his erection teased her love nest.

"What kind of man do you want?" he asked, not taking her in his arms.

"I want a man who will never desert me," she whispered.

"I will never leave you." He reached out and gently cupped her breasts, thumbing her nipples until she shuddered with passion.

"I want my son to have a father who will always love and cherish him."

"Do you doubt I will?"

"I'm afraid, Garner."

"You always were most arrogant when you were frightened." He pulled her into his arms and let his velvety erection slip between her thighs, as though their talk was a thing apart from their bodies.

"I loved my father once. He was a good man in my eyes, and I don't understand how he came to change so drastically. I'm older and wiser now. I'm afraid because my love for you is so all-consuming. If it fades or becomes perverted . . ."

"Alena!" He held her away, answering in a grave voice. "Your father was corrupted by an evil system. That doesn't excuse him, but we have to put the past behind us." He held both her hands in his, making her feel loved and cherished. "There's new hope here, darling. We can live in dignity. Life is hard, but no one wears a slave bracelet; our leaders have to earn the right to exercise power. The future of the planet is in the Outlands, but without you, I have no future. I love you beyond words and always will, my darling."

"You've said all I ever hoped to hear and more."

She came into his arms, at first pressing against him so lightly electricity seemed to crackle between their bodies.

She threw back her head, and he pressed fervent kisses on her throat, combing her hair with his fingers and murmuring words that nourished her soul like rain on a desert.

"My beloved," he said, dropping to his knees and tonguing her between her silky thighs until she quivered like a leaf in a gale.

She joined him on the pallet, forgetting it was only a thin mat on the floorboards of a rude shack.

He put his hands under her bottom and lifted

her to ease their joining. Slowly, gently, he entered her. She writhed in an agony of need, digging her nails into his back to pull him deeper into the core of her.

"I love you," he murmured, softly thrusting against her, letting her delight in their union as her eagerness grew into a frenzy.

She pulled his face to hers, punishing his lips in her eagerness to be part of him, to feel him spill into her, to know the timeless ecstasy of belonging to a beloved soulmate.

"I love you, I love you," she cried out, arching her back and becoming one with him as they soared together in a universe of their own making.

The Garner she knew had always been a wondrous lover, but now he filled her soul with bliss, carrying her to mystic regions only glimpsed from afar before this. Even when she thought she would surely die of happiness, he gave her no pause, triggering wave after wave of ecstasy.

When at last he shuddered and collapsed beside her, she was light-headed and ready to slumber in his arms for a night and a day. Instead he playfully smacked her bottom, rose to extinguish the lamp, and came back to the mat, bedeviling her with insistent kisses and teasing caresses until she again rose to heights of delirious joy.

"My woman," he murmured into her silky hair. "I want you to be my wife, Highness Yor."

"Only if your promise never to call me that again!"

"When your chin comes up and you try to rule me with haughty words, I may forget."

"I don't do that!" She laughed, knowing that she did. "But if I do, you have my permission to chastise me as you would a Prola wife."

"A Prola female doesn't have the authority to

give permission, but my darling, you have lessons to learn on what it means to be a wife who's free of castes."

"Then I chose you as my teacher," she said, reveling in the wonder of being in his arms.

Author's note

Pam Rock loves to hear from readers! Write to:
P.O. Box 4084, Morgantown, WV 26504-4084.

A self-addressed, stamped envelope for reply would be appreciated.

SPECIAL SNEAK PREVIEW FOLLOWS!

Madeline Baker writing as Amanda Ashley

Cursed by the darkness, he searches through the ages for the redeeming light, the one woman who can save him. An angel of purity and light, she fears the handsome stranger whose eyes promise endless ecstasy even while his mouth whispers dark secrets. They are two people longing for fulfillment, yearning for a love like no other. Alone, they will face a desolate destiny. Together, they will share undying passion, defy eternity, and embrace the night.

Don't miss *Embrace The Night!* Available now at bookstores and newsstands everywhere.

He walked the streets for hours after he left the orphanage, his thoughts filled with Sara, her fragile beauty, her sweet innocence, her unwavering trust. She had accepted him into her life without question, and the knowledge cut him to the quick. He did not like deceiving her, hiding the dark secret of what he was, nor did he like to think about how badly she would be hurt when his nighttime visits ceased, as they surely must.

He had loved her from the moment he first saw her, but always from a distance, worshiping her as the moon might worship the sun, basking in her heat, her light, but wisely staying away lest he be burned.

And foolishly, he had strayed too close. He had soothed her tears, held her in his arms, and now he was paying the price. He was burning, like a moth drawn to a flame. Burning with need. With desire. With an unholy lust, not for her body, but for the very essence of her life.

It sickened him that he should want her that way, that he could even consider such a despicable thing. And yet he could think of little else. Ah, to hold her in his arms, to feel his body become one with hers as he drank of her sweetness. . . .

For a moment, he closed his eyes and let himself imagine it, and then he swore a long, vile oath filled with pain and longing.

Hands clenched, he turned down a dark street, his self-anger turning to loathing, and the loathing to rage. He felt the need to kill, to strike out, to make someone else suffer as he was suffering.

Pity the poor mortal who next crossed his path, he thought. Then he gave himself over to the hunger pounding through him.

She woke covered with perspiration, Gabriel's name on her lips. Shivering, she drew the covers up to her chin.

It had only been a dream. Only a dream.

She spoke the words aloud, finding comfort in the sound of her own voice. A distant bell chimed the hour. Four o'clock.

Gradually, her breathing returned to normal. Only a dream, she said again, but it had been so real. She had felt the cold breath of the night, smelled the rank odor of fear rising from the body of the faceless man cowering in the shadows. She had sensed a deep anger, a wild uncontrollable evil personified by a being in a flowing black cloak. Even now, she could feel his anguish, his loneliness, the alienation that cut him off from the rest of humanity.

It had all been so clear in the dream, but now it made no sense. No sense at all.

With a slight shake of her head, she snuggled

deeper under the covers and closed her eyes.

It was just a dream, nothing more.

Sunk in the depths of despair, Gabriel prowled the deserted abbey. What had happened to his self-control? Not for centuries had he taken enough blood to kill, only enough to assuage the pain of the hunger, to ease his unholy thirst.

A low groan rose in his throat. Sara had happened. He wanted her and he couldn't have her. Somehow, his desire and his frustration had gotten tangled up with his lust for blood.

It couldn't happen again. It had taken him centuries to learn to control the hunger, to give himself the illusion that he was more man than monster.

Had he been able, he would have prayed for forgiveness, but he had forfeited the right to divine intervention long ago.

"Where will we go tonight?"

Gabriel stared at her. She'd been waiting for him again, clothed in her new dress, her eyes bright with anticipation. Her goodness drew him, soothed him, calmed his dark side even as her beauty, her innocence, teased his desire.

He stared at the pulse throbbing in her throat. "Go?"

Sara nodded.

With an effort, he lifted his gaze to her face. "Where would you like to go?"

"I don't suppose you have a horse?"

"A horse?"

"I've always wanted to ride."

He bowed from the waist. "Whatever you wish, milady," he said. "I'll not be gone long."

It was like having found a magic wand, Sara

mused as she waited for him to return. She had only to voice her desire, and he produced it.

Twenty minutes later, she was seated before him on a prancing black stallion. It was a beautiful animal, tall and muscular, with a flowing mane and tail.

She leaned forward to stroke the stallion's neck. His coat felt like velvet beneath her hand. "What's his name?"

"Necromancer," Gabriel replied, pride and affection evident in his tone.

"Necromancer? What does it mean?"

"One who communicates with the spirits of the dead."

Sara glanced at him over her shoulder. "That seems an odd name for a horse."

"Odd, perhaps," Gabriel replied cryptically, "but fitting."

"Fitting? In what way?"

"Do you want to ride, Sara, or spend the night asking foolish questions?"

She pouted prettily for a moment and then grinned at him. "Ride!"

A word from Gabriel and they were cantering through the dark night, heading into the countryside.

"Faster," Sara urged.

"You're not afraid?"

"Not with you."

"You should be afraid, Sara Jayne," he muttered under his breath, "especially with me."

He squeezed the stallion's flanks with his knees and the horse shot forward, his powerful hooves skimming across the ground.

Sara shrieked with delight as they raced through the darkness. This was power, she thought, the surging body of the horse, the man's strong arm wrapped securely around her waist. The wind whipped through her hair, stinging her cheeks and making her eyes water, but she only threw back her head and laughed.

"Faster!" she cried, reveling in the sense of freedom that surged within her.

Hedges and trees and sleeping farmhouses passed by in a blur. Once, they jumped a four-foot hedge, and she felt as if she were flying. Sounds and scents blended together: the chirping of crickets, the bark of a dog, the smell of damp earth and lathered horseflesh, and over all the touch of Gabriel's breath upon her cheek, the steadying strength of his arm around her waist.

Gabriel let the horse run until the animal's sides were heaving and covered with foamy lather, and then he drew back on the reins, gently but firmly, and the stallion slowed, then stopped.

"That was wonderful!" Sara exclaimed.

She turned to face him, and in the bright light of the moon, he saw that her cheeks were flushed, her lips parted, her eyes shining like the sun.

How beautiful she was! His Sara, so full of life. What cruel fate had decreed that she should be bound to a wheelchair? She was a vivacious girl on the brink of womanhood. She should be clothed in silks and satins, surrounded by gallant young men.

Dismounting, he lifted her from the back of the horse. Carrying her across the damp grass, he sat down on a large boulder, settling her in his lap.

"Thank you, Gabriel," she murmured.

"It was my pleasure, milady."

"Hardly that," she replied with a saucy grin. "I'm sure ladies don't ride pell-mell through the dark astride a big black devil horse."

"No," he said, his gray eyes glinting with amusement, "they don't."

"Have you known many ladies?"

"A few." He stroked her cheek with his forefinger, his touch as light as thistledown.

"And were they accomplished and beautiful?"

Gabriel nodded. "But none so beautiful as you."

She basked in his words, in the silent affirmation she read in his eyes.

"Who are you, Gabriel?" she asked, her voice soft and dreamy. "Are you man or magician?"

"Neither."

"But still my angel?"

"Always, *cara*."

With a sigh, she rested her head against his shoulder and closed her eyes. How wonderful, to sit here in the dark of night with his arms around her. She could almost forget that she was crippled. Almost.

She lost all track of time as she sat there, secure in his arms. She heard the chirp of crickets, the sighing of the wind through the trees, the pounding of Gabriel's heart beneath her cheek.

Her breath caught in her throat as she felt the touch of his hand in her hair and then the brush of his lips.

Abruptly, he stood up. Before she quite knew what was happening, she was on the horse's back and Gabriel was swinging up behind her. He moved with the lithe grace of a cat vaulting a fence.

She sensed a change in him, a tension she didn't understand. A moment later, his arm was locked around her waist and they were riding through the night.

She leaned back against him, braced against the solid wall of his chest. She felt his arm tighten around her, felt his breath on her cheek.

Pleasure surged through her at his touch and she placed her hand over his forearm, drawing his arm more securely around her, tacitly telling him that she enjoyed his nearness.

She thought she heard a gasp, as if he was in pain, but she shook the notion aside, telling herself it was probably just the wind crying through the trees.

Too soon, they were back at the orphanage.

"You'll come tomorrow?" she asked as he settled her in her bed, covering her as if she were a child.

"Tomorrow," he promised. "Sleep well, *cara*."

"Dream of me," she murmured.

With a nod, he turned away. Dream of her, he thought. If only he could!

"Where would you like to go tonight?" Gabriel asked the following evening.

"I don't care, so long as it's with you."

Moments later, he was carrying her along a pathway in the park across from the orphanage.

Sara marveled that he held her so effortlessly, that it felt so right to be carried in his arms. She rested her head on his shoulder, content. A faint breeze played hide and seek with the leaves of the trees. A lover's moon hung low in the sky. The air was fragrant with night blooming flowers, but it was Gabriel's scent that rose all around her—warm and musky, reminiscent of aged wine and expensive cologne.

He moved lightly along the pathway, his footsteps making hardly a sound. When they came to a stone bench near a quiet pool, he sat down, placing her on the bench beside him.

It was a lovely place, a fairy place. Elegant ferns, tall and lacy, grew in wild profusion near the pool.

In the distance, she heard the questioning hoot of an owl.

"What did you do all day?" she asked, turning to look at him.

Gabriel shrugged. "Nothing to speak of. And you?"

"I read to the children. Sister Mary Josepha has been giving me more and more responsibility."

"And does that make you happy?"

"Yes. I've grown very fond of my little charges. They so need to be loved. To be touched. I had never realized how important it was to be held, until—" A faint flush stained her cheeks. "Until you held me. There's such comfort in the touch of a human hand."

Gabriel grunted softly. Human, indeed, he thought bleakly.

Sara smiled. "They seem to like me, the children. I don't know why."

But he knew why. She had so much love to give, and no outlet for it.

"I hate to think of all the time I wasted wallowing in self-pity," Sara remarked. "I spent so much time sitting in my room, sulking because I couldn't walk, when I could have been helping the children, loving them." She glanced up at Gabriel. "They're so easy to love."

"So are you." He had not meant to speak the words aloud, but they slipped out. "I mean, it must be easy for the children to love you. You have so much to give."

She smiled, but it was a sad kind of smile. "Perhaps that's because no one else wants it."

"Sara—"

"It's all right. Maybe that's why I was put here, to comfort the little lost lambs that no one else wants."

I want you. The words thundered in his mind, in his heart, in his soul.

Abruptly, he stood up and moved away from the bench. He couldn't sit beside her, feel her warmth, hear the blood humming in her veins, sense the sadness dragging at her heart, and not touch her, take her.

He stared into the depths of the dark pool, the water as black as the emptiness of his soul. He'd been alone for so long, yearning for someone who would share his life, needing someone to see him for what he was and love him anyway.

A low groan rose in his throat as the centuries of loneliness wrapped around him.

"Gabriel?" Her voice called out to him, soft, warm, caring.

With a cry, he whirled around and knelt at her feet. Hesitantly, he took her hands in his.

"Sara, can you pretend I'm one of the children? Can you hold me, and comfort me, just for tonight?"

"I don't understand."

"Don't ask questions, *cara*. Please just hold me. Touch me."

She gazed down at him, into the fathomless depths of his dark gray eyes, and the loneliness she saw there pierced her heart. Tears stung her eyes as she reached for him.

He buried his face in her lap, ashamed of the need that he could no longer deny. And then he felt her hand stroke his hair, light as a summer breeze. Ah, the touch of a human hand, warm, fragile, pulsing with life.

Time ceased to have meaning as he knelt there, his head cradled in her lap, her hand moving in his hair, caressing his nape, feathering across his cheek. No wonder the children loved her. There was tranquility in her touch, serenity in her hand. A sense of peace settled over him, stilling his hunger. He felt the tension drain out of him, to be replaced with a nearly forgotten sense of calm. It was a feeling as close to forgiveness as he would ever know.

After a time, he lifted his head. Slightly embarrassed, he gazed up at her, but there was no censure in her eyes, no disdain, only a wealth of understanding.

"Why are you so alone, my angel?" she asked quietly.

"I have always been alone," he replied, and even now, when he was nearer to peace of spirit than he had been for centuries, he was aware of the vast gulf that separated him, not only from Sara, but from all of humanity as well.

Gently, she cupped his cheek with her hand. "Is there no one to love you then?"

"No one."

"I would love you, Gabriel."

"No!"

Stricken by the force of his denial, she let her hand fall into her lap. "Is the thought of my love so revolting?"

"No, don't ever think that." He sat back on his heels, wishing that he could sit at her feet forever, that he could spend the rest of his existence worshiping her beauty, the generosity of her spirit. "I'm not worthy of you, *cara*. I would not have you waste your love on me."

"Why, Gabriel? What have you done that you feel unworthy of love?"

Filled with the guilt of a thousand lifetimes, he closed his eyes and his mind filled with an image of blood. Rivers of blood. Oceans of death. Centuries of killing, of bloodletting. Damned. The

Dark Gift had given him eternal life—and eternal damnation.

Thinking to frighten her away, he let her look deep into his eyes, knowing that what she saw within his soul would speak more eloquently than words.

He clenched his hands, waiting for the compassion in her eyes to turn to revulsion. But it didn't happen.

She gazed down at his upturned face for an endless moment, and then he felt the touch of her hand in his hair.

"My poor angel," she whispered. "Can't you tell me what it is that haunts you so?"

He shook his head, unable to speak past the lump in his throat.

"Gabriel." His name, nothing more, and then she leaned forward and kissed him.

It was no more than a feathering of her lips across his, but it exploded through him like concentrated sunlight. Hotter than a midsummer day, brighter than lightning, it burned through him and for a moment he felt whole again. Clean again.

Humbled to the core of his being, he bowed his head so she couldn't see his tears.

"I will love you, Gabriel," she said, still stroking his hair. "I can't help myself."

"Sara—"

"You don't have to love me back," she said quickly. "I just wanted you to know that you're not alone anymore."

A long shuddering sigh coursed through him, and then he took her hands in his, holding them tightly, feeling the heat of her blood, the pulse of her heart. Gently, he kissed her fingertips, and then, gaining his feet, he swung her into his arms.

"It's late," he said, his voice thick with the tide of emotions roiling within him. "We should go before you catch a chill."

"You're not angry?"

"No, *cara*."

How could he be angry with her? She was light and life, hope and innocence. He was tempted to fall to his knees and beg her forgiveness for his whole miserable existence.

But he couldn't burden her with the knowledge of what he was. He couldn't tarnish her love with the truth.

It was near dawn when they reached the orphanage. Once he had her settled in bed, he knelt beside her. "Thank you, Sara."

She turned on her side, a slight smile lifting the corners of her mouth as she took his hand in hers. "For what?"

"For your sweetness. For your words of love. I'll treasure them always."

"Gabriel." The smile faded from her lips. "You're not trying to tell me good-bye, are you?"

He stared down at their joined hands: hers small and pale and fragile, pulsing with the energy of life; his large and cold, indelibly stained with blood and death.

If he had a shred of honor left, he would tell her good-bye and never see her again.

But then, even when he had been a mortal man, he'd always had trouble doing the honorable thing when it conflicted with something he wanted. And he wanted—no, needed—Sara. Needed her as he'd never needed anything else in his accursed life. And perhaps, in a way, she needed him. And even if it wasn't so, it eased his conscience to think it true.

"Gabriel?"

"No, *cara*, I'm not planning to tell you good-bye. Not now. Not ever."

The sweet relief in her eyes stabbed him to the heart. And he, cold, selfish monster that he was, was glad of it. Right or wrong, he couldn't let her go.

"Till tomorrow then?" she said, smiling once more.

"Till tomorrow, *cara mia*," he murmured. And for all the tomorrows of your life.

Don't miss this haunting romance written in the immortal tradition of *Interview With The Vampire*.

Madeline Baker Writing As Amanda Ashley

Cursed by the darkness, he searches through the ages for the redeeming light, the one woman who can save him. But how can he defile such innocence with his unholy desire?

An angel of purity and light, she fears the handsome stranger whose eyes promise endless ecstasy even while his mouth whispers dark secrets that she dares not believe.

They are two people longing for fulfillment, yearning for a love like no other. Alone, they will surely face a desolate destiny full of despair. Together, they will share undying passion, defy eternity, and embrace the night.

_52041-9 $5.99 US/$7.99 CAN

Dorchester Publishing Co., Inc.
65 Commerce Road
Stamford, CT 06902

Please add $1.75 for shipping and handling for the first book and $.50 for each book thereafter. NY, NYC, PA and CT residents, please add appropriate sales tax. No cash, stamps, or C.O.D.s. All orders shipped within 6 weeks via postal service book rate. Canadian orders require $2.00 extra postage and must be paid in U.S. dollars through a U.S. banking facility.

Name_______________________________________
Address_____________________________________
City ___________________________ State_______ Zip_______
I have enclosed $_______in payment for the checked book(s).
Payment must accompany all orders. ☐ Please send a free catalog.

DANCE of the FLAME

ELAINE BARBIERI

Elaine Barbieri's romances are "powerful...fascinating...storytelling at its best!"
—Romantic Times

Exiled to a barren wasteland, Sera will do anything to regain the kingdom that is her birthright. But the hard-eyed warrior she saves from death is the last companion she wants for the long journey to her homeland.

To the world he is known as Death's Shadow—as much a beast of battle as the mighty warhorse he rides. But to the flame-haired healer, his forceful arms offer a warm haven, and he swears his throbbing strength will bring her nothing but pleasure.

Sera and Tolin hold in their hands the fate of two feuding houses with an ancient history of bloodshed and betrayal. But no matter what the age-old prophecy foretells, the sparks between them will not be denied, even if their fiery union consumes them both.

_3793-9 $5.99 US/$6.99 CAN

Dorchester Publishing Co., Inc.
65 Commerce Road
Stamford, CT 06902

Please add $1.75 for shipping and handling for the first book and $.50 for each book thereafter. NY, NYC, PA and CT residents, please add appropriate sales tax. No cash, stamps, or C.O.D.s. All orders shipped within 6 weeks via postal service book rate. Canadian orders require $2.00 extra postage and must be paid in U.S. dollars through a U.S. banking facility.

Name ____
Address ____
City ______________________________ State ______ Zip ______
I have enclosed $______ in payment for the checked book(s).
Payment must accompany all orders. ☐ Please send a free catalog.